The Spad Driver

John Britt

The Spad Driver

John Britt

Writer's Showcase
presented by *Writer's Digest*
San Jose New York Lincoln Shanghai

The Spad Driver

Writer's Showcase
presented by *Writer's Digest*
an imprint of iUniverse.com, Inc.

For information address:
iUniverse.com, Inc.
620 North 48th Street
Suite 201
Lincoln, NE 68504-3467
www.iuniverse.com

ISBN: 0-595-14214-1

Printed in the United States of America

Comments by the Author:

In the 1960's I had the privilege of serving as a Naval Aviator assigned to the 7th Fleet of the US Navy. This book is dedicated to fellow sailors of the Tonkin Gulf Yacht Club and especially to the memories of two friends:

Lieutenant Commander Terry Dennison, USN
Lieutenant (Junior Grade) Fred Kasch, USNR

They did not return.

And, to Elaine, who waited.

Prologue

Tonkin Gulf, September 1967

Falling…

In the soft, gray light before dawn the falling man glimpsed the bastard who had pushed him. He tumbled and in his clear vision of the ship he could see the man watching from the spud locker, laughing. It was a long drop to the dark, green water so the sailor had a second or two to think of what had gone wrong. His was a quick mind and he knew his terrible mistake even as he tumbled over and over, down into the churning phosphorescent wake. It wasn't so much a mistake of procedure; he had planned well. And, it seemed reasonable. Quid-pro-quo…that was the way the world worked. Something of value received for something given. No, his mistake had been one of misjudgment. Damned carelessness, a miscalculation.

The blow over his left ear with an iron pipe had given the other man an opportunity. Relaxing his attention for one careless second had been the error. He had misjudged the man's determination, his fervor. He had been surprised; it had been a reasonable proposition.

Impacting the warm seawater cleared his mind even further and he knew what he must do to survive. He would live and then he would get even.

The ship's wake glowed in the still, dark morning. Photoplankton stirred-up by the ship's huge propellers emitted an eerie green lumines-cence in the fluid capsule around the struggling figure; he splashed around momentarily within the churning glow. His mind lurched into survival mode and he pushed to the surface, thinking clearly now. The effects of the iron pipe were wearing off. Anger and pain started his brain spinning, planning, coping. The Navy had taught him how to sur-vive. He was determined to live, and then…

The US Naval Training Station, Great Lakes, in Illinois had been his introduction into the armed service and they had taught him well. A war was being fought in Asia and rather than face the uncertainties of the draft board he had enlisted in the Navy. No slogging around in the jungles, dodging incoming rifle-fire and killing little yellow people he didn't even know. No percentage in that program. He was a street-smart kid from St. Louis and he knew it was only a matter of time before he found a comfortable niche. There was always money to be made for the right kind of person.

The ship disappeared from the sailor's view. He treaded water and prepared to survive. The sailor was strong and capable. He had resources at his disposal.

Survive. Prevail. Revenge.

The ship would not return immediately, but his absence at the 0700 roll call would start a ship-wide search. Helicopters would be dis-patched. Other ships would be alerted and he would be rescued. The operations area of the Seventh Fleet Task Force was restricted to Yankee Station. Ships churned the confined area off the coast of North Vietnam conducting massive air operations. Hell, he could be rescued within three or four hours easily.

An unpleasant possibility occurred to him. The sailor hoped a North Vietnamese fishing boat wouldn't rescue him. That would mean intern-ment, Prisoner of War. They were all over the area. What a joke, those silly little junks fishing amongst the war fleet. Internment was for dumb-ass pilots to worry about, not him. He was too smart to get involved with anything that might entail imprisonment. He would face that problem if necessary, most likely rescue would come mid-morning by an American ship. Just relax, float out here in the warm Tonkin Gulf for a few hours and rescue was a near certainty.

Then, he would get even with that faithless sonofabitch. No way was he going to the authorities. He could handle this situation himself, but carefully. A little time back aboard the ship and then he would create a fatal accident. He would take over the *enterprise.*

The sailor unbuttoned his dungarees and slipped them over his deck shoes exactly as he'd been instructed in Basic Ocean Survival classes at Great Lakes. He twisted the pant cuffs and tied them, and then he re-buttoned the fly. This was the tricky part; he swung the wet pants over his head in a wide arc to inflate the pant legs with air. The legs blossomed nicely with the trapped air and looked like two balloons tied together. He stuffed the waist between his thighs and clamped it tight. Floatation!

He would survive, by God!

The sailor slipped out of his shirt then tied the sleeves. He buttoned it behind his neck. When he finished the shirt was reversed, shirtback against his belly. He blossomed the shirt by swinging the tail up then back down into the water forming a large bubble, more floatation. The sailor's spirits soared. Be smart. Survive. Revenge and prosperity waited.

The young man was strong. He could repeat the floatation process for hours without tiring. He had learned this procedure in the survival training pool and he was good at it.

Now all he had to do was wait. A ship would be along shortly. The Navy would search for him. He knew it. They always tried to rescue survivors. Maybe he would receive a medal.

His mind started to drift as he was lolled by the warm, gentle, rolling sea. The current, which flowed up from the equator, soothed as it rocked him slowly into a tepid contentment. He had overcome and he would prevail. The waves pulled him into quiet slumber.

There was an abrupt stirring behind him. Alarm bells exploded in his brain! The calm, steady current should not vary, now that the ships wake had dissipated. Of course, he should have known!

The instructors had warned them of this possibility in survival training. Two sleek fins cut the surface only yards away; he cried out in anger and fear.

One of the sharks brushed against his bare leg, its rough skin testing him for edibility. He knew the attack would begin immediately. This should not be happening! He had done everything correctly.

What to do? Get out of the water and into a raft, or onto flotsam, or debris. The water survival instructors had been emphatic on this matter. But, he did not have a raft. And, he had no flotsam. And, unfortunately, no debris drifted conveniently nearby.

He had only his shirt and pants!

He had used limited resources to best advantage, but all he had were his clothes, no raft, or weapons. What else could he do? His mind raced…

Searing pain! The first shark took a chunk of leg. He was spun around in the green luminescence. Screaming…struggling to fight to the surface!

Then instinct took over.

Hide! Yes, he must curl himself into a dark recess just as he had done when threatened as a child. He rolled into a tight ball and closed his eyes. Soon, the evil would go away.

Navy survival instructors had warned them. First the brush, then a nibble and then a final assault. He knew exactly what to expect. The sailor had been well trained.

Naval Training Station Great Lakes had an excellent reputation.

Icebergs floated past the old man in the hazy light. Sleek, gray, steam-driven icebergs that he counted carefully even though he knew their exact number from yesterday's survey.

How closely the gray ships' silhouettes resembled a multitude of icy monoliths. Of course, he had never actually seen icebergs or the frigid Arctic that lay thousands of miles south of his beloved homeland. But, the ice-gray angular structures of the US Seventh Fleet recalled memories of a slide show depicting Antarctica that French Nuns had shown in his classroom so many long and violent years before.

Major Nguyen Binh of the North Vietnamese Army was collecting the ships' numbers with the aid of a pair of fine US Army issue binoculars and he marveled at their clarity. What had happened to the soldier from whom these excellent binoculars had been taken? Lately he had caught himself speculating about such unimportant matters and the meaning of his own modest life. Was it old age that caused such inconvenient memories? He had little time for such impudent thoughts. There was a war to be fought, that endless task spanning more than thirty years. First the French imperialists, then the Japanese, then the French again and, now in 1967, the Americans. Binh had engaged in the bloody struggle against them all.

In his youth he had been a schoolteacher by day, a guerrilla fighter at night. He'd savored the pleasures of victory, for he had known many of those. But, he had also tasted the penalties of defeat. A wife and infant son killed by the French had been the sacrifices he most regretted in his nation's battles against foreign imperialism.

As a young schoolteacher, before Binh became a guerrilla warrior and later an intelligence officer, he had taught his students about America and its unique democracy. It was a fine country; he'd sincerely believed that. He had once believed in the dignity of the common man and that the freedoms of expression and enterprise would prevail, even in his beleaguered country. Now he was not so certain.

How was it possible that America, a truly great nation, could conduct such a needless war? That America would intervene in a minor Asian civil war was a confusing matter. While observing the Seventh Fleet from his fishing junk, the man had time to speculate about this near-Confucian riddle. At the beginning of the American intervention years ago, he believed the answer had to be philosophical. Americans simply could not tolerate a Communist government in Vietnam, even though its economy was barely equivalent to that of Arkansas, the most backward of America's fifty states. Lately, he had begun to doubt this analysis. Was it possible that the Americans were involved in this war as a result of political stupidity and greed? Such a notion staggered the imagination.

Nguyen Binh adjusted the focus on the binoculars. Three years earlier he had taken them from an American Special Forces sergeant captured during a Viet Cong ambush. The sergeant was tall and had been resolute during interrogation…momentary vision of agony on a youthful face. Binh admired the unfortunate man even as he'd tortured him. The sergeant had broken, as they all did eventually. But, why would a young man accept such pain and humiliation? For what purpose? Defending an obscure dissident faction in a minor civil war? What mysterious force of nature motivated such a noble creature? It was that very moment, he now recalled, that his zeal had begun to falter.

After he had taken all the sergeant had to give, the exhausted major had chosen not to kill him. He simply could not bring himself to do what he had done so many times before. He had changed and his usefulness as an interrogator was finished. His superiors agreed and now he had been reassigned to the more benign task of conducting routine reconnaissance work.

An airplane crunched onto the deck of the huge aircraft carrier in the magnified field of his binoculars. Nguyen Binh admired the skill required to accomplish such a feat. He had very little experience operating complex machinery, although he had learned to drive an automobile during his youth.

Oh, what a ship!

Gray, majestic and lethal. From "Jane's Fighting Ships" he'd identified the USS Sharpsburg, a monstrous war vessel named after a small town in Maryland where a decisive battle had occurred during the American Civil War. Couldn't the Americans, who had fought such a horrendous war on their own soil, understand the bitter struggle within his nation? Binh suspected the true cause of the American war was more deeply rooted in a strong nationalist movement than the onerous system of slavery then prevalent in their Southern states. Therefore, shouldn't they realize that Vietnam's civil war was more directly related to an inevitable nationalist movement than to expanding international communism?

The carrier soon completed the aircraft recovery phase and began launching operations. Such excitement! The choreography of tiny aircraft dashing off in a cloud of steam. He watched an airplane move toward the bow of the ship, then squat down slightly before being spit from the deck by an abrupt burst of feathery steam. He simply could not comprehend the catapulting operation. How could frail machines withstand such violent forces? He must remember to ask an engineer friend to explain when he debriefed in Hanoi next week.

Ah! The Americans! The technical majesty of the carrier. He admired them so. Even as he had tortured and killed them for information, he'd genuinely liked Americans! What did they hope to accomplish?

Why did they care?

Binh sat on the stern of his fishing junk and watched a gaggle of returning aircraft circle the carrier. He noted the types of aircraft and their numbers in his journal. This was a duty that the major enjoyed. He was still an intelligence officer for the Peoples Republic of North Vietnam but his duties no longer involved the destruction of another human being and that suited the old man just fine. Sipping an afternoon tea on the deck of a fishing boat and counting aircraft was a good way to serve his nation.

Major Binh closed his eyes for a moment and allowed the warm afternoon sun wash over him. He must radio his observations to Hanoi soon. But his thoughts wandered, as they tended to do lately. He remembered a man soaked in sweat and smeared with blood. He hoped the sergeant was alive and he felt much anger at the circumstances. Why must a simple man, a schoolteacher, fight and kill people that he admired? He had long since concluded that the world must be crazy.

Binh swept the western horizon with his binoculars. More aircraft would be returning soon. Tiny aircraft scattered in the vast purpling dusk after a bombing raid on Hanoi. They would hasten into a semblance of order and help those injured during the attack to return. Binh knew their drill. What he did not know was that they hastened to a cruel destiny.

Mars, The God of War, had surely directed these frail warriors to a common destruction. Fate had locked Major Binh and these aviators in a pitiless embrace, bonded them in an inescapable tragedy and condemned them to a timeless accord. Unwitting airborne players sped to the inevitable dance of Major Binh's incomprehensible war.

*   *   *

Among those aircraft that Major Binh awaited, a young pilot scanned the horizon, searching. Scattered in the purple sunset, white puffy clouds dotted a blue tapestry that faded into a darkening sea. A pretty evening, he thought. A promise of fair skies and gentle winds and Ensign Dan Roberts thought that he had a fair chance to survive. He did *not* want to think about ditching.

Small arms fire had stopped clattering against the Skyraider's fuselage moments earlier after he had dashed over the shoreline. But AAA had done the major damage. Anti-aircraft bursts trailed behind now, filling the sky with black puffy cloudlets.

Logically, his aircraft's engine should have failed and he would have crashed in the dense forest that concealed the enemy's 37mm guns. He could not deny that and the oil smear on his windscreen was a constant reminder. But, it hadn't failed and he took that encouraging fact to heart.

When he glanced back, the Navy pilot could still see the rugged shoreline. Ahead, the milky haze of Asian sky blended into the distant horizon of Tonkin Gulf. A brisk wind washed across the Gulf, frothing whitecaps glistened on the warm sea-prairie below. The blood distracted him but he recalculated the odds with every moment the fractured engine continued to function. If the engine survived, he would survive.

Now it seemed strangely serene in the sunset's gentle, purple haze over Tonkin Gulf. Glancing over his left wing Roberts saw the skipper flash a thumbs-up for encouragement. Roberts had not expected sympathy. Commander Gerald Isaacson was a cold, impersonal sort. *Must be wrong about him*, he thought.

Then his sick engine popped noisily reminding him not to lose interest. Complacency could kill so easily. In the last few, violent moments he had entered an entirely new phase of his life. He had never thought much about mortality, but now it seemed an inevitable thing.

Roberts raised his sun-visor and wiped his eyes nervously. How quickly it had happened! How extraordinary the experience had been! The fear still gripped him.

The AAA guns, that Highpockets said wouldn't be there, had opened up on the airgroup when they fled outbound over the beach. But, the Sharpsburg's air intelligence officer had screwed up before and he would again because the NVA were resourceful.

One of the airgroup's stragglers had been damaged and they'd tried to protect him. Roberts had followed Isaacson into a strafing run and the two Skyraider pilots had neutralized the enemy's position. *Neutralized?* He remembered that he had killed many who had fled onto the beach in panic. He had strafed the black-clad figures mercilessly. He had been hit on the last run.

Roberts reduced engine RPM slightly and adjusted the mixture control. The engine sounded smoother now, but he knew it hadn't really helped. The engine was slowly tearing itself apart. Soon, it would sputter and expire and with the dying engine rode his fortune.

Blood dribbled down his boot onto the floorboard. The subject of death flashed across his mind again as he looked ahead for the carrier. Neither the Sharpsburg, nor Binh's fishing junk, was visible through the haze. They were still thirty miles southeast, a long way to nurse an engine that had suffered such massive damage.

He had not thought about dying, or killing, before. Both had been abstract notions to the healthy, young man. Now they were daily occurrences. Men had died all around him in battle or by accident and by pure stupidity. But Roberts was a rookie. The new guy in a squadron of hardened veterans and he'd just experienced his first serious combat.

How strange! He thought of black-clad figures he had personally dispatched. Roberts looked down at the spreading bloodstain above his left ankle where the enemy had shot him during the last strafing run. The leg injury was his least concern right now, although it hurt considerably and the blood distracted him. *Forget the pain!* His dying engine was the main worry. A grinding noise pulsated from the Wright 3350.

Roberts recalculated the odds. A fifty-fifty chance that the damaged engine might endure ten minutes and deliver him to the ship. Maybe fifty-fifty, if he was lucky. If it didn't, then he would ditch in the warm ocean and wait for a helicopter to be sent from the ship.

He did not want to think about ditching!

Few aviators survived a ditching at sea. The pilot was aware of that fact but he would not think of that now because he had much to do. Think positive. It wouldn't happen.

But, what if it did happen?

He must think of it! Survival at sea was a matter of circumstance and luck. Death was the more likely result. What would they say to his wife? *Missing and presumed dead.* A time-proven and useful Navy codicil. *Presumed?* Why would they say that? Too fastidious to admit a nasty little fact. If he crashed in the Gulf, they must rescue him quickly or he would die.

What if it really happened?

He tinkered with the mixture control again. There was nothing more he could do. It gave him little satisfaction but he still had a functioning engine. He was still alive. He must ride the Skyraider as far as it would take him. If it took him all the way to the Sharpsburg then he would survive. If not...?

Missing at sea. Presumed dead.

Just then, Ensign Roberts remembered the missing sailor and wondered what he would do about that puzzle. Cdr. Isaacson had assigned the investigation to him last week. And so, if he survived, he would try to solve the mystery of an unfortunate sailor who was *missing at sea,* and who was now *presumed dead.*

The ship was several long minutes away. He could not afford the luxury of daydreaming or worrying about a missing sailor. The engine coughed and Roberts scanned the instrument panel, but it held no promise for him. The engine was slowly dying and he knew it. He must think of a way to survive.

He still did not want to think about ditching.

The massive ship rolled gently in the current. Had it not been for the serious business at hand the three men clustered in a precarious perch on the aft edge of the flight deck would have enjoyed the brilliant sun-lit afternoon. A twenty-five knot wind blew across the deck while an A-4 fighter-bomber crunched noisily into the arresting-gear.

"Fast. A little sink in close…over-controlled. Fair landing, number four wire." The older man scribbled the approach rating into his LSO logbook for the pilot's debriefing later.

"Who's next?"

The assistant Landing Signal Officer consulted his notes. The landing sequence was screwed-up. The approaching Skyraider should have waited for the fuel-thirsty jets to finish recovering before entering the pattern, but aircraft with battle-damage always had priority.

"New guy in 433…don't know him…got problems…engine damage…"

"Roberts?"

"Yes, sir. I haven't waved him yet…heard he did OK yesterday."

Lieutenant-Commander Bobby Thomas, the senior Landing Signal Officer on the LSO platform, looked up to see the Douglas A-1

Skyraider begin the 180 degree turn from the downwind leg to the final landing approach. Even in the mind-numbing racket of the flight deck he could hear the engine popping when the pilot added power to compensate for increased drag as the landing gear extended. The LSO bit his lip unconsciously giving his face a pensive quality, which was a deception since Bobby Thomas tolerated few uncertainties in his life.

"I know him," he said. "Crash crew alerted?"

"Yes, sir."

Beyond the ship's wake a rescue helicopter maneuvered into position.

A stream of black smoke trailed the Skyraider. In the day of modern jet fighters the A-1 Skyraider was a curious anomaly, a throwback to an earlier era. The US Navy kept the propeller-driven fighter-bomber, affectionately nicknamed the *Spad* after the WW1 fighter, on active service for a simple reason. The fighter-bomber could still deliver the devastating close-in firepower required in the Asian war being fought in 1967. But this was to be the last tour for the Navy's Skyraiders. They would be turned over to the South Vietnamese at the end of the year-long deployment. These few were the last of the Spads.

"Skyraider. Gear down…flaps down…tail-hook down," the third LSO shouted. "Jesus. Look at the smoke!" They knew the pilot had been injured, but the airplane was their main concern. The Spad turned through the ninety-degree position, halfway through the 180-degree turn from downwind to final.

Don't get slow! Thomas thought. A dangerous trap for inexperienced aviators. Too slow in the tight turn at the ninety, inviting an approach-turn stall. Then overcompensate on final, too fast to land properly. They'd miss all four wires, a bolter. Staggering downwind for another attempt. A carrier landing was aviation's most demanding and dangerous procedure.

Don't get slow, dammit. "Power!" he radioed. Could the engine take the abuse if a wave-off became necessary? A sick airplane. An inexperienced pilot. A fatal combination.

"Boxer Two. Skyraider...roger ball...hook down." Roberts' voice sounded thin and Bobby Thomas glanced back at the crash crew.

The *mirror* on the port side of the carrier, guided Roberts. The *meatball*, a floating orange dot emanating from the convex mirror, led him down a two and one-half degree glideslope to the tiny landing area of the flight deck. It moved between a row of bright green lights on each side of the Fresnel Lens and denoted the exact glideslope down to the arresting wires. If he flew too high on the glideslope the meatball appeared above the green lights, if low the meatball was below. When dangerously low the meatball turned into an intense red ball, red lights flashed and a wave-off was mandatory.

He must not wave-off. Thomas understood that simple fact.

Black smoke curled over the left wing. The Skyraider turned above the ship's wake and settled into a tight, final approach. The LSO watched the airplane accelerate slightly as the wings leveled. What? Thomas had not expected to see the new guy use that particular technique. Start deliberately slow through the ninety then accelerate to 105 knots in the groove, an old Skyraider pilot's trick that resulted in a smoother approach.

"Looking good...easy on the power," he radioed.

Both assistants glanced at the senior LSO, then at each other. That encouraging comment hadn't been necessary, therefore unprofessional. But Roberts was a new guy and he had battle damage. And, Bobby Thomas was tired of seeing pilots die because of foolish errors. And, he did not want to write another accident report. He knew his assistants had noticed the superfluous comment but Thomas did not care.

The Skyraider roared over the ship's stern, the round-down. Thomas squeezed the engine-cut signal. Ribbons of black smoke. Banging and popping as Roberts pulled the throttle to idle. The Spad smashed into the landing zone, the number two wire screamed in protest and the Spad shuddered to a stop. For a moment it was almost quiet. The propeller swung to an abrupt stop. The engine had died.

"Well, I'll be damned…" The LSO scribbled the debrief rating in his logbook. "An OK landing, number two wire." He watched the Spad being dragged out of the wires by a tug.

"Who's next?" He turned to spot an A-4 turning downwind.

It was a good day and Thomas knew it would be good to debrief the pilots later. After dinner he would find individual pilots and debrief their landings. A severely damaged airplane had been successfully recovered and he would not be required to write a fatality report. A good day.

"That's Herb McGinnis." The assistant LSO said. "Been having problems lately, bolters a lot."

Bobby Thomas watched the A-4 turn through the ninety, wings wobbling in the ship's turbulent backdraft. He thought about the new guy. A few veteran Spad pilots used that peculiar landing technique, only the best attempted it. It was a neat trick requiring skill and a light touch on the control stick. Just a lucky move? Thomas decided to ask Roberts about it later. He quickly scribbled a large question mark under Ensign Dan Roberts' name in the LSO logbook.

$*$ $*$ $*$

Major Binh placed the binoculars aside then sipped a little aromatic tea. He smiled because the Skyraider, he knew the aircraft's proper name, had landed safely. It had been damaged attacking his country, but that was over now. The young American had recovered safely and the major was glad because deep down he had always resented unnecessary death, especially the death of young men.

He decided to take a short nap before transmitting the intelligence report. His mind drifted with the gentle rocking of the junk and the North Vietnamese officer thought about the Skyraider pilot. Was he from Arkansas? The old man loved the sound of that particular State's name. What was his religion? Did he have a philosophy, a wife, a child?

Did the pilot have a dream? What did that fortunate pilot think about the war and the Vietnamese people? He was tired now. Heavy eyelids. Confused images.

Sleep came quickly in the lazy warm afternoon breeze. He had been observing the carrier's operations for nearly eighteen hours and a quiet lassitude engulfed him. Soon, he had a visitor, a dream of the happy times, something he had grown to savor. He dreamed of his youth and the days before the Japanese had come. His wife came to him in the vision and in her arms was a male child. The fantasy enveloped him. She smiled, shy, but proud of the tiny gift. A languid smile, a memory that had endured throughout the turbulent years.

"Major." He was rudely disturbed. "Time to transmit," a crewmember said. The velvety images faded.

He felt anger at the interruption and tried to visualize his young wife again. He wanted so desperately to remember, because that was all that he had. He tried to recall the dream.

Remembering…

Creamy almond skin and a delicate face…dark eyes smiling with pride. He tried to visualize…

"Major." The crewmember shook his shoulder vigorously and pointed toward the cabin. Now he was fully awake and it was time to transmit the operations message. The old man glanced at the Sharpsburg and it was quiet. Flight operations had been temporarily suspended while the Americans prepared for another air strike. He thought about the ship and its crew and Binh wondered about the damaged Skyraider's pilot. Wouldn't it be excellent to speak to that young man? There were several things to ask of him. Not an interrogation, mind you, for Major Binh was finished with that sort of business now. Really, it boiled down to one simple question.

There must be some mysterious reason for this war, he thought. The United States of America was a noble and enlightened nation. But, why were they here? What had directed the gods to such an unseemly enterprise? Could a young Skyraider pilot answer that singular question?

Any man who could operate such complex machinery must have superior intelligence and he began to feel an odd affinity for the unknown Naval Aviator. Could that Skyraider pilot answer the question, resolve the enigma?

What was the purpose of this war?

Perhaps they would meet one day, he thought, the grizzled old NVA major and the lucky American pilot. Wouldn't that be a fine thing?

3

"Bolter! Bolter!"

The LSO's urgent radio alert, an A-4's tail-hook had skipped over the number four wire and skittered down the deck in a spark-lined trail. Jet-blast engulfed the flight deck in thundering vibration and noise. Dan Roberts looked up from his cockpit at the A-4 fighter-bomber that lifted awkwardly into the hazy sky. Roberts was not surprised. He'd heard Ensign Herb McGinnis reporting the meatball and a few seconds later Herb boltered after an unsuccessful landing attempt. His roommate boltered frequently.

Roberts felt a gut-wrenching sensation as the elevator dropped rapidly down into the cavernous hangar bay. Now he was enfolded into the dark netherworld beneath the flight deck. It was warm but the illusion of calmness lasted only a moment. Men worked furiously in the crowded maintenance bay, a mechanic dashed under his engine cowling waving furiously. An acetylene torch sprayed showers of bright sparks in a darker corner. He heard the public-address system sputter a command. Men scurried about on missions of urgent necessity while flight deck operations continued unabated in the humid afternoon.

Roberts finished the parking checklist. The elevator jolted to a sudden halt and he was towed quickly to a parking spot. The elevator shot upwards with klaxon-heralded energy, ending thirty seconds of pandemonium. He felt slightly lightheaded.

"Damn...Mr. Roberts!" Airman Timothy Bryan was yelling into his ear. "What the hell?" Bryan hopped around on the wing gesturing at various jagged holes in the Skyraider.

Roberts touched his flight suit, blood-matted and dirty and knew a deep leg wound was concealed under the untidiness.

"Sorry about your airplane, Bryan...." His mind trudged through fresh memories. He had killed and been wounded in return.

"All them holes...sir?" The Skyraider's plane captain stared at the bloody flight suit then Bryan was rudely pushed aside.

"Sorry, sailor," a burly paramedic said. "OK. Let's take a look...where're you hit, sir?"

Roberts unbuckled the shoulder harness and seat belt. His arms felt heavy. A bloody glove had smeared his helmet. He looked up to the flight surgeon's assistant and mumbled something. Couldn't the medic see that his airplane was damaged and his flight suit had been torn...reports to be filed?

"Here....?" Roberts pointed. Blood covered his boot and a wet mass clung to the flight suit. He wanted to apologize for the oil and blood pooled under the rudder pedals. "My leg...I don't know...." He wiped at bloody smears on the controls. He felt embarrassed.

"Come on, sir...let's get you outta there...Doc's waiting." The medic nodded to his assistant.

"I turned the Master Arm Switch off. Didn't forget..." He looked up casually. Roberts removed a glove and dabbed at the blood. "You know...after I shot them."

"What?"

"I didn't forget, see?" He stuffed the bloody glove into a pocket, frowned at the red smear on the Master Arm switch, wiped at it with his bare hand.

"Better take it easy, sir. Shock, you know…come on!" The medic pulled at his arm.

"Wait…I'll get out."

Roberts stepped onto the seatpan and felt a sharp jab of pain. He paused momentarily to sleeve-off a sweaty forehead. Oil from the fractured engine coated the cockpit. Roberts noticed men gesturing. Pointing at twisted medal and dripping fluids, frowning at bloody handprints on the canopy. The Spad had been rudely disfigured. Fragments from a flak explosion had lacerated the engine cowling. The fuselage was peppered with holes. During the strafing runs he had killed several men.

Commander Isaacson walked across the hangar deck from his parked Skyraider. He looked at Roberts momentarily then shifted his eyes quickly to the engine cowling, much of which was missing. Oil dripped from the battered engine case, an ignition wire dangled from a gaping hole in the cowling. Blood dripped from Roberts' leg onto the hangar deck.

"Ensign Roberts…he'll be OK?" Isaacson asked the medic.

"I think so, sir." The medic replied. "We'll get him to sickbay…Doc's waiting."

Isaacson surveyed Roberts bloody flight suit with the same impersonal attitude. Neither Isaacson nor his aircraft had been damaged. Roberts started to say something. The Commanding Officer of Attack squadron 433 had a reputation as a hard man. He was a skilled athlete, a former champion boxer who used Boxer One as his call sign. He was accustomed to blood and intolerant of failure.

"You sure did a hell of a job on your Spad, Roberts." Isaacson did not smile. Then he did something Roberts had noticed before. He nodded his head, then abruptly walked away. Isaacson frequently ended conversations with an unconscious head nod. A defensive idiosyncrasy from the boxer? He rudely brushed past Airman Bryan, who paced under the engine with his hands clasped behind his back clucking quiet noises of dismay.

"Sorry, Bryan…." Roberts shrugged; his eyes followed Isaacson. "They shot me. I didn't mean…."

Bryan stood behind the wing. He'd sent this airplane and pilot out on a mission two hours earlier and *they* had returned like this. It was not right, he thought, just not right at all.

"Come on now, sir." The medic tugged at his sleeve.

Roberts said. "I'll help you clean it later, Bryan."

"Will you just forget about the goddamn plane, sir! Let's go! Doc's waiting."

A3C Timothy Bryan, Plane Captain was stenciled under the canopy rail. Bryan wiped an oily smear off his name. This was Number 407, *his* airplane. He took care of it, serviced it, and loved it as much as he loved his '32 Ford Coupe back home in Arizona. How could anybody be so crass as to damage such a beautiful machine, even in combat? Ensign Roberts should have been more careful, he grimaced with dismay.

"Well, for christsakes, Bryan." Chief Petty Officer Peter O'Leary had watched the flurry of activity. "This one'll have to go back to Subic," he said gently. He examined the Spad and shook his head.

"Just look at it, Pete," Bryan muttered. "Damn gooks." He wiped at a smear furiously. He did not understand Orientals.

"War's a bitch, Bryan. But this'll be fixed up better than new…you'll see."

"Dammit. Pete, I ain't never seen nothin like this before."

"Gonna happen now and then," Pete replied. The chief was called *Pete* by nearly everyone in the squadron including Cdr. Isaacson. A big, friendly man. A gruff demeanor, but an easy man to like. He had the natural ability to instill confidence in lesser men.

"I don't know, Pete…look…" Bryan pointed to a large hole in the fuselage aft of the canopy and several ragged holes in the tail section. He walked slowly around the Spad noting the damage into a maintenance logbook.

"Screw it, don't worry, Bryan. They'll off-load it in Subic next week. It'll be back in service by middle of next line period…you'll see. Meanwhile, you can help with 401."

"401? The skippers airplane?"

"Why not? You'll like it…best Spad in the squadron."

"But, that's got Cdr. Isaacson's name on it," Bryan said. He preferred working with younger pilots, like Ensign Roberts, and on his airplane, the one with *his* name stenciled on the side. Ship 401 had another plane captain's name stenciled under the canopy rail. It just wouldn't be the same.

"Come on, let's finish this survey."

They stepped over blood smears on the hangar deck where Roberts had limped off to sick bay. Neither man commented but Bryan shook his head in disgust. He looked up. There, right there, for everyone to see was his name…*his* name.

A3C Timothy Bryan, Plane Captain.

Oil from the broken engine had sprayed across the stencil. Pete poked his finger into a ragged hole on the leading edge of the wing.

"They'll fix it, Bryan," Pete said.

Bryan muttered angrily. How could anybody do such a thing? Whose fault was it, Ensign Roberts? The new pilot had an unimpressive demeanor, average height, slight build, and he frequently stammered. Roberts lacked the formidable air that other pilots seemed to emit naturally. Not someone to admire, he thought. Still, there was something indefinable about the new pilot that made Bryan uneasy. He wiped a bloody handprint from the canopy. Maybe it wasn't the pilot's fault.

"Damn gooks."

The flight surgeon looked up at the noise; three men entered the cramped clinic. He'd just finished setting the broken tibia of a hapless red-shirt ordnance loader and instruments of his trade were scattered around the surgery.

"OK...lay him down there," he pointed. "And take off that flight gear." Commander "Doc" Swanson did not recognize the pilot in the bloody flight suit, probably one of the replacement pilots shipped aboard recently. He'd had little opportunity for introductions. The Sharpsburg had a complement of 3,500 men and only two doctors.

Roberts lay back quietly while the medics cut away his flight suit. An inch-long piece of aluminum protruded from an ugly leg wound. Doc removed it carefully.

"Sharp little dagger...huh?" Swanson said.

"Yeah." Roberts winced. Swanson injected something into his arm while the medics cleaned the two-inch cut.

"Won't hurt much longer now. I'm Doc Swanson. What's your name?"

The pilot looked confused and Doc wondered if he had been heard.

"Roberts, sir...Dan Roberts. I'm new to VA-433. I...uhh..."

"Give him a little booze." Doc nodded at the medic, who retrieved a miniature bottle from a locked cabinet. "Combat medicine," he said.

"Haven't had any of this lately..." Roberts slugged it down quickly. "But it's..."

"Good?" Doc suggested. "Old Mister Boston...only the finest for our sailors."

Roberts felt a tide of placid warmth. He closed his eyes momentarily and felt the sharp tingle of Doc stitching the wound. It seemed unreal.

"Looks like a part of your airplane, sir." The medic fingered the jagged piece of shrapnel. "Musta been knocked loose by flak, or something."

"What happened?" Doc asked. It was an ugly gash but he had seen worse injuries. He had seen them frequently. Roberts gasped suddenly.

"Stitching's the worst part, Roberts."

Roberts pointed at the locked cabinet. "Do you think…?"

"Get him another." Doc said. He noticed that Roberts had a speech peculiarity, usually leaving his sentences unfinished.

"Tell us about it."

"Well…" Roberts groaned. "We were patrolling along the beach…." He drained the bottle. "Waiting for the strike to return from Haiphong…just waiting…." He blinked. Doc nodded for him to continue.

"Waiting for CAG to report feet-wet…this was my second mission. I'm kinda new at this…" Roberts slurred. He looked up at the flight surgeon. "Sorry…"

"It's OK, go on."

"Started to receive some small-arms fire from a tree-line just off the beach…couldn't see anybody, though. Like sparklers…you know?" He gestured awkwardly. "Triple-A hit an A-4…but he got away…I…uhh…"

"Anti-aircraft fire?"

"Yes, sir…some small arms stuff too."

Doc Swanson knew the pain would worsen. The cut was as deep as it was wide. What appeared to be a two-inch slice was in fact a deep wound. A jagged piece of fuselage had shattered and entered Roberts' left leg six inches above the ankle. Fortunately, the Skyraider's armor plating had absorbed most of the impact. The full force of the shrapnel might have severed his leg and he would not have survived.

"You're lucky. Ugly little bastard." Doc dropped the shrapnel into a dish.

"Skipper ordered me in first…umm…dropped two Mark 82's on the tree-line…blew the hell out of it…then I…." Roberts felt his mind drifting.

"That when you got it?"

"Huh…?" Dulled eyes stared momentarily.

"Is that when your airplane was damaged?" Doc asked gently.

"Umm….no. That came later…I think. I can't remember…" He felt a sharp tug. Doc doing something with his leg.

"Saw some secondary explosions when I rolled out…" What was he trying to remember? "Looked back…black smoke…fire in the trees…think I hit some munitions, maybe." His tongue felt thick, detached. Now he wasn't certain that he was directly involved.

"Skipper followed me in. He had napalm. Guys running out of the trees…fireball caught some of them. I…uhh…" Roberts drew a sharp breath. Pain and confusion on an oil-smeared face.

"Just relax now, Roberts. We'll be finished soon…this hurt?" The stitching was complex. It was an ugly wound.

"…didn't see any more gun flashes but I hosed them down real good on the beach anyway with cannon….jeez…those 20MM…guys running…"

Doc noticed the tremors first. He looked at his assistant then nodded at the quivering hand. "No more anesthetic," he said.

"I never saw real targets…uhh…destroyed before. Couple of trucks blew up…the people…" Now he saw it again with surreal clarity. Black figures running madly across the white sand. Bursts of sand and debris from the 20MM forming a cloud over the beach. The shadow of a Skyraider sweeping over people being blown about like discarded paper.

"It's over now, sir." The medic wiped his face.

"…people…running from the fire…napalm…fire in the trees. I hit 'em again with cannon."

The surgery's fluorescent light swirled overhead. The pulsating buzz of a fan nearby. It felt cool and quiet now. Strange images of black-clad rag dolls jerked haphazardly through semi-consciousness. Little toy things cast recklessly about as in childhood play tumbling across a huge sandbox…flying dust…flashing lights and sudden eruptions of black puffballs in a haze-gray sky.

"I…didn't fire on the last pass. No reason. Nothing moving…just black specks on the beach. I got hit."

Swanson removed bloody gloves while his assistants dressed the wound. He watched through narrowed eyes as the banal narrative unfolded from a shock-induced memory. And the surgeon thought how he hated war. Korea had been much the same. Wounded men trying to comprehend the incomprehensible. How they had killed and been killed.

"They looked like dolls."

"What?" The medic misunderstood.

Roberts did not grasp the question; he continued. He could not do otherwise. The recollection demanded satisfaction.

"Little black dolls…torn rags…scattered…ripped apart. I saw them." Vacant eyes. Violent memories so insistent.

"Be quiet now, Roberts. Let the anesthesia work."

"…people running…the 20MM. I didn't know…"

"Take him into the infirmary and clean him up, dammit." Swanson ordered brusquely. A red flush crept across his face. He tossed a bloody bandage angrily into a wastebasket. "We'll keep him for a day or so."

The surgeon cleaned the operating table and began to reorganize his equipment. It had been a long day. As the pilot was being wheeled through the doorway he heard him mumble something about an explosion and torn dolls.

Swanson examined Roberts' flight suit and bloody boot. He emptied the pockets; a handkerchief, a few survival articles; knife, mirror, flares and a wallet, eleven dollars and change, a photo of a young woman, his wife or girlfriend? A very pretty girl, Doc thought, in summer clothes waving merrily to an unknown photographer on a happier day. Swanson knew little of Roberts' background, if she was his wife then he was a fortunate man. He would not ask. Swanson avoided intimate knowledge of his fellow crewmembers, better that way.

He opened the cabinet and removed a bottle. Doc Swanson was a temperate man but occasionally the ugliness got to him. The banality of evil. He had heard confessions before and this one was little different from so many others. A decent man had slaughtered fleeing people on a sandy beach because he had been directed to do so. The enemy had tried to kill him in return. For what? Anger sprung from the realization that this particular senselessness was not unique, it happened every day.

Blood had dripped from the operating table onto the floor. Doc swore quietly. He bent down to clean the evidence of Roberts' punishment from his view. A furious headache began pounding in his right temple. He was tired.

Swanson glanced into his office. On his desk in plain view was a newsmagazine he hadn't found time to read. He slugged down the liquor with grim determination. The cover page showed two men conferring, the President and the Secretary of Defense. They were hunched over a desk studying a large map. A poignant smile played across the Secretary's pasty face as he pointed at some obscure spot on the Vietnamese coast. The President looked pleased.

It was just then that Doc Swanson smashed the bottle into the wall.

4

The ship drifted gently against the dock in the warm tropical breeze that blew in from the Pacific and fluttered through tall, spindly palm trees that covered the green hillside above Subic Bay. Although the Sharpsburg was snubbed and secured with thick mooring lines, one could feel an occasional rocking from the Pacific current that flowed through the harbor into the Bay flushing the fetid outflow of ships and city into the clear, deep ocean. Stressed mooring lines and fenders scraped against the wood pylons sending a melody of sounds that blended with harsher strains of shipboard maintenance activities. The Sharpsburg had arrived in the US Naval Station in the Philippines two days earlier for a long overdue maintenance and liberty period. The ship's aircraft had flown to Cubi Point two hours before the ship entered the vast Asian port. Damaged aircraft and those requiring periodic checkups would be attended to in the extensive Cubi Point maintenance hangars before returning to the hostile skies over North Vietnam.

Scaffolding was suspended from the carrier's flight deck carrying workers that scraped and repainted the old, battle-scarred hull into a mottled and shoddy appearance. Bright flashes inside the hangar bay

from acetylene torches punctuated reflections from the blue bay and
men scurried about like colony ants.

Dan Roberts pointed a cane at a battered Skyraider being hoisted
from the deck and said something, all three men standing on the flight
deck laughed.

"And the next time you screw up we're gonna make you fly it off the
way you bring it back, Ensign Roberts," Bobby Thomas said.

A huge crane lifted Roberts' damaged Skyraider from the flight deck
and lowered it carefully onto a flatbed truck parked on the tarmac below.

"Jeez, what a mess. You oughtta be ashamed," Herb McGinnis added.

Roberts pointed here and there with a cane, which he used to accen-
tuate an animated conversation directed toward the battered airplane.

"I think next time, I will fly it ashore…I'll desert you bastards."
Roberts did an awkward little jig using the cane as a pivot. "Probably
wouldn't come back, either…better over there, I hear." The cane flailed
toward a teeming city that bordered the Naval base.

"Fly? You must mean *point*. I think *to fly* would imply some degree of
skillful manipulation of the flight controls, that's just absurd." Herb
McGinnis gave Dan Roberts a contemptuous nudge. "You Spad drivers
are rough on your toys."

"Back-off, McGinnis." Roberts brandished the cane. "In the right
hands this thing could be considered…." He paused for the correct word.

"Lethal?" Herb suggested. "Sure…it's another blunt instrument,
which is exactly what that friggin Spad is." He pointed at the Skyraider.

"Watch it, Herb," Bobby Thomas interjected, "…he's probably just as
dangerous with that silly cane as he is with an airplane…look at that
untidiness."

The Skyraider lay in several pieces on the truck, cowling removed,
battered and grimy. Patches speckled the mutilated fuselage. Oil and
hydraulic fluid still oozed from ruptured lines.

"Actually, *to fly* would never be an appropriate term for a pilot like
Roberts here." Herb flipped a derisive thumb. "Don't even mention the

word 'pilot'…just say something like *driver*. He's a Spad driver, D-R-I-V-E-R, as in bus driver."

"I might just go kiss that particular Spad," Roberts mumbled, as he did frequently. "Hey, when're you guys going on liberty? I need a break from this bullshit."

"Right now," McGinnis said. "Why don't you come along, Dan? Bobby here's offered one or two of his girlfriends for recreation."

"Girlfriends? Bobby?" Roberts smirked. "Little brown carnivores, I hear."

"Just forget it, guys. I need 'em all. Every delicate little morsel."

"No thanks, I'll stay here," Roberts said. "It's safer and I got the duty. Skipper suggested I volunteer. I'm on sick call, you know."

"Old Isaacson's being rather severe on you, isn't he?"

"Not really. Hell, I wouldn't go in town even with a crutch." Roberts waved the cane. "You don't need my help to…uhh…"

"Debauch?" Herb suggested. "I only said that because I get tired of waiting for a tongue-tied cripple to think of the proper word all the time."

"I can think of a proper word for you, asshole."

"Shut up, Dan."

And then Bobby said, *Don't curse the walking wounded, please.* And Roberts insisted, *I may be a damn cripple, but I ain't no scooter driver, like Herb. I'm the duty officer…now, get outta here before I call out the guard. We'll throw you in the brig before you tear up Olongapo.* To which Herb replied, *Scooter driver?* defensively. *Yes, Herb.* Bobby explained. *The A-4 is called the Scooter because of its diminutive size and forgiving flight characteristics. Designed for fussy, fidgety pilots, such as yourself.*

"Bobby, I like to insult Herb all by myself, please." Roberts slapped his cane for emphasis.

"You ain't got the words, Danny," Thomas said.

"Mr. Numb-tongue," Herb added.

Mild-mannered Herb McGinnis was not the sort to tear up anything. He was a North Carolina boy who had entered the Naval Academy and flight training because he liked the recruiting posters. Roberts and McGinnis had reported aboard the Sharpsburg one month earlier as replacement pilots and had been assigned to the same room. His placid nature blended well with Roberts' more acerbic temperament and Roberts had taken an immediate liking to his roommate.

"Time for you to go, Herb," Roberts said.

"Forget it, I'm not going into that stink hole…don't worry about that."

"Oh, yes you are, Ensign McGinnis," Thomas insisted. "I've taken it upon myself to see that you finally learn to comport yourself properly. Even a ring-knocker like you has certain physical needs."

"What the heck does that mean?"

"Ring-knocker? A compulsive, anal as in Annapolis, graduate. I thought you knew that already."

"I think he means that as an insult, Herb." Roberts laughed.

"I'm talking about women…Herby. What the hell do you think…booze, women, song…that stuff. You're supposed to be a sailor on liberty. Certain traditions apply here."

"I'm not gonna…"

"Ensign McGinnis…do you know what I am?"

Herb considered the question momentarily. "Yes sir, you're a pain in the ass."

"Wrong!..well…not altogether wrong," Bobby snapped. "However, the answer I was seeking is Lieutenant Commander. That means I'm senior and you will obey my orders." A large grin across a sunburned face. "In addition, *Ensign* McGinnis, I am the airgroup's senior LSO which means that if you don't want unnecessary wave-offs on dark, stormy nights you better humor me. Is that plain enough for a dipshit Annapolis twerp, like you?"

"Subtlety is not Bobby's…" Roberts paused.

"Forte?" McGinnis suggested. "Bobby, do you notice that I must frequently finish sentences for my tongue-tied roommate."

"Yeah…you're helpful."

Lieutenant-Commander Robert Thomas was indeed the senior Landing Signal Officer and he could exercise certain punitive actions upon uncooperative junior aviators, wave-offs being the most severe, and no Naval Aviator in his right mind ever wanted to go around for another landing attempt. *Get it aboard the first time!*

"So, let's go amongst them, brave and noble warrior."

Bobby Thomas was tall and slender and frequently spoke with guarded eloquence. He smiled at the two junior officers, a grin that crinkled around slate-blue eyes. His face was a structure of planes and facets that flexed with mood and concentration. An open face of an intelligent, admirable man, Roberts thought. Thomas had become an instant friend after he'd debriefed Roberts' last battle-damaged landing.

"I think I hear my mother calling me."

"Dammit, Herb…your mother can't be everywhere. That's why the Navy has the chain-of-command and guys like me for guidance. Now…let's go downtown."

"Don't forget your rubbers, boys," Roberts said. "Oh, Commander Thomas, you'll see little Herby back home by midnight, won't you?" He observed an obscene gesture from his roommate, Ensign Herbert McGinnis, who was a genuine Annapolis graduate. "I'll be so worried….don't forget my Scotch, Herb."

They hustled down the gangplank and onto the wharf. Roberts watched Herb, a cautious man in all matters, step gingerly over a coiled lanyard while Bobby, his older companion, jumped over the obstructions with gleeful élan.

Look at him walk. Roberts thought. *Herb's too careful.* But, that was Herb McGinnis, the prudent man. Intelligent. Articulate. Blond, wavy hair seemed to float in angelic disarray in spite of Herb's fastidious grooming. Herb, the lanky athlete. Dan Roberts admired many qualities of his friend and roommate. Although they had struggled through Pensacola together as student aviators, they had not known each other well. Herb was studious, an affable bachelor. He had lived in the BOQ while Roberts lived off-base with Helen. They met occasionally in crowds of boisterous drinkers at the Mustin Beach Officer's Club but Roberts could not recall ever talking to Herb until they had reported aboard the Sharpsburg a few weeks earlier.

Their room was located in the bow of the ship below the flight deck under the port catapult that slammed resoundingly against the forward stop at the end of its powerful stroke and shook the room with relentless regularity. It was one of the least desirable junior officer's quarters as befitted their lowly status. Roberts had coined their assigned quarters *The Tranquillity Room*, after Herb had been shaken by a particularly jarring catapult stroke.

"Dammit…" Herb had dropped his book. "I hate living under an airport."

"They must have warned you about this in Boat School."

"Negative!" Herb replied. "They promised me interesting Naval adventures and lots of fun. Hours and hours of pillage and rape. They're goddamn liars…only things I've seen so far is SAM missiles chasing my ass and Triple-A. My mother was right."

Roberts remembered laughing at his vehemence and suspected that Herb's mother was always right. Herb admitted being in awe of his remarkable mother. His father had died during World War Two and she had worked at various menial jobs to support the quiet boy and encouraged him when he wanted to attend the Naval Academy. Mrs. McGinnis had a peculiar way of expressing herself and, according to Herb, used curious admonitions when trying to explain life's complexities to her only son. In college Roberts had studied the Oracle of Delphi and thought Herb's mother must be a reincarnated Pythic. Many of her admonitions had been prescient and her simple homilies were generally true.

Herb and Bobby disappeared behind mounds of equipment stacked along the dock. Strains of a popular song floated faintly from Bobby's direction as he guided Herb to their targets, the city and its amusements. *Downtown…you're going to be alright nowwww.* Bobby sang Petula Clark's current hit, a favorite among the more cynical pilots of the Seventh Fleet.

Downtown.

Actually, there were two *Downtowns.*

The song inadvertently described two most important factors in the uncertain lives of Seventh Fleet aviators, downtown Olongapo and downtown Hanoi. One, a raucous liberty town with bright lights, depravity and loud noises where many forms of pillage and rape *were* available, at a price. The other had no visible lights, was visited on deadly nighttime bombing missions but offered strange noises and bright explosions that a pilot could never forget. The two Downtowns. Two exciting and dangerous Asian cities.

They were close friends now, but Roberts realized the truth about Ensign McGinnis. The boy from North Carolina had no business flying a bomber over North Vietnam. Herb was a gentle being and cautious by nature. Although he was a graduate of one of the world's premier military academies, Ensign Herbert McGinnis was not a warrior.

After a recent heated discussion about current politics, Roberts said: "Dammit Herb…you should be a long-haired college professor somewhere….writing poetry and deflowering coeds…leading peace marches…blubbering liberal…"

"Dogma?" Herb offered. On reflection, he had agreed.

"Roberts…."

A stern voice interrupted his thoughts. Roberts glanced back into the dim depths of the hangar bay. In the intense tropical light of the quarterdeck he could not see clearly into the shadowy gloom but he recognized the voice. He had expected it. Dreaded it.

"Yes, sir." Roberts replied before he could distinguish the stocky figure beckoning from the shadows. Roberts limped slowly through the quarterdeck that served as the ship's formal entry while in port. The ship's OOD stood his watch there and greeted visitors before entry into confines of the ship. A red carpet temporarily adorned the deck; at sea it was just another working space on the hangar bay.

Commander Gerald Isaacson looked Roberts up and down with a critical eye. "See you're getting around OK…feeling better now, I hope?" A smile was not offered, nor expected.

"Yes, sir. No problems…stitches come out in a couple days. I'll be ready to go back to work."

"Next time maybe you won't get so damn close in a strafing run, like I told you." Isaacson had a habit of nodding his head at the completion of a sentence, to corroborate a statement, a palpable over-and-out. "But, look, I do appreciate your volunteering for the Watch. The rest of the guys have been at sea too long…need the rest and whatever else they can find in that filthy town. God help 'em." Isaacson had been a boxer at the Naval Academy and Roberts suspected the head nodding was an involuntary defensive impulse. Isaacson had an intimidating manner, large nose, jutting chin. Average height, beefy shoulders on a muscular frame, hard eyes that invited little dissension. He did not suffer fools gladly and he had little tolerance for weakness. He was not accustomed to failure.

"I don't mind, sir. I haven't been aboard very long…they deserve the time off. I…."

"Listen, Roberts…." Isaacson interrupted. "I'm going with CAG and the other squadron C.O.'s to Manila for a conference. Be gone a couple of days. You'll have to handle the squadron…the exec and department heads're all on leave. Think you can handle it?" The examination continued through cold, blue eyes. There was always an uncertainty about replacement pilots, *new guys*.

"Yes, sir…should be pretty quiet around here." Roberts wondered if Isaacson ever addressed junior officers by their Christian names.

"You should've started on that Franklin thing by now. Anything yet?" A head nod. He examined Roberts with critical disdain.

Roberts had expected the question. He'd been directed to investigate the disappearance of Airman Darryl Franklin, a squadron sailor mysteriously missing at sea, a timely report was required.

"Couldn't do much in sickbay, sir. But, I'll start working on it this week. Hope to have something before we sail again."

"Well, get right on it. I need a full report ASAP. I suggest you get Pete to help…he knows all the men." Still no smile.

"Yes, sir." Now he'll nod his head and leave, Roberts thought.

"By the way…that walking-cane looks cute. You remind me of Fred Astaire. Maybe we better get you a top hat and tails." He hunched broad shoulders and searched Roberts for any sign of defiance. Then Isaacson nodded his head and disappeared down the ladder. He did not look back and he did not notice Roberts' reddening face.

Sonofabitch. Roberts had been confined to sick bay for three days before Doc Swanson had discharged him. Several pilots had stopped to visit, but Isaacson had not.

What had happened to Franklin? Roberts wondered. The young Airman 3rd Class had simply disappeared without a trace. He had failed to report for muster one morning and subsequent searches were unsuccessful. *Missing at sea.* Not an unusual occurrence, especially in a wartime navy. *Presumed dead.*

Dan Roberts had reported aboard the Sharpsburg a few days after the airman had vanished, replacing Lt. Ted Williamson, who had been killed in a tragic accident. The new pilot was assigned to the Maintenance Department working for Bobby Thomas and had been delegated the unenviable task of investigating Franklin's disappearance. The squadron's safety officer had conducted an incomplete cursory investigation.

Missing at sea. A puzzling affair…a missing person in a highly confined environment. On the USS Sharpsburg you couldn't easily find a place to disappear. It was difficult to avoid contact with other crewmembers or to seek solitude in the tight confines of the ship. Missing? Where could he have gone but overboard?

Roberts limped through the hangar deck; every step sent a sharp pain through his left leg but he could do without the cane. He *would* do without it. Isaacson's biting comment had contained a blunt message. Weakness, or even the appearance of frailty, would not be tolerated. The skipper was a stickler for protocol and demanded sturdiness from his men. Isaacson was not a popular commander.

Roberts hobbled toward the lowered port elevator; a cooling breeze flowed into the shadows of the hangar bay bringing pungent fragrances of Subic Bay. He stopped for a moment to watch a group of enlisted men playing basketball on a makeshift court. Boisterous shouts and grunts echoed through the cavernous bay as the two-man teams vied for position, a shot careened from the backboard toward him. Roberts retrieved the ball and bounced it awkwardly until the men had repositioned themselves.

"Come on, Mr. Roberts...dump it!" Timothy Bryan shouted, then frowned. The plane captain was still uncertain about the worthiness of any pilot who would return his aircraft in such an unworthy condition as Ensign Roberts had recently done.

"Pretty long shot for an officer," Roberts replied. He looked from Bryan to the hoop.

"Betcha can't sink it, sir."

"Well now, Bryan," Roberts laughed. "A wager? Better think about it...I'm pretty good." He dropped the cane awkwardly. "Never could resist a dare. Tell you what...I sink it and you guys polish my shoes. If I miss, I'll spring for burgers at the gedunk...deal?" He dribbled the ball a few times to whet the appetite of the situation.

"Yes, sir! But, we ain't s'posta bet with officers."

They were plane captains of Attack Squadron 433, the *brown-shirts* of the line division and they worked in the noisy, dangerous world of a carrier flight deck, a hostile environment of fuel, oil, oxygen and deadly ordnance loads. A risky job with few rewards and a convenient place for the maintenance officer to dump troublemakers. Roberts had been assigned to head the line division three weeks earlier.

"It's not a bet...an...." Roberts struggled for the word. "...an agreement." He saw an opportunity. It could be difficult for a new officer in a squadron of veterans.

"You ain't gotta chance, Mr. Roberts...better move a little closer!" Bryan smacked his lips. "I can taste them hamburgers already."

"Nope...I'm gonna shoot from here. My shoes need a good shining today...besides my foot hurts."

The men laughed. A preposterous notion, polishing an officer's shoes.

"Watch this."

Four pairs of eyes followed the ball as it floated toward the hoop. Roberts bent to retrieve his cane before the ball brushed the rim and rolled through the net. He looked up to see the ball drop into the disappointed hands of Timothy Bryan.

"Dang!"

"You men just learned an important lesson. Never, never trust an officer carrying a cane...with dirty shoes." Roberts had been particularly adept at that type of shot in high school.

"I'll shine them shoes for you, Mr. Roberts...but I'm thinkin you was just lucky." Bryan growled. He assumed responsibility for the disaster. The pilot who had flown 407, his airplane, had tricked them.

"Tell you what, Bryan. Double or nothing...I'll give you another chance." Roberts stood there, smiling.

"What...you ain't gonna shoot again, sir? You was just lucky." Bryan felt a wisp of salvation. The shot could have been pure luck. Still, one couldn't be too careful around officers and Bryan sensed that Ensign Roberts was someone to watch carefully.

"I have three pairs of shoes in my locker. Same bet...only you polish them all if I can do it again."

Suspicious eyes calculating the odds. A trap? Officers were naturally clever. Bryan cleared his throat noisily.

"Deal?"

Since, by unspoken agreement, Bryan would be the one to polish the shoes, the three accomplices allowed him to accept or reject the wager. With authority goes responsibility, the Navy adage they knew so well.

"Kay...only, one step back this time. Gimme your cane, sir." Bryan handed Roberts the ball.

A blurred movement in the corner of Roberts' eye; he bounced the ball a few times and nodded to Chief O'Leary, who had walked over to investigate the unusual situation. The men responded to the delay with nervous impatience. It was nearly time for midday chow and there was that unresolved issue of a thick, juicy civilian hamburger from the gedunk.

Roberts concentrated on the back of the rim. Then, he shifted his focus to the side of the hoop and let fly. The ball arced slowly then bounced off the edge of the rim. A near miss and a spontaneous cheer.

"Jeez...you missed, Mr. Roberts."

"Damn, I almost got it."

"You ain't gonna Welch on us, sir?" Three heads nodded in agreement with Bryan. Pete O'Leary watched from a distance, said nothing.

"I'm thinking about it." He frowned. "Hmmm...the elevator's down and I can't run very fast...I suppose you guys might throw me overboard? Well, since I lost fair and square." He handed Bryan a ten. "You take the men to chow, Bryan. I'm going down for a last look at our Spad before they truck it away."

"Hey...thanks, Mr. Roberts." Bryan accepted the ten and then tipped the cane in a dapper salute.

"Just one catch, Bryan. You gotta drop that cane at sick bay on your way."

"No problem-o, sir."

The four laughing plane captains hurried off. They would forego lunch at the enlisted mess and have one on an officer. It was a good day for plane captains.

"You flubbed that shot on purpose, Mr. Roberts." Pete O'Leary chuckled. A large grin on a ruddy Irish face.

"Oh, heck, Chief. I wouldn't sandbag...."

"With all due respect, I know a setup when I see one, sir." The chief shook his head. "Done it myself, a time or two."

"They're a good bunch, Pete." Roberts felt slightly uncomfortable addressing the chief by a familiar nickname, but everyone did, including Cdr. Isaacson. "Besides, I like to polish my own shoes."

"I'm not surprised. Giving up your cane, sir?" Pete nodded toward the departing sailors. Bryan was swinging the cane like a baseball bat.

"Yep! Damned nuisance. I must look like Fred Astaire."

"Sure," Pete said. "I'd tolerate the limp, myself."

"Say, Chief. Glad I ran into you." Roberts changed the subject. "I gotta write a report on Franklin. Could you bring his Personnel Evaluation Form to the maintenance office this afternoon? I never knew him...maybe you could..."

"Certainly. I wrote his last Eval. I can fill you in, sir."

"Thanks, Pete. Not much to say about him, I guess?"

Pete, Master Chief Peter O'Leary. Large, gregarious and intelligent. Dan Roberts had taken an instant liking to the burly Non-Com. He'd joined the Navy after graduating from high school in Chicago and had become an excellent engine mechanic. A natural leader, Roberts learned that Pete had been offered a commission and would have accepted, but he preferred the prestige of a Chief Petty Officer, a position commanding great respect.

"No, sir. I expect not. Accidents happen. I'll bring you the report."

Roberts limped through the quarterdeck onto the gangway. On the tarmac below a group of men were securing his damaged Spad onto the flatbed truck. It would be delivered to the overhaul facility, repaired and returned to service with VA-433.

A longshoreman walked over to greet Roberts who stood awkwardly rubbing a leg while he surveyed the damaged airplane.

"Need something, sir?"

"No, thanks...just saying good-bye." Roberts limped over and touched a wheel. The tire was flat and hydraulic fluid dripped slowly from an oleo strut.

"Your airplane, sir?"

"Yes...my fault." He looked up at the pitiful Spad. A jagged hole under the cockpit where a shell fragment had splintered into his leg.

"You're lucky, sir. To get it back, I mean."

Roberts stared curiously at the man. A flash. An instant recall of a long stretch of silvery-white beach, fiery smoke and fleeing black figures, of airframe vibration from 20MM cannon fire and black iron-filled blossoms against a blue afternoon sky. Of torn figures scattered on white sand. And a black explosion under the wing. Of pain and fear and guilt. He remembered a small village nearby. Would there have been women and children on the beach?

"Yep...that's me...just about the luckiest sonofabitch around."

A few minutes later Roberts sipped coffee with Pete O'Leary in the maintenance office, the dark cramped space located in the aft part of the ship below the round-down and forward of the spud locker, not far from where his Spad had been stored.

Pete shoved the personnel report across the desk. In the brown covered jacket was the evaluation on Darryl Franklin and his performance on the job.

"Not four-oh by any means, sir. But a competent sailor and capable of good work on occasion."

Roberts quickly scanned the report then examined a few documents detailing the Navy life of the missing sailor.

"Who wrote this report, Chief?"

"I did the initial work-up and Mr. Thomas finished it."

"High marks on intelligence…middling on competence and lower marks on…well, the social portions."

"Yes, sir. The kid was bright, no doubt about it. And he could do excellent work, if he wanted to. Could be a troublemaker, though."

"Really, how so?"

"Hard to put your finger on, Mr. Roberts. Smart ass, mostly. Little bit of a bully, too. Not well liked, I'd say. But, not an outcast, either. He was capable of making friends…if it suited him. He had his problems."

"Racial problems?" Franklin was an African-American. Roberts didn't like the new word. It seemed demeaning, half-African and half-American…equaled what?

"No. Not exactly. He seemed well accepted at first. Good athlete. Intelligent and he could be quite personable. Good sense of humor."

"Think he committed suicide?"

"Probably."

"Why?"

"This your first cruise, sir?"

Roberts shrugged. "Sure. Hope it's not my last. Does it show that badly, Pete?"

"No, sir," Pete chuckled. A deep throaty laugh that invited anyone who heard it into a sailor's brotherhood. "No disrespect intended. But, you'll see. After a while all of a man's strengths and weaknesses come out on a long cruise. Especially a war cruise. There're few secrets aboard a ship. Some people just can't take it. It's the impersonal power of a crowd that crushes some guys. This is not an easy life for anyone, especially in the lower ranks. Suicides are not that rare unfortunately. We try to watch out for the potential jumpers. But, sometimes….well, it just happens. Hell, there are days…"

The discussion continued for several minutes. An intelligent, tough, well-adjusted sailor was missing. And, by default, suicide was the only explanation.

"You gonna get any liberty, sir?"

"Nope. I'm the SDO. Other guys need it more than me. You going ashore?"

"I don't know, maybe. A cool San Miguel would taste good, wouldn't it?"

"You live in Oakland, Pete?" Roberts asked to be polite. Pete O'Leary was an easy man to like.

"No, sir…Berkeley. My wife likes it better there."

"Kids?"

"No…just got married last year. Wife's a professional model…goes to school in Berkeley now…part time."

He showed Roberts a wallet-sized photo of a nearly nude young woman. A professional studio shot of a languid coquette in artistic pose. A very beautiful, very young, stimulating woman with dazzling sunlight shining on red, wavy hair draped over alabaster shoulders. Roberts recalled wartime photos of Rita Hayworth. In the background the Golden Gate Bridge was crowned by a sunlit California sky. Roberts caught himself staring at the photo and was embarrassed by Pete's knowing smile. He did not know what to say.

"Ain't she something, sir?"

"She's…beautiful." Inadequate, but the best he could do. "You're a lucky man, Pete."

"That I am." A gleam of fierce pride broke over Pete's rugged face. "Bought her a new Mustang convertible just before we left on the cruise. Candy-apple red. Gotta take good care of my baby…keep her loyal."

"Don't blame you…money well spent, I'd say."

The sensual luster of Mrs. O'Leary's smile captivated Roberts. Her vibrant sexuality was difficult to ignore. He returned the photo. Pete grasped it between thumb and forefinger momentarily; a slow gentle smile crept over his brawny face.

"Yes, sir, sure is. Some women are just naturally high-maintenance, you know."

5

Evening in Olongapo. An unforgettable melange of raucous sounds and pungent odors. Few places in the modern world could match the kaleidoscope of activity surrounding the North Carolinian as he strolled beside Bobby Thomas through the Mecca of hedonism, the last of the American Navy's Asian ports-of-call. A liberty town devoted to one primary activity, an exchange of needs. A haven for sailors to release pent-up aggressions and subdued sexual energy in exchange for the mighty American dollar. A perfect synergy of commerce. Everything was available and the prices were reasonable. Music, laughter, boisterous noise. Garishly painted Jeepneys darted in and out of dark alleys and unpaved streets with horns blasting a warning to all. Pungent odors from barbecue stands that sold sizzling morsels to tourists who should have known better. The noise!

Black is black..I want my baby back…

A popular song blaring from every dive and honky-tonk. A girl's shrill laughter punctured the thick air. An angry scream echoed through canyons of debauchery.

They swaggered down the dirty street, modern cowboys in an Oriental Dodge City eager to wash away the trail-dust of an air war. Derelict children darted past sailors and tourists looking for the easy marks. Stealing, cajoling the unwary to positions of vulnerability. Pickpockets abounded and hookers hung from doorways. Music, laughter, shouts of joy and remorse mingled in a constant assault on the senses.

Gray is gray…I want her here to stay…

"Los Bravos must be making a zillion dollars on that stupid song," Herb groaned. He wished they were back in the Cubi Officers Club.

"I like it," Bobby said. "Has a certain charm."

"Charm? Rudimentary cadence and bass rhythms that appeal to Neanderthals, like some people I know."

"Yeah. Ain't it great? I love it here."

Degradation poured out of every cranny. Herb flinched a time or two. Children stealing from drunken sailors. Cheap booze and cheaper women thrust at him from every nook, corruption seethed around every street corner. Almost immediately Herb was certain that he hated every element of the ugly town.

And yet…

There was *something*. And he almost quivered with the excitement of that thing, an indefinable, intriguing aura of unrestrained depravity. *A liberty town.* The last fleshpot of the old China Fleet's liberty ports. Dodge City, or old Shanghai, couldn't have been significantly different. The small brown Filipino women were as enticing and dangerous as the hookers of the old West.

What can I doooo? 'cause I, I, I, I'm feelin' bluuuueee…

Precisely.

Bobby and Herb had spent the late afternoon in the new Cubi Point Officers Club on the Naval Air Station located on the shore of Subic Bay and separated from Olongapo by a fetid canal dubbed the Perfume River.

There they had met friends from the Intrepid, another carrier refitting for Yankee Station. Several rounds of liar's dice and San Miguel beer had primed the two aviators for their venture into Dodge City East.

"I liked the old Club better," Bobby complained. "Goddammit Herb, why do they have to change all the really good things in life?"

"*They* who?"

"Just they, dammit. *They*, those shitty little narrow-minded goddam bureaucratic bastards that always screw things up."

"Oh, you must mean CincPac?"

"Yeah…them and all the rest. Do you know what the Roman Centurions did to guys like that?"

"Like who?"

"Like MacNamara, for instance…assholes like him."

"Damned if I know."

"Cut their balls off!" Bobby chuckled with delight. "Of course, in MacNamara's case…may not have been necessary." Herb watched a barmaid scurry beyond the grasp of an inebriated fighter pilot.

"The old club was great, Herb, before the bastards tore it down."

"C'mon, Bobby, I heard it was old and flimsy and made out of plywood and you guys kept tearing it apart and they'd have to rebuild it every year. Maybe that's why."

"Yeah…it was wonderful!" A barmaid foolishly ventured within range and Bobby pinched a pint-size Filipino ass.

"Ouch! Bobby you one big sombitch…sometimes."

Bobby laughed and Herb could tell that he was truly happy. This was his world. This place and this time were precisely what Robert Thomas would have them be. He was in a war zone, more exactly in a liberty port between combat engagements in that war zone and with the promise of speedy returns to both. The alternating challenge of combat relieved by boisterous R&R in this convenient fleshpot. A perfect synergy for the natural warrior. Bobby was happy!

"Pinchers get no more drink."

"That was only half a pinch. Come back here, I'll give you the whole nine-yards."

The violated waitress turned slowly and they were taken by the inherent grace of her lithe body.

"Hey, Bobby, what you do here, anyways?" she crooned. "I hear you get killed."

There was little uncertainty in Bobby Thomas' world. This is exactly where a combat pilot should be. Herb understood that fact and he was angry with himself for coveting the unfettered life of a professional warrior like Bobby. Herb envied the clarity.

"New club kept the same bargirls, though. I take comfort in familiar faces. Don't you Herby?"

"How would you remember? I doubt you ever took a serious look at their *faces*…sir."

"That's better. Show a little respect with your insults. How about another beer." Bobby reached for the dice cup.

"No, thanks."

"Good." Bobby signaled for another round.

"I'm broke, Bobby. Don't spend my money too fast."

"Hell, so what? I'm broke too. Hell, I'm always broke." Bobby frowned. "If only I had more money, just think of the fun I could have."

Herb glanced down at the dance floor; a group of fighter jocks were preparing an inebriated victim for a *catapult* shot. He tried to ignore Bobby and the dice; he did not want more beer. What he wanted was to be left alone for a few hours, free of the enforced closeness of shipboard life. A few precious hours alone in Subic would be a release from the confines of the Sharpsburg.

The fighter pilots had formed two parallel lines on the landing above the dance floor. A semi-conscious volunteer pilot was strapped into a bar chair. The cat officer, who waved his arm in the power-up signal, sent the hapless catapultee skidding precariously across the wooden floor. At the stair leading down to the dance floor below, two pilots held a towel across his path where the pilot would attempt a *landing*. Very few ended in a successful trap. Most crashed spectacularly onto the dance floor, which was usually vacant, since it took a truly fearless man to invite a respectable woman there.

"Say Herb…wanna hear about Captain Jimmy Allison and the old club?"

"No!"

"Good. I'll tell you." Bobby joined in the applause for the pilot whose trap had ended in a noisy but painful failure. A split upper lip spewed red droplets on the dance floor and a sympathetic friend tossed a glass of beer into his face to sterilize the wound.

"Well, the old club was wonderful…perfect in every way. Form and function fitted to location. I think Frank Lloyd Wright designed it." The bait was cast.

"Oh, bullshit!" Herb interjected and Bobby laughed with satisfaction. "I studied architecture. Wright never designed anything in the Philippines. That's the stupidest thing I ever heard."

"Don't be so judgmental, Herby," Bobby interrupted. "Anyway, the old club was right over there." Bobby pointed through the expansive windows. "Wright might have designed it. You never know?"

"Baloney."

The new Cubi Point Officers Club successfully combined the flavor of the tropics with the efficiency of a California cabaret. Broad windows provided a visual frame around a singularly beautiful vista. Massive trees and colorful tropical vegetation undulated down the green hillside to the blue bay. At the foot of the hillside the vast shipping port of Subic Bay sprawled in constant motion, giant cranes lifted supplies onto Seventh Fleet ships. Watercraft of every shape and size zipped about churning the calm blue surface with mottled gray streaks. Busy docks commanded the shoreline while support facilities stretched inland to the malodorous canal separating the expansive base from Olongapo.

The center of club's activity was the dining room on the upper level, which overlooked a spacious barroom. A small dance floor, where the unsuccessful cat shot had been performed, and a snackbar adjoined at the extreme edge of the space.

This modern structure contrasted favorably with the old Officer's Club, which had been a casual plywood building and could have been easily mistaken for one of the base's derelict warehouses. It had been hastily built in the early 'fifties, an inexpensive slap-up where aviators could release destructive energies in an expendable plywood box and stay far, far away from the nicer Subic Bay Officer's Club over on the black-shoe section of the base.

"The new building's beautiful, though," Bobby conceded. "In fact, there's only one drawback. It's too...*nice*." The Navy could not allow this expensive structure to be used and abused as the old club had been. This was not to Bobby's taste. "I preferred the *old* club...hell, I preferred the *old* Navy." Bobby was an old style Naval Aviator.

"I'm thinking maybe I'll head back to the ship now," Herb ventured. "Gotta a good book waiting in the Tranquillity Room."

Bobby, who had been communicating with a barmaid, looked up in dismay.

"Captain Jimmy Allison...what a prick. He cut me out of the landing pattern once last year. He was CAG on the Sharpsburg then. I was staff LSO. Bastard came into the old club a couple weeks later just after he had been promoted to captain. Another ding-a-ling Annapolis ring-knocker, kinda like you, Herb. Anyway, he started chewing on several pilots...he was a CAPTAIN now, by god!"

"Who hit him first?" Herb asked politely.

"I recall his exact statement to one fighter jock: '*Don't talk back to me, asshole. I'm a Captain!*' Well, this poor guy was rather drunk, you know, so he punched Captain Jimmy's lights out right on the spot. Before much longer two other pilots had decked the silly sonofabitch, too. Shore patrol hustled everyone back to the ship...what a waste. Hadn't even been into town yet. The Sharpsburg's captain confined us all to the ship for the rest of the R&R. Jimmy spent the rest of the cruise getting even. Shit...what a night."

"Lemme guess..." Herb had heard the rumors but had not believed them. Captains were rarely assaulted but the Vietnam War and the 'sixties were anything but normal. "You should be ashamed of yourself, Bobby."

"Oh...I am. But Jimmy's such a jerk. He was on TV recently...war hero, you know. What a blockhead. Probably be CNO someday."

Bobby smiled at a pleasant recollection and gazed through the window at the vibrant scene below. A division of F-8s entered a formation break-up before landing on Cubi Point's runway. The vista was terrific. Fighters darting about the airstrip, ships plying the harbor and tropical beauty surrounding a crystalline bay.

"Look, Herb. Where in the world can you see such awe-inspiring things? Great place to begin an R&R, isn't it? Even a ring-knocker's gotta see that."

"OK...it's nice."

"Goddammit, Herb...think about it! It's good to be alive and drinking beer and watching airplanes and ships...relaxing between combat tours. And we haven't even seen Olongapo yet. Ain't life grand?"

Herb laughed. "Didn't know you were such a philosopher."

"Yeah...well, my talents were never fully appreciated." The barmaid who he had briefly fondled delivered two beers and waited momentarily for another friendly assault. When it was not immediately delivered she said: "Bobby, you such a teaseeerr...I love you, I think...you still love me alla same?"

"Impeccably!"

She was only a barmaid and therefore wasn't expected to understand such complicated words. But, she had heard Bobby mention pecker in a moment of intimate conjunction and since there were similar sounds in this new word, then it must indicate a good thing.

So, she smiled in contentment and offered a tempting portion of her anatomy, but wiggled away before Bobby could respond.

Bobby laughed with joy. "Dammit…ain't life grand? Let's eat."

"Oh…must we," Herb whined.

"Yes. We'll need our strength later. We have maidens to serve and wine to drink."

"What did I do to deserve…?"

"Let me give you some advice, Herb. Don't always be so prudent."

"Prudent?"

"Yes, one might even say, *cautious*. That's an insult by the way. Carrier pilots are rarely described as cautious. Try to be a little more impetuous."

"Screw you, Bobby."

*   *   *

Now they wandered through the dirty town and Herb stopped to examine a Jeepney. A garish yellow paint job appointed with delicate blue scrolls caught his attention. Bobby pulled his arm impatiently.

"Let's stop here for a while." Bobby pointed at the joint across the unpaved street. "Want you to see something."

The Willows was scrolled boldly over the establishment's wide entrance. Loud music drifted from an open door where two middle-aged tourists stood cautiously weighing the promise of gratification against the possibility of bodily harm.

"I've seen about all I can stand, Bobby. I'm thinking…"

"Don't think. Try to be more receptive. Don't you want to experience different cultures? See unusual sights…taste foreign foods. Have a little fun. You're only an ensign once, you know."

"I'm not gonna…."

"Besides, there's a war going on," Bobby interrupted. "And you need to adapt, Herb."

"Adapt? Like you, I suppose."

"Could do worse. I have an unusual talent for gleaning the best morsels from any occasion. Trust me."

"I'd sooner trust a snake."

The door swung inward into the darkened, smoke-filled room where Herb expected to see a brawl or two in progress. Instead, he found a pleasant L-shaped barroom. An unused stage loomed behind an armed Filipino soldier who slouched with a Coca-Cola on a chair in a darkened corner.

"Bobbyyyyy…" The screech seemed to emanate from within the bowels of degeneracy. Herb flinched.

An aging *hostess* hustled over to the two aviators. She wrapped a thick arm around Bobby Thomas and gave the laughing pilot a warm, noisy embrace.

"Betty. My own true love."

"I heard you was dead, Bobby. I cried and cried. You OK?"

Herb edged away from the gross woman. Odors issued from her vicinity suggesting cigarettes and booze and ancient depravities.

"Sure. But I still gotta soft pecker, you know."

"Oh, Bobby. You such a liar," she giggled. "Hey! We gotta new girl! She big, fat an' pretty. You wanna try?"

"Betty, please." He gestured toward Herb, who was now some distance removed.

"Who you friend, Bobby? He cute…maybe I marry him."

She was wearing a ribald dress that may have been in fashion when the Japanese occupied the city. Betty was short and rotund. Thick arms protruded from the sleeveless garment and hung toward a pair of lamp-post legs. Broad hips swayed with every notion. Stringy black hair flaked with gray straggled across lumpy shoulders and a steady stream of spittle spewed her audience. Herb, who had a quixotic attitude about women, was appalled.

"Let's go back to the base *now*, Bobby."

"Nooo," Betty interjected. "You stay, Bobby. Lillian be here soon."

"We're here to stay, Betty. Send Lillian out. Shut up, Herb."

Herb groaned. "Okay, be receptive, right?" He'd heard rumors of exotic and perverse exhibitions to be seen in this godless town. "This Lillian thing won't be a disgusting event involving animals, will it Bobby? We just had dinner."

"Oh, we can't miss Lillian's act, Herby. That would be a dereliction...you'll see."

"You sound like my mother, Bobby."

"What did you say?" There was a high noise level in the crowded bar and Bobby thought he had misunderstood.

"Something you said...I've heard it before. My mother..." Herb shrugged.

Be receptive to new ideas, Herbert. She'd said. *Remember, if you want some honey, don't kick the hive.* One of his mother's frequent homilies.

"Good...maybe you should listen to both of us."

Betty ushered them to a table positioned below the small raised stage. A dark-green curtain with hand-painted exotic scenes was drawn across the stage and a soft glow of footlights doused the area. Bobby sat down after pointing Herb to the chair nearest the stage. A barmaid delivered beers and stroked Bobby's shoulder with a familiar eagerness.

"Bobby...we heard you was dead. Who your friend?"

"Not very likely," Bobby sputtered. "And, I'm getting real tired of these unfounded rumors. Those bastards missed me, as usual."

The little barmaid frowned, her feelings injured.

"But, it's good to see you anyway, Mary. Still love me?"

"Sure...you betcha. You wanna...?"

"Maybe later," he said. "Mary helps me with my prostrate problem, Herb. She's a physical therapist, one might say." He beckoned and Mary thrust herself upon his lap.

"Gee...I'd never guess."

"Don't watch us, Herb. Look at that nice curtain or something."

The dark-green velvety cloth was decorated with minute figures in irregular pose and Herb thought the curtain's scenes were hieroglyphics or stylized characters in some mysterious Oriental script. Finally, Herb, who had drunk several beers, was obliged to lean over the edge of the stage for a closer examination.

"Bobby...look..." Herb pointed. "...look at this."

Dozens of characters reigned over the cloth in haphazard fashion. Sexual couplings displayed in an artist's minute depictions of joyful pornographic abandon. Blithe wantonness that flowed from the subjects' engaging exhibition captured his imagination and Herb decided that the curtain was superb artistry. It did not occur to him that alcohol and the deprivations of life at sea could influence his evaluation of an artist's creations.

"Sit down," Bobby said. "Show's about to begin."

The curtain opened. Soft music. A boisterous crowd. A melody drifted above the laughter and celebration and even the most intoxicated of patrons recognized the beginning of the show.

The show.

Lights dimmed and the curtain opened to reveal an empty stage. Then from stage left a flash of movement, a shimmering indefinable form. Music flowed in whispery strains.

Slowly, the unhurried musical passages compelled the audience into silence. A gliding form became visible under a black glow of long-wave ultraviolet light flowing gently into the simple, commanding musical composition. A ribbon of fluorescent movement drifted into the music. The dancer was adorned in a wispy thin robe spiked with small star-like sequins that flashed under the black light.

"Bobby, what...what is that...?"

A vision appeared gliding into slow, pulsating musical cadence from behind that most compelling of curtains. Herb was the moth drawn to the flame of a mysterious, lighted creature. Long iridescent fingernails whipped through the blackness, a free flowing seraph that danced before a willing captive.

Bobby laughed carelessly. "Skipped music appreciation class at boat school, didn't you?"

"Huh?"

"Ravel, Herby…like it?"

"It's fantastic," Herb muttered, trapped in the bewilderment of music and dancer.

Somehow, the gossamer star-specked garment had been discarded. Delicate limbs swirled around streaks of violet luster.

"See something you like, Herb?"

Too soon, the music ended with abrupt crescendo and the curtain closed. Applause. Loud and continuous. Even from a group of badly inebriated attack pilots.

"What?" Herb looked at the closed curtain.

"Maybe you're ready to go back to the ship now. You look kind of tired, my boy." A sly smile played across Bobby's thin lips.

"NO!"

"Oh, I see," Bobby said. "You must've noticed Lillian. Be careful. She's a force to be reckoned with."

"Phooey."

"Yep…I'd call Lillian one of nature's most fundamental forces. And then there is you, and you're like so many guys…living ordinary lives of happy illusions, then something like this happens. And there you are."

Herb resumed a study of the fascinating curtain. He had seen something similar in a textbook. Kama Sutra illustrations the Annapolis cadet had perused in an art class three years and a millennium ago. Perhaps his mother had been correct; one *should* be receptive to new things.

"Say something intelligent, Herb."

His thoughts were interrupted when Lillian reappeared with a burst of musical energy. Strong bass chords, driving the dancer into rhythmic undulations, replaced the soft classical melodies. Delicate breasts, silk-black hair, soft brown shoulders, dark eyes that flashed with intensity.

Herb's hands trembled; he reached for a cooling beer. Bobby was asking him something. A vibrant fantasy spun before him. He felt light-headed and his heart pounded to the throbbing beat.

Why hadn't he known of this before?

Herb had studied engineering at the Naval Academy, but now he was certain that this lissome creation was nature's consummate gift. Not a single line or curve was flawed. She was simply extraordinary!

How could he have been unaware of this jubilation?

The music surged, dancer swayed and observer yielded to the power of the dance. Was his condition so obvious? Was desire sketched upon his face as shamelessly as the flagrant eroticism of the curtain? The dancer wrapped about a stage pole in serpentine triumph, delicate arms guided a supple body around the pole in agonizing seductiveness and he was lost.

But, then the song abruptly ended. The curtain closed. And, Lillian was gone.

They were watching him. He wiped his brow self-consciously. Bobby was smiling at him. *Always carry a clean hankie, Herbert. You never know who might notice.*

The dance left Herb drained. Mary had disappeared in the crowd, but a new girl plopped herself upon Bobby's lap and whispered something in his hear; he nodded seriously, then laughed. Herb could tell Bobby was pleased when she ran painted fingernails through his hair. Herb took a deep slug of cool San Miguel. It was late and he felt depleted. The dancer was gone. Reluctantly he stood and glanced at the curtain.

"Sit down!" Bobby commanded. "I'm going out for a few minutes. Important personal business. You stay here, Herb. I'll be back pretty soon. Wait for me, understand?"

"Oh…all right."

Herb had anticipated this and he wondered if Bobby would keep his promise. Probably not. He sipped a San Miguel and his mind drifted in afterglow. He could catch one of the Jeepneys back to the base. A good book waited on his desk in The Tranquillity Room and Dan was waiting for his Scotch. Time to go. He wanted to ride back to the base in one of the Filipino jeeps with their garish paint jobs.

6

The room was dark. It smelled of old booze and tired bodies and music intruded from the nightclub above. Over in a far corner a bored young woman waited patiently. She filed bright-red nails and took an occasional sip of brown liquid from a tall glass. It was uncertain what was in her glass but two men who quietly conferred across the room from the girl were drinking a fine Irish whisky with a subtle aroma that wafted through the thick air like an exotic perfume. It reminded one of the men, an American sailor, of home. The other man, a middle-aged Filipino, placed a cardboard box beside the table then sat down with a puff of exertion.

"Same quality as the last load?" the sailor inquired pleasantly.

"Yes, sir…you bet…"

"You sure? Good stuff…not local?"

"No, sir! Cambodian, I think…through Hong Kong. You smoke it yourself?"

"My favorite vice is booze." The sailor sniffed the ancient whisky thoughtfully before slugging it down. "And women. Marijuana is for queers and fools."

"Wise choice."

The Filipino laughed a bit too loudly and the young woman looked up to see if she had missed something of importance. The handsome sailor was studying her, but that was not unusual and she ignored his lingering eyes. Deciding that little of interest had occurred, she turned her attention back to polishing. Fingernails were important.

She was young and slender with a casual air of corrupt indifference. Long, black hair tumbled over a bright sleeve of her tight dress and almond colored arms darted here and there on critical grooming duties. The sailor turned to continue his examination of the woman. He smiled at the girl and she returned the look through steady, dark-brown eyes. Soon, the zip-zip noise of nail-filing resumed and her attention shifted but the sailor's eyes lingered for a long, familiar moment. The regular beat of a current pop song vibrated through the wall. Olongapo was warming up to the night's activities.

"How much?"

"Price same as last time…good stuff…price will go up next week, I think." The Filipino rubbed a long scar on his cheek. "Maybe sooner."

"No, I meant…" The sailor glanced at the girl who slowly crossed a bare, slender leg for his benefit. Still no smile from the pretty girl but she offered a slanted look of burgeoning interest toward the handsome sailor through firm brown eyes.

"Oh…free for you as usual, my friend. A business arrangement, yes?"

"She clean?"

"Yes. I only work her in bar. I keep her for myself. Sometimes for good customers, like you."

"Hmmm…Pretty girl. I like pretty girls. Will she…?"

The Filipino laughed at the suggestive gesture. An ugly scar hardened his otherwise sympathetic face.

"Sure…anything you want. Just tell her…she'll do anything."

"That's a nice arrangement. Actually, I have several requests."

"She's here only a year. I use her…train her…my…uhhm…what you call…niece?"

"It's a family business, I guess."

"Yes, sir, we all family in Philippines," the man with a scarred face laughed. "Everyone belongs."

*   *   *

The music had died. It was quiet and he was becoming bored. But Bobby had said to wait. Herb finished his beer. It was time to go. Bobby was apparently occupied with important business involving God knows what, the woman no doubt. Herb watched a group of fighter pilots arguing at the bar, arms flailed and hands gestured to denote complex combat maneuvers. He yawned.

"May I?"

A polite voice jerked Herb out of the quiet reverie and he turned to shoo away the presumptuous girl who sat beside him. The light was behind her and at first he could not distinguish her features, but the moment was electric.

She was older than he had expected, several years his senior. A slim face with a light almond complexion stared at him with bemused curiosity. Dark, unblinking eyes smiled at his dismay.

"I'm Lillian. Bobby said you wanted to meet me."

*   *   *

Later Bobby returned to a nearly vacant nightclub. Several pilots played Klondike. Filipino bargirls observed the game with bored indifference. And in a darker corner a fiercely contested game of Olongapo Roulette was concluding.

"What happened to Herb?" Bobby asked the old hostess. He blew a pungent smoke stream from a cigarette.

"Oh, he left with Lillian. Gimme a smoke. Where you been? You look tired. Oh, I know, having fun with new girl," Betty snickered. "You friend won't be back for long time, I think. You know that happen. Yeah, you sure one big devil, Bobby."

Night had fallen soon after the ship exited the harbor, the brief rest period concluded. A warm tropical breeze welcomed the Sharpsburg back into the deep blue Pacific as she pointed her bow into the sunset toward Tonkin Gulf. Most of the 3,500 men had returned safely, an accomplishment, since there were usually a few stragglers reluctant to leave the bordellos and watering holes of any liberty port. But the men had been admonished to avoid a variety of demeaning punishments. A few hours spent scrubbing equipment in the blast furnace of an engine room did wonders for a young man's perspective.

The muster prior to sailing was uneventful. A number of broken bones and bruises. One careless sailor had fallen prey to the perilous enticements in Olongapo and had been fished out of the Perfume River with a large knife protruding from his leg. Trouble over a woman, or a disagreement in one of the gambling dives or simply an anonymous drunken brawl. He could not remember the precise cause and the Naval investigation declared the unfortunate incident unsolvable. It was such an ordinary occurrence.

A few hands stood on the fantail to watch the receding shoreline. Lush green mountains with tops crested by fluffy white clouds tumbled down to the sea in the watercolor scene disappearing to the east. A sandy, white ribbon of beach stretched from the north and wandered among jagged cliffs before fading into shadowy recesses of the deep-water port of Subic Bay. Rain fell from clouds into the deepening purple twilight.

A bright green-white wake followed the ship as it picked up speed to hurry to its appointed duty. As night fell into blackness the wake would become a green luminescent tail to the great gray beast, the USS Sharpsburg, a veteran ship-of-war returning to its natural calling.

On some of the less guarded faces the reluctance was all too evident. A return to months at sea faced the young men who until only this morning had been swept up by the hedonistic culture living in a tropical, alien biosphere that was disappearing on a distant horizon. Slowly, one-by-one, they turned from their fruitless vigil and plodded reluctantly down to cramped, crowded quarters. Heat-filled spaces occupied by countless other men who wanted exactly what the watchers had wanted, to be someplace else. To return to the world. To live. To be with women. To enjoy real food. Personal freedom, booze and women. The frivolous things that civilians took for granted.

The ship plowed through the warm water and normal routine resumed. Several aircraft that had been left behind at Cubi for maintenance flew aboard. The Fresnel lens on the landing mirror had been repaired after a minor landing accident. The stragglers landing on the pitching deck were testing it. Maintenance shops swung into full operation. A subdued buzz heralded a return to normalcy while in sick bay several pilots were receiving their annual flight physicals.

Doc Swanson said, "Christ, what a way to end the R&R…looking at a bunch of assholes…chow only an hour away." Four men stood before him naked except for Navy issue shorts. Much whining had occurred in the last few minutes from pilots reluctant to comply with any routine without a token protest.

"OK, Roberts, lets see that leg."

"Christ, that's a beaut, Dan," Bobby Thomas said. The ugly gash on his left leg had healed into a fresh pink scar.

"You can go back on flight status tomorrow."

"Oh…goody."

Swanson shook his head. "What the hell you here for anyway, Roberts? It ain't all glory…you guys are a pain." He looked at the rotund figure next in line.

"Yes, sir. But, Doc…"

"Shut up, Roberts." A scowl crossed his earthy face. "Goddamnit, Jensen…" He had seen this so many times. "You've got the clap again. Haven't you?" A rough sigh of resignation escaped the flight surgeon's lips. "Haven't I told you repeatedly about the hazards of bareback riding? Leave the girls alone or you'll become a medical specimen. Hell, you already are."

"Sorry, Doc. I forget sometimes." Lt. Jensen vibrated with laughter. "Besides, I'm trying to develop an immunity. I got this here theory, you see…"

"Yes…yes…I'm sure that you do. I can see no earthly reason to explain yet again the hazards that tawdry women represent to a chubby, libidinous A-4 pilot like you, you dumb shit."

"Jeez, Doc. Have a heart."

"Give Lt. Jensen his usual mega-dosage of post-R&R penicillin," Doc grumbled to his assistant. "Maybe you should just carry a medical bag ashore with you and just shoot-up whenever you feel infected. Take your damn shot and come back again Thursday with all the other profligates. Goddamit, Jensen…you're an Annapolis graduate. You're supposed to set an example for the dumb Reservists, like Roberts here…he ain't got the sense God gave a goat."

"Oh! But I am," Jensen insisted. "You'll see, Doc. I'm almost certain of my hypothesis. I'll make medical history, if only…"

"Oh…screw it…"

"Yes…that's the situation precisely, Doc. Besides, gimme a little credit. I don't have no bullet holes in me like a certain junior Reservist Naval Aviator whose name will remain unknown but he is present as we speak."

Roberts threw a tongue depressor at his superior officer.

"And!" Jensen dodged, then continued. "In addition I have never screwed a Jap like a certain senior Naval Avi…"

"Yes, yes," Doc said. "*And in addition* you need to lose some goddamn weight. You are fat…got it. F…A…T…E… FAT!"

"Doc, please be reasonable. I prefer to think of myself as one who enjoys all of nature's abundance. Rules attached to ordinary pilots simply cannot apply to me. I'm special. Surely, a man of your intelligence must see that."

"Doc, I must protest," Bobby Thomas interrupted. "That outrageous allegation is apparently aimed at myself. And, they're Japanese, Bill, not Japs. You're a crude, racist, overweight person."

"Jensen must be referring your alleged successes with women of exotic ethnic groups," Doc muttered.

"Bullshit, she be a Jap, I seen her myself." Jensen frequently used gutter English when stressing an important point.

"A duel is the only honorable….here, Bobby." Roberts handed the adversaries tongue depressors and the sword fight was on. Dashing and crashing about the confines of sickbay.

"Shit! Out…get out, all of you." Doc dodged a clumsy thrust and a neat little parry.

"But, Doc, we gotta settle this like gentlemen."

"OUT! Goddamn savages."

And, so it goes.

*   *   *

A burning cigarette fluttered down to the dark water below. It fell into the foamy green wake and joined other flotsam that trailed behind the ship. The man, who had flipped it away, had been waiting impatiently for several minutes. *Dammit, the bastard should have been here by now*, he muttered. He hated tardiness. Promptness was essential and his subordinate had kept him waiting, discipline would be required. Allegiance to cause and fealty often required potent reinforcement.

The mid-watch had secured thirty minutes earlier and the man had waited patiently in the spud locker. But time was growing short and his patience was wearing thin. There was much to be done before dawn. Their *enterprise* was tenuous at best and had suffered a recent setback with the Franklin problem. In the early stages of his budding enterprise the man had worked alone. Cautiously. Fearfully, because so much was at stake. The man was a risk-taker but not a foolish one. He knew the enterprise would work; his market tests had been very successful. A great deal of money could be made if one were prudent; he was certain of that. Subsequent events had dictated that he employ an assistant, both for his own security and for the increasing demands of the business.

"Sorry, Boss." A head appeared in the gloom. "I got delayed by the asshole on Integrity Watch. Them goddamn ensigns…they think…." The voice drifted away under the cold blue eyes that demanded silence.

"OK…let's get down to business." The man handed the small Hispanic sailor a shopping bag. "Twenty packets in there…give 'em to your two distributors before reveille. Get the money back tomorrow after morning chow…don't take any excuses, Diaz. No loans, no credit, got it?"

"Yeah…I ain't gonna pull no Franklin… hey!" His head was slammed solidly against the bulkhead.

The man grabbed Diaz's right arm and twisted it into a hammerlock. With his left hand the man slammed his subordinate's head into the bulkhead several times.

"Listen carefully, asshole…no more names. I'm the *Boss*."

"I didn't mean no…" Diaz whimpered.

"Don't ever mention any names again, especially *that* name, got it?"

"Yeah…" Pain rocked the smaller man. Fear welled up into Diaz's throat.

"Call me, *Boss*."

"Yeah, *Boss*."

"Again."

"BOSS!"

"Only Boss from now on. You're my assistant. We never mention names again after tonight. Even when we're alone. Franklin never existed, understand?"

Assistant nodded. Diaz looked over the railing to the water below and he knew genuine fear. Had Franklin said something stupid? Had the Boss thrown him overboard? Diaz did not know. Franklin had been the former assistant and Diaz was certain that Franklin had not committed suicide.

"You better learn to keep your mouth shut. Franklin never did."

Boss released the twisted arm and politely dusted off Diaz's shoulder. No need for permanent anger. The point had been well made.

"How much did you make last month?"

"Three-hunert-sixty."

"Not too bad…more than Navy pay, right?"

"I ain't got no complaints, Boss."

"We're gonna increase distribution a little. But, not too much. Greedy people get caught. You'll get one-fourth of the net as usual. I get three-fourths of the profits after expenses. I provide all capital and the marijuana. It's good stuff, I'm told."

"Hey, it's great. Tried it myself."

Cold, ruthless eyes surveyed the smaller man. Diaz visibly shrunk from the inspection.

"I don't mind if you sample a little of the product. But, I don't want to find out that you have been cutting the packets, or that you've become too obvious. I want strict accounting and no unhappy customers, understand?"

An enthusiastic nod.

"OK. Use your two distributors. Get the money from them immediately and if they give you any trouble, squeeze them. Don't take any excuses, ever."

Just like you just squeezed me. Diaz thought. However, he would not ask if Franklin had required squeezing. A cold shiver ran down his spine. Franklin had been one tough customer.

"Don't ever mention my name, not ever. As far as anyone is concerned you are the sole distributor of the stuff. I'll have more for you next week. We'll pace our distribution throughout the cruise and we'll both make some money. Be careful! Do we understand each other?"

"Yes, sir! I understand."

He looked down at the deep, dark Pacific Ocean. Diaz did not like to swim.

8

By 0530 the next morning the USS Sharpsburg was in position on Yankee Station. The muggy briefing-room was smoke-filled and stank of stale cigarettes and sweat. There were few air-conditioned spaces on the World War Two Essex Class attack carrier. The Sharpsburg was 840 feet long displacing 27,000 tons and by current standards was one of the smaller carriers in service. It was still in operation in 1967 during the lingering Asian war, one of three American carriers assigned to Yankee Station in Tonkin Gulf off the coast of North Vietnam.

The combat cruise had been broken by the nine-day R&R period in Subic Bay where both ship and aircraft were returned to a serviceable condition. Morale was surprisingly high considering the fatigue, combat losses and normal accidental deaths and injuries experienced aboard an aircraft carrier, the most dangerous work environment ever designed by man.

A loose group of two dozen pilots had reported for the mission briefing, most carried steaming cups of strong Navy coffee, including Dan Roberts who liked the brawny, black stuff that could carry a pilot through a long day. Most lit cigarettes, a few were openly nervous before the Alpha Strike on Hanoi's outskirts, some assumed a pose of casual indifference. Bravado was a common cover for the apprehensive.

Highpockets concluded a detailed briefing of the run-in checkpoints. The intelligence officer's name was Commander Harrison but everyone called him Highpockets because of the plethora of pens and pencils he carried in his shirt pockets against uniform regulations. Highpockets had described the upcoming mission in minute, excruciating detail, even though most of the pilots had the drill down by heart.

Now the briefing was over, much to Highpockets' relief. The disrespectful wisecracking which had occurred during his monologue disturbed the professional intelligence officer. But humor relieved tension; he considered himself to be a compassionate man and sympathized with the young aviators.

"Any questions?" the gangly intelligence officer asked tentatively; he knew what was coming. The man's lanky bird-like frame seemed to shrink slightly. Why couldn't pilots show a little more professionalism during his briefings?

"Yes, sir." A hand shot up eagerly. A snicker of anticipation riffled through the assembly of thirty-plus men. Lt. Jensen always asked the same questions, and got the same answers.

"All right, Jensen. You again?" Highpockets said with what he considered a stern, but fatherly, tone of voice. Bill Jensen could barely squeeze his corpulent frame into the cramped cockpit of the Douglas A-4 fighter-bomber. "Same questions, I assume?"

"Yessir," Jensen drawled. A pleasant smile played across his chubby face. It was generally known that Bill Jensen found it difficult to take the war very seriously, since he was privy to several universal truths that lesser men had overlooked. Simply stated, there were more important things to be concerned about. Things like women and alcohol and food and the critically serious game of golf.

"OK, same answers then, Jensen. One, payday is on the first of the month, like always." Highpockets ticked the answers off on scrawny fingers. "Two, I don't know what's for chow tonight, but I'm certain it will be exquisite. And three, I don't know how you could get out of this chicken-shit outfit. But, if you find out let me know." A minor ripple of laughter. Most had experienced this exchange before.

Jensen grunted skeptically and raised his hand for another important question.

"Any more questions?" Highpockets looked around, artlessly ignoring Jensen. An ensign, who was an academy graduate and bucking to make admiral some day, asked a serious question about the rendezvous sequence. He always asked pertinent questions. But he was really just a pain in the ass and everyone knew it.

Another hand shot up.

"Sir, you said *we* were going to strike that power plant outside Hanoi. Were you serious about that?" A breathless question suggesting extreme eagerness.

"Why….yes," Highpockets simpered. The question sounded professional, therefore suspect. Highpockets' bird nose darted here and there cautiously seeking a clue.

"I was just wondering, sir," the ensign said. "Are you really serious about that *WE* stuff, you know, like *We*…all of us…you and me?" He pointed at Highpockets and himself.

"Of course, we're a team here on the Sharpsburg."

"Well, then, how would you like to take my place today?" A rude giggle was heard from the back of the room.

"Well…hmm….much as I'd like to I wouldn't dream of taking your place. Besides, what would you do all afternoon? You'd just get bored and restless," Highpockets said. He wasn't a pilot, had never been a pilot and furthermore thought that nobody in his right mind would ever get into a fighter-bomber in the first place. Much less be catapulted from a pitching flight deck with hundreds of pounds of bombs and rockets attached to a flimsy piece of flying aluminum. And to venture over hostile territory and be shot at by all sorts of terrible missiles and guns. The entire concept was ludicrous. It was simply out of the question.

"Oh, I just thought perhaps I'd lie-about in my room and read a splendid book….maybe take a little nap…then later hop ashore and get an ale or two at some jolly little pub in Haiphong. I'm feeling a trifle peckish today, old boy." All of this in a terrible British accent with which the ensign liked to irritate people. Highpockets declined to answer. CAG Ferris grunted impatiently from the front row.

Jensen was practically jumping for attention.

"Sir…?"

"Yes," Highpockets groaned. Jensen was persistent.

"Just one more question, Highpockets, I mean, Commander Harrison…sir?"

Highpockets did not answer. Why bother? It was inevitable. Jensen was relentless. The porky attack pilot was a dedicated needler.

"It's the weather, sir. Why can't somebody do *something*?"

Highpockets sighed audibly and raised his eyes to the heavens seeking fortitude.

"The weather is excellent, Lieutenant Jensen. I covered that in great detail, remember? And, if you would pay just the modicum of attention you would know that, too!" he snapped.

"Oh, I know that, Highpockets, I mean Commander Harrison…sir. I listened to every word of your exciting briefing and, I must add that I, for one, would like to compliment you on your zestful presentation because it's been an inspiration for us all…but.."

"Well, then…."

"But, it's them frigging black clouds, sir. Like. You know, them little, teeny, black, puffy things with all the iron and steel in them. I keep running into them goddamn things ever time I go near Hanoi. Can't you do something about that kinda shitty weather and them black clouds?" Delivered in gutter English.

Pandemonium.

"All right that's enough!" Commander Ferris shouted, the Air Group Commander was leading the strike today and was plainly irritable.

An ensign in the back of the room had raised his hand.

"Yes, Ensign, do you have a question? I don't remember your name," Highpockets ventured, hopeful of more sober questions now. He liked those.

"Dan Roberts, sir. I'm new here. Actually, I have two questions of an intelligence…nature, sir."

"Go ahead, Roberts."

"First of all, High…sir. Do you think McNamara wears lace panties…some secretaries do, you know?"

Subdued snickering. CAG Ferris shuffled impatiently. Highpockets laughed.

"Oh, that's creative," Highpockets said. A truly dedicated intelligence briefer always encouraged audience participation when appropriate, he thought. Humor had a role in the process provided that it was thoughtful and restrained. "Creative humor relieves tension, Ensign…?"

"I'm still Roberts, sir."

"Well, Roberts. I'm not privy to the personal quirks of our notorious Secretary of Defense. Perhaps you should call J. Edgar Hoover. I think he handles Lyndon Johnson's gossip." Highpockets enjoyed the laughter and he could be one of the boys.

"Do you have another question, Ensign?" The nondescript pilot was still standing, a new guy. Highpockets always had trouble with names and other inconsequential details. A briefing officer must concentrate on important matters first; target evaluations, Bomb Damage Assessments and kill-ratios were the grist of the intelligence mill.

"Roberts. Yes, sir." Roberts smiled, he'd practiced the questions numerous times to avoid a stammer. "What color do you think they might be? The panties, I mean. Commie pink or Democrat yellow?"

The room erupted in outright laughter.

"By God, that's enough," Ferris, a short and stocky, ill-tempered man, snapped. "You...Roberts. Shut up! I want to see you after the mission." He was having a bad day and the mission hadn't even started. "Goddamn reservists," he muttered. "Dismissed!" The airgroup commander angrily stomped from the briefing.

"Roberts, you're a born smartass, I think," Thomas said.

"I'll probably be in hack forever. CAG seemed...well, sorta...upset."

"Oh hell, forget him. He's leading today...scared shitless...can't you see it? Hasn't got it anymore. Did you notice the way he walked out on his tippy-toes? Looked like Napoleon." Thomas laughed. Roberts picked up his kneeboard and followed Thomas out of the room.

"Better keep my big mouth shut."

"No, keep talking. You need the practice. CAG won't remember any of this by tonight. You'll see."

Roberts had taken an immediate liking to Bobby Thomas. He thought the senior LSO was the quintessential Naval Aviator. At thirty, Thomas had flown fighter and attack aircraft for ten years. The lanky Lieutenant Commander had never married and appeared to view women as targets-of-opportunity to be analyzed, out-maneuvered and subdued. While Bobby Thomas apparently had nothing in particular against married pilots, like Dan Roberts, he simply couldn't understand the tactical necessity of a female encumbrance. Women were meant to be enjoyed as primary recreational vehicles.

"But...that was an important question. Don't you imagine McNamara *does* put on lace panties every chance he gets?" Roberts asked.

"Probably. Almost everybody here despises the creepy sonofabitch," Thomas said. "But, then all politicians suck, right?"

They ducked their heads to squeeze through a watertight door. It led to an escalator that conveyed them to the flight deck.

"Listen, Dan," he said. "I want you to be the division leader today and I'll fly your wing. I've already briefed the other section leader."

"Smithson?" Roberts shook his head. "He'll be pissed." Younger aviators rarely led a flight until old hands had confidence in their abilities. "I'm still the new guy around here."

"Oh, hell. He needs a little humility…you'll lead today…he'll get his chance tomorrow."

"You're putting me on the spot. Welcome to the Knighthawks, huh?"

"Yeah! Attack Squadron 433, flying the venerable Douglas A-1H Skyraider, the last operational single-engine, propeller driven, fighter-bomber in the Navy's inventory affectionately nicknamed the Spad after the famous WW-1 fighter, needs fresh blood. Isaacson wants every pilot to be a flight leader. Today, you're it, Danny boy. Tomorrow, Smithson."

"I think you're gonna get me in real trouble with Smithson. I'm not…why not let him go first?"

"And, the A-1 is also called the Ensign-Killer because of its treacherous handling characteristics and intolerance of young, stupid inexperienced aviators, such as yourself."

"OK. You're ignoring me. So, what am I suppose to do?"

"That's better. The mission is rescap. We'll station ourselves along the coastline as briefed, near Pho Cat Ba, any A-4s get shot down after the airgroup's bombing run, we'll provide rescue cover, destroy enemy forces near the downed pilot, same ol' shit. Rescue helicopters will swoop in and save the day and we'll all be heroes, ta-da!"

"That's the theory?"

"Piece a cake."

A cluster of pilots emerged from the escalator, which had brought them up from the bowels of the ship. There they had finished individual briefings after CAG had dismissed them so abruptly. They stepped gingerly around stores and equipment placed near the ship's island from which the escalator dumped its human cargo onto the flight deck. Aircraft tugs, oxygen service carts, fire-fighting equipment and sundry items cluttered the area between a yellow off-limits line defining the flight operations area of the flight deck and the island. Nothing could be placed beyond the yellow fouled-deck zone, which was reserved exclusively for aircraft operations.

The flight deck was awash in a feverish pre-launch mode that a casual observer might mistake for mass confusion. However, there was a disciplined choreography underway that a more discerning observer could detect immediately. Aircraft were being moved and positioned on the deck by men in green shirts, while men in yellow shirts were preparing them for the launch. The red-shirts were loading ordnance and checking bomb-rack connections.

Roberts and Thomas led the boisterous group toward the aircraft. Thomas had divulged several interesting items about a recent adventure in the resort city of Olongapo. He held a cupped hand out from his torso to describe what must have been a close encounter with a female of considerable proportions.

"No way…" Roberts stammered. "Am I sposta believe *that* about my little Herby?"

"Talk slower, you'll do much better," Thomas suggested.

"You realize Herb's just pretending to be sane, don't you?" Roberts said slowly.

"Aren't we all? And you're wrong, Dan. I'm telling you McGinnis is a man to be watched closely. Quiet, and stealthy but deadly. A true swordsman."

"I still don't believe that part about the curtain," Smithson protested. He had frowned when told of Roberts' assignment.

"It's all true. Ensign Herb McGinnis, adventurer extraordinaire, smote the heathen curtain and carried off the beautiful maiden," Thomas chuckled. "I expect he may have smote her a time or two also."

Across the deck, CAG scowled at the laughing group. This was no time for hijinks, he thought. It was people like Bobby Thomas and that smartass Roberts that he despised the most. This was a war and he was in a sour mood and he hated levity. He kicked the nose tire of his A-4.

"Good luck today, sir." CAG's plane captain remarked then followed his cold stare directed toward the four casual A-1 pilots.

"Goddamn...Spad drivers...."

A yellow aircraft tug sped by with a loud roar. Roberts jumped to give the driver a clear path. There were many ways to be injured on a flight deck, but casualties had been relatively light during the two weeks since their return to Yankee Station. There had been no flight deck accidents and only one A-4 and its pilot had been lost in combat.

Roberts and the other three pilots would form a division of four aircraft. The A-1's were spotted forward. Two of the ungainly fighter-bombers were already attached to the catapults for Roberts and Thomas. Smithson's second section was parked immediately aft.

Four smudged, dirty Spads, Roberts noticed, the fighter-bombers were never pretty and shiny as in the Hollywood versions of war. In reality the Spads showed the strains of combat, grimy oil stains around the engine cowling, ugly scuffmarks covered the fuselage, evidence of hasty maintenance and handling abuse. A few patches here and there, evidence of recent battle damage.

"Tell me something, Dan," Thomas said abruptly. "Remember when you brought back that beat-up Spad last month, you flew the approach a little slow through the ninety, then accelerated in the groove...nice approach. Why'd you do that? Somebody tell you about that technique...some old Spad driver, maybe?"

"Nope...it felt right to me. Why?"

"Just wondered. That's an old trick, thought you might have heard of it. But be goddamn careful...you're right on the edge. Don't wanna stall at the ninety...lost a lot of Spad drivers that way."

"I'll watch it." And Roberts ambled off to his Skyraider.

It felt right.

Bobby Thomas liked the answer. A certain amount of carrier aviation was done by feel. In spite of the advances in aircraft and shipboard equipment such as the Fresnel lens and the angle-of-attack indicator, a great deal of successful carrier flying was dependent on the *feel* of the situation. But the wrong perception, an incorrect interpretation of an aircraft's performance, a screw-up, had killed many Naval Aviators. It was an unforgiving profession and the Skyraider was an unforgiving aircraft, but Thomas loved the old Spad.

The Douglas A-1H Skyraider had character.

A massive blunt fuselage. Thick wings loaded with deadly ordnance. Dull gray paint decorated with the squadron's insignia, an armored bird of prey, the Knighthawk. They were ungainly overloaded things. Under the wings were attached two five hundred pound bombs and rocket pods, under the belly a three hundred gallon drop-tank for extra fuel. When catapulted the airplane's basic weight of twelve thousand pounds would be nearly doubled by the fuel and ordnance.

More ornaments than a Christmas tree, Roberts thought as he approached his Spad. The Skyraider wasn't pretty. Hell, it wasn't even clean. It was massive and powerful. A fearsome, effective weapons delivery platform, an anachronism in the jet age. The eighteen-cylinder Wright 3350 radial engine delivered nearly three thousand horsepower through its four-bladed propeller, which swung an arc fourteen feet in diameter. Along the leading edge of the wings protruded four 20MM cannon barrels. Each gun pumped out seven hundred rounds per minute. A devastating weapon system, a homely airplane, and yet, it had something. An aura of strength, of lethal dependability, and excellence. A design perfectly matched to mission. A pilot's airplane.

"Hey, Bryan," Roberts said.

Timothy Bryan, plane-captain. He had prepared Roberts' airplane for launch. They examined the bomb-racks and Bryan handed Roberts a piece of chalk.

"I remembered today, sir," he grinned.

A nice kid; he'd offered to shine Roberts' shoes for free after the hamburger wager. *A deal's a deal*, Roberts had refused. *Yes, sir, but I think you missed on purpose,* Bryan replied. *Maybe, better watch me from now on,* Roberts laughed. And now Bryan seemed to be Roberts' plane-captain.

Roberts accepted the chalk and turned to the bomb under the right wing and scribbled on the casing near the detonator. *WRATGAS.* Bryan repeated the ceremony another bomb.

"What does that mean, sir?" Bryan asked. "You never told me yesterday…like you promised."

"That's right, you were supposed to bring me a coke…after the recovery, as I recall. I gave you the money, too," Roberts said with mock gravity.

"Yes, sir," the serious eighteen-year-old from Phoenix said. "But the chief made me clean them heads in the chiefs' latrine and I never got back before you went to the de-briefing."

"Better be nice to Pete…seems like he's the honcho around here."

"I just do as I'm told, sir."

"OK, then hold this helmet, Bryan."

The launch crew was ready. He climbed into the cockpit and began strapping in with Bryan's assistance. His would be the first of twenty-two aircraft to be catapulted off the carrier deck. Further aft on the flight deck sixteen A-4s would follow the Spads and then two F-8 Crusaders armed with Sidewinder missiles for top-cover. A twin engine E-2 radar plane had been launched earlier to provide command-and-control for the Alpha Strike. Rescue helicopters from another carrier were already enroute. In all, nearly thirty aircraft were engaged in the operation. All would check in with the E-2 after launch and be in the same vicinity of the North Vietnam shoreline as the main force of A-4 bombers coasted-in on their way to destroy a power plant a few miles north of Hanoi.

"How's that leg today, Mr. Roberts?"

"OK, I guess." He took the kneeboard from Bryan. "Tell me something, what do you know about Franklin?" Roberts inquired abruptly.

"Must hurt, though. Broke mine once on a horse." Bryan wiped a green sleeve across his brow. "Nothin much, sir. I didn't like him much…an' it wasn't 'cause he was a Negro, sir." Bryan watched the pilot to see if he would be corrected. They were African-Americans as the chief had instructed everyone recently. Equal rights, everybody was the same now.

"Think he just fell overboard?" Roberts offered.

"Well, I do know one thing, sir. Franklin never fell overboard…he's…uhhh…too…" The word wasn't there; he hated talking to officers.

"Intelligent?"

"Not 'xactly…umm…*tricky*, I guess. He was one of those smart guys…you know, quick. Always talkin, smart aleck. I never trusted him, sir. Just too tricky. And, he never *fell* overboard…guarantee you, that. No way, sir."

The plane captain wiped the windshield while Roberts secured his shoulder harness.

"You ever work with Franklin?"

"No, sir…he had his own airplane to tend. Number 409. That's the one Lt. Williamson rode in…."

"What?"

"You know, he crashed it into the water…before y'all came, sir."

"Wait. You mean…Franklin was the plane captain on Williamson's Spad the night he died? Is that right?"

"Yes, sir."

"I didn't know that." Roberts stared at the horizon, then said. "What do you think happened to Lt. Williamson?"

"Dunno, sir…kinda funny, though."

"Why?"

"409 useta be my airplane…it was a good one. Never any trouble with it like some a them others. Not this one though, sir. It's a good one, too. But don't bring it back all beat up again…OK, sir?" Bryan looked directly at Roberts then quickly diverted his eyes.

Roberts accepted his helmet from Bryan and smiled.

"It's an acronym, Bryan."

"Huh…?"

"WRATGAS. It means 'Who Really And Truly Gives A Shit.' Kind of describes our situation out here. Doesn't it?"

The bullhorn blared. *Pilots start your engines.*

"I know what you mean, sir. All them bombs…jeez." Bryan glanced at the bustling airgroup. "I'll be sure to have that coke for you."

"Bryan…?

"Yes, sir?"

"Was Franklin a competent plane captain?"

"I didn't know him so good. I didn't like him much, sir."

"But could he…"

"He did his job OK, I guess."

The catapult officer approached his station. A flurry of pre-launch activity ensued near Roberts' Spad. In the distance he could see puffy clouds that would not develop into heavy rain, or so Highpockets had promised. Gentle wavelets speckled the blue-green sea and a gentle breeze wafted over the flight deck. Nearly time to go.

"Don't forget that coke…for both of us," Roberts said.

"Good luck, sir. And don't you forget…no bullet holes, today."

Roberts watched Bryan scramble off the wing. He ran through the Before Start checklist and watched the yellow-shirt Flight Deck Officer as he signaled to start engines. Roberts pressed the starter button with his right index finger and watched the prop turn through eight blades to make certain there wasn't a hydraulic lock in one of the cylinders, then touched the primer button. The Wright R-3350 caught immediately and fire belched from the exhaust stacks with a black smoky roar. The airframe began vibrating.

Tricky. Bryan had said, and it had struck a chord in Roberts' mind.

Quickly checking for oil-pressure, he moved the fuel mixture to full rich with his left hand and stabilized the engine at 1000 RPM. Since he was already spotted on the starboard catapult, no taxiing was required; he watched for the Catapult Officer to signal for run-up and engine check. It came quickly. The ship began a turn into the wind. 2000 RPM. Propeller cycled. Oil pressure and temperature normal. Cylinder head temperature in the green. A quick magneto check, less than 100 RPM drop on each mag.

Tricky? What did that mean? A peculiar, bothersome word.

An uncomfortable notion crawled through his gut; he raised his right hand and gave the yellow-shirt Catapult Officer a thumbs-up, *ready-to-go*. The Cat Officer raised his right hand with two fingers extended and rotated them in a circular motion signaling for full-power and looked to the ship's bow, one-hundred fifty feet along the catapult track, all clear. Roberts shoved the throttle to the forward stop. *Check oil pressure, RPM and manifold pressure.* The Spad shuddered like a nervous racehorse straining at the bit. Anxious to go. Looking at the Catapult Officer, Roberts gave a quick salute and immediately returned his right hand to the control stick. The kick in the ass would come very quickly.

Franklin missing and Lt. Williamson dead in Aircraft 409. An unusual coincidence? Both men and their Skyraider forever joined in a watery grave, consumed by the dark stillness of Tonkin Gulf. Nagging thoughts consciously subdued by Roberts. The cat shot was coming and it would require all of his concentration.

Roberts waited. The Cat Officer flung his right arm forward to meet his left hand pointing at the ship's bow. The steam-catapult crew tripped a valve releasing tons of live steam, actuating a piston shuttle on the flight deck attached by a bridle to the Spad. The aircraft shuddered under full power, held stationary by a steel cable attached to the cata-pult's holdback station.

His eyes swept the quivering instrument panel while the Spad rumbled and vibrated with barely contained energy. He waited. Split-seconds seemed like minutes. When the steam shuttle pressure reached a predetermined load a holdback fitting snapped and the Spad hurdled down the deck accelerating to 125 knots in two seconds. The entire process from engine run-up to cat-shot had taken less than ten seconds.

Acceleration! Vertigo! Eyeballs compressed and he was temporarily blinded. The incomparable thrill! Three seconds after the Spad was flung from the flight deck his brain and eyes had caught up to the situation. The Spad had rolled into a left bank and was starting to descend, only sixty feet to water! The radar altimeter blinked a bright red warning, too low! He kicked the right rudder and gently, so gently eased back on the stick. A little right aileron, level the wings, back on the stick ever so slightly. Easy, carefully. The red warning light dimmed.

Don't stall.

Gear-up. Reduce drag. Then milk the flaps up slowly while still in ground-effect, the cushion of denser air over the flat ocean surface created by venturi pressure under the wings.

He looked down at the water. So close. So deadly. Roberts imagined the terror of a night ditching under the approaching bow of the speeding ship. What had happened to Williamson? A ditched aircraft flipped upside down. Black water and the ship bearing down on a helpless pilot suspended in his harness. Trapped in darkness and fear, disorientation, and finally, panic. Sinking into blackness. The horror of impending death.

He started a gradual right turn to get clear of the ship's path in case of an engine failure. *I don't want to get run over today.* Williamson must have panicked, he thought. Confused. Disoriented. He'd forgotten how to release the shoulder harness. Sinking in the Spad into the darkness. Williamson might not have had a chance.

Tricky.

The word nagged at him. What had really happened to Williamson? Nobody seemed to know, but now he was dead, and forgotten.

Looking over his right shoulder he saw Thomas had launched, beginning a right turn to an intercept for rendezvous.

Roberts maintained a moderate bank-angle permitting Thomas an easy intercept vector to join on his right wing. He saw that Thomas was approaching fast, much too fast.

Let's see how he handles this, Roberts thought.

Could Thomas handle the rapid join-up? Misjudgment could cause a collision. Like subordinates everywhere, he wouldn't mind if Bobby Thomas screwed up a little. *Teach him some humility*, a commodity in short supply around the Sharpsburg. Two hundred yards, a high closure rate, Roberts saw a small puff of black smoke spurt from Thomas' exhaust stacks indicating a rapid power reduction. Thomas increased the bank-angle, made several quick corrections and gently eased into position under Roberts' right wing. An impressive bit of stick and rudder work by a cool professional. Roberts was not surprised.

The two Spads continued in a gradual right turn and waited for the other section to join-up. They came in quickly after the fourth Spad completed a running rendezvous on Smithson. They eased up the intercept line onto Thomas' right wing.

Roberts leveled his wings and the other three Spads rolled gently around his axis into level flight. He pumped a right arm and closed fist twice and Smithson's section dropped down slightly, flying beneath Roberts and Thomas, joining on his left wing, a classic finger-tip formation.

After establishing a heading to the coast-in point Roberts keyed the transmitter button, "Shadow flight...radio check; one is up." Shadow was his call sign; he was leading and they would use it for this mission.

"Two." Bobby answered.

"Three." Smithson.

"Four." His wingman.

Radio silence would be in effect now for the rest of the mission, unless they engaged in combat.

Roberts signaled the flight to check guns. Master Arm switch…*ON*. Guns/Bombs switch…*GUNS*. He pulled the trigger and the Spad shuddered as the four cannons pumped out several rounds, tracers arced ahead of the airplane and fell away into the horizon. He looked right to Bobby then left to Smithson's section, three thumbs-up.

They climbed to 10,000 feet to conserve fuel. It would be cooler at the higher altitude. Within a few minutes Shadow Flight passed an American destroyer; the northern Search and Rescue ship, on station to rescue downed aviators and to serve as the northern screening vessel for the Seventh Fleet's Task Force. It was heavily armed with anti-aircraft missiles and guns. Roberts transmitted the assigned IFF code for identification. The ship had full authority to shoot down any unidentified aircraft.

They flew around a layer of puffy white clouds and turned to the final heading to their holding position. Whitecaps covered the ocean surface stretching to the shoreline miles away. A strong wind from the southwest had been blowing for the past few days. It was the monsoon season but the weather was good.

Now he was able to see mountaintops to the northwest and he took a moment to admire the beauty of Vietnam. A rugged horizon of sepia tones, mountain peaks floating on a sea of cottony haze, a vast water-color mural. The range of ragged hills west of the Red River formed the long backbone of North Vietnam. Enemy territory, the beautiful country, an Asian enigma.

A shimmering slash of white sandy beach separated the green hills from blue water. Further south near Da Nang the French had established resort communities in better times. The beach made him think of Helen, and his mind drifted. *What was it like?* he thought. *Not so long ago.* They'd stretched on sugar-like sand with cold beer. He recalled their last day together. Cool beer, warm laughter, bright sunlight on Helen's blond hair. A good day that had sped by too quickly.

Maybe the pub that Highpockets was asked about during the briefing was down there somewhere. *It would be good to have a cold beer again. And talk to a woman.* But, it was no good. He tried to forget the happier times; it would do no good. Today they would do what they were ordered to do, what they always did, to this land of sandy beaches and beautiful mountains. Bomb the crap out of the enemy.

He saw a flight of A-4s pass above on their way to the coast-in point. He pointed and Bobby gave a thumbs-up. Herb was in that group and he felt a strange kinship with the distant flight. A brotherhood of airborne warriors. Then he heard it.

When you're alone and life is making you lonely you can always goooo…DOWNTOWN. A cynical A-4 driver mimicking Petula Clark on the radio. *When you've got worries all the noise and the hurry seems to help I know…DOWNTOWN.*

The Seventh Fleet pilots had adopted her song as a theme. It could be heard frequently during air strikes and radio silence would not deceive the North Vietnamese.

Just listen to the music of the traffic in the city. A general chorus joined in. *How can you lose..the lights are much brighter there..you can forget all your troubles..forget all your cares…so go…DOWNTOWNNNN…* CAG Ferris didn't approve of this levity but he couldn't do much about it. *The lights are much brighter there…you can forget all your troubles…forget all your cares..so go…DOWNTOWN.*

In the distance a bright streak drug a smoky trail into the afternoon sky. Black puffy clouds erupted here and there punctuating the blue haze. A strike force of F-105s had attacked a target. The North Vietnamese had thanked them with SAMs and AAA.

Don't wait a minute more…DOWNTOWN….everything's waiting forrr youuu…

"Shut up, goddammit!"

Roberts recognized CAG's nervous command.

The strike group approached the coast-in point, a small fishing village east of Quang Yen and prepared for the nasty business of going *downtown*, then trying to get back out alive. The sandy coastline was protected by a group of islands that extended northward to the Chinese border. The islands' verdant beauty beckoning the airgroup to a looming embrace.

Roberts watched four divisions of A-4s spread out into a loose combat formation. CAG radioed his coast-in message to the E-2 command aircraft patrolling safely over the sea. He sensed the tension; it could be felt throughout the airgroup. Palms became sweaty. Eyes nervously scanned the horizon for MiGs and SAMs and AAA, angry greetings from the North Vietnamese.

Roberts guided his division around the islands and positioned the four Spads. The A-4s would coast-out near the islands after the bombing run in a few short, dangerous minutes. He gave the other section the break-up signal; his left hand extended vertically and rotated in a circular motion. Then hand to his lips and the kiss-off. They detached from their position on his left wing and turned to fly twenty miles south to their patrol area near Pho Cat Ba while Roberts and Bobby flew the northern circuit. Any damaged aircraft would attempt to flee over the coastline before the pilot ejected. The Spads could protect the pilot while a rescue helicopter raced to his position.

Roberts flew along the shoreline with Bobby searching for enemy gun positions or troop concentrations. If they received ground fire, they could destroy the hostile position before the airgroup's coast-out but their primary mission was to support the bombers and they would conserve their ordnance.

He took a drink of water from a canteen, wiped the sweat from his face with a dampened rag. And waited. He glanced at North Vietnam, a landscape he had learned to admire. Its rugged topography lay before him in green splendor. A nation he knew little about, but had grown to respect for its tenacity during the long war. The politics confused him. It had a unique beauty he had never seen in America. Islands of mysterious undulating hills covered by drifts of pillowy haze ranged under his bomb-laden wing. White, sandy shorelines stretched to the horizon broken here and there by enchanting inlets and rugged, steep limestone cliffs. Greens and browns and limestone grays of the mainland bordered by ribbons of sugar-sand beaches that rolled down to the endless blue ocean. They turned north and flew over small bays and swampy river outlets populated with quaint fishing villages and numerous junks that rested peacefully at village docks or fished lazily in the blue-green Gulf.

Roberts thought he would like to examine a Vietnamese fishing junk someday, they had a compelling gracefulness under sail and seemed to offer a promise of mystery and intrigue. But, any junk had the ability to pick up a downed pilot and some were heavily armed and dangerous. He thought it unlikely that he would ever have anything to do with a junk. He yawned and rubbed the fresh scar on his leg that ached and reminded him of his insignificance. It would be several long minutes before the airgroup reappeared.

Shadow Flight waited.

9

Commander Grant Ferris scanned ahead for the initial approach point to the target and reconsidered the disturbing fact that he was frightened. A primal fear welled up from his gut and choked his voice. Now he dreaded every day and every mission and he was always frightened. Always. But Ferris was a determined man, a professional attack pilot. The sweat that drenched his flight suit that reeked with the smell of fear would not interfere with the mission because he simply would not permit it.

On CAG Ferris' left wing a young pilot worried very little about the AAA or SAM missiles. He knew, as well as Ferris, the risks of combat. Fear of the enemy had little affect on CAG's wingman. Another more ominous force worried Ensign Herbert McGinnis. And, like Ferris, he thought about his fears now.

Herb flew the airplane into the parade position tucked tightly under Ferris' wing with unconscious skill. He was a fine pilot and in any other situation Herb McGinnis would have been considered among the best. But McGinnis was a Naval Aviator and his job was to fly from the flight deck of an aircraft carrier, and it was that peculiar situation that frightened McGinnis. He admitted that fear quite frankly now to anyone who bothered to inquire. Since nobody did, other than his roommate and certain LSO's, it was generally unknown in the group of carrier pilots who abhorred weaknesses.

Herb squeezed on another 1% RPM to compensate for the outside turn the airgroup was making for the initial run-in. A delicate pressure on the stick moved his A-4 away from Ferris' wing, a looser position in case they had to maneuver around flak or SAM attacks.

Had McGinnis been an Air Force or Marine Corps pilot he would have been admired for his considerable skills. Those unchallenged pilots were not required to fly their fighters from the pitching decks of aircraft carriers and never experienced the fear that he knew so well. The gut wrenching uncertainties of a difficult carrier landing were of little concern to the uninitiated. He was a carrier pilot and Herb was constantly exposed to the black nights and pitching deck with its almost useless mirror approach. Low visibility approaches with minimum fuel where a pilot had to feel his way down onto the deck with a near-meta-physical acumen. This was what worried Herb McGinnis at this moment, not the AAA bursts or SAM missiles rocketing toward his airplane at mach-two speeds. The pitching, rolling unforgiving deck that waited for him after the mission was Herb's special terror.

Herb was recognized as a man who could fly an airplane with consummate skill in combat, but that was not enough. He could perform lovely aerobatics with the delicate touch of a skilled surgeon. He could fly formation with the best and air-to-air combat, or dropping bombs directly on target in spite of flak bursts that seemed to flow directly into your guts, was a natural environment for him. Unfortunately, Herb McGinnis was afraid of the deck and he boltered frequently and all of these admirable abilities were forgotten.

A fine glint of sunlight filtered through his bombsight onto the glareshield during the turn. Herb searched ahead to see the Initial Point where the bomb run would begin, the IP. Quickly, he scanned his instrument panel. Every indicator was normal. The aircraft was ready. He was ready.

It was curious that he thought even now of the next landing. *The landing!* Now the target was before him but he had little fear of it. The SAMs, the AAA, the MiGs; he could handle anything they threw at him. But, the landing worried him. A fine bead of sweat dribbled down his brow.

Was it his keen intelligence that made carrier landings so difficult, he often wondered? Herb was a graduate engineer from the Naval Academy and he had the imagination and the capability to foresee all of the many dangerous little things that could kill so easily. A couple of feet too low over the round-down. Or too slow in close. Or a misjudged sinker. Or a compressor stall at the last critical second. In his dreams he had seen himself splattered in a ball of fire. Exploding against the round-down, flames tumbling down into the spud locker consuming him in his helplessness. A fiery death frightened him the most, the subconscious fears of a man who had been badly burned by a campfire in his youth. All of these things came to him in his imagination. That fear and the physical tenseness it spawned caused Herb to bolter. He boltered frequently.

Herb's weakness was public knowledge, there were no secrets aboard the ship. All landings were monitored and recorded by closed circuit television. LSOs observed every landing and anyone else who cared to watch a TV monitor could witness his failure. He found himself trapped in the pitiless, unforgiving world of carrier aviation.

Herb was known as a pilot who boltered.

He admired Dan Roberts' simple solution. Night blackness. Gusty winds. Lousy weather. A pitching, rolling, rain-smeared deck. Those things did not frighten him for a simple reason…Roberts' secret. *Ignore the danger and the landings were routine.* His roommate had little difficulty with carrier landings for the simple fact that he did not acknowledge the dangers. The landing was just one more problem to be solved at the end of a long flight involving many problems and a pilot could only be expected to acknowledge so many of those. The simplicity of it. The audacity! Roberts did not acknowledge the uncertainty and refused the fear. That was the trick that Herb envied but could not emulate. He rejected Roberts' casual indifference and reviled him for his innocent but more practical mind. Roberts was a man of pedestrian intelligence and Herb had apprised him of that fact many times. He lacked Herb's technical intellect, a perplexing but decisive advantage.

Herb looked ahead to find the IP checkpoint that would guide them to the target and worried about carrier landings. Then he saw the thick brown river that flowed from the hills through a small valley then turned in a lazy serpentine afterthought to the seashore. A few miles inland a tributary joined from the northwest and upstream was the city of Bac Ninh. A narrow bend of river east of the city supplied a hydroelectric power plant, the target.

Damn the haze, Ferris muttered, a cold trickle of sweat ran down his neck. CAG was a senior commander soon to be promoted to captain, one more step to flag rank. He was forty-two, old for carrier aviation. His distance vision was no longer sharp and his reactions were slowing. But he was an aggressive little man and he compensated for his physical deterioration and uncertainties with determination.

Where is it? Dammit. He fretted about the IP. Could he find it with his lousy vision? The airgroup was following Ferris and he did not want to make a foolish error simply because he could not see the target. Nervous eyes swept the horizon. He fretted. And then, there it was! He marveled at the clarity of the approach path before him. The afternoon sun glittered on the river and the river bend sparkled like a silver necklace. A quick flash of recollection. His wife had had a necklace like that, he remembered, a lump slowly forming in his throat. He had given it to her on their last wedding anniversary, when he had commanded an A-4 squadron at NAS Lemoore. A beautiful woman and a silver necklace.

During the change-of-command ceremony she had smiled, so proud of him, and that smile came to him now, a lonely, frightened man, remembering. She was still beautiful then and it was the best day of his life.

She had waited a full month before telling him, allowing him to savor the joy of command for a while. *I wanted us to enjoy it,* she'd said. *Probably nothing…a little chemotherapy, that's all, don't worry.* But the cancer had developed swiftly and she was dead within the year. He had finished his command in a grief-stricken haze and his men had covered for him. Since then, his life had been a hollow shell.

Don't think about that now!

The strike leader forced himself to concentrate. Only one thing was important now. The mission was paramount; he was a professional. The bomb run must be executed precisely. The flak and the missiles must be avoided. Then, the flight to safety. Get it over with quickly and get back to the ship alive.

Survival!

CAG Ferris turned five degrees left. Strange, he thought, no AAA or SAMs. There should be resistance this close to Hanoi. Maybe Highpockets was correct and this track took them over a lightly defended corridor to the target. Maybe they would surprise them today, he prayed quietly. Perhaps this would be easy, a piece of cake.

A few seconds to roll-in. CAG signaled to his second section to move to his right wing behind Herb McGinnis. Everyone could see the target now. An unimpressive power plant in a primitive jungle in a backward third world country.

The left turn brought them into attack position at twenty thousand feet with the sun at their backs to hamper the vision of the AAA crews. The next thirty seconds would pass like hours, he knew. They were veterans and they knew what to expect. Ferris was proud that men would follow him into combat. He had been a superior pilot at one time, but that was years ago. He had become an old man during his wife's misery, too old to be a carrier pilot. And he was frightened.

Now they were slow and heavy with ordnance. Maneuvering was restricted by requirements of the bombing run, they were sitting ducks in the dangerous sky before the roll-in. They all knew it and so did the enemy. Sixteen A-4s quickly prepared to roll-in on a small power plant in a jungle in the small country that many of the younger pilots had never heard of a few years earlier.

Master arm switch….ON. Gun/bomb switch…BOMBS, he muttered aloud.

"Faro One is in!"

CAG rolled the A-4 to a near vertical dive. An image of the target twisted around the windshield. Ferris maneuvered the A-4 out of the roll-in and weak eyes focused. An image floated vertically down the windscreen until it filled the bombsight. A tiny white dot on the bombsight tracked toward the target. His hand moved automatically to guide the pipper. He knew what to do. Ferris had performed this maneuver countless times. The pipper danced around the bombsight lens until he steadied it with smooth control movements and it settled on the center structure of the power plant.

THERE!

Toggle bomb switch. Bombs away. Ferris pulled back on the control stick and grunted to offset the G-loads. Vision graying-out! He ripped away from the dive. Four, five, six G's. The A-4 shot vertically into the blue tropical sky.

McGinnis rolled left to follow Ferris. He acquired the target in the bombsight, wings leveled, nose down into a vertical drop attitude. A black puff of smoke erupted to his left! The airplane jerked violently to the right and he cried out in surprise.

AAA bursts erupting everywhere!

"Flak trap!" He yelled into the microphone.

Black puffs filled the sky suddenly and Ferris knew someone would be hit. He leveled the wings of his A-4 and looked at his instrument panel, no apparent damage even though he had been heavily buffeted by the bursts. He saw McGinnis pull-up into a tight climb.

ESCAPE!

Sweat poured off Ferris' face onto his visor. Run, fly away, hide, primal fear engulfed him! He scanned the horizon for an area of clear, blue sky and saw only black bursts! Angry red flashes! Flak explosions everywhere. No avenue of escape, no clear skies. He saw his men roll into the ugly black mass. They would attack regardless of the AAA because they were instructed to do so and they were good men. Were they frightened too? He was terrified. Grant Ferris wanted to key the mic and warn them, as if they didn't already know. But he was too frightened to speak. A hot, glob of bile welled up into his constricted throat. His brain slowed from the numbing panic. He forced himself to think clearly. He throttled back to 85% RPM to allow his men to catch him for a rendezvous. An eruption bounced his A-4 like a rubber ball!

Now fear gripped him in an iron embrace. Ferris shoved the throttle forward to 100% RPM. Escape! Forget the men. Flee from the dreadful black explosions. But he must not do that! He was the Air Group Commander and he had to wait for his men and he must not show fear. He pulled the throttle back to 85% and saw McGinnis join on his right wing. A black cloud burst under his wing.

He was terrified and he must escape!

Ferris screamed silently into his oxygen mask! A flak burst directly in front. He yanked the A-4 into a steep left bank and crammed the throttle to the forward stop. No time to check the RPM gage for an overboost. He pulled the nose up sharply then rolled left. Throttle back to 90%. He looked back; McGinnis had followed him expertly through the abrupt maneuvers.

The AAA puffs merged into a single black cloud. Bright flashes of bursting flak punctuated the awful blackness. Flak everywhere! He shoved the throttle forward, full power. Roll right, then left. A flak burst sent his A-4 into a tumble. He kicked right rudder and righted the bomber. Climb quickly then descend. McGinnis followed him easily.

Jinks. Rapid evasive tactics. Wild maneuvers to avoid the terrible bursts! Anything to confuse the enemy anti-aircraft. The airgroup would be widely disbursed after the frantic maneuvers. Ferris looked over his shoulder and saw A-4s dashing wildly across the sky. Black bursts followed them with murderous determination. They would rejoin later. But for now, survival was his only concern.

Seconds later, Ferris was out of the deadly cocoon of AAA. He retarded the throttle slightly and saw three wingmen rejoining. McGinnis had followed him doggedly through the entire series of jinks. Good man! They were all good men, the best, he thought. Tears of fright mingled with his sweat. Ferris pushed his visor up and sleeved his sweaty forehead. Bile gushed forth in his throat and he was close to vomiting. Ferris took a deep breath. His heart pounded. He felt weak, depleted. Surely, the worst was behind them.

A heading of 105 degrees would take them out safely, he hoped, he prayed. Ferris turned toward the coastline. He punched the autopilot button with a shaking hand, afraid to maneuver the A-4 manually. Would they notice? Would McGinnis, his wingman who was a fine pilot in spite of his difficulty with carrier landings, *notice*? Would anybody guess that Faro One was flying his aircraft on autopilot because he did not trust his own trembling hands?

The airgroup slowly re-joined. By twos and threes they joined his division. Occasional stragglers swept in from above and below. One showoff did a dandy canopy-roll over the entire group and slid easily under his section leader's wing. Were they all there? He was afraid to look, but he must!

He had heard one cry of alarm over the radio in the midst of the exploding horror. The memory came back to him now. The fearful cry that he had been unable to acknowledge. *"I'm hit! Ohhh…Jesus…"* That terrible cry echoed in his conscience.

Now it was silent. Ferris looked to his left. One section was missing. He twisted, looked right but couldn't locate them. He cleared his throat, breathed deeply, then keyed the microphone.

"Check-in, Faro is up." He said with all the calmness he could muster. His own division of four A-4s was intact. Herb McGinnis waved a casual hello. What about the others?

"Dancer is up." The second division was intact.

"Midas is up." The third division.

"Faro, this is Slammer One, we're missing Three and Four."

Ferris twisted to locate the fourth division, one section missing. The last division to roll-in on targets, always the most dangerous position during a bomb run.

"Slammer Three...you read Faro?" he radioed. Where were they? He scanned the now-silent sky. Only empty quietness where seconds before had been chaos.

"Slammer Three, do you copy?"

Finally he heard, "Faro, this is Slammer Four. Read you, but Three is hit, I think. I can't tell damage."

Ferris struggled to think through his exhaustion. Slammer Three was Lt. William Jensen, the heavyset section leader of the last division, a good man.

"He's hit during the drop. He's ambling off to the northeast. I can't...I'm on Jensen's wing. I can't see any damage."

"Slammer Four, this is Faro. Stick with him as long as possible. Try to get him over the water. We'll contact the Spads."

"Roger."

The wingman moved slowly under Jensen's A-4. What was wrong? Jensen's head bobbed languidly against the canopy. Not a word since that last desperate call, but the aircraft was under minimal control on an erratic course to the north.

To continue north was unacceptable!

The wingman recognized the danger; his mind reeled with alarm. North was capture, torture and lingering torment before a merciful death. Or, even worse, they'd heard rumors of lifelong internment and endless interrogation in secret prison camps. North was suicide.

North was Red China.

10

"Faro, this is Shadow One," Roberts radioed. "We have you visually. Standing-by."

Bobby Thomas signaled a thumbs-up. They could see the Alpha Strike formation approaching from the west but not the missing section of A-4s. Roberts hadn't expected to see the two stragglers immediately. The airgroup was still struggling to reform and it would pass overhead when they went feet-wet.

"Shadow Three, this is One, over."

"Shadow Three is up."

"Hold position...you cover the south. We'll stay north, call you if we need you."

"But, we should proceed north immediately," Smithson radioed.

"Hold position until called." Bobby intervened.

"Roger!" An angry response. "We'll hold."

Ensign Terrence Kelly, Slammer Four, flew under Bill Jensen's wing, then slowly maneuvered above the battered aircraft. He looked down into the cockpit, a cold shiver ran up his spine. Jensen's canopy was splattered with blood, a red glow reflected in the brilliant afternoon sun. Jensen was struggling to fly the A-4 with his left hand causing the erratic motion. The right arm was a bloody, limp rag. Jensen couldn't key the microphone switch on top of the throttle.

He keyed the mic. "Bill, can you hear me? Nod your head." Jensen moved his head slowly.

A sigh of relief. "OK, Bill, we're getting out of here right now."

Kelly saw that an AAA burst had ripped through Jensen's right wing slat. A piece of shrapnel had penetrated the cockpit and partially dismembered Jensen's right arm. Blood was splattered everywhere. Kelly knew what had to be done. Could he help Jensen save himself? They had little fuel or time to spare.

"Bill, reach over with your left hand and engage the autopilot…copy?" He could see Jensen struggling to comply with the difficult command. Was he going into shock? "Come on…you gotta do it now, Bill."

In the blood-splattered cockpit Jensen fought through pain and confusion; he pushed the engage button. Blood coursed down his arm onto the radio panel.

"Good, Bill. That's great! Let's get the hell outta here…with your left hand push the throttle forward. Go ahead, Bill."

That was easier. Jensen felt light-headed and bewildered. How had his arm become so messy? Something hurt terribly.

"OK, Bill, now turn right to a heading of 120 degrees."

That was difficult. *I can't reach the turn knob. It hurts too much.* A dull throb pulsated through Jensen's arm into his entire body whenever he attempted the slightest movement. It was difficult to reach across with his left arm. A flash of agony racked his body. Jensen felt tired. This couldn't be happening. He didn't deserve to be injured. Jensen shook his head.

"Goddammit, Bill, you gotta do it now! Turn to 120 degrees. Do it right now, Bill! Don't you give up on me now!"

The entire airgroup heard the desperate call. Jensen must turn right and everyone knew it. East was the Gulf. East was the Seventh Fleet and home. Jensen and Kelly were flying further into North Vietnam and very soon into China. There was minimum fuel remaining and they must get over the water to survive.

Kelly saw Jensen struggle to reach the autopilot. The A-4 started a slow right turn.

"Outstanding!" Kelly cried.

So much blood loss. Kelly knew shock and fear were overwhelming Jensen; his head slumped occasionally. If he overshot the 120-degree heading they would turn in circles, easy prey to MiGs based northwest of their position.

"Shadow Flight…goddammit, get some fighters up here!" Kelly screamed. He saw 110 degrees on his RMI.

"On their way," Roberts replied. "We just talked to the E-2. F-8s here in ten minutes…just get over the water. We're waiting."

"Stop the turn! Stop the goddamn turn *now*, Bill!"

Slowly, ever so slowly, Jensen's wings leveled.

"OK. Good. That's OK, Bill," Kelly sighed.

A heading of 118 degrees. The coastline was visible to the east. Kelly almost dared to hope. Perhaps they would both survive this day. If there was enough fuel. If MiGs didn't jump them. And if there were no SAMs waiting on the coast.

If! So many *ifs*.

Kelly ran a dirty glove across his sweaty brow and calculated the odds.

Fuel equaled time, equaled survival. Kelly looked tentatively at his fuel gauge. There was so little of the precious liquid remaining. Only twenty minutes of life-giving kerosene left. So little time. They had to hurry!

Jensen was soaked with blood and his wingman was soaked with sweat, and both A-4s were expending fuel at an alarming rate. Kelly groaned. He couldn't leave Jensen, but Kelly must refuel. A life saving A-

3 tanker waited offshore. If Kelly left, Jensen would continue flying on the 118 degree heading for a few minutes, then flameout and crash into Tonkin Gulf. Bill Jensen was Kelly's squadron mate, a good friend. What more could he do? It was going to be a near thing.

Could Jensen eject? Would Kelly's nerve last? He did not know! They needed help right now!

"Hey, Shadow Flight," Kelly's voice crackled. "You guys see us, yet?" A plaintive plea. He must rendezvous with the Spads! No time or fuel to spare. Bill Jensen must eject. Kelly must refuel.

Time…fuel…hurry!

"We're here, Slammer. What's your posit?" Roberts radioed.

"We'll be coast-out about ten miles northeast of briefing. About three minutes from feet-wet. At 12,000 feet." *Please God, let the Spads see us.* Kelly muttered his first sincere prayer. "Can you see us yet?"

Kelly's voice cracked and Roberts could hear the strain. Soon, Kelly would soon be forced to leave Jensen. This would be a very near thing. Black AAA bursts erupted above the shoreline and Roberts heard Kelly's plea.

"Dammit, Shadow. Where are you?"

Roberts spoke slowly and clearly. "No contact yet, Slammer, but we're on our way. Just keep on truckin. We can see the Triple-A. We know where you'll be."

Roberts nodded his head forward several times for military power. The AAA bursts must have been very close to the A-4s. They began a slow descent to 5,000 feet and increased airspeed.

Then, he saw them. A sun-gleam from a shiny canopy.

"Got you now, Slammer. About twenty miles. Get Bill to punch-out over the water. We'll take over. Chopper's on the way."

Roberts quickly evaluated the situation. Jensen must eject over Ha Long Bay; an area twenty-five miles long and five to ten miles wide dotted with islands and small fishing villages. The rescue helicopter was fifteen minutes away. MiGs might be in the air and patrol boats in the water. Roberts called for Smithson's section to re-join.

"Shadow, we're feet-wet. Can you see us?" Kelly called nervously. The A-3 tanker was ten minutes south. "Can you guys take over…I gotta go refuel right now!"

"Roger, Slammer, we're here…check your two-o'clock low. Take Bill over the bay before ejecting. Probably lots of bad guys around here."

Roberts looked at Bobby Thomas. A thumbs-up.

"One more minute is all I got, Shadow." Kelly saw the Spads. "Can you take him now?" An audible sigh of relief. "I got no fuel left."

"Roger, Slammer, any time you're ready. See you back at home plate."

Kelly looked down into Jensen's cockpit. The *Low Fuel* warning light was flashing brightly on Jensen's instrument panel, as it was on his. Could he do it? Kelly feared the worst. Could Jensen eject? Would he? There was no time to argue with the strong-willed, heavyset lieutenant. He had less than ten minutes of fuel remaining. It had to be now.

"OK, Bill, time to go. Punch-out now."

Nothing!

Jensen looked up at Kelly. He shook his head slowly.

"Damn it, Bill, you gotta go right now. Eject! Do it…Now!"

He saw Jensen's left hand reach above his helmet and slowly pull the yellow Ejection Handle. Kelly quickly banked away.

11

Sunlight gleamed from Jensen's canopy that tumbled away while his ejection seat spewed a trail of gray smoke against a blue sky. Roberts watched the seat separate from Jensen. He fell for several seconds before the parachute blossomed.

"Shadow Two," Roberts radioed. "Will you stay with Bill? I'll take a look at that island." No fishing boats were visible but an island loomed one mile to the east.

Roberts had a knot in the middle of his stomach and wondered why Bobby Thomas had not taken command of the operation. No time to worry about that now.

Bill Jensen, wounded and bloody in a parachute two thousand feet above the bay, drifted slowly in an onshore breeze toward the island. He looked at his blood soaked sleeve and mangled arm, trying to comprehend. What had happened? He heard an explosion in the distance, his A-4? A Spad circled his parachute. Jensen was confused. He considered the circumstance with mild indifference and thought it strange that his bloody arm felt numb when he tried to wave at the Spad.

Bobby Thomas banked in front of Jensen and rocked the wings; the injured airman slowly raised his left arm, almost a wave. No fishing boats in the bay. Maybe Jensen's luck would improve. Maybe they would get lucky today, Thomas thought. And then his aircraft shuddered. He felt the shock of an impact! The Spad skidded into a yaw. Thomas kicked right rudder to level the wings. Hit by something! Something powerful. Engine instruments normal. No engine roughness. No trail of black telltale smoke. Controls responsive, the Spad was still flyable but it had been damaged. He sensed through the controls and the memory of the impact that there would be a large hole somewhere in his aircraft.

"Shadow One, this is Two," Thomas radioed. "I've been hit but I'm OK. It had to come from that island."

"Roger," Roberts said slowly. "I think I see them…standby." A cluster of men scurried on a cliff above the sandy shore of the island. Bright puffs of automatic cannon fire marked a reinforced anti-aircraft gun emplacement. They were firing at Bobby Thomas and they had not seen his Spad circling to the north. "OK, I got 'em visually." The gun crew hadn't noticed him. They were engaged with the obvious target, Thomas orbiting Jensen's bright parachute canopy.

"We can't allow them to fire on Jensen or the chopper, Dan!"

"Roger," Roberts replied. He could think of nothing appropriate to add. The parachute, Bobby's Spad, the rescue helicopter, easy targets concentrated in a stationery location. He maneuvered to put the sun at his back.

The weapon appeared to be a 23MM automatic rifle mounted on a flatbed truck above a steep cliff overlooking the bay. He watched it spew a tracer-laden stream toward Thomas. Roberts powered down the Wright and slipped quietly into the perch, the roll-in position above the truck. It had to be done right. Now he regretted that Smithson's section was miles away.

Roberts rolled in from five thousand feet.

The startled Vietnamese looked up at the noise; hurried efforts to re-orient their cannon. Roberts rolled into a sixty-degree descent, dive brakes deployed, hanging from the seat harness. A highly accurate bomb delivery maneuver that he'd practiced many times. But there was a price to be paid for precision. Now Roberts was the easy target. The aircraft was in a fixed, vulnerable descent with little deflection required from the enemy gunners.

It would be close. The truck's image drifted into the gunsight. He had two Mk-82 bombs but he'd have only one opportunity to deliver them before the gunners sprayed a defensive wall of 23MM.

The Spad streaked down toward the scurrying figures. Twinkling lights from the gun emplacement. *Wait!* Hold for the exact moment before dropping. Wait an eternity for the pipper to steady. Wait to get a good hit. Bright gun flashes seen through the bombsight. A tracer round shot past his canopy.

Wait.

There! Roberts toggled the bomb switch and felt the two five hundred pound bombs drop away.

Quickly now!

He retracted the dive brakes and jerked the Spad into a tight climbing turn. Shove the throttle to the forward stop! The propeller groaned in protest. Vision graying out from the G-load. Too low! Get away from the blast. Hurry! A stream of tracer rounds streaked overhead. Something thudded against the airframe. He kicked right rudder to tighten the turn. Another slug ricocheted off the fuselage armor-plating. More tracers. They were on him now. The engine screamed as he climbed and turned. The airframe trembled from a solid hit!

A huge explosion!

A shock wave burst through the still air. The Spad pitched up violently, a jarring concussion enveloped the aircraft and debris splattered his canopy. He felt the airframe shudder.

Don't stall!

He pulled the Spad through a tight reversal, armed the 20MM cannon and rolled back into a strafing run. The fiery wreckage filled his gunsight. Mop-up time! Dust and smoke, the gun emplacement had disappeared. A brilliant red secondary explosion, dense black smoke billowed above the cliff. Bright flashes from the battery's ammunition speckled through a blanket of drifting smoke.

The cliff had fallen away. Wreckage tumbled down onto the sandy beach. Secondary ammunition explosions punctured black smoke, exploding fuel tanks burned furiously into the sky.

"Jesus, Shadow! Anything left over there?" Thomas radioed. He watched the sheets of bright flame shooting like angry Roman candles through the billowing blackness. "Dan. You OK? What's your posit? Don't see you."

Roberts waited to respond, uncertain that his voice would function. He cleared his throat. "Above the beach. How's Jensen?" Roberts circled the devastated emplacement. Only death and destruction remained.

"No chopper, yet." Thomas watched Jensen drift down near the black smoke that rose furiously into blue sky, a beacon for the fishing village on the small island. The rescuers could not remain long. Enemy forces would move into the area to capture the American pilot. Thomas knew local forces routinely murdered downed airmen. "He's just about to splash-down. I'll circle until the Angel arrives. We gotta check that village, Dan."

"I'll take a look."

Roberts re-checked his ordnance status. Two Lau-19 rocket pods and several hundred rounds of 20MM available. Massive destructive power still remained at his disposal. Suddenly, he felt powerful. A squad of men and their weapons lay prostrate on the beach under towering clouds of black smoke and leaping shards of bright-red flames. He felt a wave of immense satisfaction. Roberts heard the radio crackle.

"Be nice," Bobby suggested.

Smithson's section had joined the Sikorsky helicopter and was escorting it into the wider mouth of the bay. It was slow going, if anything happened to the chopper the mission would fail and Jensen would be lost. Fishing junks sailed lazily outside the bay but none appeared hostile and they ignored them.

"Shadow Leader, this is Three," Smithson radioed. "About seven miles east with the Angel. Is that you guys up there with all that smoke?"

"Roger, Three. That's us. Hurry up, we need you. Two is covering Slammer and I'm trying to secure the area."

"We'll hurry….damn you're messy."

Jensen had dropped into the bay. Thomas thought he saw a feeble arm waving. His May West inflated and he appeared to be conscious.

"Angel, this is Shadow Two," Thomas radioed. "Slammer is in the water."

"Roger, Shadow, Angel here. We'll be there in about two minutes. We have a visual on you. What's Slammer's condition?"

"Alive. Can you drop some help for him?"

"Affirmative, we got a really good swimmer on board. Can you buy us a few more minutes?"

"Oh, I think so," Bobby laughed. "We have a really good man working that problem right now. But hurry up before he pisses 'em off."

"Yeah, we'll expedite. Looks like he's been a rude sombitch."

Now Roberts flew over the fishing village. A junk had pushed away from the pier emitting rapid puffs of diesel exhaust. They were in a hurry. He descended over the small inlet that opened to a wide bay and the village. The fishing junk was sixty feet long, sails unfurled on its two masts.

"How much longer, Shadow Two?" he radioed.

"Ten minutes, Dan. Are you OK?"

"Affirmative, I think you got some company on the way. A junk…don't think they're going fishing." A machine gun was mounted on the bow, men were uncovering a small howitzer, black smoke puffed furiously from the stern.

"Goddammit! Do you need assistance? That boat's gotta be stopped…the chopper's not here yet."

"Negative, I'll handle it. Don't leave Slammer."

"Roger, I can see the chopper but we need a few minutes, Dan."

Roberts watched the boat exit the small harbor. If they turned any direction but east, toward Jensen, he would allow them free passage. He maneuvered the aircraft while arming the four 20MM cannons. Master Arm Switch *on*. Gun/Bomb switch to *Guns*. Cannons charged. Roberts prepared the Spad. He prepared himself. He had killed several men on the pretty beach.

The junk cleared the harbor's entrance and turned to the east; black-clad crewmen, unaware of the circling Spad, scurried around the automatic weapon.

12

Roberts kicked right rudder and dropped the nose into a 30-degree dive-angle. Airspeed inched up to 250 knots. A little left rudder to compensate for P-factor. Muzzle-flashes from the junk. Ignore them! Let the nose drift slowly along the track into the target. Rudder out the torque, right aileron for compensation. Pipper on the target. Slowly, smoothly. So easy if you knew how.

Wait.

The fishing junk filled the gunsight. He felt a jolt. The Spad shuddered. Pipper on target, squeeze the trigger. The control stick vibrated in his hand. Four cannon emitted a pulsating staccato. Bright-white 20MM tracer arced down into the bay. The Spad decelerated a few knots from massive cannon recoil. Shaking, vibrating. He held the pipper steady on the junk and followed the smoky trail of 20MM tracer mixed with high explosive and armor-piercing ammunition. The Spad slowed. Ease off left rudder. Quick, gentle cross pressures on the stick. Stay on target.

Four tracks of watery 20MM geysers enveloped the junk's bow blasting away chunks of wooden hull then converged on the center of the boat. An immense explosion filled the sky with burning debris. Wooden masts tumbled, smoky fragments cascaded outward. Black oily smoke billowed.

Roberts banked the Spad sharply to the left and pulled the nose into a high-G roll through the top of the blast-cloud. He shot through and felt hurtling fragments bounce off the airframe like hail on a tin roof. Seconds later he was clear of the fireball, rolling out of the climbing turn. He glanced back over his shoulder.

What remained of the junk floated in the turbulent water under a black cloud. A few fragments splashed into the dirty oil slick.

The bay's blue-green surface roiled and foamed as the downwash from the Angel's rotor blades enveloped Jensen. The helicopter crew deployed a cable and rescue harness into the water, discharging static electricity from the chopper. Jensen's parachute was still attached and swirling in the water around the wounded airman. A frogman jumped into the turbulent green water, unsnapped the parachute's quick-release fittings, a weak smile on Jensen's face was returned by a pat on his helmet. Then, an explosion filled the sky with a concussion wave.

Black smoke mushroomed into the hazy afternoon sky. Thomas saw the bright flashes of detonating ordnance sparkling in the dense blackness. The chopper pilot corrected the hover slightly for the disturbance and eased over the frogman who fastened Jensen into the rescue harness. A quick thumbs-up and they were slowly reeled out of the water. Jensen's nearly severed arm dangled at his side.

"Shadow One, you OK?" Thomas radioed.

"Affirmative, that junk was headed your way. There's another at the dock. How much longer?"

"Give us five minutes, maybe more. Better disable that other boat. Need some help?"

"Negative, but lemme know when you're outta there."

Roberts turned to fly over the smoky flotsam and saw the village's thatched huts grouped around a narrow stream flowing down from the hills into the harbor. On a wide brown path that led to the dock a small knot of people scurried toward the village. Twinkling lights! Probably Ak-47s. He ignored them.

Roberts pushed the nose over and concentrated on the gunsight pipper as it tracked over the dock toward the moored boat. It was smaller than the fishing junk he had just destroyed. He placed his finger on the trigger; the target filled the gunsight. 20MM tore into the junk.

Something was wrong!

He sensed something out of place and held cannon fire to scan the target area. His eyes focused on the anomaly.

"Shadow One, Slammer's recovered," Thomas radioed. "Let's get the hell outta here!"

A small figure running up the dock. An erratic movement, then an explosion, a fireball. He continued the run-in, captivated by the scene. Bobby's message slowly registered.

"Roger," he said and turned-off the Master Arm Switch angrily. He could think of nothing but the runner. She was small and dressed in Vietnamese black pajamas. She fled up the dock, long dark hair streamed behind. A child? He was close now, speeding over the smoky dock, well inside normal cannon range, straining to see.

The girl snapped her head back toward the nightmare that had destroyed the fishing junk, the largest man-made structure she had ever known. It was the pride of her village and one small airplane had savagely annihilated it before her eyes. And, now that same noisy destroyer screamed above her. A secondary explosion. Fire and smoke consumed the dock. She disappeared into the fiery oblivion.

He pulled up and flew over the village. A few rounds of small arms fire clattered against his fuselage. He rolled into a tight turn, circled, and squirmed for a last look, but she was gone. Lost in the smoke and destruction. His hands shook and he wanted to say something but he could not. What had he done?

Dan Roberts looked for the girl in black pajamas. *Had she escaped?* He remembered her terror-stricken little face. The streaming black hair. Running away from an airborne monster.

Running away from him.

He tucked into position under Thomas' right wing.

"Welcome back….busy day?" Thomas radioed, tapped his helmet, pointing to Roberts. *Do you want to resume the lead?*

Roberts, wrung-out from the engagement, tapped his helmet in return and pointed back. *No, you keep the lead.*

The Sikorsky escorted by the four Spads departed Ha Long Bay. Smithson's section was to the left of the chopper, Bobby Thomas and Roberts on the right. A medic worked furiously to staunch the blood flow from Jensen's mangled arm. Thomas signaled to jettison their unused ordnance into the Gulf.

Roberts eased closer to examine the minor AAA damage to Bobby's fuselage and saw Smithson looking in his direction. He waved casually but there was no friendly greeting in return.

Roberts methodically secured the armament switches. He would have no reason to shoot again today. Bill Jensen had been rescued and the mission would be judged a success, there would be accolades during the debriefing. Bobby's hearty wave meant he was pleased. But Roberts knew the truth; he had made serious mistakes and there would be consequences. He tried not to think of the black figure. A shattered dock. A junk splintered and in flames. His hand shook while securing a switch. A little girl had witnessed the destruction and had fled in terror. He racked his brain…had she survived? Possibly, but he did not know! He truly did not know. There was no escaping it now and he would always question his guilt. *Have I killed a girl?* What would 20MM do to a small body? He imagined fragments, blood, and ugly haunting apparitions.

Eventually, Dan Roberts would look back on this instant as the seminal event that was to have major influence on the rest of his life. *Was this when it had truly begun?* He would dream of the fleeing black figure on this night and for years to come. The nightmare would haunt him and couple with memories of betrayals. The joint exigencies of the dreams and the betrayals would have profound affects. In time burning anguish would give birth to revenge, and crime.

But, for today, there would be other problems to face. Smithson, the legal officer, had a formidable intellect and an expansive ego. He didn't seem the type to forget a slight. Why had Bobby Thomas relinquished the lead to Roberts today, thrusting him into an awkward predicament? Roberts should have called the other section in earlier; now he regretted his errors. He decided to apologize to Smithson during the debrief, but there would be consequences.

He flew with deliberate precision under Bobby's wing. Bury the troubles. Concentrate on flying the Spad. Obscure the worry. Forget the black pajamas, the black memories. Try to forget the unforgettable.

They returned to the USS Sharpsburg and recovered without further incident. Bill Jensen had what remained of his shattered arm amputated that afternoon by Doc Swanson; his flying career had ended.

13

Nguyen Binh watched the four Skyraiders circle the ship, then land. A helicopter fluttered aboard the Sharpsburg ending the day's flight operations. He knew that because the ship turned out of the wind and he observed securing activities on the deck. Time to relax.

A shadow drifted over the tiny junk bringing a cooling breeze and to the southwest towering cumulous clouds signaled a sea-change. The cloud's slate bottoms blended into mid-level lighter grays and the drifting monoliths higher anvil crowns that flattened out into long white sheets that promised rain. The monsoon season brought frequent showers to the Tonkin Gulf and Binh welcomed them for they meant a slackening of the air war, but Binh did not think it would rain today. Tomorrow would bring the welcome rains. He glanced up at a noise. His crewmember placed a tin cup at his elbow then bowed timidly. *He's heard of me,* Binh thought. *And he is wondering why I don't look more fearsome.* The crewmember looked at Binh's hands, but not his eyes. *He expects my hands to be bloodstained. And why not?* Binh knew of his dreadful reputation and resented it. The crewmember smiled when Binh dribbled tea down his shirt. *He'll say nothing,* Binh knew. *But he will look at me and wonder why I'm so unimpressive and not realize that it is because I am.*

Nguyen Binh was a small man, slight of stature but wiry. Thick gray hair topped a skull that contained a massive but subdued intellect. He had a deceptively mild voice; a soft tenor vibrating with intensity that had deceived so many people. When he displayed an infrequent smile, his face softened and one might wonder how this grandfather could have been so vehement.

The old man secured his watch and drank the tea; flight operations on the Sharpsburg were completed. The slackening activity on the flight deck indicated that the ship planned a brief respite from the war. Major Binh was pleased when the aircraft carrier had returned from Subic Bay. He knew where the ship had taken its rest period; the Russian KGB kept the North Vietnamese counterparts well informed on many things. Binh had grown to feel a curious affiliation with the carrier and he had missed the ship's iron-gray mass steaming madly about in his vicinity. Somehow he thought of the ship as being *his* ship, a peculiar symbiotic connection existed between the old ship and the old man. The ship and its crew may not have been aware of the wrinkled observer but he was totally cognizant of them. Now there existed an earnest connection between two enemies. Why hadn't he seen it before?

Yes, he mused in the warm afternoon sun; it was good to see the ship again, to be near it. A decision had been made. An important thing had to be done. It had come to him with sudden clarity one warm, gentle afternoon while the ship had been absent. The connection, the cause, the redemption had all merged into an inspiration. He and the ship and a Skyraider pilot were now wedded to an enlightenment. He'd had a bold and noble vision.

Why not end the war?

Why not? It could be done. Binh was convinced of the possibility. Simply *end* it! Between two rational individuals compromise and reason were always possible. The problem was that the two hierarchies, actually three including the government of South Vietnam, could never agree to anything. That was the rub! Binh was well acquainted with the governing forces of his own country and he was quite certain that America's leaders could be just as chauvinistic. And the South Vietnamese were impossible. Unless?

The idea was really quite simple. It had come to him in one of his many dreams. He dreamed frequently now of his lost family, but occasionally he dreamed of the *troubles*, and how to end it.

Now, finally, it had come to him. So simple, yet so reasonable. He had dreamed of the ship and of its men. And in particular his mind had wondered through the drifting mists of memory to that recent day when a pilot had returned to the ship with a smoking, crippled, rough-running Skyraider. That Skyraider pilot was a warrior like Major Binh, they were brothers-in-arms. He had not forgotten that day. And now he saw the truth clearly.

Why couldn't two rational individuals, warriors who had tasted the agony of war, sit down and reach a reasonable understanding that could be presented to their governing bodies to end the hostilities temporarily, and with good fortune permanently?

At first it seemed so improbable. Was it madness? Binh dismissed it as idle folly, wishful dreams of an old, battle-scarred man. But as time passed and he had mulled over the idea, it began to make sense. After all, who better to sanction an end to the bloodshed than those charged with the responsibility of shedding the blood?

The warriors themselves could end the fighting!

An inspired notion. It was so logical. Peace would be so sweet. All that was required was the seed of truce and the tender cultivation of compromise.

Of course he realized that the Skyraider pilot and himself were mere pawns in the larger game. The plan would require another man of considerable stature as an intermediary. If they could agree to a suitable method of disengagement, how could this plan be presented to the governments who must implement it?

The plan would require a sponsor.

But, who? The dilemma had troubled him until the absence of the ship had inspired him. The solution was right there where it had been all along, steaming briskly in his clear vision. The ship *was* the answer!

The USS Sharpsburg. A mainline ship of war. One of the most powerful and destructive forces in existence. On that single ship existed more firepower than most of the world's nations had in their entire inventories. Who would be responsible for such power? The Captain! That man, whoever he was, was an individual of great importance and trust. Certainly, he would be held in high esteem by the government of the United States.

There was his answer!

If the old man could find a way to visit the ship and request a conference with the Skyraider pilot, with whom he felt a strong and natural affinity, he was certain that a logical understanding could be reached quickly. Then jointly they would petition the Sharpsburg's captain and enlist his sponsorship to end the bloodshed.

Was this madness? Perhaps, but what bold enterprise was not initially thought to be mad? And only boldness could yield such grand results.

The captain would have the ability to present their agreement to America, the most powerful of the three parties. He already had the framework of such a plan in mind, an immediate cease-fire enforced by the United Nations, then honorable negotiations under the auspices of the Geneva Convention. Such an agreement proposed by the combatants themselves would carry considerable moral force. It could be over within days. It would be a warrior's supreme attainment. A warrior's peace. It could work! He fairly quivered with anticipation!

Binh must find a way to approach the Sharpsburg.

He compiled his daily report. One A-4 had not returned from the last mission. Major Binh had carefully observed the departing aircraft through his American binoculars, categorized them by type and ordnance load. He rechecked his notes. Then he compared the returning numbers for the flight operations report.

Binh felt a sickening feeling of despair. In spite of decades of blood and war and anger and more blood, the old man had never succumbed to nihilism. His was too strong a spirit to allow defeatism to cloud an unflagging faith. The future, that is where salvation lay, waiting for the moment. He, who had given so much, could be the catalyst for peace. One could see it so clearly now, just a simple matter of trust and logic. It could be over, finished, complete. And it could begin with only a modicum of good will between two warriors. It could be done. He had conceived the plan and with him lay the responsibility for implementation.

Why not he and the young Skyraider pilot? Why not?

They could begin the process. He was confident as the plan mellowed in his eager mind. Major Binh had complete faith in the nobility of the common man and he would not allow the cowardly notions of abrogation to dampen the possibility of peace with the giant nation he admired so much.

He looked at the carrier eagerly as the sunset washed his tiny boat in a warm red glow. On the Sharpsburg resided all the essential elements he must employ. It would be difficult, but with tolerance and understanding, it was possible. Honorable warriors could end the dishonorable war. He smiled contentedly at the concept.

There could be peace in his lifetime.

What would peace look like? He could not imagine a condition he had never known. Peace was an enigma to the old warrior. But he would welcome the wonderment of it with an open heart and willing soul.

For now, Major Binh must wait, the proper time would present itself. Of course he must be receptive to any propitious offering. He must be ready to exploit any opportunity and when the time was right, he would not be found wanting. Major Nguyen Binh was a wise and courageous man.

He must watch for *The Moment!*

14

A curtain of cigarette smoke drifted over the men in the cramped room. There had been loud talk and laughter that night; eruptions of bravado and youthful arrogance, not an unusual occurrence, but Roberts had little taste for it now.

"That's enough cheating for one night." Roberts yawned. He had stretched the game, and his limited sociability, as far as he could and he had something else on his mind.

McGinnis threw his cards down. "Yeah…win a few bucks then leave. Take your damn money. What did I tell you guys…never trust a Spad driver…especially Roberts. Did you all know he got several more holes in his little Spad yesterday?"

Dan Roberts laughed; he scooped loose change from the table.

"You've been sniffing too much 115-145 lately," Herb continued. "I imagine your shoot-'em-up over Bill Jensen has gone to your head, right?"

"Listen, two bucks is a large investment for a married guy," Roberts said. "Damn cardsharps oughtta appreciate my…uhh…my frugal position. Besides, my mother told me to never trust grown men who ride around in scooters."

"Skyhawk. Please! The A-4 is the venerable, and deadly, Douglas Skyhawk to all you dipshit Spad drivers. Just look at him, guys." Herb pointed at Roberts. "Small brain…large right leg…torque gets to them after a while. Yeah! Ittsy, tiny brain…and a little teeny weenie but a really big right leg."

"We need it for kicking rude roommates," he stammered. "Especially jet jockeys. Did you know that the dumber guys get assigned to jets because they can only remember two things at a time…push-pull…left-right?"

"No…" One of the card players said. "See…Roberts, we couldn't qualify for Skyraiders. All of our parents were married. Did you have any parents? I mean were your folks normal people that didn't live in trees?"

"Parents?" he said slowly, time to think.

"Even a dumb Spad driver should get that one, Danny," Herb drawled.

"Parents? Married? Don't gimme that…Scooter pilots weren't born of human flesh. They evolved. They crept up out of the ocean slime, probably at night under a full moon."

"Damn, Danny…you must have practiced that for a week, such eloquence."

A little mild scuffling ensued for male bonding. Roberts found himself sprawled on the floor.

"Take your ill gotten wealth and get the hell outta here, Roberts. I'm weary of you and your salacious bullshit."

When outnumbered, why not just leave?

"All right, Herby." Roberts rubbed a sore shoulder. "Don't forget your flashlight."

"I better. Someday I'll have to lead you outta here, Danny." Herb sneered. "Second thought, maybe I'll do aviation a favor and just leave your sorry ass. But I won't…I'll lead your silly butt out of some dark hole up to sunlight and salvation."

McGinnis had decided to carry a flashlight after the recent Oriskany accident. The intense magnesium fire, which had been carelessly ignited in the flare locker, had burned for hours and suffocated dozens of men in the forward berthing areas. Most victims were Naval Aviators.

"Dark hole? Did I hear a reference to…" Roberts struggled. "…depravity? I'm not the one who got lost in the Willows and I don't want to hear any more stories about magic curtains and exotic dancers or your adolescent wet-dreams."

"Screw you, Danny," Herb said.

"Damned profligate." One poker loser added.

"Cheats at cards, too." Another concluded.

And so it goes.

Roberts left the poker game after recovering from a losing night with five pilots from Herb's squadron. He'd had something on his mind. A nagging thing. It had been difficult to concentrate on poker. A single word had been spoken casually with an immense undertone and it had given him little peace since he had heard it.

Tricky.

Such an innocuous word, an offhand remark. Roberts doubted that Timothy Bryan even remembered making the comment before yesterday's launch that had preceded Bill Jensen's rescue. But, Dan Roberts had not forgotten. A sense of unease. A burning ember nudging his memory for comprehension.

He wandered through the forward hangar deck toward the starboard side and ducked through a watertight door near the flare locker. Junior Officer's quarters were located on either side of the dimly lit passageway. Roberts proceeded forward to the third door and knocked quietly. A tall stooped-shouldered lieutenant opened it.

A cool greeting, "Hi, Roberts."

Lt. Ralph Manley had been reading at his desk. He was stripped to shorts and a tee shirt. The warm humid air stirred past Roberts from the wall fan over the desk.

"Still up, Ralph?"

"Yeah…catching up on the classics." He dropped a Playboy magazine on the bunk. "Sit down." And pointed at the second chair. "What can I do for you tonight?"

They were squadron mates. Acquaintances, but not friends. Actually, they had not exchanged more than a few words since Roberts had reported to VA-433 and a subtle discord had developed between the two officers. Something unspoken and unacknowledged had developed after Roberts was assigned the Franklin investigation. They were two incompatible personalities keeping a wary distance. He did not care for Roberts.

"Mind if I ask you a few questions, Ralph? Skipper still wants me to write some kind of a…umm…report on Franklin. I…well, don't really know what…." Roberts exaggerated his halting speech pattern while deliberately downplaying his assignment, an unimportant thing.

"Sure," Manley interrupted. "Glad to help. I never found much to report on that deal, funny thing though?" Manley spoke with quick certainty. He was a senior lieutenant, the squadron's Safety Officer. His responsibilities included both air operations and shipboard safety. Commander Isaacson evidently had not been satisfied with Manley's investigation and assigning the responsibility for the final report to Roberts, Franklin's assistant division officer, had been a minor rebuke. Roberts sensed a mild hostility.

"I think you did all you could, Ralph." A peace offering. Roberts wondered how to obtain information from an unfriendly source.

"Wasn't much to go on."

"That's for sure. Know what? I've thought a lot about this lately and I think the skipper decided to take the millstone off your neck and shift it downhill to me." Roberts grimaced. Earlier, he'd practiced the sentence several times to get it right. A critical moment. Manley smiled at his stammering voice.

"Well, an official report from a safety officer does carry a lot of weight." Manley frowned at the burden he bore gallantly.

"Exactly…I can't blame Commander Isaacson. I just wish he had chosen another ensign…not me." Roberts laughed. "My usual lousy luck."

"Isaacson can be tough on everybody." Manley hadn't thought of this angle. He laughed a bit too long and considered the new possibility that he might have been saved from an embarrassing failure. "Ensigns are made for jobs like this, I guess." Manley propped a long skinny leg on the table and looked closer at the new guy. He'd disliked Roberts initially and there was the annoyance of the Franklin report. Mostly, he resented Roberts' background. The new guy wasn't Annapolis; therefore his pedigree was shadowed. Manley had heard through the grapevine that Roberts' flying skills were adequate and that Bobby Thomas, his division officer, had some regard for him.

Roberts kept the thought going. "Bobby Thomas said shit flows downhill in the Navy. And, I…well, I guess I'm the downhillest of them all right now. What do you call…?"

"SLJO? Yeah, *Dan*. You are the current SLJO. New guy equals Shitty-Little-Jobs-Officer, equals flunky." His smile was genuine.

"Thanks for reminding me, Ralph." Now it was *Dan*, the SLJO. Maybe, just maybe. Roberts waited.

"Course, I was a midshipman for four arduous years at the Academy, so being a lowly ensign was no big deal for me. But, I understand your problem, believe me." Manley laughed openly. "Hey, you want a little snap. I got some booze left in the safe."

"Sure…but I don't want to intrude…" Of course not.

Several minutes of chitchat ensued. The subject of Annapolis had been broached and Manley reviewed the glory days at the Academy where he had been a top-notch basketball player.

"University of Washington." Roberts responded to Ralph's inquiry. "I wasn't accepted for the Academy. I applied but I was a B-minus student and not such a great athlete, either."

"U-Dub, huh?" A frank admission, Manley concluded. "Hey, is Washington gonna be granted statehood someday?" He knew little of the backwater college.

"Oh, sure. They're even talking about paving Seattle's streets."

"Amazing." Manley laughed.

Roberts decided not to hurry the situation. He needed information. Manley might have it, and his curiosity had been provoked.

Tricky?

"I read your preliminary Franklin report. Excellent work, Ralph." Groveling a bit.

"Not much to go on," Manley replied, in case Roberts hadn't heard it the first time.

"Look, Ralph, I was wondering…was he a gambler, do you think?"

"I thought of that, of course." Manley smiled at the obvious question. "Nope, Franklin seemed to be a guy with no notable vices. Well, no unusual stuff anyway. Nothing worth dying for. No particular enemies…just didn't show up at muster one morning….weird, but accidents happen."

"Yeah…he worked for Lt. Williamson, I see." Roberts pretended extreme interest in Manley's preliminary report, which he had brought with him. *Franklin* had been scribbled across the front of the buff envelope by a squadron yeoman.

"Yeah…he was the line division officer, guess you've taken his place there, too. Nice guy, good pilot. Teddy Williamson was a year behind me at Annapolis. Wife in Oakland…coupla kids. Tragic."

"Tough…" Roberts shook his head and was genuinely sorry about the pilot that he had replaced.

The only photo on Ralph Manley's desk was of himself. An official Academy eight-by-ten glossy of a youthful Ralph taken midair during a hook shot. The ball hung suspended above Ralph's smiling face, good form. Roberts had been an avid basketball player whose skills were inadequate for the varsity team. A lull dropped over the conversation while Manley studied the photo as though it was the first time he had ever seen it. Now was a good time to ask the question.

"What do you think happened to him?"

Manley was relaxed. He had slugged down two large Scotches while Roberts had dallied with his.

"I think he just jumped one night…depression, maybe." Manley misunderstood.

"No," Roberts said carefully. "I mean with Ted Williamson." And eased the conversation where he wanted it to go.

"Oh…who knows, really. Wanna read my preliminary report on Williamson, too?"

"Well…sure, I guess. Might help." Yes!

"Not much in it either. We eliminated any physiological factors. Teddy was in top shape. Jogged on the flight deck every day. Teetotaler. All around terrific guy. No problems at home…nothing."

"What about the airplane?"

"Nothing significant. No recent battle damage. No outstanding gripes in the maintenance log. Hell, I flew 409 myself on the afternoon just before his fatal night launch. A clean airplane."

"So, what's left?" Slowly.

"Weather had to be part of it. Darker than hell that night, I remember. No moon. Light rain showers around. Beginning monsoon season. Ceiling about a thousand feet."

"Steady sea-state?"

"No, pretty rolly that night. Kind of an ugly night if you want to know the truth."

Truth! Exactly what Dan Roberts had in mind.

"Soooo….?"

"Vertigo." A sluggish hand motion, Ralph's lethargic eyes drifted to his photo. "Rolling deck. A black-ass night, you know. That's my opinion. Had to be. No other apparent explanation...it happens."

"Christ, yes...vertigo," Roberts frowned. "I get it bad on every night cat shot. Do you?"

"Oh, I'm pretty used to it now." Manley, the Academy graduate, reappeared. A condescending smile was allowed to play across his assertive face. "But I know what you mean."

"Last time I couldn't tell if I was right-side up, upside down, sideways...nothing." Roberts laughed at the self-deprecatory remark. It was absolutely true. He hadn't been able to tell what the attitude of the airplane was during the catapult shot. Only disciplined attention to the flight instruments had prevented him from flying into the ocean. Vertigo was normal on night launches. It happened regularly to every pilot. Human senses were inadequate for the deceiving forces at play during mind-scrambling night catapult launches.

"Hell...don't feel bad." A satisfied smirk appeared on the safety officer's face. "Happens to us all occasionally. The ol' human inner-ear just doesn't know how to handle G-forces and side-loads at night."

Manley had the reputation of being awkward around women. He covered his weakness with bravado and frequent boasts of his triumphs with prostitutes. Success with females was an important attribute for a successful Naval Aviator.

"Too bad about Williamson....and Franklin, too. Line division lost two good men in what...? Roberts feigned a quick computation. "...about five days, I guess?" He opened both hands in a gesture of dismay. Apparently this thought had just occurred to him.

"Yes...uhhh...that's about right." Manley consulted each report; one titled *Franklin* and the other *Williamson*. "Sure, it was five days, exactly. Williamson crashed and five days later Franklin disappeared. Just a coincidence, I guess."

"Coincidence?"

"Yeah, kinda weird." Manley sloshed a bit of Scotch in their glasses, feeling quite effusive. Roberts and he could work out their differences and might become friends eventually. Dan Roberts wasn't that difficult to get along with. The new guy recognized his place in the scheme of things, being an ensign and a Reserve officer among other things. Manley appreciated junior officers who knew their place.

"Those things happen, I guess," Roberts said.

Ralph, the rodent was Manley's nickname. Spoken frequently behind his back. Although he lacked success with the opposite sex, he was feared as a tireless Martinet by the enlisted men of the squadron. He frequently wrote-up men for minor infractions and took pleasure while doing so.

Roberts accepted the drink politely and encouraged Manley to review his reports in detail but he already had the information he wanted. Ralph Manley was evidently prepared to believe that a skillful, well-adjusted pilot in a good airplane had crashed during a night launch and that the *only* suitable explanation was pilot disorientation. And, the Safety Officer was also willing to accept that Franklin, Lt. Williamson's plane captain, had disappeared five days later and it was all a tragic coincidence. It was maddeningly illogical but Manley was content with that simple conclusion. Whenever an airplane crashes without an obvious explanation, blame the pilot. Why not? It was a safe, routine explanation for many accidents. Franklin's disappearance could easily be one of many unexplained deaths at sea. In the era of body counts and MIAs the two missing men had become insignificant casualties during a war. Why not?

"I really appreciate this, Ralph."

He had learned little of the late Ted Williamson that he hadn't known previously, but he knew what he *didn't* know and that was important. Now he had in his hands what he had really come for, something dark and portentous lay hidden in the Franklin and Williamson reports. Roberts had a sense of unease, an uncomfortable, incomplete feeling like seeing distant lightning on an unsettled day, but not hearing the thunder. Perceiving subtle abstractions was a critical skill for someone handicapped by a speech impediment and Roberts had a questioning, acerbic mind that was quite capable of believing illogical things when necessary. However, there was one situation he could never accept. Ensign Dan Roberts did not believe in *coincidence*.

15

Thick gray clouds billowed over the Sharpsburg broken by sunbursts that shot through breaks in the ragged ceiling and gusty sheets of rain swept across the Gulf's wind-whipped surface. The monsoon weather had been a problem after the Sharpsburg's return to Yankee Station. Attack missions had been launched but rain had caused many aborts, bombs were jettisoned into the ocean and aircraft frequently returned without engaging the enemy. The Sharpsburg's frustrated captain had ordered a three-day stand-down, quiet time to refurbish and repair, to rest. Time to read a few books and watch old movies in VA-433's ready room. Time for unhurried sleep. Deferred maintenance items in aircraft logbooks were cleared and delayed bureaucratic tasks finished.

All of the Skyraiders were parked below in the hangar bay when a group of pilots strolled through on that dreary, humid afternoon on their way to the wardroom. The hangar bay echoed with youthful bantering.

"Hey, look Danny. A Spad with your very own name on it," Herb McGinnis chuckled. "I wanna take your picture in front of that antique before it gets shipped back to the boneyard."

McGinnis held a Japanese camera, which he had purchased at the Subic Bay Naval Exchange. He was having only moderate success operating the complicated devise. Focusing lenses and F-stops and other infernal devises continued to confound the graduate engineer.

"You're gonna miss these…umm…things when they're gone, Herby. A Spad driver might save your sorry ass someday…"

"Not very likely," Herb interrupted.

"…and you'll be glad to see an old Spad flying over your Scooter, which will be scattered all over North Vietnam. Especially, if you don't stop doing those stupid low-altitude drops."

"Quit stammering. Just stand up there in front of that greasy Spad and shut up, Roberts." Herb was weary of his roommate's twisted syntax. How did he always manage to bend things around?

"Bobby said I oughtta talk to you about that stuff, since you won't listen…"

"You, talk?" Herb laughed. "Gimme a break."

"I don't know how you afford all these trinkets, Herb. First an engagement ring for your girlfriend…now a new camera. How do you do it?"

"They pay us Regular officers more. May is my fiancée and she needs a ring and I need a camera…now shut up, Roberts."

"May seems like an intelligent girl…what does she see…"

After several minutes of tinkering and adjusting, the rancorous camera was apparently ready for action. Roberts heard low unintelligible mumblings about open apertures and F-stops and slow speeds and a guttural curse or two.

"Why don't you deep-six that silly thing, or better yet mail it home to May? She can probably operate it."

"Shut up. There…now smile dammit. Say cheese or something."

"Oh, shit, Herb."

"Perfect!" A series of shots were taken from various angles. The photographer even had the temerity to stand upon a platform for better exposure. Cap pushed back, tongue pressed through clamped lips. Eyes squinting in deep concentration. Blond hair flopped over a wrinkled brow. Roberts posed as commanded and became increasingly self-conscious during the outrage.

From behind an adjacent Skyraider a ruddy face appeared and pleasant laughter greeted the two pilots. Chief Pete O'Leary had been directing a crew on the finer points of dry-washing an airplane and had stopped to observe the maladroit photographer.

"Can I take one of you both, sir?" Pete asked. "Because I'm not so sure a pilot can handle a high-tech camera like that."

"Be careful, Pete," Roberts said. "That frigging camera might be loaded. It's probably got a warning label somewhere, like everything should around Ensign McGinnis."

"Sure, Chief...shut up, Dan." Herb handed the camera to Pete. "Let's do it, Dan," he laughed. "This way, I'll have proof someday when you're infamous. I can prove I knew you after the despicable deed that I expect you to commit eventually. I'll be able to say to everyone....*I knew Danny Roberts when he was an honest man.*"

"Oh, bullshit," Roberts grumbled; he could not think of an adequate response.

"Don't scoff, Danny." A quick rejoinder. "Just look at him, Chief. I know...I truly know about his fatal character flaw. It's right there in those virtuous green eyes...a blind man could see that. I'll read about you someday, Dan. Gar-un-damn-tee it."

After a patient moment Pete said. "Now, if you two will be still...I'll try to work this thing. There, I think you needed a little faster lens setting, Mr. McGinnis." Pete made an exaggerated display of photographing the two younger officers.

"There you go, Mr. Roberts," Pete laughed. "Now there's an official record for Mr. McGinnis...when you do whatever it is you're going to do."

Pete seemed to like Roberts, Herb McGinnis noted, and he thought it unusual. Roberts had few friends.

"Phillips, get over here!" Pete shouted. Two men were dry washing an airplane, Roberts noted that was his Spad. "Didn't I tell you and Diaz to cover those static ports with ordinance tape? Mr. Roberts is going to be pissed if he loses his pitot-static system on the next cat shot." Pete admonished one of the men who had been rubbing a creamy paste onto the upper fuselage.

"Say, Chief…what is that greasy stuff, anyway?" Herb had been examining the camera for any secret settings Pete may have used.

"Dry-wash? Come on…take a look, Mr. McGinnis." He rubbed the jelly-like substance between his fingers. "If this gets into that static port, it's a pain to clean out. Really screws up the airspeed and altimeter indicators." Pete pointed to the small air-sensor inlet that Phillips was covering with tape.

"Is it soap?"

"Well, it has an official Navy name about this long." Pete held his hands apart to indicate considerable length. "But, it's a strong detergent paste with some anti-corrosive additives. Since we can't actually wash airplanes aboard the ship, we use this. Rub it on and it removes all the crud and leaves a protective film…salt water's a real problem for us. Good stuff. Costs a lot of money, works great."

"Hey, maybe I'll try it on my Vette."

"You don't really have a Corvette, do you Herb?" Roberts asked. Herb doted on his black Corvette. "It's just another one of your…."

"Fantasies?" Herb suggested. "How come you always choke up on the critical word, Dan?"

"Yeah, fantasy. Just like some other stories I've heard lately."

"It's stored in North Carolina…at my mother's." *Herbert, this car looks too fast.* Herb's mother had actually said that. *It must be dangerous.* But Herb explained that he was a pilot and could be relied on to control a mere automobile. The faster the better. *Fast cars and fast women are never conducive to good health, Son.* Herb promised to consider her advice, to ignore his mother's maxims was perilous.

"I can tell you that dry-wash works great," Pete said. "I've used it on my wife's Mustang. Remind me when we get back to Alameda, Mr. McGinnis, I'll get you a sample for the Vette."

"Hey…thanks, Chief."

New camera in hand, Herb wandered off to attempt even more complicated exposures in the darker recesses of the hangar deck. Roberts remained behind; he had a question.

"Pete, I'm almost finished interviewing the men about Franklin." The tedious process had been conducted over several days while in port and after they had departed Subic Bay.

"Find anything of interest?"

"Nope. Skipper's really on my back about this thing. I can't tell what he wants. The truth, or just some fancy report which covers everything and says…"

"Nothing? Gotta give him something, sir. Commander Isaacson's a good man, but he's tough. Better do your best. But, in the end…well, you know my conclusion."

"Suicide?"

"Probably."

Roberts frowned, "It's just…?"

"Problems, sir?"

"Oh, nothing. I guess…" He waited for the chief to take the bait.

"I'll help, sir. You know that. Just ask. What is it?"

Roberts looked at Chief O'Leary, a charismatic man, easy to work with and he liked Pete. The twenty-year veteran was a tall, second generation Irish-American from Chicago. Broad powerful shoulders topped a stocky frame and a reddish-blond shock of wavy hair peeked out from under his hat. Although there was usually a pleasant smile on his ruddy face, this was not a man to take lightly. He had played football in high school but had enlisted in the Navy rather than pursue a college career. Roberts thought Pete was probably the most respected individual in VA-433.

"Pete, I'm getting funny vibes whenever I ask the men about Franklin. Something's…I don't know…?"

"Strange, you mean? He wasn't particularly popular, sir. How could he be?" Pete said. "A smart-ass and a Negro and a loudmouth. Not a good combination."

Roberts nodded. "I know there's a racial thing here, maybe. You're right, but it *is* strange. None of the men volunteer anything. If it was suicide, wouldn't someone suspect? I mean..umhh…when I've asked the men directly about that possibility, I get a lot of squirming and stammering. There's something unspoken. It's…uhh…" He shook his head.

"Frustrating?" Pete offered. "You'll learn the men can be a little reticent around officers…better get used to that, sir. Look, may I speak frankly?"

"Of course…anytime."

"You're the new guy, an ensign, a nugget…an unknown quantity to the men. Give them a little time. But, you're getting squared-away and you've caught on quickly. The men will come around, you'll see, but don't rush it. As for Franklin, finish your investigation soon and write a good report but don't overdo it."

"Makes sense, but…" Roberts smiled. Encouragement from a seasoned sailor was reassuring. Roberts had grown to admire Pete who bore a certain physical resemblance to his father, a World War Two marine. "Skipper's putting pressure on me."

"He's got to, just finish it. And I'll help any way I can."

Here was the opportunity. He asked the question. "Pete, were you aware of any relationship between Franklin and Lt. Williamson."

"Nooo." The chief gazed thoughtfully for a long moment. "Nothing out of the ordinary. Why do you ask?"

"Oh, it's probably nothing. Except…?"

"Lt. Williamson was liked by the men. Good pilot, I hear. I doubt that Franklin and he ever had much direct contact. I could ask around about that if you'd like."

"No. Don't bother, Pete. It just seems strange to me, two unrelated deaths, both in the line division. Five days apart. Coincidence, I suppose."

Pete nodded. "You're gonna see a lot of that. Accidental death and injury are pretty common aboard a carrier, Mr. Roberts. Even in peacetime this is a very dangerous environment. In fact, it's absolutely the most dangerous workplace in America. One moment of carelessness…and, well, you know. Those things happen too often, I'm afraid. Even suicides aren't that unusual. People get killed and injured regularly around here. You'll get used to it. But, it's never pleasant. Can I help with your report?"

"I suppose so…" Roberts said, unconvinced. "Oh well, you mind if I take those two men for a few minutes? Last guys I want to talk to today."

"Of course not." Pete motioned to the men. "Diaz…you and Phillips take a break now. Ensign Roberts wants to talk to you."

They sat on an empty bomb rack in a quiet corner of the hangar deck. Phillips, a twenty-year-old pimple-faced kid from Detroit, knew nothing and did not like talking to officers. He especially did not like talking to officers about dead Negroes. The sailor had a thick batch of brown hair, which needed a trim. Brushy eyebrows formed a base for a low, angular forehead. His eyes shifted when he spoke and he rubbed his sideburns nervously with quick animal strokes. Roberts asked if he had known Franklin.

"He ain't no friend a mine and I didn't never even talk to that…uhh…to him, sir."

And that was that.

Diaz was more intelligent, a short cocky Hispanic from Imperial Beach, California. When summoned for the interview, he scowled timidly at Pete but said nothing. The chief never permitted disrespect toward officers.

"Sit down, Diaz," Roberts said. He pointed at the bomb-rack rail. The sailor gave the junior officer a haughty look before complying.

"This won't take long." There was no need for preliminaries, everyone knew that Roberts was conducting an investigation.

"Did you know Franklin very well? I heard you were friends."

Diaz was a slight man. A wiry frame, physically strong with quick, darting eyes that shifted rapidly, unwilling to linger on the despised image of an officer. Roberts sensed a feral shrewdness. A dyspeptic, dangerous terrier. He peered momentarily at Roberts analyzing the question.

"Yes, sir…him an' me went on liberty together sometimes. Why?"

"Where did you men like to go…on a pass?" Roberts smiled casually, but he could tell Diaz was unimpressed.

"Anywhere's…we sometimes went to the White Hat Club in Olongapo an got girls. An' in Hong Kong we got laid once inna place over in Kowloon…once or twice."

"Was Franklin much of a drinker?"

"Na..err, no sir. Coupla beers, maybe…but not lots…uhh.." A nervous tic began in Diaz left eye.

"Any other vices that might have caused him some personal problems. Gambling maybe, drugs, girls?"

An uncomfortable smirk dashed across his pockmarked face. Diaz blinked rapidly. A moment passed while Diaz formed an answer. Roberts waited silently.

"No, sir. Why ya wanna know this stuff?" Obvious dissembling.

"You knew Franklin. Would you say that Franklin was well adjusted? Did he have any personal problems? Girlfriends. Family trouble. Alcohol. Drugs?" Diaz squirmed on the bomb rack.

"I dunno…maybe. How come you wanna know all this, sir?" Diaz obviously hated talking to officers.

"Commander Isaacson wants a full report. Did you ever see Franklin get into an…altercation?"

"Huh?"

"Umm…a fight or some kind of disagreement?" Roberts' speech difficulties were an advantage in this situation. He reminded himself not to use large words. Speak slowly. Don't hurry. Don't stammer.

"Oh, he beat up onna guy from the Intrepid once. Other guy started it. But, it wuzza fair fight. I seen it."

Of course.

"What was the reason for the fight?"

"I dunno…girl inna club, maybe. That guy from the Intrepid didn't like no niggers dancin with some girl he liked, I guess."

"You get involved?"

Rapid eye blinking. "Naa."

Another obvious lie.

"Did you…umm…ever see Franklin and Lt. Williamson together?"

"Huh? Whaddiya mean, sir?" Furious blinking. Diaz gripped his hands into tight fists.

"I mean in…well, abnormal circumstances. Did you ever see Franklin and Lt. Williamson together in any…unusual situation?" Forget discretion, Roberts thought, just ask the damn question. "You ever hear Franklin mention Lt. Williamson in any way?"

"No, sir! Franklin don't like no…goddamn…." He wrapped his arms in tight defensive posture and blinked a time or two.

Officers, Roberts completed the thought.

"Can you think of any reason for him to commit suicide?"

"No, sir!"

"Well, that'll be all, Diaz. Thanks for your help. You can report back to the chief now."

The sailor shuffled away. His fists still clenched in defiance, a nervous look over his shoulder while retreating. Roberts watched him walk toward the aft hangar bay and wondered why someone would lie about something that seemed so unimportant. Diaz was an arrogant unsophisticated man with limited facility for deceit and Roberts had learned an important fact. Diaz was a liar. He had the body language of guilt, and he knew something worth concealing.

*   *   *

Ralph Manley was working and he took his job very seriously. Assignment as Safety Officer of an Attack Squadron during wartime deployment was a heavy burden. However, paper work was one of the tasks that Manley truly enjoyed and he excelled at it. He was tapping a pencil rapidly and humming when Roberts, whom he tried to ignore, paused in front of his chair.

"Hi, Ralph. Busy as usual, I see." Roberts said. Manley wasn't going to acknowledge his presence.

"Oh, hello, Roberts. Yep, same old shit." Shoulders slumped to emphasize the burden of responsibility and the rudeness of the intrusion.

Roberts sat next to Manley and glanced openly at the report to imply extreme interest. It was a routine mission report.

"I…umm…gotta problem with that Franklin investigation, Ralph. I don't know where to turn. I hoped maybe you could help me. Do you mind?"

"Warned you…didn't I?"

"I gotta give you credit, Ralph. You knew better than I…this thing is nothing but a bag of worms, got me by the balls." Humbleness before the great one. Manley smiled, a flash of smugness.

"Not much to go on, I guess…huh, Danny?"

"Not a goddamn thing."

"I told you so, didn't I?"

Roberts nodded to confirm his incompetence. "I've talked to every man in the maintenance department and every pilot in the squadron…the flight deck officer…the line division…everybody. Nothing." He spread his hands to emphasize what an incompetent he was. "But I've gotta submit a report to Isaacson and I still don't know anything."

"Lousy job, sometimes. But I can help." Manley leaned back and twiddled his fingers and did his best imitation of an old salt. "I'd call it suicide and gundeck it, if I were you." He rambled on for several long minutes about the demanding aspects of a properly executed accident investigation. Roberts hung on every word. When Ralph Manley was well into the mood, Roberts decided to move.

"Say, Ralph," he said casually. "Whatever happened on that Williamson investigation, anyway? You must have completed the Preliminary Report." Cut to the chase.

"Very little to go on. But, I've finished the report. Pilot disorientation, probably." Manley shrugged.

"What about the weather? You mentioned it before." Lead him to it.

"Yeah," Manley sighed. "It might've been a factor…but nothing that the other pilots couldn't handle. I talked to them all."

"So you wrote it up as pilot disorientation with a contributing factor of poor weather conditions. That was your conclusion?" Roberts did not stammer; he had carefully rehearsed the sentence a few minutes earlier.

"Yep." Manley thumped a pencil impatiently.

"Too bad the skipper didn't accept your Franklin report…would've saved me some frustration." Set the hook.

"Suicide…had to be. I said so, but Isaacson wouldn't buy it. Gave it to you. I don't understand that at all."

"Yeah. That was unfair to you and me. I don't understand the skipper's attitude either." A deliberate lie to assuage Manley's feelings.

"I could give you my preliminary Franklin report. It might help."

"Gee, thanks, Ralph." Roberts looked up to pretend deep thought. "Listen…I was just wondering, what *could* cause a Spad to crash like that anyway." Casually, it might have been an impulsive question.

"What do you mean?"

"Oh, the Williamson crash. Well…you're more experienced with this stuff than I'll ever be. How many possibilities are there? An experienced pilot…good stick-and-rudder man…a good airplane. You flew it your-self, didn't you, Ralph?" *Take the hook, dammit.*

"Sure did. Just before Williamson…nothing wrong with that air-plane…guarantee you that."

"So what did you look at for possible causes. I mean, how many pos-sibilities could there be?"

"Very few, really. Of course the obvious…pilot error, disorientation, vertigo during the cat shot."

"What else?"

Manley looked at Roberts momentarily but saw only open curiosity on a bland, ordinary face. He was a detached individual, Manley decided. Roberts could never be one of the inner circle, even if he wanted to be. "Only other possibilities are an engine failure or mechan-ical failure of some sort. Why?"

"Just interested…thought I might like to be an assistant safety officer some day. Wondered how you did it. You kinda got my interest…piqued." Outrageous pandering, but Roberts felt little remorse.

Ralph Manley beamed. "Sure…you might be good at it with some training. I could help."

"Would you?"

"Certainly."

"Engine failure or mechanical failure, you think?" Roberts prompted. *Get on with it, Ralph.*

"Not an engine failure. One of the yellow-shirts was working in the forward catwalk and saw the whole thing. Williamson went in with full power. The yellow-shirt said he heard the engine the whole time. No backfires…no popping or roughness…just good, solid power all the way in. By the way, he was only an eighth of a mile off the ship's bow. Went off the catapult in a level attitude, then rolled straight into the water…poor guy."

Roberts could see it in his face. The conceit. Of course, Ralph Manley would never make an error like Ted Williamson. Ralph, the Rodent, thought he would never die. He'd succumbed to the false invulnerability of arrogance.

"The witness said that…full power, no indication of engine problems?"

"Yep, exactly. Remember, I flew that Spad on the previous mission that afternoon. That engine was solid…no problems at all."

"Can't get a better endorsement than that…from the safety officer." Roberts laughed and Manley joined him. They were almost buddies.

"But, what kind of mechanical failure could cause it…do you think?" Roberts moved the conversation where he had wanted it to go.

"Wing could fall off, I guess." Manley laughed and Roberts felt like an idiot but laughed anyway.

"Seriously?" Roberts muttered and acted the fool; he wanted information desperately. Roberts knew his halting speech patterns could be disarming, an occasional advantage around less astute people.

"Nah…the airplane was solid," Manley smirked. "Just been though its periodic maintenance check. No problems. No maintenance items of any importance in the logbook. Those things don't happen without some warning, you know. A true airframe failure is extremely rare."

"What about a generator failure?" he asked. "Or instrument failure?" Finally!

"Certainly possible, Dan. But, say it was a generator failure? You'd still have a battery backup and no essential instruments or cockpit lighting lost for at least twenty minutes of the normal battery life. He wouldn't even notice it except for the generator fail warning light. Williamson could have handled that with both eyes closed…great pilot. Instrument failure? Maybe…but there again, backups. We've all seen those types of problems and handled them with ease…right?"

"Sure…what if it was…umm…maybe the attitude indicator?" Roberts stammered deliberately.

"OK…say that happened. Sudden failure of the artificial horizon…you go to needle-ball and airspeed. You've done that haven't you?" Manley frowned; even an ensign should know that. He allowed the contented glow of sanctimony into his expression.

"Yes…in fact I prefer the needle-ball…right off the cat shot any-way…more reliable. Level the wings with attitude indicator *and* needle-ball, check airspeed and then radar altimeter warning light to confirm I'm climbing…that's all I have time for."

"There you go! I'm sure Williamson did the same. We all do. Look…all of us are good instrument pilots. Have to be to survive out here. Williamson was damn good!"

So, Roberts concluded, Ralph Manley believed that a highly experi-enced carrier pilot had crashed into the water immediately after a night catapult shot due strictly to pilot error. A competent, well-adjusted man, with no personal or physical problems, in a good airplane with lit-tle probability of engine or mechanical failure, had foolishly crashed and it was his own fault. Therefore, the squadron safety officer, who apparently saw no contradiction in his last statement, could in good conscience attribute the accident to vertigo.

Vertigo?

A common situation for every carrier pilot on every night catapult shot. Rapid G-force stresses and a lack of visual references confound the brain's sensory perception of spatial orientation. A routine problem. A common irritant easily overcome by disciplined instrument flying.

"I guess you've given this a lot of thought, Ralph."

Roberts took a moment to review what Manley expected him to believe: A highly experienced pilot had succumbed to a minor spatial disorientation problem, something he had experienced countless times before, a problem so routine that pilots rarely discussed it among them-selves. And, five days later Airman Franklin, the plane captain who had preflighted the airplane in which Williamson had died, apparently com-mitted suicide.

"That's my job, Danny. I did my best for Williamson. He was a friend."

Amazing! Ralph Manley, the Safety Officer, could not see the apparent relationship between the two events. He was content to ascribe the concurrence of the two deaths to the vagaries of fate. Roberts mulled over the unlikely existence of a commodity known as *coincidence*.

Manley had made another serious mistake. It was easy to underestimate a person such as himself, and Roberts knew it. A slight speech deficiency can be disarming. Slow speech did not signify a slow brain as foolish, arrogant people occasionally discovered. And, Manley, who had intended to be incommunicative, had eventually told him everything.

Roberts knew instinctively that the demise of the two men was not, and could not have been, mere fate. Now he knew exactly what he had to do. *Motive* was the connective tissue between the two seemingly unrelated deaths. Find a common factor connecting the two men and he would find the truth that Cdr. Isaacson demanded.

For Roberts the nagging thoughts that had begun with an innocent comment had now blossomed into full-blown incredulity. One single word had triggered an uncomfortable question that he was now compelled to answer.

Tricky.

A virus of deceit had invaded his conscience and only truth would free him of its infection. Something evil had invaded VA-433. A misty aura surrounded the events, but now he acknowledged the corruption. The artifice drifted to him in the words of men who had been there when the *thing* had occurred. Words of unconcern. Curious looks. A knowing expression here, a gesture there. Lies!

A cold tremor of doubt crept into Roberts before he excused himself from the presence of the one man who should have known better.

He didn't know what the *thing* was. But, he did know this: Something dark and cold had passed by in those five days and it abided in the secret recesses of dereliction. Now Roberts had acknowledged its existence and he was determined to root out the depravity. It had killed two men in his squadron.

           *   *   *

Later that night Herb McGinnis would deposit a roll of film at the ship's photo lab. He would give his roommate a photograph and Helen Roberts would dutifully place it into an album of her husband's remembrances; two smiling friends standing in front of an ancient Douglas Skyraider secure in their immortal youth. In another place, another time, that grainy photograph would herald a major turning point in Dan Roberts' life.

"I'll have proof someday when you're infamous. I can prove I knew you after the despicable deed that I expect you to commit eventually. I'll be able to say to everyone…I knew Danny Roberts when he was an honest man."

And then Herb McGinnis laughed the quiet, prophetic laughter that Roberts would never forget.

16

The wardroom emptied rapidly after dinner. Roberts was sitting at a corner table assigned to junior officers. He ordered a last cup of coffee before returning The Tranquillity Room. A brief nap would be in order, one never knew. It could be a long night and he was scheduled to fly on Isaacson's wing. A double-cycle, three-hour flight riding shotgun over an undisclosed nighttime Army operation.

During dinner Roberts had listened silently while Bobby Thomas engaged Herb in a lengthy discourse on the proper role for a modern carrier pilot. Thomas had a way of needling the somber Herb.

Roberts interrupted after a frustrating exchange. "I wonder, Bobby, you can't be…umm…serious about the true purpose of war."

"Why not? You're thinking of Vietnam, our war? The reason for this particular war isn't important. It's war itself that matters, since war is man's noblest, ultimate endeavor. Human nature…face it, we're hunters and warriors by nature."

"Jesus, Bobby, what…what do you mean? How about Herb here? He wants to be an architect someday, if he ever grows up. On a scale of human worth isn't…umm…building better than destroying?"

"Screw you, Danny," Herb said, not many knew of his secret ambitions.

"Maybe so, who can say with certainty?" Bobby continued. "Depends on the circumstances. But, I do know this, only through human conflict can an individual truly affirm his commitment to community. All other forms of public service pale in comparison to the risks of combat. It is the only true vestige of heroics, the warrior's sacrifice for family and country. Who do you think the history books should be most appreciative of, the warrior, General Eisenhower, or the architect, Frank Lloyd Wright?"

"That's not a fair comparison and you know it," Herb interjected.

"Sure it is. They're both giants in their field. Ike freed Europe. Wright designed beautiful structures for his own gratification, but primarily for profit. We just happen to appreciate them, too."

"But, Wright's work is timeless, a national treasure," Herb replied. "No comparison."

Roberts said, "Bobby, I think Herb means that warriors are a separate…well…category."

"Gee, thanks for explaining that, Danny. So is freedom from Nazi's."

"Look, Bobby." Herb pressed on. "We break things and kill people because…who knows…we're in the military? But your argument falls apart when you consider the ultimate sacrifice. We're supposed to die for principle. Right?"

"Perhaps. We are fortunate, indeed. The Vikings believed that death on a battlefield was the only true path to Valhalla."

Roberts decided to play the Devil's advocate. "Oh, bullshit, Bobby. How can there be any honor in fighting and dying in a foolish war? Like….."

"Vietnam? That sacrifice may be the greatest privilege of all. I recognize that we are fighting a war of containment dictated by political twerps. But, look at it this way; for better men to defend the security and honor of those who are weaker or corrupt is a paradox of Homeric proportions. It is also a subject worthy of debate by Cicero and his Skeptics."

Huh?

"Bobby...that makes about as much sense as a...tennis tournament."
Roberts looked around sheepishly, not accustomed to talking so much.
Several officers had gathered to listen to the debate.

"Danny, you must learn to control sarcasm. It's a very disagreeable
habit of yours, like pissing in a punch bowl. You could stand to make a
few more friends around here."

"Then, don't try to confuse me with bullshit."

Sigh. "Want me to talk slower? Use monosyllables maybe."

"I didn't understand a word you said," Roberts muttered.

"I'll try to speak in simpler terms. Duty, Honor, Country. Get it?"

"Baloney!" Roberts grumbled. "I'm not sure that I want to die for
Johnson and those greedy jerks." Two pilots from Herb's squadron
snickered. A lieutenant laughed openly at his stammer. Roberts felt
embarrassed.

"That's not what the credo means. At any rate, you don't have the
privilege of discrimination, my friend. And, war conducted for greed
and ambition is nothing new. In fact, that is probably *the* prime motiva-
tion behind most wars including the Civil War that your Confederate
relatives vainly fought and you're so proud of. Hell, Dan, read *Caesar's
Commentaries* sometime. Do you really believe Julius Caesar was altru-
istic, a patriot? He was a cold, calculating, self-serving politician who
used his Legions to further his own political ambitions. He may have
been a military genius but his primary goals were political. He was a
politician first, a general second. The Roman Army and war were simply
means to an end for that particular ambitious asshole. And yet, you
can't condemn the officers and soldiers who were loyal to Rome *and* to
Caesar. That's why I say that a soldier is his nation's most honorable
man. He fights and dies for a selfless reason. Loyalty to his country and
to the country's leaders, no matter how ignoble those leaders might be."
Bobby Thomas shrugged. "Johnson and McNamara are prime examples

of the unworthy. Can't you see the reason for that simple credo, 'Duty, Honor, Country?'"

"Not right now, I can't," Roberts mumbled. "There is no God."

"Of course there is. He's just preoccupied, that's all."

"That's pure Sophistry," Herb sneered.

"Actually, it's Platonic, Herb. Don't flatter yourselves. We aren't that significant."

Roberts looked like a man who had missed a train. Bobby laughed.

"You'll understand, Dan. Believe me, someday you will."

"But, this whole thing is….."

"Outrageous? Of course, not all wars make sense. If you want irony, consider this. Our politicians, many neo-socialists, are supporting a fascist regime in the South against the socialist North. How's that for a whopper?"

"That makes no sense at all."

"Sure it does. Money. Always follow the money trail, Dan. Especially in politics. Some politicians and their military-industrial pals are getting rich."

"Why don't we see more about that in the papers…the news."

"Oh…and who owns the media, the leftist elite, maybe? What difference does it make if a few slopes get killed in the process? Money talks, ideology walks. At least it does with American socialists, they have no shame. Politicians are whores. They'll never allow philosophy to interfere with profits. They prostitute themselves for greed and ego. Even if they start out principled, the culture consumes them in time. Remember, only a few years ago Eisenhower warned us about this."

"I don't know about that, Bobby."

Thomas shrugged. "That's because only a mature mind can fully appreciate the ability to simultaneously espouse two completely contradictory principles while maintaining a counterfeit self-respect."

"Why didn't we listen to him, then?"

"Ike was a conservative and the left-wing media rarely treats them with much regard."

McGinnis had heard enough. "Jesus, Bobby, you sound like a damned Republican. We got rid of those critters in North Carolina after the Civil War."

"Hell, no. They're not much better. But, then, they're not in power. This is strictly a Democratic folderol. Pay attention, darn it. Dunce caps may be issued soon."

"Well, I'm leaving," Roberts growled. "Gonna sleep a while before the launch. You two settle it. I'm totally confused." He slurped coffee. The discussion was giving him a headache. "Say, Bobby...who was that Caesar guy, anyway?"

"Shut up, Danny."

"That's the most I've ever heard Dan speak," Herb said. "He normally doesn't say much." Roberts had disappeared down the passageway. "Ever notice how people get impatient with his stammering and finish his sentences for him? I do it unconsciously now."

"Yes, he doesn't want anyone to notice his problem," Thomas replied. "But you gotta respect his honesty."

"What problem?"

"Little speech impediment he's got. He keeps quiet so you won't notice. His candor is symptomatic of an inarticulate man."

"Really? I dunno...Dan never seems uncertain."

"Of course not," Bobby replied. "Don't you understand the Dan Roberts mentality? He'll never get ulcers worrying about unknown terrors." *Like you!* Thomas thought.

"*Understand* Dan Roberts? You gotta be kidding. I'm not Solomon, you know."

"It's not that difficult. Our Danny boy is really quite uncomplicated."

"Sure, I guess..." Herb interjected. "He never bolters, does he?"

"Not yet...he has good hands. Good stick-and-rudder man."

"I think it's that he doesn't recognize the dangers...refuses to, maybe."

"No...no, Herby. Almost, but not quite...see, nothing fatal will happen to Dan. You gotta understand that to understand Ensign Roberts. He senses that somehow, and I don't comprehend that part completely myself. Call it *luck* if you will, but that's too simple. It's more potent than that. And, even if you can grasp that peculiar advantage of his, you would still be overlooking something because it's really more complex."

"Now you lost me."

"It's a blessed quality some guys have. Something inherent. I think the Goddess of Fortune rides around on his shoulder just to make certain that he's OK. If something potentially bad should happen to your roommate, the nice Goddess simply steps in and makes everything right. He's just plain lucky...for lack of a better term."

"Jesus...I've noticed that about him. And it really pisses me off."

"I remember that landing of his. I waved him aboard when his engine was all shot up. Remember, Herb, you boltered right behind him? Fortune straightens everything out for Dan Roberts and then probably provides a compensatory gift for any inconvenience he might have suffered. His engine quit but only after it had delivered our fair-haired boy safely aboard. It should've died way back over the beach. The Romans had a term for people like him. I forget...something like *Fortune's Favored*. That's your roommate's secret, Herb. Take my advice, stick close to him. You could use a little luck."

"I remember that bolter...I shouldn't have. It was just...I don't know...sometimes I screw up."

"He's not perfect either, Herb. Whenever he makes a less than excellent landing and I debrief him, he usually can't think of an appropriate response so he just gives me that sappy look. I hate that. Dan Roberts has some very irritating qualities."

"Jesus, Bobby, Dan does that to me when we disagree. He can't win an argument because he's not very articulate. But even when I outmaneuver him verbally, he hides behind that stupid smile and I wonder what he's thinking; he *knows* something. I don't get it, but then I know somehow I've lost."

Bobby chuckled. "Dan has a slight speech impediment, minor dyslexia, perhaps. But don't underestimate Danny boy. That would be a serious mistake. He's got an incisive intelligence. I can detect that in his airmanship. He's a watcher, doesn't miss much. And he's restless, a common thrill-seeker. A dangerous combination."

"I'll tell you, though. He's a good roommate, loyal. I like him."

"Ever wonder what he's thinking behind those inoffensive green eyes, always watching?" Bobby smiled. "I think I know. He's thinking that it doesn't really matter."

"What doesn't matter?"

"Anything! For example, his landing was *good enough* and he thinks it always will *be* good enough. How could it ever be otherwise? Damnedest thing I've ever seen…weird."

"His luck will run out someday."

"I wouldn't be so certain, Herb. He might be the last survivor around here. Don't ever underestimate luck."

*　　　　　*　　　　　*

Roberts had been present when Lt. Smithson, the Schedules Officer, had assembled tonight's flight schedule.

"Oh, by the way…" He'd heard Isaacson remark casually, "…better put me on the schedule tomorrow night. I'm a little shy of night landings. And I'll take Roberts here with me." Isaacson gestured rudely in Roberts' direction.

"We got a single section mission to cover, sir." Lt. Smithson answered. Isaacson would have checked the calendar, Smithson knew, and noticed that the moon would be full, a *Commander's Moon*. Isaacson never made casual remarks. Everything Isaacson said or did had serious content. But, why choose Roberts as wingman, Smithson wondered? He had taken an early dislike to the new guy. Roberts was entirely too self-sufficient and had not shown proper respect for his seniors in Smithson's judgment. In addition, Roberts had gotten much of the credit for Bill Jensen's rescue. Smithson had led the second section that day and felt it was more properly his place to have engaged the enemy opposition. Roberts' awkward apology had done little to assuage Smithson's anger.

"OK, we'll take it. You don't mind a little night flying, do you, Roberts?"

"N...night f...flying?" Roberts stammered deliberately, and they laughed.

"OK, you guys are on, Skipper." Smithson chuckled at Isaacson's pretense. A common and inaccurate joke among carrier pilots claimed that senior officers flew only on high-visibility nights when the moon was full. In Isaacson's case, the rumor was true. Gerald Isaacson was the commanding officer and he could fly when and with whom he chose, but why Roberts? Full moon or black-ass nights, it didn't make much difference to Smithson. It was not the business of a mere lieutenant to question a full commander. Let him fly with Roberts all he wanted. The two arrogant jerks deserved each other, Smithson concluded.

Now Isaacson looked around impatiently as Roberts ambled up and took the adjacent chair. A letup in the late October monsoon permitted the special mission to be flown and they were the only pilots to be briefed tonight.

"Gonna be a black one tonight, Roberts."

By now Roberts understood the lexicon and listened respectfully.

"Yes, sir. Wind's picking up, too."

Isaacson, like all carrier pilots, had an earned reputation. Even in his youth, Isaacson had avoided night landings, the most difficult phase of carrier flying. And now he was forty, old age for a carrier pilot, with failing vision. Roberts sensed that Isaacson's fears coupled with aging reactions and deteriorating eyesight had corrupted the confident man's abilities and the pucker factor had increased before the briefing.

"Blacker than a coal miner's cock." The skipper laughed too loudly. He rarely told jokes.

"Windier than a wives club luncheon."

Roberts had the dialogue down pat. These conversations followed a precise ritual. Both pilots pretended that the conversation was spontaneous.

The briefing officer looked up. Highpockets Harrison also wondered why the commanding officer of VA-433 had chosen Ensign Roberts for his wingman? It was apparent to Highpockets that Isaacson disliked Roberts, a man who lacked the political skills necessary to succeed in a complex organization like the Navy.

"We can begin whenever you're ready, Commander," Highpockets suggested.

"Have at it…we're ready to turn and burn." Isaacson responded with a flourish. Roberts smiled at the bravado. Isaacson had an admirable style.

"First of all, the weather. I heard your comment, sir. Actually, it should be quite lovely tonight…full moon and clear skies until later tonight. Guess you haven't been topside yet."

"Great." Isaacson laughed as though this bit of weather trivia was a total surprise.

"Good night for flying," Highpockets concluded.

Roberts watched Isaacson closely; why had he had been selected for the skipper's wingman? Isaacson's animosity was palpable.

"Simple." Bobby had explained earlier, after the flight schedule had been posted. "He doesn't give a damn about anyone or anything except his career. You're just a commodity to him, Dan. He respects ability and wants a competent wingman. Consider it a compliment, that's all the recognition you'll ever get."

Highpockets continued. "Possibility of patchy fog later tonight…not likely to be a problem until after your recovery. Your mission is a routine patrol along the coast north of Vinh. There will be an insertion of Special Forces somewhere in this vicinity." Vigorous slapping of the map. "Operation Lazy Boy. A sniper team is targeting an NVA political operative visiting this village. They'll be dropped here by a patrol boat…" The pointer flailed vehemently at the multi-colored map of the northern coast. "…conducting a clandestine operation which you need not be too concerned with. We just want air-cover over the PBR in case of resistance during the beach landing phase, not likely though. You'll check-in as usual with the North SAR and hold in this position. Also, we've had Elint reports of possible enemy patrol boat activity. Seem to be coming out at night, patrolling along the coast…a few radar emissions…then disappears before dawn. You might look for them on your patrol. Could be the same type boat that attacked Turner Joy." Highpockets slapped the map with his pointer. "Sink 'em if you see 'em." He pointed at a neat little oval area sketched on the display. "Any questions?"

"Yes, sir." Roberts smiled pleasantly. Both commanders looked sharply at him. There was a warning in Isaacson's glare. "I just wanted to compliment you on the…umm…concise briefing, sir." Highpockets responded with another smile. He always responded overtly to praise. "Gee…do you really think there'll be fog?"

"Later…maybe…shouldn't be a problem though," Highpockets said cautiously.

"I'd rather have fog than snow…wouldn't you?"

"In Tonkin Gulf…what..?"

"I heard about a snow…"

"Shut up, Roberts," Isaacson interrupted. "No snow jobs tonight." No sarcasm either, not before a night flight. He stood up deliberately. Briefing over, time to go.

They began to collect their gear. Isaacson finished a cup of black coffee; his hand shook slightly, coffee spilled. Roberts whistled while studying Highpockets' chart and pretended not to notice.

Highpockets thought the melody was familiar but the process of collecting his briefing materials distracted him, it was time for other things. This was a special movie night in the Wardroom, Annette Funicello and Frankie Avalon in *Beach Blanket Bingo*. He was extremely interested in Annette, the Mouseketeer who had become such a fine actress. During a previous viewing he had noticed that her Bikini jiggled when she trotted across a sandy beach in pursuit of her pursuers. Fantastic motions. A kaleidoscopic display of physical abundance and further study was justified.

"Oh, good luck tonight, Commander…you'll do well." A polka dot Bikini, Highpockets recalled. He bustled with impatience.

"See you on the debrief," Isaacson mumbled.

Highpockets shuffled from the briefing room. Once into the passageway he scurried forward to the wardroom. Then he remembered the tune Roberts had whistled, The High and Mighty. *That goddamn Roberts. Smart-aleck pilot and his cute little question about fog and snow.* No time for anger right now, Annette's movie was scheduled to begin at 2200. He attempted to visualize poetry in motion. Would it be possible to design a smaller Bikini while increasing its load-carrying capacity? It made him feel slightly light-headed and a thin coat of perspiration appeared on his shiny forehead. He must remember to ponder that engineering problem in greater detail when time permitted.

Half an hour before the launch the two pilots began a routine. First, Roberts donned a green G-suit, zippered over legs and abdomen. A Smith and Wesson pistol, ten rounds of .38 ball ammunition and five tracer rounds. A yellow Mae West. A PRT emergency radio. One plastic bottle filled with water stuffed into his green Nomex flight suit. Flashlight. Survival knife. The accouterments of a carrier pilot.

Roberts checked his kneeboard for briefing notes and radio frequencies. Marshaling time and altitude circled with the ship's Foxtrot Corpen. Initial Approach Time to depart the Marshal holding fix for the landing. He dropped the kneeboard into his helmet. Isaacson glanced up sharply at the noise.

"Let's go, Roberts." An escalator carried them from the ready room to the flight deck. The October night was pleasantly warm and a gentle breeze wafted across the deck. Isaacson commanded himself to appear relaxed. He was a goal-oriented person and the routines to be accomplished were a subtle comfort for anxiety. He attempted a bit of light conversation on the way to the catapults.

"You're married aren't you, Roberts?"

What?

Roberts was surprised. A personal question from an austere man who had never shown an interest in his private life.

"Yes, sir…wife's home in Seattle with her parents right now."

"Ahhh."

Roberts had heard that Gerald Isaacson had a beautiful wife, a willowy blond with the disposition of a panther. Her reputation as an ambitious and dedicated Navy wife was common knowledge in the squadron. She was known to cut-and-slash her way through an officer's wives luncheon with ruthless dexterity. The junior officers and their wives treated Mrs. Isaacson with cautious respect.

"Tell me, Roberts….what's going on with Franklin?"

"Still working on it, sir. Gotta couple of…umm…angles I want to explore further. Been kinda busy lately but I'll get the facts for you…promise…I…"

"Try not to stammer so much, talk slower. Get on it, now. I want the truth, Roberts."

"I'll do my best, sir," he said slowly. The truth shall make thee free. And the sooner the better, Roberts thought. It wouldn't hurt a commander's career, either.

"That report should have been on my desk already."

A full moon washed the cluttered flight deck with a gentle glow. Warm, soft wind-currents hummed melodically through rigging and tie-downs. Eerie figures scurried around the secured aircraft and laughter could be heard in a dark corner. Roberts paused to study the ethereal scene. An opulent moon. Endless dustings of starry heavens surrounded a magnificent ship-of-war preparing to engage an enemy. Somewhere a flag flapped in the breeze. Ghost-like figures drifted through blackened foreground. Roberts listened to capture the wistful ship-melody before aircraft engines disturbed the surreal richness. He would write to Helen about it, if he could think of the words. He mumbled something. Isaacson looked at him curiously.

"Don't get slow in the groove." Isaacson concluded their litany.

"Bet your ass." Roberts truly understood the communion.

Now he nodded to Timothy Bryan, Plane Captain. A quick glance at the Spad's vertical stabilizer to confirm the Pitot-tube cover had been removed, then a brief inspection. Four 20MM cannon were loaded with the standard mixture of armor-piercing, explosive and tracer rounds. Four bulky fragmentation bombs hung under the wings. Two high-intensity magnesium flares were attached to the outboard stations. Under the belly a 300-gallon auxiliary tank was filled with 115/145 high-octane avgas.

"Oil level OK?"

"Yes, sir. Full internal fuel and the drop's full. Got a good airplane tonight, Mr. Roberts."

"You do 'em." Roberts handed the chalk to Bryan. WRATGAS, quickly scribbled on all four bombs.

Roberts climbed over the canopy rail, onto the seatpan, into the tight cockpit. A red-lens flashlight provided a soft glow. Roberts wiggled down into the parachute harness.

"You ever help Lt. Williamson like this, Bryan?" He looked up with a bored smile.

"Sure...once or twice."

Roberts hesitated. "Was he a good pilot?"

"He was a nice guy…heard he could fly real good, too."

Roberts adjusted the kneeboard. "Have any idea what might have happened? Night launch, wasn't it?"

Bryan draped the shoulder harness over Roberts and helped him to fasten into the Spad.

"No idea, sir!"

Roberts looked directly at the plane captain. Over his shoulder stars burst up from the distant horizon and in the milky glow he could identify the Southern Cross.

"Were you on duty that night?"

"Yes, sir, I was helpin on the flight deck integrity watch…checkin them tie-downs mainly. Kinda windy."

Roberts completed the cockpit preflight. He wanted information, but he did not want to be noticed gathering it.

"Who else was up here that night…remember?" A natural question. Small talk.

"We only launched two of our airplanes…funny, just like tonight."

Slowly, now. "So, the two pilots and two plane captains from VA-433…anybody else around?"

He readjusted the shoulder harness for a distraction. Five minutes until engine start. Roberts pulled Nomex flight gloves out of his helmet.

"Just them guys an' the yellow-shirts for the launch. An' some red-shirts checkin ordnance. I don't remember anyone in particular, though."

"Any mechs around?"

"Well…yes. And Mr. Thomas came up later…he's talkin to Mr. Smithson 'bout something, the other pilot, you know. An' the chief…he's always around during launches, I guess."

"What about Diaz?"

"No…well, I didn't see him till after the launch…he was over there by Tilly, messin around." Bryan pointed at the yellow crane. "He don't come up here unless he has to work. Not very interested in watchin flight ops."

"Do you like to watch, Bryan?"

"Sure…it don't make me no never mind if I miss a little sleep. I like the planes, you know. How they fly an' stuff."

"I know what you mean, me too. How would you like to go flying some day, Bryan?"

"You mean with you, sir?"

"Sure…when we get back to Alameda. Base flying club has an old T-34. How about an orientation flight some time?"

"Yes, sir!"

Roberts laughed, "Good, when we get back home. Don't let me forget."

PILOTS START YOUR ENGINES. A klaxon broke the stillness.

"Good luck, sir."

"See you on the recovery."

"Don't get no more bullet holes tonight, 'kay Mr. Roberts?"

"Do my best."

A red wand waving in a circular motion on the darkened deck. A yellow-shirt directed Roberts to start engine. External power plugged in. Lights adjusted. Finger on the starter button. Count through eight blades. Tap the primer button until the engine starts with a rumble. Steady prime until eight hundred RPM. Advance the mixture-control knob and stabilize at idle. Signal with a flashlight for external power disconnection…flashlight lens to flat of hand then pulled back sharply. Battery and generator switches *On*. Check engine indications. Oil pressure normal. One thousand RPM. Generator indications good. Radio *On*.

"Boxer One, radio check." Crackled in his headset. Isaacson had started.

"Boxer Two," Roberts acknowledged.

They were spotted on the catapults. The yellow-shirt signaled for wings unfold. Drop the wing-fold handle down, then locked. A flaps signal. Roberts lowered flaps to full down. Control check. Wipe the cockpit with the stick, finishing with full up elevator and left aileron, full right rudder. A flashlight thumbs-up from a yellow-shirt. An arm signal handoff to the catapult officer. Circular flashlight signal for full power. A quick engine run-up; magnetos checked, propeller control cycled, then up to full power for launch.

Isaacson's Spad rocketed down the starboard catapult. Steam trailed over the catapult track. Roberts watched the green and red wing lights speed into the night.

Full power; fifty-seven inches of manifold pressure, three thousand RPM. Head back against the headrest. Stick lightly grasped for the shot. Left hand wrapped around the throttle bar. Flip on the navigation lights, and wait.

Wait for that eternal second that seems like an hour. Wait for the cat shot. The ultimate stroke. The supreme exhilaration reserved for those who dared.

The catapult officer watched for go-signals from the aircraft launch crew and the yellow-shirts. Right hand waving a flashlight in the launch signal. Everything looking good. A rapid drop of the right hand down to the extended left arm.

Roberts felt the catapult harness take up tension, saw the cat officer's launch signal. Focus on the artificial horizon and wait for the kick.

Acceleration!

Blasting down the catapult track into the blackness. Pinned into the seatback. G-loads increasing. Vision blurred. Rapid spatial disorientation. Sensations of untrammeled speed, of limitless power, of uncontrolled elation. Dizziness from the cat shot. Goosebumps of joy.

He was off.

*   *   *

Major Nguyen Binh relaxed with a pipe and enjoyed the evening. It was a calming thing, something to look forward to after a long day. He had been writing something, but not an intelligence report, something far more personal.

Such a beautiful night, a good time to think, an evening of special clarity. A huge yellow moon had crept over the eastern horizon. Stars twinkled under the black curtain and the old man felt good. He had actually enjoyed himself today. That in itself was a rarity. There had been little happiness in Binh's Spartan life.

The letter had begun quite spontaneously. Somehow a sheet of paper had appeared in his hand and a pen leveled itself above the blank sheet. Binh had begun to write, furtively at first, then with satisfaction as he began to comprehend.

Curiously, he had been writing a letter to himself.

Dear Nguyen,

It has been too long since we have communicated, you and I. Don't you think it is time that we finally broke the silence? Why have you avoided me, your *Conscience*, lately? Is it because we are no longer friends? Or, is it an act of cowardice?

The answer is readily evident to us both. You are ashamed! For three decades, and longer, you have killed and murdered and tortured for the Democratic Republic of Vietnam. Admit it now for it is true! The fact that your enemies have done the same and even worse is no excuse. It is to your credit and your damnation, that in the twilight of your life, *you have come to see both sides of the question.* Is that why you have summoned me today?

This is what I think you should do. You should follow me, your *Conscience*, and allow us to do something worthy for once. We have decided on a course of action that is quite unique and dangerous. But, you and I cannot go back now, can we? Once committed to contrition only honorable deeds can provide atonement. Admit this also for it is true. There is no turning back. You must do the noble thing, now before it is too late and your soul is lost forever….

The letter rambled through vivid memories of war. It admonished himself for not pursuing his secret goal more vigorously, for cowardice. Granted, the idea that an NVA intelligence officer *could* approach the Sharpsburg with a strategy of reasoned disengagement was risky. It was also visionary and Nguyen Binh had never been one to avoid peril.

The letter finished by prodding the reluctant old warrior to find the opportunity soon and admonished himself for temerity. So be it. He must seek an opportunity, *the moment*. The letter closed by invoking memories of his dead wife and child and how they would applaud his decision.

It was signed:

Nguyen Binh, Seeker of Peace.

Major Binh reread the letter several times while smoking a pipe of hashish, his only vice. The pot was of excellent quality and had been purchased from a reliable dealer in Hanoi. The stuff had been imported from the Cambodian Highlands, a place Binh had never visited. Perhaps after the war was concluded he would go there and see for himself the land of such reputed beauty.

He glanced over at the Sharpsburg as an aircraft catapulted into the night sky but he knew it was not to be a major air strike. Only two Skyraiders joined in formation above his old fishing junk. Not enough airpower for concern.

The Skyraiders' huge engines roared overhead, heralding a noisy epiphany to the moon-blessed night. They made the old man think once again of the Skyraider pilot, the one he now considered *his Pilot*. The pilot whose damaged, smoking Skyraider had started Binh's introspective process on that special day not long ago and had concluded with this evening's letter. He thought it unlikely that his pilot was in one of the aircraft he watched disappear into the night. But he thought of him anyway and questioned the vagaries of war that would send an educated American pilot into his beloved country, the Democratic Republic of Vietnam.

He rolled the name of his homeland over in his mind and thought of the irony. *Democratic.* Why was that simple word so abused? His country had never been a democracy. Now it was a communist dictatorship. He wasn't ashamed to admit that fact for there were few political options available to the besieged, backward nation. Still, the irony was painfully evident to the lover of true democracy.

Binh puffed vigorously then touched the glowing tobacco to the letter. It would not do for another crewmember to read of his ambitions. He blew a cloudy wisp of pungent smoke toward the Southern Cross and celebrated his decision.

It was good to be in touch with one's conscience.

17

He had flown directly over the old man's junk, but Dan Roberts was unaware of Major Nguyen Binh. He chopped power and slipped into a loose parade formation under Isaacson's right wing. The skipper watched Roberts' join-up and dimmed his navigation lights. They continued to climb into the calm night air. Over his right shoulder Roberts could see the ship begin a slow turn back toward the recovery area. The ship would be precisely there when they returned three hours later. A pilot could have confidence in the veteran carrier. The Sharpsburg's captain ran a tight ship and it would be there as promised. He was demanding and arrogant, but the man ran a good ship and that was all that mattered.

Roberts thought of friends on the Oriskany, their sister ship, plowing the Tonkin Gulf only a few miles to the east. An unlucky vessel, a black cloud hung over the carrier from the day it had arrived on Yankee Station. To date the Oriskany's airgroup had lost nearly one-third of its pilots to the war and shipboard accidents. Roberts had bingoed to the Oriskany recently and found that the ship hadn't the élan of the Sharpsburg. It was a subtle thing, but a sinister oppression hung over the airgroup. The A-4 pilots in Ready Room Three where he had waited were a silent dispirited bunch and a contained anger prevailed everywhere. A poorly run ship trapped in an ill-conceived war and its unfortunate pilots and sailors paid the bloody price of ineptitude. Roberts had waited impatiently to return to the security of the Sharpsburg.

Isaacson and Roberts climbed silently over the black-silvery sea. In the distance, as through a dimmed lantern, he saw the carrier's shimmering wake gliding through golden moon-flakes sprinkled upon the placid ocean. A golden path leading to home and to safety.

Across the western horizon bright flashes of artillery salvos dotted the night. The marines had a night operation underway to the south. "Boxer Flight will ignore it, it has nothing to do with your primary mission." Highpockets had alerted them during the briefing. Streaks of light shot down from the sky where Marine air support launched rocket fire into the rugged hills, not a pleasant night for the Viet Cong. "Easy for you to say." Roberts had chuckled.

"Stick to your mission, Ensign," Highpockets said. "I think you'll find that adequate tonight."

"Shut up, Roberts," Isaacson added.

He looked up. Stars shimmered above the ocean's obscure southern horizon forming a sparkling canopy crested by the golden moon, an eternity of darkness strewn with diamond-studded splendor. In the distance the Sharpsburg's outline vanished into a splash of moon-glow trailing a fading streak of luminescent wake. He looked for the familiar comfort of the Southern Cross and soon found it resplendent in the elegant starry night.

Roberts glanced back over his shoulder for a last glimpse of the ship. But, it was gone now, invisible in the black ocean vastness. The two fighter-bombers sped away from the security of home. Somewhere to the west friends might need help and an enemy waited.

Isaacson blinked his nav lights twice, a signal to test their cannons. Roberts eased out to the right, armed the cannons and fired a two-second burst. Tracer rounds streaked into the star-curtain, tiny meteors hurtling down into blackness. He watched them arc down into the void.

He secured the Master Arm switch and looked up into the dome of silver-dotted infinity covering his canopy. Its dissimilarity triggered memories of night flights over the Pacific Northwest. He recalled the Aurora Borealis and swirls of dancing light in a wintry night sky formed by charged particles from the sun sweeping through earth's atmosphere. He saw none of that amazing display tonight but the tropical sky had a special grandeur of its own. He recalled the Northwest and memories of home. Of his wife, Helen. Of life postponed. Melancholy swept over him in the solitude of a black sky and an even blacker aloneness. Only the overwhelming magnificence of heaven's star-spangled umbrella reconciled the moment.

Isaacson's crackling radio broke the stillness. He had called the North SAR to check-in. The ship informed them that Operation Lazy Boy was underway. Somewhere to the west on an isolated beach three men were wading ashore on a mission of assassination. Boxer Flight would ply the quiet skies above the clandestine insertion to destroy anyone who tried to kill the assassins. Isaacson and Roberts were the top-feeders in a complicated savage game.

Then it was quiet, so he thought of Helen again, and the baby. Happy thoughts. When was it due? Roberts struggled to recall the approximate date and calculate the time span until he became a parent. The bizarre images confused him. He had never imagined himself capable of actual fatherhood, but Helen's last letter had reconfirmed the impending event. He must write to her and tell her of this night and its commanding grandeur because he relished night flying. He looked up at the starscape. How to tell her? The inarticulate man struggled to find suitable words. A feeling of diminished presence in the vast aura of heaven's black vault enthralled the pilot, but bewildered him and he could think of no adequate expression to describe the magnificence.

He must remember to ask about the baby. Helen would expect that inquiry. Had she selected a name? What if the baby was one of those confusing creatures, a girl? Why was that possibility so difficult to imagine? He eased closer to Isaacson's wing. The skipper did not look in his direction.

Finally, he stargazed and listened to the engine's steady drum and considered several descriptive words; beautiful, magnificent, awe-inspiring. None seemed to satisfy the boundlessness of this night. Dan Roberts was compelled, once again, to recognize his limited facility for the expression of abstract notions; he was inadequate.

An hour later they descended to the northwest in search of a boat. The North SAR had informed Boxer Flight that the secret insertion had been successful and that air-cover for Lazy Boy was no longer required. However, a RA-3 ECM aircraft had detected a Firecan radar emission somewhere to the north. Could it be the weapons control radar of a North Vietnamese patrol boat? The ECM aircraft had suggested it might be. Would they investigate?

The shoreline stretched before them in bright moonlight. It was the last thrust of the tropical landmass that began to the west in rugged hills before tumbling down into the flat fertile plain that finally spilled into the Pacific Ocean. A ragged coastline glistened in moonglow. They had descended to four thousand feet scanning rugged inlets and murky channels for the boat. Ahead they could see the darker outline of a river as it dumped a muddy discharge into Tonkin Gulf. Somewhere near that dark inlet was the source of the elusive radar emissions.

Roberts scanned the horizon. The NVA were known to have AAA batteries spaced along the shoreline to destroy unwary aircraft. SAM missile sites were secreted further inland and were of little concern to the low flying fighter-bombers.

"Boxer Two, why don't you reconnoiter north along the shore for five minutes?" Isaacson's voice crackled in his headphones. "I'll recce up this river and meet you back here in ten minutes."

Roberts answered. "Will do. See you in ten."

He flew north along the uneven shoreline. Searching for signs of a wake, easier to detect than the small boat itself. Roberts adjusted the propeller and throttle for something to do. Rechecked the Master Arm switch *Off* and gun/Bomb switch to *Guns*, just in case. If a target should pop up suddenly, he could bring the cannons to bear much more quickly than setting-up for a bomb run. The engine's steady drum soothed the tired pilot. Night fatigue washed over him and he yearned for sleep. A sweet face appeared in the dreamy night. And he saw her there, smiling at him as he tried to say something important. Blond hair. Blue eyes crinkled with quiet amusement. Helen.

Her last letter had a hint of loneliness. Was it because of the pregnancy? He did not know and the uncertainty bothered him. She was a self-reliant woman. And living with her parents removed some of the worry while he was deployed. He must remember to reassure her in tonight's letter. Mentioning Bill Jensen's rescue recently had been a mistake. Now she knew that friends very close to her husband were being injured and killed. The war was no longer an abstraction. Genuine personal risks were involved. He scratched a few notes on his kneeboard, reminders for the letter. It was quiet and finding a small boat concealed in the rugged coastline was an unlikely event.

A large inlet had appeared in the gloom and he circled it a few times because it seemed a place he would seek concealment, if he had been an enemy patrol boat captain. But, it was apparently just as it appeared, a quiet, beautiful lagoon on the enchanting shoreline of an enemy's homeland. The full moon's reflection glistened off the bay's undisturbed surface. No evidence of boat activity. In the distance to the west a flash of light appeared several times, then it was gone. Unusual, the North Vietnamese rarely showed a light at night fearing an attack from the air. The light had a forlorn quality, like a beacon in the wilderness. Roberts yawned. He scratched another kneeboard note for the letter to Helen and tried to remember the precise blueness of her gentle eyes in the dark loneliness of night-flight. Eyelids heavy with fatigue. He drifted.

Thud!

A flash of light. The Skyraider bucked. A rumbling concussion. The stick jerked wildly in his hand. Suddenly the Spad was engulfed with bright flashes of intense light.

Everywhere! Streaks of tracer rounds screamed past the lone Skyraider, 37MM explosions above and behind him. Calm air erupted with loud percussion and orange-white flashes of AAA bursts filled the sky. He gasped. Confusion! For a moment Roberts' mind could not comprehend the violent intrusions. Then his brain shifted into survival mode; instinctively he kicked the right rudder and rolled full right aileron.

Turn!

Descend into the darker sky to the right. The light flashes followed him into the steep descent. AAA explosions closing. An arcing stream of fire followed him in the turn but the gunners, confused by the evasive maneuver, had not found the range. They searched for him knowing he was there. Bright ribbons tracked his flight path. Seeking *him*, but he was concealed in the darkness. Probing streaks of tracer pierced the gloom. Desperately, Roberts pushed the nose down; flashes streamed overhead like dying meteorites. An orange burst directly ahead. He felt a thump but knew immediately it was concussion and not impact damage. The altimeter unwound as he descended into the safety of the night. At one thousand feet he added power. The radar altimeter flashed an urgent red warning…he leveled out. Then he looked back at the bay. It was quiet. A darkened gloom in the distance where the white-orange muzzle flashes had been. He felt a boiling well of anger replace the fear.

Goddammit!

A climbing turn to the south brought him back to the direction from which he had intruded into their silent trap. Now Roberts knew where they were. During the rapid turn and descent he had glanced back momentarily to see the muzzle flashes from a southern edge of the bay. If it was a patrol boat, they were concealed in a small inlet.

How could he have been so reckless?

But he did not believe a boat was there. More likely there were heavy automatic weapons hidden in the trees waiting for an easy kill, a wounded aircraft struggling to reach the safety of the open sea or a helicopter dashing to a rescue. An easy mark for expert gunners. Or, even better, a foolish pilot such as himself blundering into a trap.

The anger was subsiding now. Anger directed mostly at himself for allowing the enemy to surprise him so easily. He had been daydreaming about home and that momentary lapse had nearly killed him. It had been a near thing; they had almost destroyed his Skyraider. Only instinct, the snap turn to the right and desperate dive had saved him. During the climb he checked the Spad. Engine indications were normal. He had not felt the familiar jarring impact of anti-aircraft shrapnel, only the thump of disturbed air. The airplane was intact. He had been lucky.

"Boxer Two...do you read Boxer One?" A nervous crackle on the radio.

Roberts cleared a lump of fear from his throat. "Roger, One...somebody took a few shots at me...no damage. I'm going to check the area."

"Careful, Two...I'm on my way. What's your posit?"

"About fifteen miles north of the river inlet."

"Wait till I get there for backup."

"Roger..."

Like hell he would! Roberts was angry with himself, and at his attackers, who probably believed he had crashed into the Gulf. He imagined the gunners drinking tea, congratulating themselves on the easy sucker kill.

When directly over the dark inlet where he had seen the muzzle flashes, Roberts dropped a parachute flare.

The sky lit up with the severe brightness of burning magnesium. The flare drifted in the light breeze above the beach and jungle that lay in open view, dark shadows flickered under tall trees. Roberts shielded his eyes with a gloved hand and searched. No boats concealed along the shoreline. No trucks along a narrow road winding down through dense forest to the beach. Nothing. He circled and waited.

Then a stream of tracers laced up through the night sky toward the flare. They were shooting at the flare! A mistake, a truly dumb move, nearly as dumb as a pilot daydreaming over enemy territory.

Now Roberts saw the AAA position exposed below him. An anti-aircraft battery in a narrow cut in the thick growth between the road and the beach. He detected movement among the trees as several men scurried for concealment.

Master Arm switch *On*....Gun/bomb switch to *Bombs*.

The drifting flare distracted the gunners, blinding them in a smoking brilliance that lit the night sky into noon brightness. They continued to fire at the drifting flare unaware that the real threat was rolling-in from the west, under the full moon that blazed in ethereal backdrop.

Speedbrakes deployed. Throttle reduced to idle. Propeller shoved to high RPM. Roll-in from the perch at five thousand feet. Lots of left rudder to compensate for P-factor, needle-ball centered. Ease right aileron for lineup. Trim out the nose-down elevator forces.

The gunners, confused by the flare, attempted to reorient their gunfire toward the thunderbolt noises of a diving Skyraider. An arcing spray of tracer pattern swept across the night sky. Bright flashes of muzzle fire pulsated the darkness. Tracers spun out, seeking, but not finding.

Roberts concentrated. Track the bombsight pipper onto the target. Steady hands now. Disregard the tracer rounds that were swinging closer and closer. There was time. Bright tracer spray arced into the night. Hold on target. Don't waver. One more second. Tickle the bomb switch gently. Feel the release.

Bombs away.

Four MK-82 fragmentation bombs dropped from the Skyraider's wings. Trip wires armed the detonators. One ton of high explosive dropped into the blackness.

Tracer flashes above his canopy. Close now, too close. The gunners had his position. Speed brakes retracted. Slam the throttle forward to the stop! The engine screamed. Roberts felt the power surge. Full right rudder and right aileron. Ease the stick back and roll into the darkness away from the bright streaks. Ribbons of tracer fire falling toward the Skyraider. Roll the nose down…further! Descend toward the black water of the bay. Down into darkness and safety. Down to sea level where the cannon fire could not follow. He watched the altimeter unwind through one thousand feet. Pull the stick back. Check the accelerometer. Four G's…five…six…seven G's…round out the descent.

A burst of intense white light preceded the bomb concussion. An immense gush of airflow enveloped the fighter-bomber. He felt the Spad pitch nose-down! The aircraft jerked to the left and he knew the bay was only dozens of feet below the tumbled aircraft. Roberts kicked right rudder, slammed the stick full right to raise the wing. Level the horizon. A bright-red light flashed on the panel. He glanced at the Radar Altimeter. Fifty feet above sea level…forty feet…and he felt the ground-effect cushion under the wings. Roberts pushed the throttle against the stop and pulled the stick into his belly. Trade airspeed for altitude, trade airspeed for life. The propeller clawed into the humid air, surging, protesting loudly at the outrageous demands. The Spad shuddered, airflow burbled over the wing.

Don't stall!

The red light disappeared. He eased backpressure, airspeed increased rapidly, and he began to climb.

"Boxer Two…this is One," Isaacson radioed. "Do you copy?"

Roberts turned back to survey the damage. Fire crackled around the AAA emplacement. Pulsating flashes of bright light from secondary ammunition detonations. Smoke billowed into blackness. A fireburst cloud blossomed high above the beach. Twinkling lights near the fiery tempest caught his attention. Small arms muzzle flashes. Probing. Seeking.

Mop-up time.

Roberts checked the ordnance panel. Master arm switch *On*, Gun/Bomb switch to *Guns*. He climbed toward the burning AAA emplacement. A fiery beacon led him to the enemy.

"Boxer Two…this is One. What's your posit?"

Roberts rolled the Spad onto its back. He pulled the stick into his belly, a Split-S down to the target, inverted, nose pointed down to the dark forest along the moonlit bay. G-forces building. The G-suit inflated tightening around his abdomen and thighs, slight graying-out then full vision returning immediately. Focus on the gunsight and the altimeter. Four thousand feet and descending vertically to the target. The gunsight adjusted to a dull glow, a bright pipper sliding toward the muzzle flashes. Flaming images filled the glass gunsight. Tiny flashes of small arms fire stuttered in the blacker fringes of the flame-bright emplacement. Airspeed indicator steady at two-fifty. Left rudder. He toggled the nose trim to ease elevator control pressure.

And waited.

The pipper slowly tracked across the flaming AAA position onto the small patch of darkness. Steady, easy control inputs. Track smoothly to the target. Roberts remembered his gunnery instructor's rules.

Don't hurry. Steady hands. Hit it exactly. Don't miss.

The Spad shuddered. Twenty-eight hundred rounds per minute from four cannons spurted down into the darkness. Tracer ammunition burst into the NVA gun crew firing AK-47s at the Skyraider they had attempted to destroy moments earlier.

Even in the darkness Roberts could see the destruction below. Dust kicked up by the 20MM reflected in moonglow. Trees fractured under the massive cannon assault. Human bodies scattered like torn rags. The twinkling lights disappeared in the maelstrom.

"OK, Boxer Two…that's enough. Join up."

Isaacson had witnessed the strafing run from over the beach. The destruction had been decisive, but this engagement had not been in their operational brief.

And, it was time to go home.

18

Thirty-eight minutes after Roberts had destroyed the gun emplacement Boxer Flight entered Marshal, a racetrack holding pattern in trail of the ship, at three thousand feet.

"Boxer One, descend to two thousand feet," the radio commanded.

Isaacson reduced power and descended as instructed by the GCA radar approach controller. Roberts remained at three thousand feet five miles behind the ship.

"Boxer One," the approach controller's radio crackled in the darkness. "We're showing one-hundred foot ceiling, variable overcast, one-quarter mile visibility in fog. Going up and down. It's below minimums. Check your fuel state. Do you want bingo clearance? Danang bearing two-two-zero degrees, one hundred fifty miles."

A nasty little surprise. The fog that Highpockets had promised would not occur until later was already in full blossom. Boxer Flight was holding in clear air above the thick, cottony stuff that bloomed in the heavy, moist tropical night air. A gentle offshore breeze stirred the whiteness into a consistent layer of impervious goop.

"Negative," Isaacson replied. "We'll take a look-see."

"Roger, Boxer One, cleared for the Tacan One approach, signal Charlie at 0315, time now 0312, Foxtrot Corpen one-one-five degrees. Report at Initial and on Final."

Isaacson read back the approach clearance and prepared for the descent into the fog. He wiped a sweaty glove across aging eyes and convinced himself that failing vision would not hamper the approach. The red ink entries in his aviator's logbook recorded a history of many successful night landings.

"Boxer Two, your signal Charlie at 0317."

Roberts had copied down Isaacson's clearance. His would be the same, two minutes in trail of his flight leader.

"Roger, copy, 0317."

Gerald Isaacson completed the approach checklist with swift efficiency. He was a man not easily dissuaded from proven methods. Careful, even plodding, technique was essential for success in his opinion, now more than ever. He mumbled checklist items to himself, resenting weakness, swearing not to allow poor vision and slowing reflexes to inhibit performance of duty. Isaacson was a professional warrior and veteran player in a culture where weakness, physical or mental, was unacceptable.

His eyes moved slowly over the instrument panel. Fuel selector to main tank. Tacan receiver set to Channel Two, CDI inbound-bearing set to the Foxtrot Corpen of 115 degrees, the ship's heading, for recovery. Distance Measuring Equipment indicator showing five miles from the ship as he turned outbound on the final circuit in the holding pattern.

"Goddamned fog," Isaacson said aloud. He had counted on a full moon illuminating the ship for the approach and landing. It should have been almost a daylight landing with a Commander's Moon. It should have been so easy tonight. Goddamned night landings.

Airspeed 150 knots. Too fast. Shape up, Gerald. Slow it down to 140 on the inbound leg. Course Deviation Indicator drifting off to the left. Correct the outbound heading! He muttered aloud. The altimeter drifted up to 2,200 feet and his bleary scan pattern failed to catch the climb. A bead of sweat rolled off his forehead into his eyes.

Can't let them think I'm afraid!

Feed in a little nose-down trim. Ease down to 2,000 feet. He stared into the fog, hoping. No wake. No ship. Not yet.

0313. Reverse course to inbound heading. Two minutes to Initial.

Gotta hit it right…only a twenty second window to start the approach or lose sequence…a humiliating failure…can't let Roberts know.

Slowly the CDI centered, on course. 115 degrees. He'd carelessly descended to 1800 feet in the turn. Angrily, Isaacson pulled the stick back and shot up to 2,100 feet.

Dammit!

"Boxer One, Initial," he spat into the mic. Had he sounded angry, frightened?

"Roger, Boxer One. Your signal Charlie. Call Paddles at mirror."

Mixture, rich. Prop, full RPM. Gear, down and locked. Full flaps. Tailhook, down.

Scan the instruments, dammit! Stay ahead of the airplane.

He had trained many younger pilots. Isaacson knew what to do. He knew exactly how to execute a night carrier landing and he had done hundreds successfully in past years, but he had been younger then. His eyes had been better. Scan. Anticipate. Murky wisps of fog drifted by the canopy. Hazy distractions. He couldn't afford a mental lapse.

Concentrate!

He knew what to do. Descend to 500 feet…keep the CDI centered…watch for the meatball. A piece of cake! He'd done it many times before. His eyes had been good and his younger hands had been quick in the ring and quicker in the cockpit. Hands that had once instinctively moved the stick in minuscule increments, smoothly guiding the aircraft with ethereal grace. But he had been younger! Now he was forty, flying with a squadron of twenty-year-olds, like an antique racecar sputtering awkwardly around the Indianapolis 500 among sleek new speedsters. Inadequate. Outmoded.

Meatball. Lineup. Airspeed.

What he must face was this: The Sharpsburg had a gyro-stabilized landing mirror. When the ship rolled left or right, or pitched up and down the stabilization system was designed to dampen the mirror's erratic movements so that the pilot was presented with a reliable indication of the true glideslope. That was the theory. In actual practice the stabilization was unreliable. When dampening a pitch deviation, it could aggravate the roll compensation and vice-versa. A few years earlier Isaacson had done an engineering study of mirror deviations. He was well aware of its flaws and the traps it held for unwary aviators.

Level at 500 feet. Power up to thirty-five inches MAP. Not enough; he added a little; he perspired a little more.

Watch for the mirror. Meatball, lineup, airspeed. Slow. Too slow. Airspeed dropping to ninety-five. Don't stall! Add power. More power!

Thirty-eight inches MAP. Airspeed jumped to 115 knots. Too fast. He jerked the throttle and swore angrily.

CDI drifting to the left. Correct quickly. Lineup was critically important. He had emphasized that fact to junior pilots.

The moon had disappeared above the cottony fog. Isaacson floundered in the blackness. Gray fog surrounded him. He glanced down for the wake and found no comforting phosphorescent glow to guide him home.

A red flash!

The radar altimeter warned him he had descended below 200 feet and still two DME from the ship. Too damn low! He eased the throttle forward. CDI had drifted right…an overcorrection.

"POWER!" An urgent voice crackled in his headset.

"Negative meatball," he radioed.

"POWER! You're too low, Boxer One! This is Paddles…check airspeed!"

Forty-two inches MAP. Airspeed jumped to 115 knots and he climbed a bit. He saw the meatball change from bright red to orange as it rose from the bottom and shot to the top of the mirror.

"Boxer One…roger ball."

"You're fast…check line-up."

At one-half mile Isaacson finally saw the meatball. He could even see the ship's glowing wake now that he did not need it. The red dropline lights were at a slight angle to the deck's white centerline lights. Lined up left. Correct quickly.

Three tasks must be skillfully executed to land aboard a carrier. He mumbled the mantra to himself: *Meatball. Lineup. Airspeed.* Isaacson knew what he had to do; he must do it now; he had done it before. But he had been younger!

"Looking better, Boxer One…" Isaacson recognized Bobby Thomas' voice. "Don't get fast…check airspeed."

The ship rolled gently in the warm gulf current. The meatball dropped slowly from the top into the center of the mirror. Glideslope lights glowed invitingly. Just center it up. He knew what to do. The ball slowly centered between the green horizontal bars. He was there! Just right. Be smooth, hold the ball centered and the mirror deviations didn't matter. He could do it! He had done it so many times before. Isaacson eased a little right stick to bring the red dropline lights into vertical alignment with the deck lights. On centerline! He felt better.

A little fast. Ease throttle. Watch lineup. Check the meatball. Just do it, goddammit!

Isaacson mumbled the mantra again and again. He'd briefed student pilots…do those three things correctly and you'll get aboard every goddamn time.

Meatball. Lineup. Airspeed.

The ship rolled to the right. The mirror stabilization system compensated for the roll by slewing the green horizontal light bars and the centered meatball rose to the top of the mirror. An uneasy feeling.

Something tickled the back of his mind. A false indication? Too busy now to think.

Am I high on the glideslope…is the mirror right? Airspeed! Push the nose over. Get back on glideslope. Get on speed. Something's wrong!

"Power…you're low, Boxer!"

He jammed the throttle to the stop. Powerful hands that had been able to down an opponent with a single uppercut now found it difficult to handle the Skyraider's controls with the gentle, caressing touch necessary on night landings. He overcompensated and, knowing his deficiency, Isaacson was unable to soften the stranglehold on the stick that grew in intensity and exaggerated every gross mistake. He raged at the inability to do something he had once done well, and he felt the dismay of failure. Quick, deadly hands had become aged club-like instruments incapable now of delicate control.

The ship wallowed into a wave trough. The false-high meatball snapped to the bottom. Red flashing lights! High on glideslope? NO…too low! He slammed the throttle forward followed with full right rudder. Red flashing lights!

"Waveoff! Boxer One, waveoff! Go around!"

Throttle slammed to the forward stop. Lots of right rudder. Ease back on the stick.

Lights!

Isaacson was mesmerized. The lights! Red flashing waveoff lights. White centerline lights that disappeared beneath his wing. Bright-red radar altimeter warning light flashing on his instrument panel. Lights everywhere.

Noise!

The radial engine roared. Fifty-seven inches of manifold pressure thundered through eighteen massive cylinders. Fourteen feet of screaming propeller roared into full-increase RPM. Bobby's voice yelling in his headset…something about flying the proper attitude…nose too high…airspeed too slow.

Confusion!

Shaking hands strangled the throttle and stick in a death hold. Flying on instinct. Unable to comprehend. Vertigo overwhelmed his senses.

"Waveoff! Power…POWER! Waveoff! Goddammit!"

Isaacson's bleary eyes instinctively locked on the attitude indicator, seven degrees nose-up. Wings leveled with clumsy hands. Full power! Establish a desperate climb!

And he did the only single, solitary thing that Commander Gerald Isaacson's aging overloaded brain could remember to do.

Fly attitude!

19

A scratching noise, Highpockets noting something on his debriefing sheet. Roberts looked up from his coffee cup and noticed Bobby Thomas was watching him closely. He was tired. The LSO's gray-blue eyes swept over him in curious appraisal, while smoking quietly, and Roberts knew he was being evaluated about something. But what? He deliberately avoided attention; he did not want it; he resented the intrusive aggravations of another person's curiosity, particularly an LSO's. Had they noted his reluctance during the mission debrief? He'd deliberately omitted much detail of the engagement. The landing had been OK, to have gotten aboard in the dense fog was no small accomplishment, but he took little pleasure in his success. Isaacson had screwed up and bingoed to Danang.

"So, lemme get this straight…Boxer Two," Highpockets muttered. "You say that the gun emplacement surprised you…almost knocked you down. In return, you attacked the enemy without waiting for backup from your leader. That about it?" Highpockets did not like to debrief in the middle of the night. But, Thomas had called his room at 0345 and the LSO's voice had an immediate edge to it.

"That's right."

"Why?"

"Why, what, sir?"

"Why didn't you wait for the Boxer…for Cdr. Isaacson?"

"He was too far away. I thought they'd scatter."

"Yes, but you dropped on an alerted, armed target alone. Not normally considered good headwork, is it Roberts?"

Alerted? Roberts remembered flare-blinded figures scurrying under his gunsight. Desperate men in shadowy bas-relief fleeing from devastation. Dead men running.

"Headwork? I…I thought I had the advantage."

The intelligence officer did not look up. Sipped from the coffee cup thoughtfully. Scrawled unhurriedly onto the debrief sheet. He was in his late thirties but a rapidly receding hairline and deep wrinkles made him appear older. Roberts thought Highpockets to be a compassionate man; a good man who was ill suited for his job. The rumor mill reported that his wife was a rapacious alcoholic.

"37 millimeter cannon augmented with small arms support against a single aircraft. How do you figure an advantage?" Highpockets asked deliberately.

Scurrying figures flashed into his memory. Desperate men. Small helpless men torn apart by the Spad's cannon fire. Trees splintered. Secondary explosions punctuating darkness with brilliant light. Smoke. Noise. Destruction. He'd felt a god-like superiority, but now he felt only an apathetic deflation. And confusion.

"I blinded them with the flare."

"Yes, but…."

Roberts waited. Highpockets fidgeted momentarily, blinked a time or two, and did not finish his query.

"I think they thought I was splashed…dead. Before the flare." He glanced at Bobby Thomas, but found no support.

The LSO listened carefully to the intelligence officer's debriefing. Thomas would wait. After Highpockets had finished he would debrief Roberts' landing. Now it was Highpockets' turn, a mission to be evaluated. As he listened it became clearer to him that he had been correct about Dan Roberts, and he had been correct all along. Ensign Roberts had a major weakness. Thomas had suspected earlier and had forgiven the new pilot blaming it on shyness and the insecurity of a handicap, but now he knew it was more serious. In a demanding occupation where close cooperation often meant the difference between success or failure, life or death, Roberts had a dangerous character flaw; he was not a team player. Highpockets finished the debriefing with a grunt, had Roberts sign the report, and dismissed them both.

"Wanna talk to you again when Isaacson returns." Highpockets shuffled through the passageway with an imperious wave. Thomas waited.

Roberts yawned. "Come on to my place, Bobby."

Ready Room Three had taken on a dreary hue in the early morning lull. The green walls scuffed by careless flight crews and the detritus of last night's briefing details scribbled on the blackboard. Half-empty coffee cups scattered on vacant tabletops. Full ashtrays waited for the housekeeping detail. Dank cigarette odors permeated the confined space. An ugly, depressing room.

They walked into Roberts' stateroom for the debrief. Herb was dressed and soon left to brief for an early launch. The LSO said, "Landing looked fine, Dan. A little fast in close, dropped the nose an RCH on the chop, an OK pass, number two wire. Landing looked real good." He snapped the LSO book closed, the official debrief had concluded.

"When did you actually pick up the meatball?" A quiet conversational tone. A smile for the pilot who'd had a long night.

Roberts lied, "About a quarter mile out...200 hundred feet, maybe...kinda busy."

"You did not!" Thomas snorted. "I saw you correct line-up at an eighth mile, max. You were on the glideslope alright, but you were too damn low out there without first seeing the meatball." Thomas knew Roberts had broken the rules to get aboard. There was testiness to his voice. Both were tired.

"I might have descended a little below 200 feet, Bobby," Roberts said slowly. "But I had the wake and I was riding the right edge to the ship. I knew where I was." *Expect me to go that low without some clue, not hardly*, he thought.

Roberts had departed the holding pattern at 0317, well within the twenty-second window, he recalled. Dropped the landing gear and flaps. Tailhook extended. CDI centered nicely out of the turn to final. Set thirty inches of manifold pressure then squeezed on a little more to hold the indicated airspeed exactly at 105 knots. Trimmed right rudder. One click of nose-up elevator. He'd eased a little right rudder, slid slightly to the right, glanced down and there it was, the wake. A soft phosphorescent glow in the wispy gloom. Better than the CDI, an exact trail leading him to the ship. He flew down the right edge of the wake, sharp knowing eyes, quick hands. Feeling his way down the ghostly glow below the left wing. The ship's wake had guided him home.

Meatball. Lineup. Airspeed.

"I'm not arguing with your technique. You made a great pass considering the horseshit conditions tonight. But do not *ever* go below minimums again! Don't get cocky, Dan…nobody is that good. 200 feet Above Ground Level is the approach minimums for a good reason. You know how high the ship's tower is?"

"Yep."

The meatball had been one dot high. He had eased deliberately low on glideslope knowing that the visibility would be better below 200 feet, behind the ship's air-wake where turbulent airflow over and around the huge carrier thinned the stable fog-layered cocoon. Hold a level 200 feet and drive straight into the meatball until it centered. He had eased one inch of MAP and settled into the groove. So simple. Once you got through the fear and you knew, just knew in your gut, that you could do it, *then you could do it!* The ability, and once you had it, it was yours. The danger only added to the delight. And then you could enjoy the kick of a night landing.

Boxer Two. Roger Ball. Hook down.

Looking good, Boxer Two. This is Paddles. Keep it coming.

He'd waited for it. So easy, once stabilized in the groove. Trimmed up, on speed, a centered ball. A quick correction on the red dropline for lineup. Hold the meatball centered with elevator. Easy, until you hit the sinker. He had felt the airflow sliding over the round-down above the spud locker. The Spad settled, he crammed on two inches MAP, held the ball centered. Saw the flashing green cut-lights. Chopped the throttle. Eased back on the stick and smashed onto the deck.

Head and shoulders slammed forward. Vision blurred. Shoulder harness biting sharply into flesh. The landing wire played out. Tires screeched on the deck. He had caught the number two wire at 105 knots and rolled to a twelve-G arrested stop in one hundred feet.

Roberts unconsciously rubbed his bruised shoulder. He had made five arrested landings in two days. A physical battering.

"Don't go below minimums again unless you can see the meatball and the centerline lights...and keep the red dropline lights squared away, too. Dammit, Roberts, you'll end up in the spud locker someday."

"OK." Roberts nodded. "How about a drink, sir?" He stood up at rigid attention. "You like Scotch?"

"Sure...debriefing's over, drop the humble act, and I like anything you got."

"OK. When will Isaacson return from Danang? We'll miss the Boxer."

"Tomorrow morning. First morning recovery, if I know Gerald Isaacson. He won't want to leave his squadron unattended for long. Not on his watch. Hell, I'd at least drink a few beers first...but not the skipper. Man of iron, you know."

Roberts clanked around in his locker and a bottle of Scotch appeared.

"You know, Bobby, I kinda like the Boxer, sometimes…tough guy act and all. Deep down he's a good man. He doesn't… I think he doesn't care for me, though."

"He's OK. Don't take it personally. He treats everyone the same. Besides, he wanted the Franklin report like *yesterday* and you haven't finished it yet. You're tardy. That's not the way to Gerald Isaacson's heart."

"I still don't know what really happened…not yet."

"I'm the Maintenance Officer…your boss, in case you haven't noticed…hurry up with that report, Dan. Fake it…gundeck it. Do anything, but finish it!"

"Yes, sir." Roberts' laugh drifted into a tired sputter.

"I mean it…better keep in Isaacson's good graces. You'll find life much more pleasant around here if you do."

"I'm not going to gundeck this thing, Bobby. I'll do it right, as long as it's *my* investigation. I think something's…I don't know…weird."

"Like what?"

"I told you, I don't know. I'm going to get to the bottom of it, though. If he doesn't like it…" Roberts shrugged, "…there's always Manley."

"See, there you go again. Don't buck the system, Dan. It may not be your style but it has its good points. You stick your neck out at the wrong time and I guarantee it'll get cut off. Your problem is that you're not an organization type. You're a loner."

Thomas held up his hand to silence Roberts' protest.

"You're a rebellious loner and you don't fool anybody around here, especially me. You usually don't like the system and you fight it. That's dumb, Dan. Really stupid! Your only saving grace is that you're a competent pilot…and we need guys like you right now."

"Look, Bobby…Isaacson said he wanted the truth. I think he meant it." *A goddam Albatross around my neck.*

"Don't be so damned sure. Play it smart. You better learn to work within the organization…or else. What Isaacson wants is an *acceptable* report, and quickly. Truth may be incidental in this situation. You better think seriously about *your* position. Sometimes the truth can be very tricky."

"Tricky? Funny you choose *that* word." Roberts laughed. "I'll do it my way until I find out what actually happened...or I'm fired, which wouldn't break my heart. Let Manley do it."

"Don't say I didn't warn you."

"I'm not worried," Roberts said, tired.

Thomas gazed around the small room. A loud screech from the port catapult above the Tranquillity Room interrupted his thought.

"Listen, smartass, you sure-as-hell better be, the Navy protects itself. First, last, always! The Navy will survive and your ensign's ass is grass. You better get used to it. An organization like the Navy can gobble up a non-political guy like you in a heartbeat. It's risky bucking the system. I know, I've tried. This situation is very serious. It's a *real* thing happening here, Dan." Thomas chuckled, shook his head. "It is as tangible as that red light staring you in the face tonight."

"What red light?"

"You didn't fool me, asshole. I knew you descended below 200 feet AGL and no frigging meatball."

"What do you mean?"

"The radar altimeter. The red warning light, dummy."

"It didn't come on...till I crossed the round-down. I never descended below sixty feet. I'm not that crazy, you know."

Bobby frowned. "You had the radar altimeter warning set at sixty feet?"

"Well, sure. I always set it at sixty feet for the cat shot...that way I know immediately, as soon as I cross the bow, that I'm in a climb...don't you? The red light goes out, therefore I'm above sixty feet AGL, the level of the flight deck...and I'm climbing."

"Oh, I see...it's not a big thing. I guess it was before you came aboard. We had an All Officers Meeting...decided it was squadron SOP to set the radar altimeter at 200 feet AGL, the approach minimums for landing. That way you get a double check on the glideslope. The GCA controller tells you to stop descent at 200 feet AGL, unless you pick up the meatball. You have the barometric altimeter to give you raw altitude information and the radar altimeter warning light as a backup. The red warning light will come on when descending below 200 feet. You didn't hear that on your initial ops briefing when you reported aboard?"

"NO!…What?…*wait a minute!*"

Bobby continued, "Of course, it's a pilot's option. If your gut tells you to set the thing at sixty feet for the cat shot and then reset it for 200 feet AGL for the landing, then it's your call. Personally, I like to set it and leave it. Don't forget it that way."

Roberts held up his hand, trying to comprehend what he had just been told. "Wait a minute! Just…wait a minute, Bobby."

Roberts thought silently for a moment. There it was. The thing had nagged at him, and now he knew. At least he knew part of it. He poured Scotch into their glasses and eyed Bobby carefully while he allowed the realization to mellow.

"Getting a little low on my Scotch supply, Bobby."

"You need some R&R to replenish."

"I'll get by."

"Got any paint thinner?"

"Look. Are you telling me that Williamson probably had his radar altimeter set at 200 feet when he crashed on that night cat shot?"

"I imagine so." Thomas nodded. "Why?"

"He crashed and maybe…maybe, he would never have even seen the red warning light extinguish, *because he never got above 200 feet?*"

"Can't be certain…but probably."

"That's crazy."

"No, it isn't. It's a pilot's option. Sure, sixty feet gives you an instantaneous 'no-climb' warning on the cat shot. But, from sixty to 200 feet is only a matter of a few seconds off the catapult, then the light would extinguish anyway. He may have had it set at sixty feet, but I doubt it. It's more important to have it set at 200 feet for the descent so some stupid jerks don't bust minimums on the approach, which you just did, Dan. That 200 foot descent minimum is critical."

"But, if Williamson had the radar altimeter set at 200 feet and something else happened…?"

"Like what?"

"Almost anything," Roberts stammered. "If…if a generator failed and he got a momentary interruption of electrical power…or cockpit lighting failure…or instrument failure of some kind. He wouldn't have gotten the single, easiest, most reliable warning that he was too low *and not climbing*…can't you see it? The red light was always *on* because he never got above 200 feet…it didn't tell him a goddamn thing!"

Thomas closed his eyes, sipped the Scotch. "Wow, I'm impressed! That's a pretty long statement for you, Danny boy. Sure. It could've happened that way, but that's so remote. You're guessing. Even if you're correct, so what?" Thomas sloshed a jigger of Scotch into his glass, stretched his shoulders with fatigue. "Remember. Your main concern is Franklin right now. Not Williamson, that's Manley's job. He's finished with it, incidentally."

"I know, but…"

"But, what?"

"There's something wrong here, Bobby. It really stinks."

The LSO hesitated, "You better be real careful, Dan," he said quietly.

"Heck…I'm the picture of caution."

"That's a Class-A, goddamn lie."

"I'm…."

"I'll tell you what you are, Dan Roberts. You're a damn fool." Thomas leaned back in the chair and shook his head. "Who the hell do you think you are, Dan? Really, what makes Danny tick?"

"I don't go for this…umm…introspection stuff, Bobby. And, you can't have any more of Scotch if you keep insulting me."

"Sure, that's too demanding for a tongue-tied guy like you."

"I'm just plain old Dan Roberts, Ensign, USNR, service number 682734. Bull Ensign of VA-433, what else?"

"Oh, no. That's a cop-out....it's not that simple. You walk around with that dopey grin on your face most the time, but I know that behind that innocent mug is probably the guy who *ate the hula dancer's skirt*. Ever hear that story?"

"No. But after two months at sea, I'm ready!"

"Look, I mean it. Don't distract me. Deep down you're a damn existentialist. You refuse to be molded. Isaacson didn't know what he was getting into when he gave you the Franklin investigation...big mistake. I'm gonna pull you off."

"I'm just doing what I was told..."

"Jesus, Dan...you still don't get it. I've never met one of you guys in Naval Aviation before. You really don't care what anybody around here thinks, do you? The Navy is just a convenient organization which allows you to do something that you love, and can do very well."

Roberts squirmed out of the chair. Thomas pointed a finger at his subordinate.

"Sit down. You're really such a simple being, Danny boy. You just like to fly lethal airplanes off aircraft carriers. Don't you? What do the longhairs say? Like, it's your bag, man."

Roberts shrugged. What was the use? Thomas was determined.

"But you don't want to pay the piper...oh, no. You won't conform to Navy enlightenment and you really don't care if, or when, you make higher rank, do you?"

"Nope. That radar altimeter, Bobby...you don't understand..."

"Quiet. You can't make your own rules so easily...hell even *I* know that. You're so full of crap, Danny."

"I wanna finish it...so please leave me alone, sir," Roberts said.

Thomas sipped the dark-amber fluid, a sigh of despair. Liquor was the one vice to which the ship's captain turned a blind eye. Men at sea for extended periods required a little slack.

"Finish it? You'll finish *something*, I'm warning you. Be careful! You might be making a big mistake."

"It's even worse that you imagine, Bobby. Yeah…I want to fly the airplanes and I like to shoot the guns. But I have two rules now."

"Phooey…rules…ensigns don't…"

"Don't interrupt…uhh…sir."

"OK…your turn, asshole."

"One, I'm going home alive. Two, I refuse to kill any more people who don't require killing. Tonight was…I don't know…something…"

Thomas straightened. Frowned.

"A vendetta? Listen, Dan. I know what you're trying to say but it's not that simple. We all want to live; especially me…just try to imagine all the women who'll require my future services. But, as far as selecting your targets, you can't have it both ways. If you want to live, you'll have to kill anybody who gets into your gunsight."

"No…"

"Listen to me, dammit. If you leave a target undestroyed, your wingman may get that fatal round you could have prevented by destroying that target…see? We're comrades out here…we're all alone. The White House, those bastards in Congress, even the American people don't support us one-damn-bit. Some of them hate us even though we do their bidding. We're pro's, but we're all alone and we gotta trust and protect each other. Besides, you can't always tell about targets. Things get a little murky out there sometimes."

The room had become thick with words and Roberts felt the strain of uncomfortable knowledge.

Thomas said, "You ever see me needing some help, don't think and don't hesitate, just shoot the bastards and I'll do the same for you. Remember that!"

Roberts dusted off a photo frame on his desk and set it carefully in place. His eyes locked on the photograph of Helen washing their sports car on a sunny afternoon captured in sepia tones in a silver frame. Memories of a simpler and better world. Thomas glanced over at the photograph. He scratched his head as though making an important decision.

"Don't distract me with pictures of beautiful women, Roberts."

"Just watch me...I'm, well...I'm slippery...more than you can imagine."

"I doubt it! You're full of crap, Dan."

"No more Scotch for you...sir," he chuckled.

"I think I'll have to put you on my wing again. Keep an eye on you at all times. I'm gonna speak to the skipper about it tomorrow. If he makes it back aboard, that is."

"Don't trust me, huh?"

"Isaacson's made several *cut* passes lately. Last night was even worse...a wave-off to a bingo...a real goat-rope. His eyes are going bad...won't admit it. Maybe he got poked once too often in the ring."

"Think you can straighten me out?"

"Oh, sure. As you say, it's even worse than that. You're screwed up but you're a good aviator and I admire ability."

"Just don't try to convert me into a ring-knocker, like Manley."

"Dan Roberts, the solitary, the inarticulate, has his standards. That what you're trying to say?"

"Yep..." Roberts gulped the Scotch. "And you're wrong about that radar altimeter, Bobby."

20

The cooler morning air flowed around two men strolling casually across the flight deck. They both glanced back at the sun bursting over the horizon washing the ship in a red glow before they headed for the wardroom and breakfast. Bobby Thomas made light conversation and Cdr. Isaacson nodded his head, both pretending to ignore how the previous evening's recovery had gone.

"What's the bad news?" Isaacson asked. An abrupt question, a direct, unblinking challenge. They were alone after a Filipino steward had served coffee and there was no need for further pleasantries.

Thomas had expected defiance. He opened the LSO debrief book, even though he knew precisely what to say. The action gave the landing debrief an official status. A good idea when giving a senior officer an unacceptable rating, especially Isaacson, a physically intimidating man.

"Cut pass this morning. Not your best work, sir. Slow in the groove…good lineup. But you went low, number one wire…better watch that…too close to the round-down, Skipper. Let's see…" He paused. "Not very good last night. Lined up left, FAB, then got slow in-close…waved-off…bingoed to Danang, sir."

The skipper frowned. "Bobby, I couldn't see a damned thing last night." The debriefing had been fair; his expression said he knew it.

"I know that, Skipper. You were all over the sky, *faster-than-a-bastard*. Overcorrected. Way behind the airplane, unacceptable. I could see it when you waved-off. It was bad. You gotta get the airplane under better control. Take some friendly advice. It's your eyes, sir. Why don't you skip the night flying?" *And recognize, for once, that you no longer have it.*

"Can't. I need to set an example. The younger guys…"

"Screw the younger guys! You won't set a very good example rolled up in a fireball on the round-down."

"I can handle it for two more months, till the end of the cruise, Bobby."

"Sure. You could handle it just fine when you were a kid, too. Hell, so could I for that matter. But, we all reach a point…"

"I know! How did Roberts do?" Cold, ruthless eyes that had once searched the ring for an opponent's vulnerabilities warned the LSO.

"Just fine…OK pass, no problems except he deliberately descended below minimums without a meatball to find the wake. Good stick-and-rudder work, though. He's usually pretty good coming aboard."

Thomas signaled the steward for more coffee. Isaacson had returned from Danang and made an acceptable, but not skillful, landing. Thomas had scheduled himself as LSO on the first recovery to personally wave Isaacson's landing.

"You know what he did last night?" Isaacson asked.

"Most of it. I heard the debriefing…as best he could tell it with his usual tongue-tied problem. But, yes sir, the word's out about Boxer Two."

"Took on that flak nest alone. Went nose-to-nose with them after they nearly knocked him down. Stupid or gutsy, take your choice. I saw some of it. They surprised him I think."

"Surprised his skipper, too, I'll bet."

"I told him to wait. Oughtta hang his ass, Bobby."

"Don't do that, skipper. We need him."

"Smartass."

"Yes." Bobby laughed. "He said they made him mad."

"He shouldn't have gone in alone."

"He's self-sufficient. I guess you'd call Roberts a highly-integrated personality. A borderline loner. What do you expect?"

Isaacson glowered. "I don't particularly care for his attitude."

"You're not alone. He's not very political, so his attitude will always be unsat. Plus, he can't express himself very well, you know that. Gets him into trouble."

"But, doggonnit, he does good air-work, Bobby. Reliable, too. When I look out there, off my wing, he's exactly where he should be."

"And that's why he's flying on the skipper's wing, right? Look, why don't you take him off that Franklin investigation, sir? You realize what could happen?"

"I want the truth, by God! I don't trust Manley. I think Roberts can do it…he's pretty stubborn."

"Oh, sure. Guaran-damn-tee it! Dan is fully capable of stirring up a huge pile of shit. He is definitely stubborn. Do you think that's really what you want? Why take chances?"

"He reminds me of a guy I fought at the Point. Mean little bastard…stubborn as hell. I had to beat the crap outta him."

"Skip the night flying, sir." Thomas sighed. "Do us all a favor."

"Franklin didn't commit suicide and I know it."

"Probably not, but the *truth* may be more than we can tolerate. This situation stinks. The Navy has a belly full of troubles right now, Skipper. So do we."

"I want the truth, Bobby. I insist on it. We owe it to Franklin. He was a squadron mate."

"Franklin was a dipshit, sir. Don't say I didn't warn you."

"It's part of this job, Bobby. I'll do my job my way. Your job is to kick Roberts' butt, and get me that report."

"How about sending Roberts to Cubi for his overhauled Spad? It'll be ready in four or five days. Give the new guy a rest. He needs to go ashore. Get his mind off Franklin and maybe it'll all blow over. I god-damn hope so."

"It's Smithson's turn to run the ferry flight."

"I know, but it was Roberts' airplane when it got beat-up. Roberts has had three major shootouts and several minor scrapes in less than three months. He's done more than most of us who have been here the entire cruise. Hasn't been ashore since he reported aboard. He's got ship fever. I think he needs some R&R. Besides, he's running out of Scotch."

"What about Smithson?"

"He can do the next one. He got ashore plenty on the last R&R, while Roberts stood the Watch."

"OK, you handle it, Bobby. And you can tell Smithson the bad news."

"I'm sure he will accept it gracefully."

"Hah! Smithson isn't the accepting type."

"One other thing, Skipper. I'd like to reassign Roberts to fly on my wing for the time being with your permission."

Isaacson snorted. "Oh…why?"

"Hargrave and I don't get along," Thomas lied. "He's thrown out some subtle hints, lately. I think you'll like Hargrave…he's pretty good. I worked with Dan a bit when he first reported aboard…kinda like his style. Maybe I can channel his energies, move him along. Do you mind, Skipper?"

Thomas could see it in his face. The uncertainty. Hargrave was a good pilot but he did not have the singular quality that Isaacson wanted in a wingman. Something that Isaacson required in increasing quanti-ties lately, a rare commodity. Dan Roberts was *lucky*, and Isaacson wanted a pilot with that particular asset on his wing at all times. But he couldn't reveal that insecurity and Thomas knew it.

"Sure, Hargrave's OK. Take Roberts and get him squared away, and get me that report. But, I want him back later. You can handle that assignment with Smithson, too."

21

Gentle rolling swells bobbled the huge ship as it maintained position in a box of ocean called Yankee Station. The Sharpsburg had been assigned a long overdue stand-down day to permit crew rest and to allow a twenty-four hour respite for deferred maintenance. A dark gloom permeated the cavernous hangar bay in the early predawn hour before a tropical sun burst upon Tonkin Gulf warming the ship and its three thousand inhabitants. A day of rest awaited those who would emerge from the bowels of the ship later that morning to enjoy a quiet, sunny day. Warm moist breezes flowed through open hatches and coffee odors drifted from the galley. The hangar deck was quiet. There would not be a formal muster in the morning.

Dan Roberts stepped through a hatch onto the dimly lit hangar deck with a steaming cup of coffee. He strolled aft stopping occasionally to inspect aircraft tiedowns, whistling softly to break the solitude. His flashlight beam darted about examining aircraft. Nearly fifty warplanes of various models were tied down waiting maintenance. He passed an A-4; a new engine poised alongside ready for installation. Roberts placed his cup on the wing of a damaged Skyraider and tugged at the tiedown chain under the port wing. It was the Spad he had flown on his last mission with Isaacson. A brief examination of a bullet hole repair near the wing root, evidence of his scuffle with the gun emplacement. He poked his finger at a fresh aluminum patch on the wingtip. *Pretty close*, he thought.

"Evenin, Mr. Roberts."

Roberts' head snapped in the direction of the quiet voice. Timothy Bryan saluted casually, a boyish face broken by a crooked grin. He shuffled his feet; embarrassed to approach an officer so casually? Shyness? Roberts could not tell.

"Didn't mean to scare you none, sir. Whatcha doin to our Spad?"

"Hello, Bryan. Aircraft Integrity Watch…on duty till reveille. What are you doing up so early?"

"Couldn't sleep. Thought I'd go look at them stars before sunrise. Do you maybe know where Polaris is, sir? I seen somethin about it in a book."

"Sure. Come on, I'm going topside. I'll show you."

They climbed a ladder near the Damage Control Station and stepped through the hatch onto the flight deck, into a world of noise, strange shapes and blackness. Only the red tower beacon on the ship's superstructure pierced the void of dark night. Wind blew through the superstructure, then flowed into gun tubs and drifted into a myriad of nooks, antennae and crevices, murmuring an eerie nightsong symphony. They strolled slowly across the deck into the warm wind. Roberts' flashlight beam danced across the deck illuminating tiedown chains, checking closed canopies, alert for fuel leaks.

"All them stars, Mr. Roberts…ever seen so many? Kinda like Arizona."

The nightwind whistled through rigging and they were alone in a quieted world of lethal machinery.

"But, not Seattle. We don't have many clear nights like this, Bryan."

"Can you tell which way we're headed, sir?"

"Southeast. Just maintaining position. We'll probably move farther west tomorrow…resume flight ops. See that big "W" up there?" Roberts pointed into the black cosmos.

"Hmmm?"

"Cassiopeia's Chair." His hand swept across the speckled vaults of heaven. He said, "Follow the point of those three middle stars."

"Okay?"

"Now, look over there. The Big Dipper. Ursa Major. Follow the line from the two outer stars toward Cassiopeia." Sweeping gestures to show the path. "The Little Dipper is in between. See? Last star on the handle is Polaris. The North Star."

"Damn. It always work like that, sir?"

"Always. Polaris is over our shoulder….we're steaming southeast."

Rolling waves rocked the ship gently through bright moon-flakes. They sauntered aft on the shadowy flight deck. Warm tropical breezes crossed the dark expanse carrying the nightwind song. Roberts pointed to starry constellations and individual stars. Bryan nodded, but spoke infrequently to Roberts, an officer who was almost a friend. The Navy's social strictures separated the enlisted teenager and the older officer but a professional bond had formed between the plane captain and the pilot. They shared the responsibilities for a Skyraider.

"You should be getting some sleep, Bryan."

"Sir, I seen you was on the mid-watch. I wanna…" Bryan stammered. Roberts smiled curiously, aware of speech impediments.

They stopped to look over the deck to the water below. Roberts glanced down into a five-inch gun tub. A golden trace gleamed across the ocean surface from the half-moon. Gold specks reflected from wave crests that stretched to a starry horizon. The soft tropical breeze caused Roberts to yawn with early morning fatigue. He glanced down to find the wave crests breaking against the ship's hull. Then, a dim flash. A smoky odor. A dark figure scurried out of sight below. He shined the flashlight down into the empty gun tub.

"What was that?"

"I dunno, sir."

"Let's take a look, Bryan."

The plane captain followed Roberts down a ladder into the gun tub. A five-inch cannon barrel pointed vaguely over the moon-dusted ocean, a quiet sentinel that had not been fired in anger since World War Two. A rancid smoky odor lingered in the tub's deep recess, a musty odor that Roberts recognized immediately, an odor that should never be present on a Naval vessel. He flashed his light around the space. Bryan was quiet; he stood behind the officer and glanced nervously at a closed hatch when it was illuminated by Roberts' flashlight.

"Sir?"

The officer stepped toward the hatch. Stopped. Looked back at Bryan. "Do you recognize that odor?"

Roberts swept the space with his flashlight, explored a corner behind the gun. Bryan's eyes followed the beam. It illuminated something. Roberts walked to the reflection and stooped to retrieve a small rectangle of translucent white paper.

The two men looked at each other. A look of recognition passed silently between them.

"Come on. Let's look around, Bryan."

He opened the hatch. The handle had not been dogged down. A careless error, or a hasty mistake? A dark passageway. Red light emanating from the corridor into the interior of the ship. A sharp corner was visible a few steps into the passageway. Roberts cast the beam into the void. Immediately, they heard a scuffling noise. Roberts ran to the end of the corridor, heard a hatch being slammed shut. He stopped.

"Sir…maybe…?"

"Shhhhh."

In the distance only darkness and ship noises. His flashlight swept over a closed hatch. Roberts opened the hatch slowly to a landing and a ladder, which descended into darkness. He flashed the beam below. Another closed hatch. Nothing. He remembered the hatch at the bottom opened onto the hangar deck. They stepped down into the darkness. A bumping noise. Scratching sounds drifted in the dark space. His flashlight casting eerie shadows.

Silence.

Roberts eased the lower hatch open and stepped into the hangar bay; his flashlight sweeping the space. They stood silently in the cavernous void; parked aircraft, equipment stretched upwards like ragged stalagmites. Watching. Listening for the intruder that was not there. A silence that was not noiseless surrounded them; the ship was never completely quiet. The low vibration of the steam engines mingled with hissing from steam lines and rumbling ventilation ducts. Roberts snapped off the flashlight and stood motionless. He signaled for stillness from Bryan with an upturned hand. They were alone in a silent steel cavern. He waited.

A tool dropped noisily onto steel deck plate, echoing through the bay. They turned at the sound. In a far corner two men stood looking in their direction. They were standing under an A-4. Tools scattered under a wheelwell. One man had a hammer poised to strike a stubborn bolt. Roberts' flashlight reflected the gleaming hammer. His hand trembled slightly. He quenched the light and approached them cautiously.

"What are you men doing here?"

"Fixing an uplock, sir."

"I was by here fifteen minutes ago. You weren't here then."

"No, sir…we was having chow. Just started before you walked up." The man was tall and stocky. He looked squarely at the officer. A confident voice. "You're Mr. Roberts…ain't you, sir."

"Yes. I'm in VA-433. So's Bryan. Flight Deck Integrity watch."

"We're supposed to be here, sir. Our maintenance officer wants this aircraft flyable tomorrow." The man was a veteran second class petty officer. The junior officer did not intimidate him. A scar above his right eye marked him as a brawler.

"Hmmm. You men see anyone around here in the last few minutes?"

The older man looked closely at Bryan. Shook his head. Pointed aft with the hammer. "Only the fire watch, sir." A moody defiance in his voice.

"Somebody was smoking in the gun tub. I'd like to talk to him. Ran down here…through that hatch, I think."

"We didn't see nobody."

Roberts looked at the petty officer. Quiet eyes stared back; defiance mixed with resentment, an unyielding man. Roberts started to say something, thought better of it and looked away.

"Who's your maintenance officer?"

"Lieutenant Garrick, sir. He told us to fix that uplock first thing."

"Were you men smoking up there?"

"No, sir. It wasn't us."

Roberts walked under the A-4. The left landing gear door was unlatched. Hydraulic fluid leaked into a drip pan.

"OK. Let's go, Bryan."

They retraced their steps up the ladder into the corridor. Roberts surveyed the narrow passage. Near the hatch he found what he was looking for.

"What's this, Bryan?"

"Dunno, sir."

The gun tub was dark and quiet on their return. Roberts stood alone under the cannon. He looked out to sea. Long rolling wave crests broke the blackened expanse.

"You didn't just happen by tonight, did you, Bryan?"

"No, sir. I mean…yes, sir, I seen you was scheduled for the watch. And I thought…"

Roberts turned the cigarette paper in his hands. His eyes focused in the distance, then narrowed. How should he ask it?

"Bryan, you…well, you must know what this is. Don't you?"

"Yes, sir. I know."

"I saw a bit of this in college." He sniffed at the fragment of marijuana he had found near the hatch. "It's absolutely forbidden in the Navy." And he asked carefully, "You're not part of this, I hope?"

"No! You shouldn't....sorry, I don't mean no disrespect, Mr. Roberts, 'cause you're a good officer. But, you should be more careful."

"Careful?"

"Yes, sir. Most of the guys're good folks 'round here. But some don't like officers very much."

"Like those two back there?" Roberts chuckled.

"I don't know them, sir."

Roberts examined the cigarette paper. Wondered what to say to the plane captain. He could not find the exact words.

"Do you know Diaz, Bryan?"

"Yes, sir."

"He a friend of yours?"

"Diaz don't have no friends, sir."

"What about Franklin?"

"He wasn't my friend and they wasn't really friends neither. More like...the same kinda jerks, sir."

"What do you know about Diaz?"

"Nothin, sir. I don't know nothin."

Roberts looked closely at the plane captain. How could he warn Bryan about something that he did not understand himself? The words were there but he could not find them.

"Stay away from Diaz, Bryan."

The plane captain looked squarely at his officer.

"I don't need you to tell me that, sir."

"Do you have any idea what's going on around here?"

"No. But, you need to be careful, sir."

"Why? Did you come here tonight to warn me?"

"Yer askin too many questions. Everybody's suspicious about you."

"That include you, Bryan?"

"No! I'm sorry, sir."

Roberts stood quietly in the dark gun tub. Ugly thoughts swirled in his quick, but inarticulate, mind. He tapped the flashlight slowly against the bulkhead. It began to make sense.

"OK. I want you to tell the chief about this. I'll drop it, for now…keep my mouth shut. But, you tell Chief O'Leary what we saw, Bryan. Maybe he'll know what to do. I don't want to cause any trouble for the enlisted men. But this is…unacceptable. I've got orders." He paused, and finally decided to ask it directly. "Did you ever see Lt. Williamson on the night watch…like this?"

The plane captain looked silently at the officer. Roberts sensed the uncertainty.

"Are you afraid, Bryan?"

"No, sir. I ain't got nothin to be afraid of."

"Good."

"It ain't me that needs to be afraid, Mr. Roberts."

22

Ralph Manley had ridden in the C-2 COD aircraft for four vibrating, tiring hours and now he stepped out onto the hot tarmac of Cubi Point's transient aircraft ramp. It felt good. Heat waves radiated from the concrete taxiway and he looked to see where he should go. He felt a familiar strangeness, to walk on solid ground again without the gentle rhythm of a ship at sea. He remembered the exhilaration of promise that a liberty port offered for a sailor long at sea, and for Ralph Manley that meant nothing more than women and booze. Manley prided himself on his political skills and he had used them to advantage recently for the simple reason that he desperately needed some R&R. And he must finish some serious politicking and telephoning while ashore. There was the tempting potential of a staff job opening at CincPac in Pearl Harbor.

The COD had delivered mail and other high-priority items to the Sharpsburg on its scheduled run from Cubi and had returned with homebound mail and two passengers. Manley hid the disdain in his eyes as the new guy stepped down.

"I'm ready," Ralph said, and looked into Roberts' innocuous green eyes to see if he understood. But he saw no comprehension in the return glance. Roberts was difficult to read. His face was open and amiable but it reminded Manley of another face from long ago. A fellow cadet he'd tangled with at Annapolis had a face like Roberts', a man he had badly underestimated. A confident face, unassuming, almost indifferent to everyone around him. In some ways a careless face and, in the depths of those green lenses, not truly friendly, but rather a polite awareness. Roberts had the face of a natural hunter and Manley had known instinctively that he would be a good pilot. Such men were rarely unskilled. And he made Manley nervous.

"Boy, I can taste a cold San Miguel already." Manley decided that Roberts would not contribute to the conversation until he saw fit. "Hospital first, Dan...a beer later? I'm buying." A direct question. He licked his lips and rubbed his hands in evident glee.

"You better take care of that rash at the hospital, Ralph. I gotta check on my Skyraider."

"Screw the hospital."

"Alright. Let's get setup in the BOQ. I'll buy *you* a quick beer in the Cubi Bar...you're the patient. Then I gotta check on my Spad."

Manley decided what he most disliked most about Roberts was his sarcasm. Misguided and indirect. It was evident that Roberts reconciled the vagaries of life through acerbity.

"You can check on your friggin Spad if you want but I gotta see a girl about a problem." He laughed and made a rude gesture involving hands and rapid hip movements.

"You're not that badly infected...I guess."

"Not so's you'd notice, Dan. At least not anywhere vital."

After checking in at the BOQ they changed into civvies and walked to the Officer's Club on the green hillside above the bay. They sat at the bar and looked out over Subic Bay. Colorful birds fluttered overhead and a light sea breeze flowed up from the bay bringing a dank, jungle odor through the open verandah. Two palm trees graced the entrance to the Club and colorful tropical flowers fringed the sidewalk. It was an impressive building on a hillside with commanding views of Subic Bay.

"I like it here, Dan. Think I'll stay a while."

"Hospital might want you for…uhh, extensive observations of your rare tropical disease, if you play your cards right, Ralph."

Roberts understood the game. Ralph Manley had apparently decided to tolerate him but his face registered mild distaste. Roberts' sarcasm reflected a strong independence and he had learned it could be a turn-off for social people like Manley.

"Well, they better observe quick. I got my priorities," Manley said. He could never really like Roberts and he suspected few did.

Manley slammed the dice cup onto the bar. "Play, dammit."

"You're a natural liar, Ralph. I'm at a definite disadvantage."

"Probably. I really like it here. The old club was OK. But, I think it was overrated. Just an old plywood building with screened windows. Japs probably built it after they kicked our asses out in '42."

"I was never in it…new guy, you know."

"Well, this one is better. Better looking barmaids too." He eyed a slender form bending over a table; a short dress inched up an almond-colored thigh. "Don't ever play liars dice with a superior intellect, Danny. You're overmatched; I can see it right now. I'm the best."

"Wrong. Bobby Thomas is the killer dice man, I hear."

"Shheeet! Bobby's a babe in the woods."

A Filipino barmaid strolled behind the pilots. She dropped an outstretched hand casually on Roberts' shoulder and brushed past with a giggle. She scurried away but a furtive glance captured Manley's attention and he jumped at the clink of a glass being dropped on the bar.

"Friend of yours, sir?" The bartender looked directly at Roberts, while he placed a clean ashtray near them. Neither pilot smoked.

"Nope," Roberts replied. He had not seen or talked to a woman in many weeks. His eyes followed her lithe form across the room. She turned and smiled but he looked away.

"You fellows just arrive?" The Filipino bartender nodded warmly at the pilots. He was middle-aged and his face showed the effects of a life of abuse.

"Yep. In from the Sharpsburg...couple days. Picking up an airplane. Ralph, here, is going to the hospital for a check-up. Wounded Naval hero, you know."

The bartender laughed and engaged them in an extensive discussion of World War Two. He had been a guerrilla fighter and claimed to have dispatched many hated Japs. Extensive discussions ensued of throat slashings, head bashings and machete hackings.

"What's your names? I try to remember all the pilots."

"I'm Dan Roberts...this Yankee Air Pirate is Ralph Manley."

They shook hands and the bartender slid two fresh beers to the pilots.

"Compliments of the Club. Pilots are special around here. She likes you, Mr. Roberts." He nodded toward the barmaid. "Shall I arrange something? She'd be willing."

"No, thanks." Roberts laughed and Ralph's contemptuous glance admonished him for temerity. "Tempting though...been at sea too long, I guess."

"You married, Mr. Roberts?"

"Very."

"Yeah...well, not me," Manley interjected. "I'm not a man of steel and I got my needs."

"I don't want to hear about it, Ralph."

Apparently Roberts selected his friends with care. Manley knew that Bobby Thomas and Herb McGinnis were his only regular companions.

"Have you ever thought of all the things you can do with a woman, Dan?" Manley's eyes followed the girl.

"I better get over to O&R...check on my Spad."

"The one you beat the crap out of?"

"The very one."

"I saw them off-load it last time. Shouldda just shit-canned it. Goddamn antique. Come on into town. See the sights."

"Don't bad-mouth the old bird. Got my ass home in one piece."

"Sort of, as I recall." Manley shook his head with exaggerated disdain.

The barmaid placed an empty glass on the counter. She glanced at Roberts, laughter like tinkling crystal. Roberts smiled at the girl.

"You pilot?" she asked.

"Yes, he is," Manley answered. "And, you might wanna know we Spad drivers are noted for an abundance of testosterone." Manley shot a skeptical glance at Roberts. "At least some of us."

"What's that?" She looked suspiciously at Manley.

"He doesn't know either," Roberts said.

"Come into town with me, you'll find out," Manley blurted.

"Maybe later…my Spad…remember?"

The girl wandered off. Manley slammed the dice cup emphatically. "Ten bucks says I got at least a pair of sixes under there?"

"Ralph, I don't wanna take your money. I expect you're gonna need all your tens tonight." Roberts downed the San Miguel and stood to leave.

"You'll be sorry. All kinds of exotic tropical delights await those who dare."

"Maybe you better go to the hospital first. Get pumped up on penicillin early…who knows where that…rash originated?"

"Stop stammering, I'm a lieutenant, right?"

"Yes, sir." Roberts sighed.

"And, as I recall, you are a mere ensign. Please correct me, if I'm wrong."

"Yep…Bull Ensign of VA-433."

"So, I outrank you, isn't that right?"

"Yes, sir, Lt. Ralph."

"You will meet me later, then. I'll see you in a couple hours, understand?"

"Where will you be, Ralph? Some hell-hole, I'm sure."

"Nah. Same place your buddy, Bobby, goes. Good booze, clean girls. You'll like it."

"Maybe."

"It's called The Willows…beautiful downtown Olongapo. Meet me there."

"That's a nice place, Mr. Roberts." The bartender insisted.

"Look, Ralph. You probably won't even be conscious in two hours…who are you kidding?"

"I can do everything necessary in a semi-conscious state. Just be there."

Roberts stood up to leave. He looked at the long wall covered with squadron plaques. VA-433 had not yet provided a plaque for the Club and he recalled that Isaacson assigned that task to Bobby Thomas recently. *Who's better qualified than you?* The skipper had inquired reasonably during a squadron meeting. *You spend so much time there, Bobby.* Thomas had laughed with the joy of a man truly blessed. *Who indeed, skipper?*

"See you later?"

"Maybe, Ralph."

And he walked away. Ralph Manley watched Roberts stroll through the Cubi Bar, glancing here and there at squadron plaques and Naval artifacts that decorated the walls. He stopped to touch a large engine cylinder converted into a table lamp. It cast a yellow wash of light over a dark mahogany wall. An ancient aileron punctured by shrapnel was oddly out of place on the beautiful wall. Several old propellers with battered hubs were scattered throughout the room. Abused tailhooks and scarred gunsights hung at haphazard angles here and there.

A velvet painting filled the space at the end of the bar, an object impossible to ignore and known throughout the Seventh Fleet. Roberts paused to admire the large painting that dominated the room, a life-sized creamy nude recumbent on purple velvet. Long, dark hair flowed over an alabaster shoulder. Arms stretched to receive a lover. Large breasts with erect pinkish nipples inviting a caress. Legs draped languidly across the canvas with infinite promise. Dark beckoning eyes entreating fulfillment. Roberts examined the painting for a long moment and then he walked through the door. He did not turn to wave good-bye.

Manley watched him leave and reflected on the fact that he did not understand Dan Roberts. He would have been unable to observe that painting, and then depart with Roberts' apparent indifference. He speculated about the two dissimilar roommates. Herb McGinnis, who he did understand, a cautious likable extrovert. And Dan Roberts, a reserved, but aggressive enigma. Manley sensed Roberts' fierce independence and he knew that it was unlikely that they would ever be friends. Roberts had quickly established a reputation as a good stick-and-rudder pilot and he was noted to be reliable. But he was not political, and Ralph did not trust anyone who did not play the game by conventional rules. Manley suspected that Roberts recognized him for what he was…an astute politician who was temporarily employed as a Naval Aviator.

Manley prided himself on his ability to get along with anyone, *a natural politician*, Isaacson had said, who could go far in the Navy. But, Roberts was not so easily categorized. He had a quick mind, but VA-433's Bull Ensign had difficulty expressing himself and when he did, it was usually with an abundance of irony. He had dismissed Roberts as a lightweight, but Herb and Bobby, whose opinions he respected, seemed to admire Roberts and that fact baffled Manley. The simple truth was that Roberts confused Ralph Manley and he could not like people that he did not understand.

Now he regretted having pressured Roberts to meet him later. Manley had an immediate, pressing agenda involving booze and women. There was much to be accomplished before returning to the Sharpsburg. Was Roberts a player? He watched Roberts disappear into the bright, tropical sunlight. Such an ordinary man, medium height and weight with a commonplace appearance, who possessed not a single notable attribute. Certainly not a man one would ever admire. Roberts was a straight arrow, out of place in an intense environment of egotistical over-achievers, who would probably not be any fun on liberty. Ralph sighed, then drank his beer and thought about women.

Another pair of eyes followed Roberts closely. Dark eyes in a wrinkled, Filipino face. The bartender did not smile as he watched the pilot depart. He washed a glass before placing it casually on the rack and glanced at Ralph Manley to make certain that he had not been observed. Then he picked up the telephone.

23

With a lurch and a belch of black smoke the Jeepney shot into the evening traffic. The driver grinned back at his passenger, displaying gaps in a jagged row of yellow teeth, unashamed of his driving skills. The street, potholed and dirty, snaked down into Olongapo from the bridge over the rancid flow dubbed the Perfume River, which wandered aimlessly through the town before dumping its contents into Subic Bay. Roberts winced at a near collision with another Jeepney that rocketed toward the bridge under minimum control. Raucous noises everywhere. Ragged children ran beside the war surplus American Jeep that had been lengthened into an open-sided covered taxicab. Two bench seats were anchored to the sides and passengers sat precariously with their backs to the traffic. The thing rattled with every bump and the lone passenger grasped a handrail as a desperate swimmer might hold a life ring.

The Jeepney careened past knots of pedestrians and bolted through a crowded intersection. Screams of protest from all quarters. Arm waving, obscene gestures and crude references to the driver's parentage. A fringed canopy draped overhead with full intention of shedding rain, an ambition of little prospect. Every metal surface was painted in fluo-rescent tones demanding individual recognition. Numerous Jeepneys veered through town, horns braying like frightened sheep, drivers shouting greetings and epitaphs frequently in the same breath. The Jeepney was decorated with bright swirls of yellow and orange over a base of bright blue. One side displayed a sinuous stallion rampant in tones of white shaded with gray and on the right front fender the rig's name was boldly embossed in silver script.

PRETTY PONY.

"Where you go tonight, sailor?"

"I'll ride with you for a while," Roberts muttered. "See the sights. Can't you go any faster?" His shoulder slammed into a sidepost during an uncertain skid. The driver was happily unconcerned.

"Sure…you betcha. Wanna girl?" the driver bellowed. "I know best places…best girls."

"No. Just drive me around."

"Clean girls. No water down booze. Good places. Cheap. I tell them you my friend, OK?"

Music blared from an open doorway. A girl stared openly, dark eyes, an insolent grin, teeth like piano keys. She twisted bright-red fingertips through a white necklace.

Roberts felt a headache begin. "What's that music?"

"*Black is Black*…everybody play it here."

"What does that mean?"

"Who knows…just a song…girls like…means nothing."

"Do you know The Willows?"

"Sure…sure…it's OK place."

"Drive through town first."

"You bet. What you name…you pilot, huh?"

"Roberts."

"OK, Roberts. Pilots all look alike. Olongapo nice town. I born here. My father was sailor…American sailor…not Jap."

"He was based here?"

"Nah. He gone. I never meet him…before war. Japs came. Killed my mother. You like my Jeepney?"

"Filipinos have had…." Roberts rolled a few inadequate platitudes through his mind. "…bad breaks."

"We like Americans…you like Olongapo?" He gestured broadly. Two girls signaled a promise from the street corner. Smoke drifted into the street from a barbecue stand. The Black song blasted from a barroom. It clashed in offbeat rhythms with another rendition from down the street. A cacophony of noise, pungent odors and brilliant colors flashed past the Jeepney.

"What kind of meat?" He pointed at the stand. Roberts had been warned.

"No good. Hey, you want some hash…you smoke. Maybe other kinda drug. I get anything. Cheap."

"No, thanks." Roberts felt the headache blossom.

Was everything available here? Probably. And at prices that an American sailor could afford. Drugs, women, booze. The town's display of timeless sins was discomfiting. It reminded Roberts of his dilemma. What was really going on? Were those same illegal drugs available on the Sharpsburg? Were they supplied from Olongapo? Or, was he imagining things? He thought of the larger question. Was there a connection between Franklin and Lieutenant Williamson? How did Diaz fit into the puzzle? He had been on deck the night his division officer had crashed, was Diaz part of the duty crew? Tim Bryan did not think so. Perhaps Pete O'Leary kept records of duty rosters. Roberts would remember to ask Pete when he returned to the ship. If Diaz wasn't on duty that night, what did it mean? Many sailors went on deck to observe flight operations and to witness the mayhem of accidents and battered aircraft struggling to land. But, few ventured on deck to observe night ops, too dark and dangerous.

Was Timothy Bryan involved? He hoped not. Bryan was his plane captain and he liked the kid from Arizona. But Bryan seemed to be present whenever things occurred. He was there the night Williamson died. He obviously knew Franklin well, although circumspect when questioned. Bryan was friendly with Diaz, although he had lied about it. And he was there last week when Roberts interrupted the marijuana exchange. He hoped Bryan wasn't involved. And the ultimate question, was he imagining things?

What Roberts suspected was quite extraordinary. This was his problem: Two men killed and his gut told him they had been murdered. Were drugs involved? Or, had he merely witnessed a random act of drug abuse and that coupled with two accidental deaths spurred an overactive imagination? Had Bryan been there during the mid-watch to shepherd him away from danger, or to prevent him from witnessing something? His head ached with an overflow of knowledge and confusion. Dan Roberts was well aware of his limitations. A quick mind, an incisive intelligence, but he was inarticulate and he knew it. Analytical intelligence crippled by an inability to articulate, a lifelong handicap and a reason for caution.

Timothy Bryan had started it with a single word. *Tricky!* What about Bryan's later, more cryptic, message? Had it been an attempt at humor?

It ain't me that needs to be afraid, Mr. Roberts.

Was Roberts mistrusted by the men, he wondered? Even worse, was he viewed as a threat?

The Jeepney skidded through a turn, saved from colliding with another multi-colored missile by a skillful swerve. The driver grinned back at his startled passenger with satisfaction.

"If I wanted some marijuana…could you get it for me?"

"Sure, Roberts. I get. Easy."

"What if I wanted a lot…say, a pound or more?"

"Oh, that be dangerous. Too much. How you get into ship?"

"I don't want it…just curious. What else could I get here?"

"Everything. You want anything...women, little girls, whiskey, drugs...anything. I get for you. But be careful. Sometimes not safe here, if you're stranger."

The headache moved from over his right eye to the base of his neck. He stretched to relieve the pain and he felt the loneliness wash over him.

"Willows over there...you go in now?"

The bar faced the dirty street with unabashed invitation. A bright sign offered promise of needs that could be quickly satisfied, if one were merely to venture inside.

San Miguel Beer. Dancing. Entertainment.

Neon flashes stoked the headache. He saw obscure movements through a gilded window and the ubiquitous song blasted through an open door.

Black is bla-aack....

A sailor stumbled through the doorway and vomited unceremoniously into the gutter. He sleeved away spittle and struggled to his feet, lurched toward the door, tripped and rolled into a comatose heap. Another sailor emerged from the doorway and helped the drunk to his feet. Roberts recognized him, a pilot he had known in Pensacola.

He tapped his fingers impatiently on the seat. Undecided. It wasn't too late to avoid the booze, and Manley. Torn by a promise to his squadron mate and reluctance to be involved, he lingered undecided in the rain.

"I guess so," he mumbled. "Tell you what...come back here and get me in one hour. Will you do that?"

"Yes." The driver checked his watch. "You wanna girl then?"

"No. Come inside and get me if I'm not waiting right here. If I'm not alone, say that you heard the shore patrol is looking for me to fly an airplane. Understand?" He handed the driver five dollars to insure his memory.

"OK. I do. I can get you twelve-year-old girl. Very pretty."

He felt himself a stranger befuddled in a vile place. A confusion of sensory inputs flooded his intelligence. Loud music. A burst of shrill laughter from within the bar. Strong odors from a barbecue stand assaulted the dripping, fetid night air. Roberts watched a beggar stagger across the dirty street, falling into the muddy gutter at his feet. He wore a battered Philippine Army hat. A barefoot, twisted leg protruded from torn and filthy khaki pants. Two ragged children pushed him down then ran laughing into the darkness. The old man lay there momentarily then struggled to the sidewalk. He looked up to Roberts and extended his hand in supplication. Roberts put a dollar into his dirty hand and wanted to say something, but could not.

A wave of loneliness engulfed Roberts; he watched the Jeepney shoot around a corner. Now he wished he were in the taxi returning to Cubi Point, somewhere else, anywhere else. He wished he were home with Helen. A sudden flash of blond hair, a laughing smile. The memory flushed by a disturbance from within the bar. He heard Ralph's loud voice. More laughter. A high-pitched cry of joy or pain. A series of giggles. Ralph shouting; demanding more of something. A feminine squeal.

The loneliness subsided, replaced by resignation. He turned for one last look at the street, it was not too late to back out. Someone tapped his shoulder.

"Come in, sailor. Welcome." A smiling middle-aged Filipino with a scar on his cheek beckoned from the open door.

And, he walked into The Willows.

24

Roberts turned to look at the door that had closed behind him. An uneasy feeling. The Filipino gestured toward the bar. "See, sailor. Your friends waiting?" He started for the door. Escape!

"Hey, Roberts…over here!" Manley blared. "Get your ass over *here*, Ensign Roberts." Heads turned to watch him. "Right now!"

The Willows rocked with intense activity. A dancer swirled. Her slender body twisted through a series of delightfully improbable exertions on the raised stage in the shorter leg of the L-shaped barroom. Along the longer wall a brass-rail bar invited drinkers into oblivion. There was a clutch of humanity at the bar and in the center of the mass an arm waved for attention, Ralph Manley with three girls. All were watching Roberts, the target of Manley's invitation.

"Get your ass over here, Ensign!" Manley repeated, in case someone had not heard him before.

Roberts edged into the group. Manley's hand emerged from one of the girls' blouses and gestured vaguely in Roberts' direction.

"See, ladies. Isn't he everything I promised?"

"Got your hands full tonight, Ralph?"

"Full…and full again," he blustered. A vigorous hand shot rapidly from blouse to blouse. "Nice tits, huh?"

"You know how to pick 'em, Ralph."

"Dammit, watch that…we're on liberty. You're supposed to have fun. *R&R*…you know what that means, dipshit?"

"Rape and ruin?

"Hey, tarbender," Ralph shouted gleefully. "This is Danny Roberts. War hero. Sinker of boats. Strafer of enemies. Killer of men. Famous Spad driver." He paused for a loud belch. "Give him a beer."

"What's that mean?" One of the girls eyed Roberts closely.

"Spad driver?" Ralph exclaimed. "Hell, who knows? I think it's some kind of ancient affliction…all the guys called that are sorta special, though."

"You're Roberts, huh?" The bartender placed a San Miguel on the bar. "Been expecting you. Ralph's talked about you all night."

"Dangerous Dan, the panty man! Watch him, ladies." A girl squealed as Ralph's hand shot up her thigh. She giggled with joy. Ralph lifted her skirt before she sat on his lap, a wriggling doll.

"Look at those pink panties, Dan," Manley shouted. "Ain't they cute?"

"Beautiful, Ralph. Maybe she'll loan them to you."

"Why not? She won't be wearing 'em much longer."

Roberts drank two quick beers and concentrated on the nearly naked dancer. He knew of her famous dance. The music had evolved into throbbing rhythm. Arms and legs intertwined a maypole. Strobe lights melded the movements into surreal harmony with the star-crested stage. He heard the familiar strains of a classical guitar but he could not identify the piece. He could not concentrate. Ralph shoved another beer at him. A light-headedness engulfed him and he felt alone in the crowd. A tug on his arm; he turned to a girl who was asking something. He downed the beer quickly and bent to hear her inquiry but he could not comprehend her question and she frowned. A swirl of noise and light. Music flowing with exuberant passion. The room vibrated with energy.

The girl said something emphatically, then turned and disappeared into the throng.

Now he felt tired, distracted. Music reverberated through the bar and his head ached with fatigue. The gloom of the rainy night and the burden of company he did not want to keep depressed him. Each of the girls sat in his lap at various times and engaged him in extended discussions of little interest, but their sexual presence was impossible to ignore; he had been at sea too long. He quickly grew impatient with Ralph's pleasant nonsense and turned to watch the erotic dancer. Herb had confessed after Bobby had told of his conquest. Was she the Lillian of such notoriety?

"Yes," Manley replied. "She's a friend of mine. You wanna meet her?"

She swirled and twisted and he was immersed in the realm of libidinous energy, his consciousness locked in the compelling eroticism of Lillian's dance. He would return to the ship tomorrow morning and now he wanted to leave the club; he knew his weaknesses. The booze and the stimulation of an erotic dancer and the proximity of the pretty girls. The illicit temptations he found difficult to resist were here in seductive abundance.

Everything available here...what you want? I get. The Jeepney driver had summed it up. Any vice, any drug, any perversion could be satisfied at a reasonable price. Any peccadillo would be available to any sailor and by implication, to any ship. The Sharpsburg's captain ignored the circumspect consumption of alcohol. Would other drugs be so difficult to obtain? The ramifications were obvious. Here, in this place of debauchery, surrounded by excess, Roberts understood at last. He resented the burden of suspicion; the responsibility of knowledge.

Isaacson's charge was clear. *Find the truth.* He understood the burden, but he had wavered. Now he was forced to confront the awareness and recognize the reluctance. *What if he was wrong?*

"Hey, Lillian," Ralph screamed over the crowd noise. "Great danc-ing…come here a second." He pounded Roberts' shoulder. "Watch this, Dan."

She walked to the bar; her face flushed from the dance. Lillian had covered her ephemeral costume with a silk robe. A slender body, smaller than she had appeared on stage. She was older than Roberts had expected; thin wrinkles crossed her wide forehead. Dark, confident eyes and a laughing smile.

"Hello, Ralph. Still here? Thought you would be entangled with sev-eral of those girls by now."

"I'm saving myself for you, Lillian."

"The answer is still *no*, Ralph!" Lillian turned to leave.

"Wait, Lillian, remember Herb McGinnis? This is Dan, his roommate."

She stopped. Dark, Eurasian eyes drifted over Roberts in frank appraisal. A slight smile and a gentle feminine laugh when he stood for the introduction.

"Herb? Really, how is my good friend?"

Roberts stood awkwardly; he rarely drank more than two beers. He shook her hand formally.

"Oh, he's busy just being Herb. That's a full-time job, you know." Roberts offered his barstool. "He's mentioned you a lot. I…I can see why." A nervous laugh. She smiled again at his unease.

"Herb is my very good friend because I think we have so little in com-mon. Did you know he talks in his sleep? Maybe he talks about me?"

"I know he likes your dancing."

"Perhaps. He is so handsome…like a, what do you say…Boy Scout?"

"That's Herb, all right. Mr. America."

"Do you think he will come see me again, Dan?"

"Next month. At the end of the deployment," he stammered. "I…I think you can count on it. Herb's nobody's fool."

"I miss him."

"Hey! Shut up, Dan," Ralph interrupted. "Last chance, Lillian." He grabbed two girls.

"Better get it while you can, Ralph," she said without a smile. "If they're willing, maybe you'll be able."

"Willing, able, ready. You name it. Ralph's got it. So long…I might be a while." He bustled through the door with an arm around each girl. A man on a mission.

"Jerk." Lillian's eyes followed him with cold disdain.

Roberts laughed. "You must know Ralph. He can be a real…"

"Son of a bitch?"

"Yep…sometimes words fail me."

"I know. Herb told me. But he thinks you're a good man."

The bartender placed a cup of tea at Lillian's elbow. He gestured toward the door, a man waved at Roberts. He recognized the scar-faced middle-aged Filipino who had opened the door for him earlier.

"That fellow says you have a Jeepney waiting."

"Yep. Guess I better go."

"Wait, Dan. Why don't you stay a few minutes?" Lillian said. She glanced at Scarface. "See that girl behind the bar? She's the owner's niece. Very nice girl, and pretty. Very willing. Only used for special customers. I could arrange something." A twinkle in her eye. She brushed his face with painted fingertips. Her robe drifted open to reveal a delicate breast. Roberts looked away reluctantly. Lillian closed the enticing gap slowly, watching him. "You would probably like a woman tonight. Wouldn't you, Dan?"

"Can't. I'm….gotta early launch tomorrow."

"Oh. I see." She nodded. "Herb said you're kinda strange. She's very nice, though. Would do anything you want." Lillian smiled. "If she's not right, I might even…"

"No. Thank you," he interrupted. "You're very beautiful, Lillian. Everything Herb said is true. I'm….well; I'll tell Herb you want to see him again. He'll like that."

The Jeepney was waiting at the curb. He waved at the driver then clambered aboard. He was glad the night was over and he could return to the BOQ. Scarface was sitting behind the driver.

"OK, sailor?" Scarface said.

"Sure." Roberts yawned.

"Back to base?" the driver asked.

"Yes…no hurry. Drop this man first if you want."

"Thank you," Scarface said with a friendly smile.

Two men jumped into the Jeepney before it sped into the traffic. A large younger man sat next to Roberts. The other, a wiry fellow with an ugly birthmark sat across from him. Roberts tried to dismiss the fact that he had been quickly surrounded.

"You have good time in town, Lieutenant?" Scarface asked pleasantly.

"It's OK."

The first blow came immediately. Roberts had drunk several beers and he was tired and he had not expected it. Still, as he recalled later, it should have been evident. He had been careless. He doubled over with pain from a chop to his solar plexus. He was pinned to the seat; his arms locked by Scarface's two assistants.

"We could kill you so easy, Lieutenant."

Only Scarface talked throughout the ordeal. His English was good. His voice had the mellifluous quality of an educated man and frequently evoked a sympathetic concern. The young tough, who had struck him, removed Roberts' wallet and watch while holding his arm in a painful lock.

"We have killed sailors before…many times. We could cut your throat and dump your body into that stinking river and nobody would ever know or care." Scarface nodded toward the bridge.

The base was only yards beyond the bridge. Across the river, he would be safe. He looked at the bridge. How could he manage it?

"Don't think about it. We could easily kill you first. You want to live, Lieutenant?"

They drove slowly through the teeming night crowd and turned up a dark street.

"Yes," he gasped. He felt sick from the sharp blow.

"Good. That's very good. I like Americans. I fought with General MacArthur during the war. I killed very many Japs. I enjoyed killing Japs very much. I still do. We killed some Japs not long ago on that road over there that goes to Manila. I have also killed Americans but I do not enjoy that so much because I like Americans. But I will kill you to save business. And I could kill you easy." He pointed a stiletto at Roberts' throat.

His breath came slowly in rasping gasps. He looked at the driver who had not turned around but had heard it all.

"He can't help you. If he try, we would kill him too. But first we kill his wife and kid while he watches us. He will forget everything tonight." Scarface prodded the driver with the tip of the stiletto. "Won't you, my friend?"

"We could burn his Jeepney too…an example to others. Do you know how important this Jeepney is to the driver? Can you possibly imagine what it means to him, Lieutenant?"

"I'm an ensign and I don't have any more money."

The man looked at Roberts' cash. "Take the money…give him back the wallet." He smiled slightly. It was then that Roberts thought he might not be murdered. It was a friendly smile, one that reflected humility and genuine concern. Had Roberts seen such a smile in ordinary circumstances he would have instantly felt a kinship with the man of the scarred face and calm voice. Just a quickly the smile vanished, replaced by the closed face of a serious man with a distasteful job to complete.

"Thirty-six dollars. Why don't you have more money? You poor, Lieutenant?"

"No. Not exactly, just broke."

"Listen…you talk too much, Lieutenant." An accusation rarely directed at Roberts. "You ask too many questions. Why don't you mind your own business and not stick your nose into other people's business?"

"I don't know what you're…" A sharp slap across his face. Painful and humiliating. He tasted blood.

"Shut up. I think you know what I mean. On the ship you ask too many questions. Do you want to live, Lieutenant?"

Roberts lunged against the large man, pushed him aside, and turned to jump from the Jeepney. He was doubled over by a punch to the kidneys. He fell to the floor and received several painful kicks. He rolled on his stomach, covered his head for protection and groaned in agony.

"That was stupid. Maybe we kill you now. Should we?" Scarface snatched Roberts up by the collar, spat into his face. Neon lights glinted on the stiletto blade.

"I will ask you for the last time. Do you want to live?"

A weak animal groan. Roberts looked up at his assailants and tried to conceal the fright. Ashamed. He was helpless.

"Do you?"

"Yes." Now he knew he must do it exactly right, say everything perfectly, if he was to live. He wasn't certain he could.

"Good. Tomorrow, you'll go back to ship. See…we even know that. You go back and don't tell about this and don't ask any more stupid questions about other people's business and you'll live. Who cares what any sailor smokes or drinks or kinda girls he likes? Sailors should get what they want. No officer's business anyway. Do you understand me, Lieutenant?"

"Yes, goddammit."

"Good. If you lie, we'll find out. When you come back we would kill you next time. *We* could kill you on the ship, even." He poked Roberts' knee with the stiletto. "What makes you think you could freelance so easy, Lieutenant?"

"I think you got the wrong guy. I'm an ensign."

"Ensign…lieutenant…both same. I like you, Lieutenant. I always like Americans. Good people. My wife goes to America to visit relatives, sometimes. You live in Seattle, right?"

"No, California," he lied.

"I think you mean it, Lieutenant. You want to know why?"

Roberts spit bloody saliva onto the young tough's shoe.

"Because I see respect in your eyes. You have an honest face. I tell you what I think will happen. You won't be hauled out of the river tomorrow. You'll keep your mouth shut and nose out of other people's business and everybody will be happy."

The man wrapped a five-dollar bill in a piece of paper and handed it to Roberts.

"Pay the driver. We'll keep the rest of your money for expenses. You'll go back to the ship tomorrow…don't need any money."

Scarface whispered something to the driver. Pretty Pony turned onto a lighted street.

"Why didn't you get a girl tonight?" Scarface asked. "I watched you since the BOQ. Why no fun tonight?" The question was laced with genuine concern.

"Guess I was saving myself for this."

"You gotta smart mouth." Scarface slapped him.

"Hit me again, you bastard!" Roberts spit blood. "I don't wanna forget this."

Scarface nodded. The tough jabbed him hard in the stomach. Roberts doubled over in pain. His eyes watered and he coughed. Blood dribbled down his chin.

"I saw you with Lillian. She's beautiful, isn't she? You didn't want her?" He laughed. "Oh…I know. You're married. Wife's in Seattle. Good man."

"Hey! Main gate." The driver pointed nervously.

The man slipped the knife into a pocket. "Remember, Lieutenant. No more questions." He poked the driver and nodded toward the bridge.

The driver honked and bullied his way through the crowds and Pretty Pony came to an abrupt stop at the bridge.

Scarface looked up into the dark rainy sky and yawned. He glanced back at Roberts with casual indifference.

"I wish the rain would stop."

They paused for a moment. A fine, sticky mist rolled over the river that formed a timeless border between the American military colony that occupied the strategic harbor and dominated the Southwest Pacific, and the Filipino town that provided a most unmilitary commodity. Two vastly dissimilar cultures that fed upon one another and brought out the worst elements of each, but this was of little concern to the three men who jumped from the Jeepney and faded into the raucous crowd.

A dank smell. The night dreariness surrounded them. A drunken sailor with a girl paused to look curiously at the Jeepney and Roberts said something quietly. The sailor scowled, the girl called him a name. A cocktail napkin was wrapped around the five-dollar bill Scarface had stuffed into his pocket. He gave the five to the driver.

"You know those guys…don't you?"

"I don't. If I did, I would die."

He noticed a marking on the napkin and held it under the street lamp. A green willow tree on a plain white napkin; it looked familiar. Concise scribbling, blotchy with ink spots on the dirty white napkin. It was legible and in spite of the misspellings the threat was clear.

You get new baby-dont be stuped.

How could they know so much about him? He felt a surge of cold anger in his gut. He wiped his face with a handkerchief and knew it was not bruised. They had been careful, expert. His injuries had been painful and demeaning, but not visible, and his world had changed radically. Until tonight, Roberts had been motivated by an obligation; he had felt a duty to Franklin and Williamson. Isaacson had demanded the truth and he had been determined to find it. Now the situation was markedly different. He been threatened and abused, and they had involved his wife and unborn child in their ugly coercion. There was a new factor in the equation. It had become something more than duty.

The driver pocketed the five. His hand shook and he could not look into Roberts' eyes.

"Sorry, Lieutenant. I couldn't…"

"Not your fault. Let's forget it."

Roberts walked through the gate. He felt a new emotion and he understood it. The Naval base seemed warm and secure. But he knew that was not the case. The corruption emanated from the filthy town, across the bridge, over the Perfume River, onto the base, into the Navy and into his own squadron. He walked slowly down the street. A street lamp emitted a warm glow in the thick, moist air and he thought of home. His headache was gone, replaced by sharp pains in his back and stomach.

Anger!

It hit him like a gust of cold wind. Why? Experience had taught him that most people do things for a reason. The more extreme their actions, the more pressing the reasons. Tonight, he had been exposed to assault and threats and the reason had to be something important. Those men did not want his money or watch. He was doing something they viewed as a threat and he was certain what that something was. They had waited for him in Olongapo, had known he was coming, had found him easily. Scarface seemed familiar; he remembered the smiling man opening a door. He had ventured innocently into The Willows, foolishly into their realm. Tonight had been a warning, a final warning. Had Lillian deliberately attempted to delay him, caution him?

Actually, he recalled several warnings lately. The Filipino had been brutally forthright. But Roberts recalled a more gentle admonition received several days earlier. *You should be careful, sir.* Was there a connection between the Filipino and Timothy Bryan? But, Bobby had also strongly advised him to finish the business, *and to be careful.* Bobby had arranged this trip to pick up his rebuilt Skyraider. Were they involved, Bobby and Bryan? Had he been setup by men he thought were friends? *Or mere coincidence?* He scowled at the thought. Roberts did not believe in coincidence.

He felt a growing contentment, a resolution. Anger subsided and the black mood diminished. He'd made a decision. He had been beaten and disgraced. They had assaulted him and invoked a veiled threat against his family. He had been forced to grovel and he had lied to survive.

What makes you think you can get away with this, Lieutenant? And Scarface had slapped him for emphasis. *I don't think…*he'd stammered. *Don't mumble, Lieutenant, speak up.* And he had been slapped again. But it was the recollection of Scarface's last statement that was the most demeaning; it gave birth to a slow fury. He had been assaulted and humiliated and then casually dismissed with a banal observation on the weather, an insult worse than any slap on the face. Scarface had made a serious mistake; he had humiliated a proud man and then allowed him to live. It would have been wiser to have killed him. He would get even and he knew exactly where to begin. Scarface had revealed more than he knew. The insolence now spurred him to vengeance, an idea evolved.

He whistled a tune and then laughed with the joy of one that has been very near death and survived.

Black is black…

Of course it is! A black world surrounded him. They knew him! In the mist he could see the BOQ and he was no longer frightened. Roberts felt determined and he knew what to do. A simple plan. It could work. He looked up into the black mist. A single star glittered through a break in the billowy cloud cover, then another, and finally, a constellation. He recognized the bright cluster of Cassiopeia and he thought again of Timothy Bryan, who must have guessed the purpose of his inquiries. Had he talked to others? Probably. He remembered Bobby's emphatic warnings. *Bobby?*

The BOQ's porch lights washed away the gloom. He stepped into the bright, clean lobby and he was not afraid. There was a message waiting, Number 407 was ready. Scarface had been correct. The bastards…they had known. They knew so much! He was scheduled to launch at 0700.

Before he went to his room, he glanced through the lobby window at the dark street that meandered up the hill to the gate, and smiled. A bright half-moon glistened through the broken clouds of a clearing sky. How nice, he thought, Scarface would be pleased.

The rain had ceased.

25

A windy night. Seafoam swirled in the blackness and spray drifted over the bow as the ship turned briskly into the wind for launch. Pete O'Leary jumped onto Roberts' wing, a broad smile. Roberts looked up to his amiable face.

"All set, sir? See you're back in 407 tonight. Been back a week and you haven't broken it yet."

"Ready as I'll ever be, Pete," he said. "You think I'm nuts, don't you?"

"No, sir. You're a good man in a tight spot. Our talk this morning made sense. You can always talk to me, sir."

"I just don't get it…maybe I'm wrong." Pete had been supportive; he was a friend. They'd talked frankly about Roberts' suspicions.

"Can I make a suggestion, Mr. Roberts?"

"Always, Pete."

"Ease up a bit now. We've already had three men killed on deck…flight ops are dangerous and the men sometimes need a little slack. Bend the rules…we all do. Three dead men before you signed on, plus Franklin and Lt. Williamson. And I guarantee there'll be more before we get back to Oakland. One suicide really isn't all that significant. Some things in life are just too complex; they're ugly and a man shouldn't look at them too closely. Drive you nuts…know what I mean, sir?"

"Like napalm and strafing, I suppose?"

"Exactly."

"I'll think about it. The skipper…." He could not think of the proper words.

"Sometimes asks a lot, doesn't he, sir?"

"Yep, except he didn't *ask*, Pete."

"Better ease up on the questions now…get your report finished this week, I'll help. Say it was suicide, then drop it. Be better for all of us."

"I know one thing for sure…it wasn't suicide, Pete."

"Maybe. Well, I'll be waiting for you later then, sir," Pete said, Mickey Mouse headset and goggles framed a broad Irish face under the pale glow; he patted Roberts on the shoulder. "Guess we better finish this thing."

"Maybe I should go alone tonight, Pete. I think I got a handle on it now. Diaz is the key. Why don't you forget about tonight…my problem."

"No, sir. It's a squadron problem. I'll be there to help. You'll need backup. Don't underestimate Diaz; he's a tough little spic."

"But, it's my responsibility. Think I should brief Cdr. Isaacson…bring him, too?"

"No, sir. Let's tackle it alone. Get some answers before we bring in the big guns…maybe we can keep it contained." He nodded. "Better for the squadron that way."

"OK, Chief. I appreciate it. I do need your help."

"They shouldn't have beat you up, sir. But guys get mugged all the time in Olongapo."

"It wasn't a mugging, Pete." The yellow-shirts were signaling for engine start. "And, I'm gonna nail these bastards!"

Bryan waved to him. A light breeze flowed across the flight deck and Roberts was positioned on the starboard catapult. Bobby was on the port cat. They were to be the only strike aircraft to be launched tonight.

A night road-recce along Highway One, a routine reconnaissance and harassment mission. There would be little excitement tonight.

"Sure. I'll see you on the recovery, sir." Pete looked away. "Maybe we can finish it tonight. Best for all concerned."

Time to go. The engine started with a cough, red flames and black smoke from the exhaust stacks wafted into the nightwind. A quick engine run-up on the catapult officer's signal. Mags OK, controls checked, wings locked down.

Timothy Bryan had not helped him strap-in after preflighting the Skyraider. Pete had relieved him before the launch. It was just as well.

After returning from Subic Bay, Roberts had questioned Bryan extensively and the plane captain had resented the questions, denying again any knowledge of Franklin. Roberts hadn't mentioned the Olongapo confrontation, hoping that Bryan might inadvertently tip his hand. Bryan had been antagonistic the last two days. Had his direct questioning gone too far?

I know what you're gettin at, but you ain't got it right, sir. I don't know nothin about this and I told you so. Bryan's voice cracked and Roberts, knowing that Bryan had lied, regretted the questions.

Finally, Roberts had discussed his suspicions extensively with Pete that morning in the maintenance office. Bryan was probably involved in the drug problem; he was certain the plane captain knew more than he admitted. Diaz certainly was involved; he was the key. Pete listened sympathetically.

"Sure they weren't just muggers, sir?" Pete asked after he'd described the Olongapo incident.

"They threatened me, Pete. Knew me. Mentioned my wife. I'll get them...bastards." Anger spewed forth. "They knew exactly what they were doing. And I know who to start with. I'm gonna squeeze that sonofabitch Diaz till he pops and then I'll get the rest of them."

"Wish you'd be careful, sir. Back off a bit. Diaz is tough."

Careful? There it was again. Several people had warned him lately. *Better watch your ass. Be careful, Dan!* Herb had pleaded with him after Olongapo. *You should be more careful, sir.* Bryan had warned him earlier. And Bobby had attempted to discourage him several times. *Be careful!* Only Isaacson, who demanded results, seemed unconcerned.

"Thanks, Chief. I will," he'd said. "But, I'm not gonna quit, there's more to it than Diaz. Goddamn drugs!"

Diaz was the key but Diaz wasn't intelligent enough to handle it alone and order the assault. Pete had agreed, there would be others, someone higher up. Who could he trust?

Pete frowned. "Funny you mention him, Mr. Roberts. Heard an interesting rumor yesterday," Pete had replied. "Tonight, later on, during mid-watch. Some kind of deal going down. Diaz is involved. Maybe I should attend?"

"Damn right, Pete. We'll both go. I'm gonna nail this thing."

"But, you're on the flight schedule tonight. I can handle it alone, sir."

"No, I'll be back aboard by midnight, Pete. I'm in."

"Alright. Let's meet in the spud locker after you land, about 0400. Something's going down in a familiar place to you, Mr. Roberts," Pete laughed. "The aft gun tub."

"Let's do it!"

"I wonder, should we ask Mr. Thomas about it?" Pete asked.

"No. Not Bobby Thomas," he'd replied cautiously. "I don't know about him. Just you and me, Pete. We can do it." He remembered Pete's last comment.

"You got spunk, sir."

Now Roberts glanced aft and noticed Pete giving the Spad a final visual check before he disappeared behind the aft fuselage. Timothy Bryan waved, then showed him the landing gear pins he had removed but did not display his usual grin. Bobby Thomas' Spad careened down the catapult. *Checklist complete. Position lights on.* Roberts scanned the instrument panel. Eased his helmet against the headrest and waited, but something troubled him. A nagging thought. A quick recheck of the instruments. A needle wiggled in the flight instrument cluster. An anomaly. One needle in the vibrating maze of flickering needles had flickered erratically. Something abnormal. His eyes searched in the panel's labyrinth for the offending instrument. He felt the catapult tension. Something wrong! Quickly, he reached to switch off the position lights to suspend the launch. The Spad settled slightly.

Whoosh!

The crushing blast. Roberts was slammed into the seat cushion. Numbing acceleration. Momentary confusion. Eyeballs unfocused before he could identify the erratic instrument. *Something wrong!* Rapid disorientation. Surrounded by blackness. He was hurled from the flight deck into the immense darkness of the night.

Alarm signals rang in his brain!

Struggling to focus, to identify the problem that could destroy him. Vision swimming in an obscure gloom. A red smear of cockpit lighting on blurred instruments, not yet lucent enough to understand. The settling feeling in his ass, knowing the heavy Spad was wallowing down into ground effect. Desperate for vision. Frantic for the knowledge he needed immediately, but must wait to see.

Were the wings level? Was he climbing?

No horizon in the blackness. Vertigo, his mind spinning into confusion. Gut-clinging fear. Cold sweat. Eyes slowly focusing, he searched for the deadly aberration. *Check the needle-ball!* Needle deflected left, ball out to the right. Skidding, a dangerous attitude! He kicked right rudder and right aileron, and slapped the gear handle up. Where was the altimeter? Frantic for life-saving altitude. And then he saw it.

Airspeed!

The airspeed indicator bounced radically at sixty knots! *Impossible.* The Spad would stall immediately and crash into the ocean. He pushed the stick forward, desperate for airspeed. Then, knowing that it could not be….*at sixty knots he would have already stalled, crashed into the Gulf…*he eased the stick back and focused on the attitude indicator, a most unreliable instrument, but he must use it now to set a climb attitude. The airspeed indicator jiggled. Sixty knots, then immediately jumped to one hundred ninety knots, then back to eighty knots. Altimeter climbing rapidly through two thousand feet. Rate-of-climb indicator pegged unbelievably at three thousand feet per minute. *Impossible.* His left hand trembled; he jerked the emergency jettison handle. All under-wing ordnance, two five hundred pound bombs, two rocket pods and a fuel tank, fell into the ocean. The Spad lurched, three thousand pounds dropped away and he felt an immediate climb. Slowly now, milk the flaps up…decrease drag, accelerate. He cleared the lump of fear from his throat and keyed the mic. What to say?

"Hammer One. This is Two, I got….problems."

"Copy, Two," Thomas radioed. "Can you join-up?"

"Roger. Give it a shot. I got no airspeed, no altimeter…instruments all screwed-up."

"Got you visually, join on my wing."

Roberts set climb power and held the trimmed attitude. Thomas was in a gradual right turn; Roberts closed on the green wing light. He slid slowly under Bobby's right wing and retrimmed the Spad to match his airspeed.

"You dump it all?" They turned directly into the Delta pattern, holding on the ship's starboard side.

"Affirmative." Roberts' voice quivered. "Almost took a swim, Bobby. Pitot-static system's completely inop."

"Hammer Flight, this is Homeplate," Approach control radioed. "Understand you have an emergency. You have a ready deck…or you can bingo to Danang."

"What do you say, Hammer Two? Your choice," Thomas asked.

"Lead me down, One. Call airspeed in the groove, OK?"

Bobby Thomas jettisoned his load and reduced power. There would be no mission tonight.

"Homeplate. Hammer One, we'll take the deck. I'm jettisoning ordnance. Two will land first. I'll lead him in and wave-off in close. Paddles…you listening?"

"Paddles up, Hammer One," the duty LSO radioed. "Got a ready deck."

"Hammer One, copy. Let's plan a one-mile straight-in."

"Roger. Don't try to fly it fast. Just give us a normal pass. Wave-off at five hundred feet; we'll take your wingman from there. You got twenty-five knots of wind down the centerline."

Bobby Thomas flew a wide downwind leg on the ship's starboard side. Roberts glanced to his right and saw the eerie shadow of a ship slide past in the dark night. The wake glowed, a green ribbon on dark velvet, stars gave a faint reflection of moonless sky. They leveled at one thousand feet and Bobby called for the gear and flaps and the Spad bounced slightly in tight parade formation.

Gear, prop, flaps, hook.

"Landing check."

"Hammer Two's complete. Gear down, hook down."

The two Skyraiders turned to final over the wake's glowing path. Roberts watched for and saw the wake appear under his left wing and a quick glance found the mirror's bright glow against infinite blackness.

"OK, Two. Airspeed steady at 105 knots."

"Roger." He felt the elevator forces. Two clicks of nose-up trim. There, just there, was the exact airspeed, the precise stick-force he would try to maintain all the way down to the deck. The nightwind was steady and the Spad's attitude should be stable until he hit the downwash over the round-down.

The meatball drifted down from the top of the mirror and the red dropline lights lined up with the white centerline deck lights. On centerline, on glideslope, on airspeed. Bobby Thomas, the man he'd told Pete he did not know about, flew a smooth lead.

"Hammer One. Five hundred feet. Roger ball."

"Looking good, Hammer Flight," the LSO replied. "Hammer One wave-off to the left. Two, call the ball."

Roberts saw Bobby's green wing light blink twice and watched him slowly turn from the glideslope and fly away. He checked the phosphorescent wake, the red dropline and the five centerline lights. No use scanning airspeed or altimeter, they were still fluctuating wildly. Don't look at the useless airspeed indicator. Maintain the power-setting Bobby had provided on the lead-in. He modified his landing mantra.

Meatball. Lineup. Easy on the stick.

"Hammer Two. Roger ball. Hook down. Negative airspeed."

"You're fast. Hammer Two. Reduce power one-inch," the LSO shot back. "Don't get fast on me, now."

Roberts pulled the throttle back and watched the manifold pressure gauge. Thirty-three inches MAP…about right. He would hold that until Paddles called again.

"Looks good. About three hundred feet….keep her coming. Smooth, now. *Eaasy* on that stick."

The ball started to rise from the centered position. He eased the slight backpressure on the stick and let the nose settle gently. It was all feel now, nothing to look at on the instrument panel. No valid information there for him. It was all visual and feel. The meatball drifted gently between the green glideslope bars. He touched the right rudder to correct a drift to the left. The wake glowed beneath the left wing, exactly where it should be.

Meatball. Lineup. Easy on the stick.

"Getting a little slow…crack on some power. Easy."

Gently, so slightly, Roberts eased the throttle forward. *No wave-offs tonight.* A trickle of sweat ran down his forehead into his left eye. Disregard!

In the groove. The round-down and the spud locker disappeared below the nose. It felt good, flying skillfully, knowing it. The cut would come soon. His left hand trembled in anticipation of the downdraft.

"Little power! You're settling. Power!"

Throttle forward! Watch for red wave-off lights.

Instead, the green cut-lights flashed! Roberts jerked the throttle to the idle stop and held the stick tight. The Spad slammed hard onto the deck. He felt the shoulder harness bite into flesh. His head snapped forward. The tailhook caught the landing cable and the Spad skidded to an abrupt stop.

"Beautiful…." the LSO said.

His mind spun-up to accommodate rapid information inputs. He had survived. The yellow-shirt's wands signaled urgently. Quickly, quickly now. Hook up. Power on. Wings up. Taxi clear of the landing area because Bobby's Skyraider was right behind him. He followed the taxi director to the Number One elevator, sensed men scurrying around the aircraft, tasks being completed. Two yellow-shirts chocked the Skyraider. Timothy Bryan slashed a wand across his throat, engine cut. He pulled the mixture control knob and watched the prop spin to a halt.

Pete O'Leary jumped onto the left wing. The klaxon screamed and he felt a sickening in his stomach as the elevator dropped suddenly into the hangar bay.

And then it was quiet.

A soft glow. A quietness. A calming. Hangar deck odors. A warm, moist breeze flowed through the cavernous space. He punched the Spad's elapsed-time clock. Eleven minutes. He had launched, almost crashed into the Gulf, recovered, flown a difficult approach, and survived. *Eleven grueling minutes.*

Pete was yelling something at him. Other yellow-shirts signaled for him to deplane. He could not formulate an answer. He could not comprehend the implications that intruded into his consciousness.

"Damn, Mr. Roberts! What happened?"

Eleven minutes. Almost a crash. His mind stumbled in conflicting knowledge.

He could not ignore the similarity!

Roberts removed his helmet and sleeved away the sweat that rolled down his face. He leaned back against the headrest and closed his eyes on an awful image. He could smell the ocean breeze flowing through the elevator hatch. The deep, dark, deadly ocean into which he had nearly plunged. He had rejected coincidence earlier. Now, he could think of nothing else.

He remembered Lt. Ted Williamson.

*   *   *

Major Binh tucked his American binoculars into the cabinet. A crewmember looked up when he tapped his pipe on the junk's gun barrel. Time for a smoke. He knew the incident was over and he must make a note of it, even though he did not understand what had happened. Two Spads, as the pilots fondly called them according to a captured Time magazine article he had read recently, had launched and immediately returned to the Sharpsburg. Why? He did not understand some of the peculiarities of American flight operations. Binh had interrogated several Navy pilots in Hanoi and had a good knowledge of their routines. It was when they deviated from *routine* that he became confused. The word jogged a memory.

Nothing's ever routine.

He remembered a young A-6 pilot who had made that assertion under agonizing duress. What was his name, something unusual like Kowolski; Binh regretted his fallible memory. A fine young man and a courageous American; he had died shortly after the interrogation. Binh pushed the disturbing memory aside. No time for that now. He had a mission and he was waiting for an opportunity. He was impatient for redemption, but he must wait.

The Moment would come.

26

The darkness folded around him. The spud locker had always made Dan Roberts uneasy. It was a dark, hemmed-in space below the fantail sheltered by the round-down but exposed to the dangers of a ramp strike and normally off-limits during flight operations. A watertight door connected the space to the aft hangar deck and maintenance shops. The shadowy structure possessed a mysterious quality, especially at night, which defied rationality and he felt the uncertain apprehension of isolation.

Although it was normally vacant, the spud locker was used for many things. Galley workers dumped kitchen waste over the railing during the day. Broken tools, garbage and other useless things were dumped over its guardrail. Sailors occasionally took cigarette breaks in its well-ventilated deck and personal disagreements that could not wait until the next liberty were occasionally settled in the private alcove after hours. Or, a lonely sailor might stand at the guardrail and watch the ship's wake disappear and wonder about home. Few of these activities occurred in the late night hours, a foreboding darkness discouraged visitors.

Roberts entered the spud locker at 0400. He was tired; the emergency landing earlier that evening had exhausted him. There was no moon to light the area but a warm red glow from the dropline stanchion washed the deck and shadowed the deeper recesses. He was alone and he wished now that he had informed Isaacson of the meeting with Pete. The last few days had been difficult for him. The Olongapo trip, exposed to disheartening temptations, assaulted by enemies and angered by suspicions. Roberts had the innate ability to sense the connections of seemingly unrelated things and to find the truth in a maze of distractions. An ability that at once beguiled and emboldened him. Now his sensory antennae churned with intelligence. Diaz was the key.

Slam!

He jumped at the noise. Squeaking noises from a door locking mechanism being dogged-down. Someone had entered the spud locker and had locked the exit.

"Hello?" His voice sounded hollow.

Roberts could see a man standing there in the gloom, watching him. He waited. The man moved toward him and he heard a slapping noise.

"Is that you, Pete?"

Why had the man clapped his hands?

"Yes, sir. Hope I didn't frighten you, Mr. Roberts."

"Oh…good," he sighed. "No. But I'm glad sure you're here. I was getting worried. Should we go to the gun tub…think Diaz is there by now?"

"No. He won't be there."

"Well…what?" He heard the clap again and saw an object in Pete's hand. "Should we call it off."

"No, sir. Not yet. We still have some business to settle."

"Can't do much…without Diaz," he stammered. He was confused. Hair raised on Roberts' neck.

"He never was coming. It's really me you want to see anyway, Mr. Roberts."

"I don't…"

"Understand? Of course you don't. Not your fault, we've tricked you, I'm afraid."

"Who tricked me? What are you talking about, Pete?"

"All of us. Directly or indirectly. It should be clear to you by now. Isn't it? I'm the guy you're looking for, not Diaz. He just works for me….selling dope to the dopes." Pete laughed.

"Well, then why…"

"Are we here? Just the two of us?"

"Yes…us. You want to talk about it?"

"Confession?" Pete chuckled. "Repentance? Turn myself in…do the right thing?"

Pete stepped into the red glow. A grim smile on his ruddy face. He slapped the object into a palm and smiled directly at Roberts. Roberts saw the iron pipe, and now he understood why coincidences were always suspect.

"What's that for, Pete?"

"Actually, it's for you."

"I don't need…?"

"A piece of pipe. Sure, you do. Just like Franklin needed a piece of pipe."

"I guess you did him, huh?"

"Yep. Bopped him and dropped him. Right over the guardrail. Just where you're going pretty soon."

"Why?"

"Franklin? He screwed up. He talked too much. Had to go."

"No. Why me?"

"Oh. I see. You still don't get it. I got a nice little operation going here. We tried to scare you off, you know. I didn't want it to come to this, and I honestly tried to warn you. Talked until my teeth ached. But, you're stubborn. You were getting too close. I think you already knew Diaz wasn't running it, didn't you?"

"No. I didn't," he stammered. And Roberts thought of the consequences of carelessness. "I really thought we were going to trap Diaz and end it tonight."

"Too bad. Guess I overestimated you. But, it's too late now. How about stepping over to the guardrail, sir."

"You don't really think I'd come alone, do you, Pete?" Roberts calculated the odds that he could defend himself against the larger man. "Bobby Thomas will be here shortly." Not good, he concluded.

"Bobby Thomas? Oh! And Bryan too, I suppose." Pete laughed. "Where are they then, Mr. Roberts?" He spread his massive arms in mock dismay and slapped the pipe against the bulkhead.

Roberts eased toward the hatch. Boxed in.

"That's far enough, sir."

"Don't do this, Pete. I've got help coming, I wouldn't be such a damned fool, would I?"

"Yes, sir. I'm afraid you would. In fact, I counted on it, 'cause you've got guts. I saw that from the beginning. Besides, you thought it was just Diaz, or Bryan, or someone else. You were even worried about Mr. Thomas, I could tell by the way you been talking about him. So, he's not coming. But, you really didn't know about me?" he asked. "Guess I screwed up. You're not as smart as I thought. Anyway, this shouldn't have been necessary, but I just couldn't let you squeeze Diaz and you wouldn't back-off. I'd hoped the Olongapo thing'd scare you off. We tried but no luck…now this. Been a lot easier if you'd crashed into the water tonight." He waved the iron pipe in front of Roberts. "Guess what this is for?"

"What happened to Franklin?" *Stall for time.*

"This…only I despised that little nigger. You're different. I won't enjoy this so much."

"It doesn't have to be this way, Pete. I'm willing to cooperate. Maybe…we can cover it all up. I'm the only one who knows. Let me go."

"Why should I?"

"Because I want to live," Roberts pleaded. He was only an average fighter. No chance against the larger, stronger, intelligent man.

"Oh, I see. If you're the only one who knows, then who's coming to help?" Pete chuckled pleasantly. "Come on…don't you underestimate *me*, Dan. May I call you *Dan* under the circumstances?"

Roberts rushed toward Pete with fingers extended to gouge his eyes, a desperate move. Pete parried the thrust then crushed his shoulder blade with the heavy pipe. Agony shot through Roberts' shoulder, pain and numbness surged from head to knee. Roberts slumped to the deck.

"Don't make me hurt you no more, Dan. It don't have to be this way."

He struggled to his knees; Pete kicked his exposed belly. He felt the breath explode from his lungs. Dizziness. Breathless pain.

"I used to be a pretty good alley fighter, Dan. You probably never had the occasion, huh?"

"Bastard!" Roberts spit bloody saliva from a cut lip. His right arm hung limp and useless. He grasped the bulkhead with his left hand and forced himself into a crouch. He would die on his feet, the best he could do.

"Why, Pete?" he moaned.

"Why?" Pete gestured. "Oh, you mean, why all this?" He chuckled. "Money, of course! Isn't that always the reason? It's the money, dummy. I needed more."

"Money?" Roberts gasped. "You killed two squadron mates just for money?" *Keep talking. Stay alive. Survive.*

"Sure…why not? You saw the picture of my wife…young, classy. Beautiful, isn't she? Do you really think she loves a scruffy old bastard like me? I want her and I need the money to keep her, that's all. You get what you pay for in life, Dan. Simple."

"But, Pete…that's wrong. She'll leave you when the money's gone and then you'd be a murderer…for nothing."

"No, not *nothing*. You pansy-ass college boys just don't get it…what it's like for a guy like me. I'm smarter and better than most of you spoiled brats but I'm never going to be anything. Except, right now I've got the best looking broad in Berkeley and I intend to keep her as long as possible. If that means popping a few wise-asses, like you and Franklin, then I'll do it. I gotta right, too."

"My God, Pete. You can't buy loyalty. What good is a woman if you have to buy her?"

"That's bullshit, Dan. You can buy loyalty just like a loaf of bread. A beautiful woman is worth having any ol' way you can get her, and I want her! You don't know what it's like…trying to be as good as someone who has every advantage. I want…"

"Hell! You're just a damned murderer!" Roberts' shout was lost in din of ship's noises.

"Murderer? You got some nerve. How many people have you killed, Dan? Dozens? Hundreds? I've seen the debriefs. I killed one lousy nigger who tried to blackmail me and take over my business. You killed dozens of men, women and children…for what, American foreign policy? That's bullshit! And you call *me* the murderer." Pete laughed bitterly.

"No, you're wrong, Pete. It's different; I'm in a war. You killed Franklin and Williamson…for money…for nothing." His mind scrambled into survival mode. *Talk, keep talking.*

"Ha! What do you know about Williamson? I only killed Franklin. That damned nigger killed Williamson all by himself and that's what started this whole mess. I could've handled Ted Williamson. He was just curious, but Franklin talked too much. Williamson would have been easy to confuse or frighten off; he was more reasonable. Then, that goddamned Franklin taped over Williamson's static ports…thought of it all by himself…he wasn't completely stupid." Pete's eyes gleamed with arrogance.

"What? How the hell…?"

"Sure. Worked good, so I did the same to your aircraft tonight after I seen you weren't going to back off. But, Timothy Bryan will take the blame because of the dry-wash I smeared around after you landed. Careless preflight, you know. I'll give him a slap on the wrist, and then

I'll scare the shit outta him and put him back to work for me, as usual. He'll keep his mouth shut, or else. He's a good kid."

"What do you mean? You taped over my static ports? How...?"

"Easy. Plugged the ports. Stuck a piece of tape over each port during final-check before launch. I removed it on the elevator after you landed tonight, then smeared a little dry wash into the ports to shift the blame to Bryan. Neat, huh?"

"Jesus! Don't do this, Pete. You won't get away with it."

"Sure I will. And I don't intend to get into a metaphysical discussion of right and wrong; they don't exist. It's what works that counts."

"Pete...don't...you can't..." Roberts remembered a nude photo. A tantalizing pose. A girl too young and too beautiful. An expensive commodity for sale to the highest bidder, Pete. "Nothing is worth this."

"Wanna bet your life?" Pete laughed. He slapped the pipe against the guardrail.

Roberts had struggled to a standing position. One last chance to survive. One last fight left in him.

"Thing is...both of you dumb pilots could have solved the problem by breaking the glass on your rate-of-climb indicator giving you another static source. Didn't think of it, did you?"

"I can cover it all up, Pete. I promise." *Beg for time.*

"No, you won't, Dan. You're too honest, Bryan told me so, and I can see it in your face. But, you'll lie to live. We found that out in Olongapo. Too bad you aren't more like me...maybe if you were older you'd understand. We could've had a good thing going here. I could've used an officer...could really make this little enterprise work...marijuana, cocaine, booze. I can get anything and sell it to these dopes. Don't pretend to beg...that might'a worked in Olongapo but you don't fool me."

"I'll help you, Pete. I want to live. I have a wife too. I'll cooperate for half the profits..." he stammered. "I'd be providing the cover. Bryan would help me." *Talk. Keep talking!*

"Bryan? He's already helping." Pete smirked, now he'd seen it all, Roberts using his weakest asset for survival. Talk, delay, promise anything. Beg, plead. He had seen that particular ploy before. It would not work, not with him.

"The skipper trusts me, Pete. I...I got influence."

"So what? He trusts me too, more than you, even. No, Dan. Sorry, but I don't believe you. Anybody ever tell you that you're not a very convincing liar. All that stammering won't help you. Time's up. How do you want it?"

"What?"

"Do you want it the easy way or do I need to kick your butt a bit first, like Franklin? That guy was a fighter."

"I'm not going quietly, Pete."

"That's what I thought. Make all the noise you want. Nobody can hear you down here."

"This is wrong, Pete."

"Right or wrong, my back hurts...better get this over with so I can get some sleep before reveille. Alpha Strike in the morning. But, you won't be there."

"Wait! Think about it for a minute. This is...."

"An outrage? I suppose so, depends on your point of view. *I want more!* I been wet-nursing you pip-squeaks for too many years. I got my rights too. Good-old-Pete. Well, I don't feel very guilty."

"I think we could make a go of it, the two of us."

"Come on, turn around, Dan. Don't beg. I promise you won't feel a thing. I know how to do this. Just turn around for a second. I don't want to hurt you."

"That's great, Pete!" Roberts snorted. "You wanna kill me but you don't wanna hurt me."

"No. I don't. You're a squared-away guy. Too bad."

Pete lunged. Roberts feinted to the left...the iron pipe flailed past his head. Roberts kicked his kneecap and Pete fell screaming; an arm protecting his head from the blow that he knew was coming. Roberts' left fist grazed Pete's eyebrow, a spurt of blood. Roberts kicked Pete's ribcage then aimed another kick at the larger man's head. Pete rolled away gasping for breath. The red glow of the dropline lights reflected from his bloody eyebrow. Roberts stumbled to the dropline ladder. He jumped for the first rung, grasped at a higher rung with his injured arm.

Climb!

Red lights glowed, loud grunts, a moan, rude sounds of men locked in mortal combat. Roberts kicked at his opponent. Pete smashed Roberts to the deck…he hit the steel plate with an explosive grunt.

"Pretty good, Dan." Pete rubbed a fractured rib and gasped in pain. "You've got some spunk."

The chief lifted Roberts with one arm and leaned him carefully against the railing. Then, Pete lowered his right shoulder and plowed into Roberts' chest. Breath burst from his lungs and he fell to the deck in agony.

"Just like high school football, Dan."

Pete twisted Roberts' left arm into an armlock, slammed his face into the guardrail. Roberts moaned…he saw green water churned by huge propellers…stars danced merrily through pain-racked vision.

"You just don't have the size, Dan." Pete laughed. "I got fifty pounds on you. I kicked a lotta quarterback's asses just like that. You need a couple of guards in front of you."

The red dropline glow lent a surreal light to the green wake Roberts could see below the guardrail that was soaked with blood, his blood.

"It's over, Danny. Now I'm gonna pop you behind the ear and drop you into the ocean. Too bad. It could have been different."

Pete's tone was brisk, impatient. Reminding Roberts of another man in Olongapo with a distasteful job to finish.

"Go to hell, Pete!" he moaned.

"Sure, eventually…I'll see you there!"

Pete raised the pipe. Roberts closed his eyes and hoped that it wouldn't hurt. He waited. It was time to die.

The pipe clattered to the deck and Pete loosened the arm lock. Pete was going to lift him over the guardrail and drop him into the water alive to suffer just a little longer. Roberts prepared for the fall.

"You bastard!"

But, he did not fall, *Pete* did. Roberts stared dumfounded at the chief sprawled unconscious on the deck. Above his ear a bloody smear dribbled onto the deck.

"You OK, Dan?"

Bobby Thomas stood over Pete with a Smith and Wesson grasped by the barrel.

"Are you OK, Dan?"

Roberts grunted. "Oh, sure…I'm in great shape." Angry tears streamed across a cheek. His right arm hung limply at his side. Roberts wiped away at the tears and blood, and humiliation.

"Pete tried to kill me. I…"

"You're OK, now." Bobby leveled the revolver at Pete. "Pick up that pipe and stand behind me, Dan. Back away a bit."

Pete groaned, then struggled to his feet. "Almost had you, didn't I, Dan? Waited too long, I guess." He grasped the guardrail defiantly with both hands.

"Screw you, Pete."

Roberts raised the pipe in his left hand, took a step forward. Bobby, watching Pete, shoved Roberts brusquely.

"Dammit, Dan. I said stay back. He's trying to bait you. Don't get near him." Bobby backed toward the hatch, a flashlight in his left hand, the revolver pointed at Pete. "You shouldn't have done this, Pete."

"I gave him a chance to let me go, Bobby."

"Shut up, Dan," Thomas snarled. "You've done enough damage."

"What?"

"I suspected Pete and I worried about this, but I couldn't stop you. Isaacson wouldn't listen to me and I had to let you continue your foolish investigation. Now look at the goddamn mess we're in."

"I thought it was…Diaz."

"Diaz is too stupid to handle this kinda thing. I figured it was Pete after Williamson died. I just didn't know how he did it. Your little mishap tonight told the story."

"You did that to me?" Roberts glared at Bobby. "You hung me out there knowing about Pete?"

"Well, I watched your back pretty close, so did Herb. He told me about this little meeting…that's why I'm here. Now go get the Duty Officer and tell him to bring some handcuffs before I decide to shoot this bastard…that would be the simplest solution."

"Wait." Pete held up his hand. "I wanna say something."

"It's over, Chief." The flashlight illuminated Pete's bloody face. "Get down on the deck. If you move, I'll shoot you. I promise I will. I'd love to."

"I don't wanna go to the Brig."

"Brig?" Roberts blurted. "You're going to hang, asshole!"

"Shut up, Dan," Thomas said. "Don't give him a reason to be desperate."

"There's gotta be another way, Mr. Thomas. I don't want my wife to know about this. She shouldn't suffer. I want her to get my pension. Can't we work a deal?"

"Too late, Pete. If you hadn't killed Williamson and Franklin, maybe."

"No. Listen. I mean, what if I just disappeared too?"

Thomas thought for a moment. "I don't know, Pete. You hammered Roberts pretty bad. Look at him. Everyone will know…something… and you missing at sea, if that's what you mean. No, it won't work."

"Look. I'm begging you, sir. Think about it. It'll be better for everyone; me, you, the squadron…everyone, if I just disappeared. And Mr. Roberts could've fallen down a ladder or something…right?"

"What about *you*, goddammit?" Roberts rubbed his right arm.

"I'll just be missing, like Franklin...you're handling that investigation. You'll think of something...please, Mr. Roberts. I'm sorry I hurt you. You gave me no choice."

Just look at the bastard, Roberts thought. *Jutting chin, hunched shoulders, strong eyes that did not waver in defeat. A good man who had done evil things. An arrogant murderer begging for the easy out, suicide.*

"Please, Dan."

"You see, the thing is, Pete. I trusted you," Roberts said quietly, as if he couldn't believe he had been betrayed.

"Then you should have listened when I tried to warn you."

"I know." Suddenly, he was very tired. A moment passed, Roberts rubbed his forehead; he could not think clearly.

"I don't want my wife to know about all this, Mr. Roberts. Promise me that, will you?"

"Don't ask me anymore, goddammit."

"Mr. Thomas?"

"I dunno, Pete. Looks to me like you either gotta surrender, or jump." He handed the pistol to Roberts. "It's your call, Dan."

"Just give it up, Pete. Dammit!"

"No, sir. No surrender...shoot me now, Dan, or let me go."

"I don't wanna shoot you, Pete!"

"Then, gimme your word. I *trust* you."

"I don't know," Roberts said, knowing that he had been a fool, and knowing that several people had betrayed him. "Maybe I *could* bury it with the Franklin investigation."

"Thanks. I am sorry I hurt you, Dan."

"Go to hell, Pete." His voice cracked. There was no force remaining in the man who had been deceived.

"Yes, sir. Like I said before, I'll see you there." Pete climbed upon the guardrail, took one look back at the two officers standing in the shadowy spud locker.

"Pete….don't…for Christ's sake!" Roberts stumbled toward the railing. "Don't do it!"

Chief O'Leary gave a crisp salute and dropped over the fantail. He fell silently into the gray-green foam, struggled momentarily, then slipped beneath the churning wake.

"Pete!" Roberts screamed into the darkness.

They watched the wake. But the man who had needed more was gone.

"Sonofabitch…the…goddammit!" Roberts shouted and threw the pistol angrily into the sea. "I tried to talk him out of it, Bobby. I really tried."

"You, did what?" Thomas laughed bitterly. "*You tried to talk your way out?* Next time you decide to take on a heavyweight like Pete O'Leary, you'd better bring a better weapon."

Roberts gazed into the darkness, weighed by the layers of betrayal. Men he respected, and liked, had used him. Now he felt the pain and humiliation of his own inadequacy. The churning wake faded into night. Cassiopeia and the eternal heavens had witnessed his failures and he knew, soon everyone would know, that he'd gotten it all wrong.

Bobby Thomas thought he heard a stifled sob; he turned toward the hatch. "Imagine, Dan Roberts, talking," Thomas said, embarrassed.

"Shut up, Bobby….just for once, you bastard!"

"You must mean; 'shut-up-goddammit-you-bastard, *sir*?'"

"I'm sorry, Bobby," he stammered. "I'm…I've had…"

"A rough night? I'd say so."

Thomas stepped through the hatch. He looked back at Roberts' flint-hard stare. Roberts turned, watched the foamy wake drifting lazily into blackness, rubbed an injured shoulder absentmindedly.

"Bobby...?" He started to say something, thought better of it, then turned back to the darkness. He hunched his shoulders, picked up a short piece of iron pipe from the deck, and dropped it into the ocean.

"Come on, Dan," Thomas said. "Let's go stage an accident." He thought he might have been mistaken about the sob.

27

To: Capt. Eric Lambert, USS Sharpsburg.
From: Cdr. Gerald Isaacson, Commanding Officer, VA-433.
Subject: Board of Inquiry concerning the disappearances of Chief Peter O'Leary and A3c Alfred Franklin.

The Board convened on 15Nov1967. The Board consisted of Cdr. Isaacson, Lcdr. Thomas, Lt. Manley and Lt. Smithson. It interviewed four enlisted men and one officer concerning the disappearances of Chief O'Leary and Airman Franklin. See attachments for personal information.

Ens. Dan Roberts was directed by Cdr. Isaacson to conduct a preliminary investigation after the disappearance of Airman Franklin. For expediency his investigation was subsequently expanded to include Chief O'Leary. He concluded that both men committed suicide by jumping overboard. His report, while brief, could suggest no immediate cause for these men to commit such extreme acts, although drug abuse was suspected. While drug abuse may have occurred, Ens. Roberts could offer no tangible evidence to substantiate his conclusions, therefore the Board is inclined to disregard the larger scope of Ens. Roberts' suspicions.

It is believed that the arduous nature of sea duty, especially during war, may explain the unfortunate, but not unprecedented, deaths of these two valued shipmates. It is the conclusion of the Board that both men probably committed suicide for unknown personal reasons.

The Board, while generally concurring, determined that Ens. Roberts' investigations and brief report were incommensurate. Cdr. Isaacson has directed his division officer to counsel Ens. Roberts. Should subsequent events warrant, this Inquiry may be reopened.

I have enclosed Ens. Roberts' testimony for your review.

Respectfully submitted,

Cdr. Gerald Isaacson, USN

Transcript of testimony of Ens. Roberts.

Presiding officers: Cdr. Isaacson, Lcdr. Thomas, Lt. Manley and Lt. Smithson.

Submitted by Lt. Smithson, VA-433 Legal Affairs Officer.

Lt. Smithson: Mr. Roberts you've been called to testify about certain events surrounding the disappearances of Airman Franklin and Chief O'Leary. We have interviewed several enlisted personnel today. You are the last to testify. Do you have any knowledge that you would like to impart to the board before we begin?

Ens. Roberts: Yes, sir. I'd like to read this statement:
I was instructed by Cdr. Isaacson to investigate the disappearance of Airman Franklin when I first reported aboard VA-433. I did not know Franklin. The investigation was expanded last week to include the disappearance of Chief O'Leary. The cases were not related, but I had established a procedure and I am on medical release from flight status, so it was natural to combine my efforts. My conclusion in both cases was that they committed suicide for reasons unknown.

Lt. Smithson: Thank you for your statement. I have a few questions. Did you interrogate members of the squadron before reaching your conclusions?

Ens. Roberts: Yes, sir. Practically every man in the squadron.

Lt. Smithson: Did you find any evidence suggesting foul play?

Ens. Roberts: No, sir. No…I have no evidence.

Lt. Smithson: Did you talk to Airman Diaz?

Ens. Roberts: Yes, sir.

Lt. Smithson: And what did he tell you.

Ens. Roberts: Very little. Just that Airman Franklin was a good friend and that they went on liberty together.

Lt. Smithson: Did you ask him if Franklin had emotional problems?

Ens. Roberts: Yes, the answer was negative.

Lt. Smithson: Did you ask him if Franklin had ever used drugs or alcohol to excess?

Ens. Roberts: Yes. The answer was 'couple of beers.'

Lt. Smithson: Why did you ask that question?

Ens. Roberts: Well, I thought….I was just trying to get a feel for the man. I had never met him. I didn't…I'm new to the squadron. I didn't know him.

Lt. Smithson: Did you ask Diaz if Franklin had any contacts with Lt. Williamson?

Ens. Roberts: No, sir. Well, actually, I might have.

Lt. Smithson: How was that question relevant to your investigation?

Ens. Roberts: No definite reason, just curious. I was trying to....

Lt. Smithson: Curious about what? I implore you be straightforward with us Mr. Roberts. This is not a process to assign punishment. The Inquiry is mainly a forum for collecting information. You may testify as to hearsay and your personal opinions as the investigating officer, even if unsupported, are important to us. Now, why did you ask that particular question?

Ens. Roberts: It bothered me. The fact that the two men had died within days of one another. It seemed such a.....

Lt. Smithson: Coincidence, perhaps? But, why was that of interest?

Ens. Roberts: I'm...I'm not sure, it seemed strange. Later, I determined there was no connection.

Lt. Smithson: Did you also talk to Airman Bryan about this so-called coincidence?

Ens. Roberts: I think so. Probably I did.

Lt. Smithson: What did he tell you about Franklin?

Ens. Roberts: I don't recall.

Lt. Smithson: Let me refresh your memory. I'll read Airman Bryan's testimony. 'I told Mr. Roberts that Franklin would never have committed suicide.'

Ens. Roberts: Yes…now I remember.

Lt. Smithson: Do you think Franklin might have been involved with drugs or something of an illegal nature?

Ens. Roberts: I'm not… I thought it might have been possible.

Lt. Smithson: Why?

Ens. Roberts: I don't know. Intuition, I guess.

Lt. Smithson: You guess? Intuition prompted by what?

Ens. Roberts: Well, nothing definite I….I'm…

Lt. Smithson: Are you telling us everything, Mr. Roberts?
Ens. Roberts: Yes, sir. To the best of my ability.

(Pause: Lt. Smithson consulted with Board members)

Lt. Smithson: Let me remind you, this is not an UCMJ Trial or a Captain's Mast. It is simply an internal Squadron hearing to determine if further investigation is required. Your testimony is vital for this determination. We appreciate your efforts, thus far. You are under no threat here of disciplinary action, nor is any other member of this squadron. Do you understand?

Ens. Roberts: Yes, sir.

Lt. Smithson: So, you found no tangible evidence of drug usage by Franklin but you suspected it might have occurred. And, that may have been a cause for depression or anxiety leading to suicide. Is that it? Am I reading your report correctly?

Ens. Roberts: Yes, sir.

Lt. Smithson: Why isn't that stated clearly in your report? (Lt. Smithson submits the report for Ens. Roberts to examine.)

Ens. Roberts: I…I didn't think it was relevant. I had no evidence. It's so indefinite. I'm not sure…

Lt. Smithson: All right. Then let me ask you directly, do you believe Franklin used drugs?

Ens. Roberts: Yes, sir.

Lt. Smithson: What kind?

Ens. Roberts: Marijuana…maybe others.

Lt. Smithson: Why? Have you evidence of marijuana use by Franklin or any other member of VA-433?

Ens. Roberts: No. I'm not certain I can give you a reason…just a suspicion.

Lt. Smithson: Suspicion? Based on what?

Ens. Roberts: I don't know for sure. I guess you'd have to call it… I had suspicions.

Lt. Smithson: You have no evidence? You don't really know, do you?

Ens. Roberts: No, sir.

Lt. Smithson: All right. Now about Chief O'Leary. Your report suggests suicide also.

Ens. Roberts: Yes, sir. But I can't speak with any true authority. He just disappeared and...well...

Lt. Smithson: Do you think he was involved with drug usage.

Ens. Roberts: No, sir. I...well, I don't believe Chief O'Leary used drugs personally. I'm pretty certain of that.

Lt. Smithson: Personally? Did you know the chief quite well?

Ens. Roberts: Yes, sir. I'm new here but I worked closely with the chief every day in Maintenance.

Lt. Smithson: What did you think of him?

Ens. Roberts: I, well, I respected him.

Lt. Smithson: Let's talk about the night he disappeared. Where were you? I mean, when were you aware of his absence?

Ens. Roberts: I don't remember everything. I flew that night. Went to a movie in the wardroom later. I couldn't sleep so I went for a walk on the flight deck. He was reported missing at muster the next morning. I think that's when I first heard he was missing.

Lt. Smithson: Anything unusual happen that night?

Ens. Roberts: What? No, sir. Not that I recall.

Lt. Smithson: Seems you had an incident that night, isn't that so?

Ens. Roberts: Oh, yes. I did. I forgot.

Lt. Smithson: What happened?

Ens. Roberts: Instrument failure on a cat shot. Nothing much, really. Emergency landing.

Lt. Smithson: No, not that. You had some injuries, I believe?

Ens. Roberts: Oh, yes. I fell down the ladder near the flare locker on my way back to my room after the walk.

Lt. Smithson: Is this your medical record? (Lt. Smithson provided Ens. Roberts with his medical records.)

Ens. Roberts: Yes, sir.

Lt. Smithson: What is the nature of your injuries?

Ens. Roberts: Dislocated collarbone, cuts on my forehead and lip, a few bruises. Cracked ribs.

Lt. Smithson: Right. We've noticed your obvious discomfort. Let the record show that Ens. Roberts is still recovering from his injuries last week. What time did the accident occur?

Ens. Roberts: About midnight, I guess.

Lt. Smithson: Midnight? Then, why did you wait until 0515 to report to sick bay?

Ens. Roberts: Can't really remember. I went to my bunk…tried to sleep but felt kind of bad. So I went to sick bay later.

Lt. Smithson: Any witnesses to your accident?

Ens. Roberts: No, sir. I saw Lcdr. Thomas on the way to sick bay.

Lt. Smithson: But, that was at 0515. Didn't you think…oh, well, disregard that. You say you accidentally fell down the ladder?

Ens. Roberts: Yes, sir. I fell and then…I…

Lt. Smithson: Seems like you had a rather busy night. Do you remember anything else? Did you see the chief that night?

Ens. Roberts: No sir. I can't remember… I…well, sorry.

(Pause: Brief delay. Ens. Roberts paused to wipe perspiration from his face. Lt. Smithson conferred with Board members.)

Lcdr. Thomas: Just a moment, Lt. Smithson, before you resume. Are you all right, Mr. Roberts? Do you want a drink of water?

Ens. Roberts: No, sir. I'm OK.

Lcdr. Thomas: Do you want to recess for a few minutes? We can take a break if you need it.

Ens. Roberts: No, sir. I'm all right. I'm on some drugs…an anesthetic…antibiotics. It can cause some….discomfort according to Doc Swanson. I'd like to get this over with.

Cdr. Isaacson: You may proceed, Lt. Smithson. Let's finish this.

Lt. Smithson: You seem fairly certain about the chief. Did you have any relationship with Chief O'Leary, other than professional?

Ens. Roberts: No, sir.

Lt. Smithson: But, I gather you liked and respected him.

Ens. Roberts: Well…I'm… Yes, sir. I did.

Lt. Smithson: On the basis of your investigations, do you believe that he also committed suicide?

Ens. Roberts: Yes, sir. I do.

Lt. Smithson: Why? Can you offer any evidence? Something you may have failed to mention, perhaps. A note or verbal hints of suicide. Any medical or personal facts. Eyewitness reports. Do you have any knowledge not in your report? Anything? You must tell us if you do.

Ens. Roberts: No, sir. No evidence.

Lt. Smithson: Alright. So, let me understand this clearly, you contend that Airman Franklin probably committed suicide because of depression aggravated by drug addiction. Since no body was recovered you assume he jumped overboard. And, in the case of Chief O'Leary, you have also concluded that suicide is the probable cause of his disappearance, but you have no direct evidence of depression or drug addiction or any other facts to substantiate your conclusions. Am I correct?

Ens. Roberts: Well, yes. I….I'm…I guess so.

Lt. Smithson: Ens. Roberts, in all honesty, do you believe that you have done an adequate job of investigation in these two separate incidents? Is this report truly all you have for us?

Cdr. Isaacson: Lt. Smithson, there is no reason for sarcasm here. Just ask the questions, please. Mr. Roberts, you don't have to answer.

Ens. Roberts: Yes, but…I think…I *know* that I've done the best that I could under the circumstances.

Lt. Smithson: Please excuse the tone of my last question, Mr. Roberts. But, be advised that if the Board subsequently finds that you have withheld information, you may be recalled and these proceedings will resume. Are you certain you have nothing more to tell us? And, do you understand that you must tell us everything? You have a responsibility. This investigation must be concluded.

Ens. Roberts: Damn it! I've done all that. Look, I was ordered to find the truth and I did! I've done the best I could.

Lt. Smithson: Oh, I see. The truth? You've found it, but you can't substantiate it. Interesting. Well, I have no further questions.

(Pause: Brief consultation by Board)

Cdr. Isaacson: We want to thank you for your efforts, Ens. Roberts. When will you be returning to flight duty?

Ens. Roberts: Next week, Doc Swanson says…maybe.

Cdr. Isaacson: This has been difficult for you and we can tell you are still suffering from your recent accident. You may stand down. The Board thanks you for your efforts.

28

Dan Roberts' hand shook slightly as he reached for the Report, the cover-up that he had written. Four sets of eyes watched him with great interest.

He knew. Everyone knew.

His dilemma was this: He had been ill prepared. An effective liar must command certain assets; a quick tongue, a pathological mind, a remorse-less character. Ensign Dan Roberts, as it was now apparent to all present, including himself, possessed few of those qualities.

*   *   *

Bobby Thomas escorted Roberts to his quarters. They had not spoken. Thomas felt guilty.

"Don't let Roberts out of your sight today." Isaacson had ordered after the Inquiry. "He's a loose cannon until we get this thing buttoned-up."

"Better not dally, sir," Thomas grumbled.

"The report is going to Captain Lambert tomorrow."

"Signed and sealed, huh?"

"It's buried, I hope."

"The captain won't say a word."

"What about Roberts?" Isaacson asked.

"I doubt it, not his style. But we shouldn't have used him like that. I warned you, sir."

"Yes, well, it's over now. He's expendable."

"Now why the hell would you say something like that, Skipper?"

"He's a loner…not career material. He'll never be successful in the Navy and you know it."

"He's fiercely independent and maybe he's not very political but don't underestimate him. And, you're right, like many good pilots he's a solitary type. He tries to escape into himself," Thomas replied.

"Oh, I realize he can do the job and we need stubborn guys like him right now but I'm not going to lose any sleep over him."

"Do you really believe it's over, Skipper?"

"I will if you will." A nervous laugh. Isaacson stomped off to supervise the report. He would waste little time in delivering the cover-up directly to the Sharpsburg's captain.

Thomas watched Roberts closely. He sat at the desk, looked at his wife's photograph tapping his fingers nervously.

"Why'd you guys do that to me, Bobby?" he asked quietly.

"You were warned. Remember what I told you in the beginning. The Navy protects itself. Stick your neck out and it'll get chopped off. You did, and it did."

"Hell, yes. I get it now. You guys needed a flunky. And Smithson finally had his chance…the sonofabitch ambushed me." Roberts lip trembled. His face was flushed with anger. "Thing is…you guys made me feel guilty."

"Well, you're not."

"But, it's more than just Pete and the murders and the drugs, isn't it? I'm confused. We should be the good guys, but we're not. It's the war and all the stupid killing, I guess. I can't get a handle on it. Maybe we're all guilty? It's too…"

"Complex? Jung had something to say about this. A good man can do awful things and still not become inherently evil. It's the circumstances and the human predicament. The duality of man."

"You guys are trying to shift the guilt to me, aren't you?"

"Forget Smithson and the Inquest. You're the SLJO. Sure, you're taking the heat…burying the scandal. You're going to protect the squadron and Isaacson from reprimand. Think of yourself as a kind of martyr, if that makes you feel better. Everyone expects that. It's the breaks of Naval Air. I'll warn you again, don't fight it. You'll regret it if you do."

"Goddammit, Bobby. I already regret it. I did exactly what I was ordered to do. I didn't do…well, anything wrong, but I'm stuck with the blame for a phony report. I've got a real bad feeling about this." His voice faltered, face flushed, hands trembling with anger.

Thomas replied calmly, "Oh, you'll be OK. Don't forget that I write your fitness reports. You'll get a lotta Outstanding marks in the next one. Isaacson will have to knock them down a bit, but then I'll add an addendum to the final. Isaacson will be relieved on schedule at the end of the cruise and the Exec will assume command. All of your fitness reports after that are gonna have Outstanding marks; I guarantee it. I can protect you. Give it some time, you'll be OK." Thomas shrugged. "One advantage you've got is your notorious lack of eloquence. Just keep your mouth shut, which should be easy for you. Bide your time. Don't rock the boat. It's too late to turn back now."

"The chief had me beat-up and then he tried to kill me, Bobby….twice."

"I know, but he didn't. You're a lucky man. Herb says you're untouchable."

"Yeah, well, Herb's not always so…spent too many hours here in the Tranquillity Room. He's getting kinda goofy. He's just pretending to be sane, you know."

"Don't sell Herb short. He's got spunk. Anyway, this'll blow over shortly. There's an impossible war going on and people have short memories. The Navy doesn't want a scandal, especially a stupid drug scandal, right now."

"But, they don't know the *truth*, Bobby…they'll…well, they'll think I'm a screw-up. Everyone who reads that transcript will think I'm hiding something….*which I am*. My report is a complete lie! I *know* the truth, but now I'm just another Ensign Numb-nuts. Right?"

"Yeah. That's about it."

"Nobody will know about Williamson and Franklin being murdered or that I almost ended up in the water myself, twice; dead, dumb and forgotten. I even got beat-up in Olongapo. Nobody knows all that."

"Isaacson knows."

"WHAT?"

"I told him the next morning, to protect your ass, Danny."

Warm, humid air sloshed around by the fan. Roberts stared at his superior officer.

"But…dammit…Bobby, are you telling me that the skipper let me go through that hearing…you know, everybody thinking I'm a liar and a screw-up, and he knew all along. *He knew!* Why did he let Smithson…"

"Crucify you? Had to. I warned you, don't forget. You persisted. If this scandal gets out, Isaacson's career is finished. He's worked hard for twenty years; he didn't do anything wrong, either. But it's his Watch and he'll get the shaft and the squadron gets a black eye. Hell, we all do. The Navy protects itself; I told you that. You're it…the SLJO! You *have* got to take the fall on this one. You have no choice now. It's gone too far."

"My God, this is like a nightmare that doesn't go away in the morning. What's Isaacson going to do to me?"

"He asked me, and I've recommended two weeks in hack. The minimum. You're confined to quarters. Don't leave your room except for official business. You're shunned. Nobody talks to you socially. A steward will bring all your meals in here."

"Room service?"

"Hell, you'll probably love it. Being in hack is a slap on the wrist. A solitary like you can do that easy. A piece of cake."

"So, I'm a…pariah for two weeks and everybody else skates." He stuttered with anger. "What am I suppose to…"

"Of course, you'll be permitted to fly. Get your ass shot off like the rest of us." Thomas sleeved away the sweat from his face. The room was close. Warm humid air mingled with anguish. Both men knew the hopelessness of guilt. "You're not afraid of solitude, are you?"

"Actually, sometimes I prefer it."

"Well, you'd better start making a few friends around here. Especially now."

"See if I got this straight…nobody talks to me and I don't have to talk to them. Somebody brings me food and I get to fly. Is that it?"

"You got it."

"Sounds great."

Thomas examined Roberts' face for irony, but saw only an open, unabashed expression. "Don't you ever get lonesome, Dan?" he asked. "I mean, in that closed-loop little world you live in?"

"I'm in hack. The entire ship thinks I'm Ensign Stupid and forgets about all the rest of the shit. That's what you guys have to offer me?"

"Yep…that's the Navy way," Bobby said. He watched Roberts closely. This had to be finished quietly, today.

"Lonesome?" Roberts asked. "I guess I never think about it."

"I didn't think so."

"Well, think about this…it's not right. Isaacson told me he wanted the truth. He ordered me…pushed me hard to get it…and I got it for him. I know without a doubt what…what really happened to those three dead men. I could've busted that Inquiry wide open. I coulddda. Really, Bobby."

"I know that. And you know what? I think they all know, too. The whole damn ship. You did a good job, maybe too good. Now, keep your mouth shut and it'll all die quietly."

"Why am I…"

"The fall guy? Shit rolls down hill and you *are* the SLJO. You never heard of 'killing the messenger?'"

"What about Diaz. He knows a lot."

"Yes…well, that guy needs the Dutch Uncle treatment. Don't be surprised to see him working down in the boiler room for a while. That's a pretty effective attitude adjuster. I'll see that he gets a general discharge back in Alameda."

"We both get punished. He's guilty; I'm not."

"I'm glad you understand."

"Two weeks in hack?" Roberts grumbled. "Isolation. That's Herb's opinion of shipboard life."

"What's that?"

"Being on a Navy cruise is exactly like being in prison. Except no visitation rights and lousier food."

"Herb's right. You can do two weeks easily. Of course, I'll have to stop by your room occasionally to monitor your repentance. Skipper assigned counseling and guidance and such. By the way, how's your Scotch supply?"

A catapult rumbled overhead. The bulkhead rattled. Roberts replaced Helen's photo, which had fallen from the vibration. He fetched a bottle from his locker.

"The Tranquillity Room is never dry."

"There's hope for you yet, Danny," Thomas chuckled. "You're a good man."

That was the third time Roberts had been called a *good* man recently. He wondered, how could that be true?

29

Herb McGinnis had an honest appreciation of his abilities. He knew full well, modesty aside, that he could fly an A-4 with consummate skill. Tucked under CAG Ferris' wing, as he was now, he usually felt comfortable in an airplane. He glanced up at a flash of light. Sunlight gleaming from a polished canopy, an F-8 pilot doing a light-hearted aileron-roll in the distance. Herb was a fine pilot and in most situations would have been considered among the best.

He squeezed on a little RPM to compensate for the outside turn the airgroup was making for the bomb-run and widened out on the lead. He scanned the horizon, anticipating flak.

Herb knew that he was a superior pilot but it wasn't that simple. His problem was obvious to himself and others. A Naval Aviator's job was to fly high-performance aircraft from an aircraft carrier; day and night, fair weather or foul, in spite of the pitching deck, or the terrors of the night, or the unstable mirror, or any of the hundreds of little things that could obliterate the reckless. Feel your way down onto the deck, overcome all contingencies, and prevail. But it was the *uncertainty*, knowing the gut-wrenching dangers. The knowledge that so many uncontrol-lable things could go wrong and kill so easily had gotten to him.

Herb could fly an airplane with exquisite skill in combat. At this moment, only seconds from the target, he thought little of the impend-ing bomb-run. Of dropping bombs directly on target through flak bursts that seemed to flow directly into your gut. Of turbulent air filled with metal fragments and blackened by AAA bursts. He could perform lovely aerobatics with the delicate touch of a skilled technician. He could fly formation with the best. Air combat was natural for him. Had he been an Air Force or Marine Corps pilot, he would have been admired for his skills, but he was a Naval Aviator and he had a problem: Fear of the flight deck! It had come to control him. Herb had the fear and he boltered frequently and all of those superb abilities were over-looked. Instead of recognition for superior skills, he was known as *the pilot who boltered*. There was the rub: Herb was a Naval Aviator, and he did not do well around the ship.

Now Cdr. Ferris signaled and Herb prepared for the bomb-run. He was undeterred, unafraid of the bomb-run.

Master Arm switch "on".

Instead, he thought of the damned landing that would be required after the mission.

He had little fear of air combat. The SAM's. Flak. The possibility of MiGs hovering high over the target waiting to pounce. MiGs flown by competent, experienced North Korean pilots eager for a kill. But Herb was a skilled and aggressive combat pilot. The MiG pilots had more to fear from him.

Herb returned the signal to Cdr. Ferris. He was well prepared for the bomb-run or combat, that was not the problem.

It was the landing that worried him, even now. A fine bead of sweat dribbled down his brow. He was cursed with the imagination and the technical ability to foresee things that could kill so easily. A couple of feet too low over the round-down, too slow in close, a compressor-stall at the last second or just plain inordinate bad luck could cause him to be splattered in a ball of fire against the ship's fantail. All of these things came to him in his imagination. And that knowledge, coupled with physical tenseness during the carrier approach, is what caused Herb to bolter so often.

It was the fear. And it had him.

Herb followed Ferris through a series of swift evasive turns. Flak followed them. Black blossoms everywhere. Herb jinked left. CAG rolled to the right. Black puffs spotted the blue sky between them. He swore silently after a burst pushed his A-4 into steep turn.

Herb often thought of his roommate, a man of more pedestrian intelligence, and the irony of it all. Dan Roberts had little difficulty with carrier landings…he did not acknowledge or even comprehend the intricate physics involved. He simply did them.

Was it the imperturbability of an ordinary mind that gave Roberts such competence? Night blackness, or a pitching, rolling, rain-smeared deck did not phase him. Roberts was a thrill-seeker, restless, unimaginative, and instinctively eager for challenge. Seek the stimulation, ignore the danger and the landings became routine. Herb envied Roberts for his casual indifference but reviled him for his innocence.

Gun-Bomb selector to "Bombs".

The target was clearly visible in the verdant valley three miles below the airgroup. Herb rolled-in after CAG Ferris. Flak bursts sputtered harmlessly above; the gunners could not follow their rapid dive. The bombsight pipper floated slowly across the green tableau. CAG dropped his bombs. Herb saw a puff of smoke from CAG's tailpipe as he applied full power to escape. To climb to safety and survive. CAG's bombs would miss; he'd dropped too soon. His bombs would explode in the rice paddy leaving the target untouched, but available for Herb's precisely delivered bombs to finish the job.

Herb descended through ten thousand feet, normal drop altitude. His altimeter unwound rapidly. Slight airframe vibration…airspeed approaching redline. Nine thousand. Black puffs to the left. The gunners were finding the range. Eight thousand. The pipper drifted slowly onto the target, a fuel dump. Seven thousand. Bright tracer streaks rising. Six thousand, well below the standard drop altitude. He would destroy the target and in the debriefing everyone would be compelled to acknowledge that Ensign Herbert McGinnis had destroyed the target and forget about the goddamn bolters. Five thousand. A bright-white tracer round streaked past his canopy. Concentrate. Four thousand. Pipper directly on-target. Bombs away!

Full power. He pulled the A-4 into a gut-wrenching climb. Right rudder. Roll. Escape the black puffs and white fire-streaks. Dodge and weave. Confound the gunners and escape through the maze of flak bursts. The target would be destroyed by superior airmanship and he had done it. He felt contentment.

Thud!

The shock of an impact. Airframe vibration. No time to check for damage. Turn. Climb. Accelerate. Escape!

Climbing through fifteen thousand feet he glanced quickly at the instrument panel. The A-4 was responding to his demands. Turn and burn. Get away!

A bright streak below. Closing quickly on a collision course. A shrill warbling in his headset. Missile alert! A SAM!

Only seconds to evade. He could see the missile below accelerating through mach-two, tracking him. Closing rapidly. No relative motion…an intercept course. The bright-white smoke trail streaked upward like a telephone pole on a Roman candle intercepting him! Herb's skilled hands responded instinctively to the danger. Throttle to the forward stop. Slam the stick to the left. Turn against the SAM's flight path. Force the offset. Force the speeding SAM to overshoot.

Turn. Goddammit, turn!

Not enough, the SAM tracked accurately. He pushed the nose down directly at the incoming missile. Only seconds remained. Pull the stick back and kick hard right rudder into a high-G barrel roll, corkscrew around the missile's axis, force it to slide harmlessly through his desperate maneuver. Airframe shudder, wing-slats popped out. Buffeting. The angle-of-attack indicator flashed a stall warning! The SAM started a clumsy turn to follow the offset of his rapid roll. He grunted against the G-forces. A split-second to safety. Pull the stick, breach the stall, force the offset. Almost free, just a little more back stick, a tighter roll would do it.

The stick froze in his hand!

30

A bright flash!

The A-4's left wing disintegrated in a red gush of fuel detonation. His helmet bounced against the canopy. Herb was slammed upward into the canopy bow struggling against negative G-forces. Red lights flashing on the panel. Warning horns blaring.

Hands desperate to find the ejection handle!

Crushed into the seat. The A-4 tumbled from the sky. Alternating glimpses of blue sky and green earth. Vision blurred. Grayness. Disorientation. Panic. He struggled to read the altimeter. No time!

An eternity passed before his hand found the alternate ejection handle under the seat cushion. An explosion. The canopy blew away. A blast of frozen air. The rocket-seat propelled him out of the cockpit into an onrushing wall of air. Tumbling into cold, blue sky. Arms flailing, twisting painfully. Legs jammed behind the cushion. A harness strap slapped across his helmet, the oxygen mask ripped away, oxygen hose flapping wildly. The ejection-seat fell away. Wild gyrations. He tumbled, gasping for oxygen.

Falling!

Extraordinary sensations of deceleration. Plunging and slowing from the three hundred knot airspeed of the A-4 into the one hundred twenty-five knots terminal velocity of a falling object. Wind whipped under his visor and tears streamed from wind-blurred eyes. Herb groped wildly for the ripcord, unable to find it in the tumbling, tear-blinded fall. He clawed at his left shoulder harness. The earth rushed up. He screamed in desperation. And, then...

Floating!

Herb stared numbly at the white parachute canopy. It had deployed automatically when he had fallen through ten thousand feet. So easy, drifting slowly over a valley. Below him the green valley ambled south between two ridges and he could see a road skirting the eastern edge separating the steep ridge from rice paddies. He rubbed a sleeve across his face to clear away the tears, the mind-numbing confusion of the ejection. His arms ached.

Drifting.

A quiet peacefulness under the canopy. Arms and legs throbbed with pain. But he had been bent, not broken. Slowly his mind commanded the terror and he had much to do, if he was to survive.

Focus. Do the important things immediately. Do it now!

Check the parachute. The canopy had deployed normally and he was slowly drifting toward the east. Good! The road would ease his escape.

Where would he land? In a rice paddy, near the road. He must get out of the valley, into the trees and concealment.

What about enemy forces? The valley appeared to be deserted but he remembered a village, near the target, several miles to the north and he knew they would come for him. He felt the .38 Smith and Wesson in his shoulder holster. He would use it only if cornered.

Rescue? The PRT radio would provide communications with the Spads. They would know he was down, an A-4 had circled his parachute before climbing away. The Spads, Bobby Thomas and Roberts, were off-shore waiting to be called. They were at least fifty miles from the valley.

Fifteen minutes flight time. They would find him and call for the chopper. An hour for the Sikorsky to arrive.

Herb twisted in the harness to survey the valley. Less than a thousand feet to descend. Get ready!

Helmet secure. He would land in the dry rice paddy. Knees together, bent slightly to absorb landing shock. A short sprint across the road into the trees. PRT radio and water bottle secure in his harness. Think!

Land. Get out of the parachute harness, grab the survival pack, and run like hell! With luck he would be back on the Sharpsburg for dinner. What a story to tell.

The news media would report an A-4 downed, it would be on television. He must write to May tonight. She would be worried.

The ground rushed up. A gust of wind twisted the chute. He slammed into the soft earth. A wrenching shock. Pain shot through his leg…he screamed. And the canopy fluttered gently onto the paddy.

31

In a day filled with bad luck, Herb now had one good break. A short run to safety. He'd made it to the trees unobserved and that is what saved him from immediate capture.

He rubbed his ankle and surveyed the hideout he'd stumbled upon one hundred yards up the steep wooded hillside. A hole barely large enough for McGinnis' lanky frame, but deep and cool in the humid afternoon shade. By carefully pushing his legs toward the rear of the hole he could lie flat and peer through the thick brush concealing the cave's small entrance. He removed his helmet, then struggled out of the torso harness and G-suit. His ankle ached. He had landed just as he had been instructed but in the gusty wind he had stumbled on the slippery rice paddy, badly twisting his right ankle. After discarding the unnecessary flight gear, he took a small drink of cool water. A slight breeze billowed through the brush and he felt better.

Within minutes he heard excited voices filter up through the jungle. It hadn't taken long. The North Vietnamese had found the parachute and survival pack he had dropped in his painful escape from the paddy. Now he was trapped in a cave with a sprained ankle and he had dropped his personal survival pack containing a spare emergency radio, a water bottle, food, and extra .38 ammunition.

The immediate emotion was not fear, it was loneliness. He could not recall ever feeling quite so isolated. Most of his life had been spent in the close company of friends. Now he was completely alone, pursued by enemies and he must find a way to escape! How the hell would he manage that with a sprained ankle? He must devise an escape plan, and quickly, before the NVA found his trail.

But, what if he could not escape? Could he survive as a POW? Herb had studied reports of the men imprisoned in Hanoi, the more fortunate casualties. Other pilots trapped in the remotest regions of Laos and Cambodia faced far worse conditions where death was a blessing. And, many captured airmen were brutally murdered by local forces, never to become POWs.

He had led an admittedly privileged life and the POW dilemma unnerved him. Americans were never prepared to face a truly ruthless, cruel enemy. Foreigners imprisoned in America were treated with respect. He recalled a story told by a squadron mate of German U-boat prisoners interned at Papago Park near Phoenix. They lived in comfortable barracks and had excellent food but several planned and executed an escape in 1944. While most were captured immediately and returned in time for dinner, three men eluded the roundup and dashed into the desert hills. Hunger prompted one man to surrender in time for breakfast the next morning. Another slipped back *into* the camp unnoticed. Their leader, a stubborn U-boat captain, was the last hold out. Soon, even he tired of the adventure and walked unmolested into Phoenix, had a Chinese dinner, then fell asleep in a hotel lobby. Finally, a bored policeman woke him and inquired pleasantly if he was ready to surrender. "*Ja…*" the U-Boat Hero replied with a yawn. "*Why not. What have I got to lose?*"

Herb McGinnis, trapped in the Vietnamese jungle, had a great deal to lose. There would be little pleasantness if he were captured today.

And the trouble was, he did not really know *why* he was here. What had
Roberts said recently?

What do you think of the war, Dan…really think? Herb asked.

They'd talked at length late one night.

It stinks.

Why?

*It's got no rational motive except it's been started and …we gotta finish
it with some kinda…honor for the President…a lousy deal.* Roberts stammered, as usual.

You can't say that, Dan. Bobby says it's the only war we got.

That's crazy, Herb…I don't….

Buy it? If we had more than one war you could afford to be choosy.

That sounds exactly like ring-knocker bullshit to me.

*That's because you are just a Reserve officer, not Regular Navy. War is
why we exist. For Bobby and I there's no alternative. War is our karma.*

Herb, that's a load of…

Bullshit? Maybe, but we're stuck.

*But, I thought you were going home to be an architect…chase May
around the bedroom…raise a passel of redneck kids.*

*Dan, don't be such a complete mo-roon. Maybe later, but not now. That
would bore me to death. How can anything compare to this?*

You're a shallow, blood-thirsty Air-pirate.

The argument had ended in frustration for Herb.

Herb pulled May's photo from his breast pocket and studied it for
several moments; a sweet face floating into his memory, strangely out of
place in this dirty hole. She wasn't pretty and had never pretended to be
something that she was not. Still, she had an inner beauty that was difficult to describe even for a man of Herb's verbal acumen. After much
effort, the best he'd come up with was goodness. She was a truly *good*
person, even if she wasn't pretty.

He had made it a point to compliment May on something every day, anything would do. Anything to validate his affection for her. What had his mother said? One of her maxims that stuck in his mind.

Be sure to tell her she looks nice, especially when she does not. Even if it is a lie, it is a lie from the heart. God gives extra credit for those.

The photo had driven home the seriousness of his situation. A moment of quiet desperation. A knot of sorrow welled up in his throat and he wondered what it would be like to die in an enemy jungle.

It was just then that he heard the Spad!

A low rumble through the thick canopy of trees. The noise increased momentarily then drifted away and he heard the loud staccato of 20MM. Was the Spad driver strafing something in the valley below? He heard an explosion. The high-pitched stutter of AK-47s answered his question. He wrenched the PRT from his harness and extended the radio antenna.

"Mayday….mayday," he said slowly into the PRT. "Mayday…this is Faro Two. I'm on the ground. Skyraider…do you copy?"

32

"Roger, Faro Two. Read you…how me?"

The PRT screeched; Herb quickly turned down the volume. Dan Roberts! Herb recognized the hesitant voice and he shouted with joy.

"Loud and clear! You were just overhead my posit."

"Understand, Faro Two…do you recognize my voice?"

"Affirmative…Dan, affirmative."

Roberts tried to think clearly. His friend was down. Probably concealed in the jungle, but possibly captured with an Ak-47 to his head. He'd just strafed a group of black-pajamaed Vietnamese near the parachute but had not seen Herb. Bobby Thomas was orbiting the A-4 crash site several miles south where a dark ribbon of smoke billowed from the valley floor. Time to confirm that Herb was free.

"Faro Two, are you solo?"

"Roger…but I can hear bandits nearby."

"OK…listen up. Authenticate. What's the name of your homeroom?"

What?

Of course, Herb thought, Roberts wanted to know if he was speaking freely.

"The Tranquillity Room."

"Good. What's your condition?"

"I'm beat-up a little, and I'm holding a lousy pair of deuces at this table. I'm where Alice fell into Wonderland."

Roberts could see increasing traffic below on the road through the valley and Herb was in a hole with enemy forces nearby. Soon, the road would be as busy as Broadway if he continued circling over Herb's position.

"Faro Two…I'm Clara." *I can't see you.*

Herb radioed, "Check right." *Turn right slightly.* "IP in thirty seconds."

"Negative contact."

"I'm IFR." *I'm concealed.*

"Request mark."

"Check left, ten seconds…" Herb watched the Spad through the green canopy of trees. "…at Perch, now." *Directly overhead.*

"Roger…bad posit, Faro. Can you leapfrog?"

"Can do…give me some time…got damaged undercarriage."

"Be back with friends next cycle."

"Give me a vector, Dan…I'll rendezvous. Can't maintain current posit much longer."

Roberts struggled to find the words. The road below was filling with enemy. Herb's only escape route was east to the top of the ridge. How to tell him so that the NVA, who were probably monitoring with captured PRT's, wouldn't understand? Roberts knew he must contrive a coded instruction. The inarticulate man searched his imagination.

Knowing his shortcoming, Roberts scribbled the message on his kneeboard. Then keyed his mic.

"Faro, listen up for your clearance," Roberts radioed. *Say it quickly, don't give the NVA time to comprehend, don't stammer.*

"In order to effect a *Trap*, you must *Cat* to the *Perch*. Steer first three digits of your *Delta-Oscar-Bravo*. Copy?"

Herb McGinnis laughed before he keyed the mic.

"Copy…will launch ASAP."

"Roger. Careful…lotsa bandits in the valley."

"You bring the heavy stuff…I'll buy the beer."

"You're on. See you about Happy Hour."

Happy hour…late afternoon. Now Herb knew when and where. But, *how*?

A climb through primary forest to the limestone ridge would be difficult. He took a calming drink of water from the plastic bottle and laughed, but quietly, because he could hear searchers thrashing through the thick undergrowth below. Highpockets had briefed that most escapees traveled downhill and into the valleys because the densely forested hillsides were nearly impassable. The Vietnamese knew that fact from experience and that is where they would be searching for a frightened, lazy American pilot. He would be safer traveling uphill into the thick forest, difficult, but not unlike climbing the hills of North Carolina.

How had his roommate thought of the code so quickly? Herb hadn't expected such glibness, but it was easy to underestimate Dan Roberts. Perhaps Bobby had been correct about his roommate's reticence. Herb recalled one of his mother's maxims: *Remember, Herbert. If you don't talk, you won't say anything foolish.*

Herb chuckled. Only a Naval Aviator would have understood that cryptic message. Herb's mother would be fascinated by the elegant simplicity of his roommate's directive:

For a rescue (trap), you must move (cat), to the top of the ridge (perch). You must climb to the east (the first three digits of Herb's Date-Of-Birth). October 2….10/2, or 102 degrees. EAST!

33

Through an opening in the trees Herb could see the valley below filling with activity. Trucks careened down the dirt road toward the crash site trailing streams of dust. A distant, thin wisp of smoke from his A-4 curled into the blue afternoon sky. He could not see the parachute. Nor could he see the lost survival pack that he so desperately needed. He longed for a drink but he did not take the water bottle from his flight suit pocket. It could be a long afternoon and he must ration the water during the climb.

Herb decided to rest for a moment. Fallen leaves covered eons of hillside debris and provided a soft bed under towering trees. He leaned the broken branch that he used as crutch against a tree and closed his eyes. Fatigue surged through him and he might have slept except for the pain. He rubbed the twisted, throbbing ankle and felt every heart beat rushing blood into the injury. Loosen the boot to relieve the pressure? No, he would be unable to lace the boot later over his swollen ankle. He thought of the escape plan, determined to ignore the pain.

The ridge crest was another half-mile up the faint trail he had followed the last few minutes; he'd limped more than halfway up the hillside through thick undergrowth in two pain-filled hours. Now Herb would follow the easier trail to the ridge because pain had quickly sapped his stamina and he had little strength remaining for heavy going through the thick undergrowth. He'd noticed deer-like droppings on the trail that led down to watering holes in the valley, but no sign of human use, and he felt safe using the trail for the remainder of his trek.

Herb closed his eyes and tried to ignore the ankle. What had happened to his A-4's hydraulics? The control stick had frozen in his hand at a critical moment. AAA damage probably, a severed hydraulic line, an uncontrollable aircraft and dodging a SAM. Bad luck. But, it wasn't just bad luck, there was more to it than that; he knew the true cause. His own stupidity! He had descended too low.

Soft shadows caressed the hillside cut by shafts of brilliant sun-streaks through the tall trees into the mottled underbrush of dark green shrubs speckled with bright flowers. A green arboretum and beautiful in its way. His mother had loved the forest and she had instilled in him an early knowledge of nature's gifts, so he thought now of hunting on Carolina hillsides. Of gentle evenings. Of campfires burning and pungent smoke curling through treetops and bright red flames licking into darkness reflecting whisker-stubbled faces of uncles and friends. He'd enjoyed the hunting trips where game may, or may not, have been bagged. Now he understood the logic; what his mother had always known; the truth of living. *It is just being here that truly matters,* she'd said long ago. And he longed for home, to be there. A soft moan welled-up in his dry throat. Pain and sorrow hit him with a sudden fury, and he could not sleep.

The swollen ankle throbbed reminding him that this was his own fault. Damaged hydraulics and frozen controls and just plain damned foolishness had brought his A-4 down.

Move it!

He had gotten himself into this mess. Now he must dispense with self-pity and get himself to the top of the ridge, to the perch, so that

Roberts could lead others to his rescue, and save his intemperate, sorry ass. To relieve tension he forced himself to laugh at Roberts' message and to enjoy the knowledge that he had underestimated his friend again. *Must be more careful about Dan in the future,* he thought.

A sunburst flowed through the trees and flooded his face with warm brilliance. The bright reflection on his fair complexion in the dense, green background would be a beacon to the searchers. *Get up! Move up the trail.* He hobbled painfully onto the path. Crutch. Step. Crutch. Step.

After a quarter-mile he paused to rest. The path meandered around a fallen tree where thick blue-green grass covered the broken ground in patchy mantles. He leaned against the tree and took a swig of water. Cool freshness. Regeneration. It surged through him and in its gratification he forgot for an instant, the pain and anger and frustration of personal folly.

Roberts should be returning in an hour or so. *Happy Hour!* He estimated thirty minutes to the rocky ridge top he glimpsed through the green thickness. *Time to go.* He pushed off with the crutch and limped toward the final stretch of trail. *Think.* Careful preparation would be necessary on the ridge. *Plan. Be ready!* A small clearing would be wonderful. The chopper would land and helping hands would pull him to safety. They would have water, and food and anesthetic for the pain. But he must not think of the pain now. Later, when he was safe he could indulge the pain, but not now. Now he must think only of survival. His stomach gnawed at the knowledge that his survival pack had contained emergency rations. The chopper crew would have a bottle of medicinal brandy. He would take it, if offered, and celebrate. *Happy Hour!*

He would find a spot. A place of quiet concealment. The emergency PRT radio must be ready to call in the chopper. And, when he got to the perch he would have another drink of water, a large drink...rescue would be imminent and he could afford the luxury and that is all that he had with which to celebrate. And he thought that he would sleep for a few minutes on the top, or until the noisy chopper woke him. He was weak from fatigue. Never during sports, or exercising, or doing chores at his mother's house could he recall such exhaustion.

What if there was no clearing for the chopper? He would not think about that now. Later, he would face that problem if necessary, now he must concentrate on reaching the ridge.

But, what if the chopper could not land?

He must think about it now. If the chopper could not land, then an opening in the trees would have to do. The crew would drop the rescue sling and somehow he would struggle into it, to be hoisted through rotor downwash into the chopper, and safety. What if they could not see him inside the forest density? The ridge would be open, he hoped. *Must be open!* And there would be a clearing. He willed it to be open. It must be!

But, what if there was no clearing? He did not know what he would do, but he would do something.

The trail curved sharply around a weathered rock outcropping, and up to the final steep thrust of limestone that crowned the sunbathed mountain ridge. Refreshed by the knowledge that the crest and rescue were so near and muttering little noises of self-encouragement, he hobbled around the rock and stumbled directly into the path of two Vietnamese men.

He heard a cough.

It happened too fast! Later he would recall with disturbing clarity how the moment spun out of control. A split-second that rolled endlessly. Rapid decisions were made. Three men trapped in a whirlwind. The older black-clad Vietnamese stood momentarily, wide-eyed, speechless. Herb held up his free hand in a senseless, friendly wave.

"Ahhhiiii!" The younger man screamed. Fear and uncertainty exploded into elemental action. The older man rushed forward with a raised machete. Herb fumbled the Smith and Wesson from his shoulder holster and killed him with one point-blank shot. The younger man turned to flee. He fired again. The man screamed. Herb dropped him with a quick shot that blew away a chunk of leg. Piercing wails of pain and fear penetrated the forest.

"Stop it!" Herb shrieked. He fired into the man's forehead. The screaming stopped. But not the echoes. The screams, the pistol shots, reverberated against the ridge into a jumbled eruption that blended in hopeless confusion and ricocheted down the canyons. Warm, tropical air carried the sounds of death and brutality and desperation down to the valley.

Binoculars scanned the ridge high above the valley floor. Orders were issued. NVA soldiers hurried. A flatbed truck with a 37mm gun sped down the road trailing a stream of dust.

Herb wiped sweat from his face and glanced up at the crest; he'd almost made it undetected, and now this. He looked down at the men he had killed. Blood and gore oozed from a shattered face. How could he have done such a thing? He vomited into the dust, then turned and limped slowly up the trail.

34

It was a day when everything happened quickly.

Now the day was almost finished and Herb McGinnis regretted every terrible moment. Enemy soldiers had died quickly. Moments earlier his rescuers had perished just as quickly…their pitiful screams had lasted only seconds and then ended in an awful silence. Echoes of their torment now silent in the helicopter's burning hulk on the hillside below his rocky summit. An intense bright-red flame shot into the smoky sky and he thought it must be the worst kind of death. As a child he had been burned while playing near a campfire and had recently witnessed a pilot's fiery death after a ramp strike. Now he had seen the horror again. Smoke billowed up the slope into his hiding place and filtered a tropical sunset into splashes of blood-red sunbursts. He felt personal responsibility for the slaughter and the clamorous bloodletting and destruction on the hillside below his stronghold. The rescue mission had quickly collapsed into utter failure. And it was his fault!

The helicopter burned furiously and they were finished. Herb realized now that he was finished too. A solitary Spad circled his position. Dan Roberts, the lone survivor of his rescue team, waggled his wings as he passed over Herb's rocky fortress, a silent communication between friends. Encouragement? Condolences? What did it matter? They had failed! The helicopter was destroyed and Bobby Thomas had fled with a smoking engine.

He'd watched Roberts drop napalm on the NVA truck down in the valley. A fireball filled the darkening sky. AAA ammunition still popped sporadically. The final violent spasms of fiery deaths of innocent men, friend and foe. He must bear the guilt; his damned foolish pride was to blame.

It had happened too quickly.

He hadn't been prepared. In fact, he had been asleep before they came, exhausted by the pain and effort and fear and remorse of his self-imposed predicament. The two Skyraiders had come without warning. Thundering over his position. Engines roaring. Awakening him with a cacophony of sounds that enveloped the rocky outcropping. Noises echoing down the canyon. He had grabbed the PRT and radioed to them gleefully.

"Faro Two is here…you just passed overhead!"

"Roger, Faro…." Roberts replied. A hesitant drawl. "Time to authenticate. What's your girl's name?"

"May! And I'm four-point-ohh, Dan. I'm on the ridge top." He gave Roberts his exact position. Roberts consulted with Thomas, then called for the chopper, and the nightmare continued.

He remembered it all.

*   *   *

After the brief, terrible encounter below the outcropping, Herb had staggered to the mountaintop. It had been quiet in the valley below Herb's ridge. So quiet that Herb napped after removing his right boot. The swollen ankle throbbed with pain but it felt better without the boot and Herb thought he could run if required. He would do whatever was necessary when they came.

An up-thrust of limestone had eroded into a small rock-strewn fortress on the bare mountaintop. Here the ridge formed a long narrow spine of exposed rock above the jungle that crept relentlessly up the hillside. Steep cliffs fell hundreds of feet from his narrow sanctuary down to leafy treetops forming a barrier on both sides of the spine. He had hidden in the crest's rocky enclave, a tumble of massive gravestones on the sharp ridge, and waited. So tired…

In his exhaustion he'd fallen into a deep slumber. Disjointed dreams of his childhood home, a shimmering image in Carolina woods. His mother waved from a shady porch. Relatives and friends drifted in ethereal focus. Gauzy, familiar, happy images.

She was there…

Such joy! Nervousness, too! The pageantry of a Naval wedding. They waited at the altar for May to appear and Herb thought he would explode. Did it show? Friends and relatives smiling at him, nervous laughter in the chapel. Dan Roberts smiling awkwardly, the best man in dress whites fiddling with the tassel on his sword. Helen Roberts sitting in the front row next to his mother. Then she appeared.

May's father kissed her gently, then handed her to him. She looked up, so small next to his lanky frame and he felt a burgeoning lump in his throat. Shimmering colors. A white wedding dress resplendent in the afternoon sun. Dazzling sunbursts through towering chapel windows. Brilliant white dress uniforms with swords gleaming in ceremonial promise. He smiled at May, who was almost pretty in her wedding dress and her mother's pearls. Bright eyes flashing, she stroked the sleeve of his dress whites and murmured something.

His heart pounded. The noise! Could anyone hear? Louder and louder, his pulsating heart would betray his secret, so loud that it sounded like an aircraft engine. He held his breath to stifle the self-consciousness. Then came the thunder…

A crackling of lightning! It made no sense. A bright flash! May looked up tentatively. An explosion! What was happening? Her eyes closed. She smiled. Dan Roberts started to say something…the PRT awakened him.

"Faro Two. Do you copy?"

From beauty he'd awakened to nightmare.

Now it was all cannon fire and flame. AAA streamed up from the valley. Red flashes in black puffs. Pilots' frenetic radio transmissions. The hillside erupted in a fiery ambush. A stream of bright tracer swept into the chopper. One of the Spads was hit and staggered away leaving a smoky trail.

Herb watched the Sikorsky spin into the trees. Flashes of exploding ordnance pierced the smoke-filled sky. Screams of agony from within the inferno. Intense flames fed by helicopter fuel torched the forested hillside. Underbrush ablaze from the chopper's burning kerosene licking skyward into trees that ignited into giant crackling matchsticks. Black smoke poured from the jungle canopy marking the conflict.

Ammo from the crumpled door-gunners station popped like firecrackers and each time he looked to see if a crewmember had survived. But, he knew they had not. How many men did the chopper carry? Five? He could not remember! He did not know how many men had perished while trying to save him. Five men in the chopper and the Spad with the smoking engine. Was that Bobby Thomas? Would he make it back to the ship?

A shrill whistle to his left. The NVA ground forces were surrounding him. But where was he going anyway? The cliff behind him was impassable and the ravine in front made escape impossible. And of course there was the awkward fact of his busted ankle. But the Vietnamese would not know about that. So they were boxing him in on both ends of the narrow ridge. When the sun went down they would come for him. He had twenty minutes, thirty at the most, and then they would rush his position. What would he do? Captivity had little appeal for Herb. Torture and a slow death. He had heard of their more interesting execution methods and he wanted no part of that. Herb could not stand humiliation and he feared pain. He looked up. The last Spad circled his position, no need for deception now. His location was obvious. The radio crackled…

"Herb, listen…we'll be back tomorrow morning…hide somewhere. I gotta go check on Bobby now."

Damn, Roberts, he thought. *Didn't he get it?*

"They're about to rush me, Dan. It's almost over…don't come back again. Go take care of Bobby."

"Goddammit, Herb…hide! We'll…we will be back tomorrow. I'll get some more help. I'll be back." Roberts radio voice sounded thin, desperate.

It would have been better if he had died in the A-4. Herb thought of the two unfortunate men on the trail he had killed. The terrible screams of fear and pain. The burning helicopter. The echoes…

"No! Don't come back, Dan. I don't want any more killing. I'm gonna finish it myself," he paused. "So long, Danny boy." There was nothing more to say.

"Wait! Herb…don't do it…listen! I think we could…"

CLICK!

Herb switched off the radio. Never could win an argument with Dan Roberts, that pugnacious ass irritated him but his cruel logic had been correct. Herb had chosen to be part of an irrational war. *In for a dime, in for your life, we're stuck,* Roberts had said. Naval Aviators were volunteers and could quit at anytime. But if you wanted to be a Naval Aviator now, to have the prestige and honor that came from that position, you had to fly missions against North Vietnam whether you recognized the validity of Congress' decisions or not. Roberts might have been correct but no professional sailor could admit it, especially an Academy graduate. He was a volunteer and his job was the delivery of 20th century high-technology weapons onto the heads of 12th century peasants. Roberts had been right, but it still pissed him off. They'd argued recently:

"Then, why are you here, Dan? Can you tell me?" Herb had baited him.

"Who the hell knows?"

"I know." Herb had laughed and pointed a finger derisively. "You're here because of love."

"What a dumb...."

"Sure you are. Think about it. Men love various things like women, power, money, fame. But some guys love objects. You love airplanes and that's what brought you here. Isn't it?"

"I don't have a...."

"Clue? Of course you don't." Herb chuckled at the recollection. "Mr. Numb-tongue. Bet you were looking up into the sky for airplanes before you graduated out of diapers, weren't you?"

"Herb, you're so full of...."

"Crap? Have you ever noticed how I finish most of your sentences for you?"

"Shut up."

"Want to know why?"

"No."

"Good. I'll tell you. Impatience. You're the most inarticulate sono-fabitch I've ever known."

"I only get tongue-tied when I'm talking to a jerk...like you."

"You couldn't talk your way into a Bangkok whorehouse with a fist full of fifties."

Roberts laughed. "That's the nicest thing you've ever said to me."

"Laugh if you dare." Herb pressed on. "But that doesn't detract from the fact that I'm right. Nothing quite compares with a natural pilot's love for an airplane...any good fighter or bomber will do. You'll stay because you love flying and this is the only show in town. I'm here because I'm a professional. You're here because you love it."

"Maybe. I'll tell you one thing though. I don't love those goddam politicians. They could have gotten us a better war."

The debate ended with the kind of incisive but outrageous comment only Roberts would make. A man with a speech impairment. A man Herb had ridiculed, had spoken wisdom.

Keep at least one truthful person around you, Herbert, someone to keep you humble. His mother's smooth logic.

Dan Roberts, his best friend, had always been such a pain in the ass.

He watched Roberts' Spad disappear behind the ridge, and then Herb smashed the PRT radio with a rock and tossed it over the cliff. It clattered down the rocky hillside and he knew it was the ending of something, a finality. A few yards beyond his fortress an NVA soldier peeked around a boulder at the noise. Careless of him, Herb thought. He checked the revolver, two rounds remained, one to spare.

Why not? What have I got to lose?

The NVA could not see him in the twilight; a jumble of rocks protected him on all sides. He leveled the revolver and cocked the hammer. He watched for movement, little usable daylight remained. In the sunset of the day when things happened quickly, he picked up a rock and threw it into the brush and the soldier's face quickly reappeared. Herb's bullet punched out his left eye. A scream. A volley of small arms fire. Loud laughter burst from his rocky preserve. Angry shouts from surrounding soldiers. Echoes of the small conflict in the ravine.

Echoes…

Several seconds later three blasts from a whistle silenced the AK-47s. Herb waited. Why hadn't they tossed a grenade into his lair, the conventional method of dislodgment? They had chosen to wait and Herb's logical mind knew why. When it was dark, they would close in on the hated Yankee Air Pirate, capture him and exact a lengthy revenge.

Highpockets had been quite forthright in warning the pilots of barbaric interrogations, an excuse for torture and slow death.

The sun slid below the horizon in a blood-red glow of finality. The end of an endless day. A foul odor drifted up the ridge from rice paddies fertilized with human and animal waste. A murky haze in the lower valley crept up the slope in the cooling evening air and Herb admired the beauty of the tropical expanse beneath his blood-soaked ridge. Small irrigated rice fields sectioned the flat valley floor into a green checkerboard and small paths meandered here and there. *Pretty country*, he thought. It seemed the wrong place for a battleground. More like home than a killing-field.

Home! Remembering. Translucent images. Glorious autumn evenings in his beloved North Carolina hills, happy evenings of peaceful joy, his mother and their friends. The pleasant fatigue that came after hunting in the hills or after football games with beer and hotdogs. Friends laughing about a fumbled football; *his* infamous high-school fumble. Gauzy images floated through his memory. Joyous times. God, how his ankle hurt...

Sorrow washed over the injured pilot. He unzipped a pocket and removed May's last letter and her photograph that he carried for good luck. They hadn't helped today, though. No luck for his A-4, or the helicopter crew, or Bobby, or the North Vietnamese they had killed.

How many Vietnamese had he killed today? The two unfortunate men on the trail and the careless soldier. His bombs and the secondary explosions probably had killed many more. He had seen figures scurrying in his bombsight just before he had pickled hundreds of pounds of high explosive onto their fuel dump. How many had been killed by Bobby Thomas and Dan Roberts on the rocky ridge and valley?

He thought about Bobby and his smoking Spad...another doomed pilot? How many had died today because of his foolishness? Died because he had known that after the bombing *it* would be there waiting.

The ship and the fear and the need to compensate. How many? Fifty? A hundred? And Roberts, the damn fool, might decide to come back and hang around killing Vietnamese until he ran out of ammunition.

More killing...

Herb opened May's letter in the evening's soft glow that was slowly blending into deepening purple twilight. He had received it from May last week, after he had sent her the engagement ring. Delicate penmanship. Fine swooping loops of capital letters to emphasize an important point. Pink lipstick where she had imprinted a kiss. A last reading.

It seemed important:

Dear Herbert,

Yes! I accept!!!

The ring is Beautiful. But, you should not have spent so much. I know Navy Ensigns don't make very much MONEY. Daddy told me so.

Everyone is so excited. *Me most of all.* I wish the war would end today and you could come home right now. Don't you?

I'm so confused about it tho. People here are awful. They protest on campus every day and call the military terrible names. I try to stand up for you and I tell my friends you don't want to be there either, but they don't seem to care. Sometimes I think they are just doing it for fun. Oh well!

If you are coming home for Christmas, couldn't we get Married then?

Married!!!

Isn't that such a neat word? Daddy said we should get married in the Navy Chapel at Norfolk. Would you like that? I think it would be nice.

Daddy is going with me next week to buy my WEDDING DRESS. Isn't that Wonderful!!!

Enclosed is a photo of my smiling, ENGAGED, face so you won't forget me!

I wish Mom was still alive, she would have loved seeing you and me. She always liked you.

Herb, be careful. Please come home soon.

Love, May

35

Bobby Thomas thought with a little luck he might survive. He struggled to adjust the throttle, easing power back slightly with his right hand to reduce the strain on his damaged engine. It was missing badly now and a thick oil smear covered the windscreen. It would be difficult to see the ship's mirror. *Divert to Danang?* No, it was too far and the pain was too great; he could tolerate it much longer. Wind whistled through a ragged hole in his canopy where AAA fragments burst through shattering his left hand before tearing into his thigh. He rested the mutilated hand on his lap to ease the pain. Blood streamed onto his flight suit from his hand and flowed freely from his lacerated thigh. The cockpit floor was a red smear.

The engine knocked constantly sending a vibration through the entire airframe. Nausea and pain. He avoided looking at the hand. The lesser fingers and palm had been severed completely, stubby white spikes of bone protruded from his glove. A bloody mass lay on the floorboard below his blood-soaked knee. The thumb was undamaged but his index finger was shredded and he knew the hand would be of little use to him. The approach and landing would be difficult. He would be forced to pre-position a final throttle setting with his right hand, then work the glideslope with pitch control alone, airspeed would vary, but if he was lucky…

Must staunch the blood-flow!

Bobby wrapped the mangled hand in a handkerchief and tied it off using his teeth and right hand. *Oh, God! How it hurts!* He felt light-headed from pain and blood loss. It must end soon; he felt dizzy and increasingly disoriented. He had damn little time. Was shock setting in? Dan Roberts had remained to destroy the AAA guns on the truck that had destroyed the chopper and damaged his Spad. He had seen Roberts dropping napalm in the valley. The AAA truck was probably demolished now, but too late for the annihilated chopper and its crew. And he would be lucky to make it back to the ship before passing out. Herb McGinnis was still on the ridge and Roberts still being battered by ground fire.

A lousy day. He remembered it all:

Hazy visions of men hastily assembling a desperate plan. A rescue mission thrown together by Roberts and himself and Highpockets. *Goddammit! No time…* They'd gotten a Sikorsky rescue chopper diverted from the Coral Sea and they tagged on after an Alpha Strike launch. Roberts knew Herb's position and he led the rescue flight. Bobby flew wing. They joined the Sikorsky and flew into the green holocaust. No time for a proper plan.

Hey, Highpockets, is this why they call it a briefing…so brief? Ha…Ha…

Time will work against Herb, Highpockets had said. So, lets get going now, Roberts had replied. And how about some help? Bobby insisted. Can't do it, another mission with the airgroup…too important…you'll have to go alone and if there isn't much opposition, a chopper and two Spads will suffice, Highpockets said. Well, I didn't see anyone near the ridge, Roberts said. Good, then you can do it, Highpockets replied. Easy for you to say, Bobby scoffed.

And they had launched; two Spads loaded to the gills with ordnance and the Sikorsky. Bobby had Mk-82 frags and rockets, Roberts had napalm and the Sikorsky had a door gunner.

It should have worked.

They skimmed over the rocky ridge and located Herb immediately and it was quiet. No troops milling around, no ground fire. The green forest crept up the hillside on both sides of Herb's lofty perch, no enemy forces to be seen under its verdant density. It could have worked.

"What do you think?" Roberts radioed after he'd talked to Herb.

What did I think? Bobby laughed in bitter recollection. *A pile of shit…a stinking trap…we should have known!* His hand throbbed. Blood spurted from his thigh…no way to bandage it…no time. He pressed his throbbing mangled left hand on the gash to slow the bleeding.

They'd flown over Herb's position and Bobby looked down into Herb's rocky fortress and it had looked easy. But, it was never easy. He should have known and he was angry with himself and the memory of his failure.

"Let's go…make it quick."

Roberts called in the helicopter. It moved in quickly, hovered over the ridge and deployed the rescue sling. Herb appeared from the rocks and waved in Bobby's bloody recollections.

Then Bobby saw movement in the valley.

Abort! He'd screamed into the mic.

Too late. The sky erupted. Bright streaks of tracer sprayed into the chopper. Red flashes in black puffs of AAA covered the sky and he was hit immediately, his Spad bucked from a black eruption. The Sikorsky exploded! A fiery mass, swirling in uncontrolled circles, crashing into the hillside. A final tortured explosion and the Sikorsky rolled down the hillside in a fireball of twisted exploding metal.

Bobby had to reach across with his right hand to key the mic. *"Dan, I'm hit!"* The bloody, distorted remnant of a hand lying there, a mess. The slow-motion, abnormal, extraordinary realization of shock and pain. He had stared in disbelief. Blood splattered the cockpit.

Roberts' voice, quiet, hesitant. "Goddammit...take off, Bobby. I'll finish this...catch up with you."

And he had.

Now Roberts was miles behind, but he knew Roberts would find his smoking Spad and escort him to the ship. Bobby had confidence in his wingman.

But, what about Herb? He'd inquired.

He's finished, now, Roberts radioed. A simple statement. Just like Roberts, Bobby thought. Blunt, tactless, to the point. An aggravating quality until, after the Inquiry, he had recognized through the artlessness of Roberts' speech the complexity of his wingman's intellect.

The sun was setting in a bright red smear behind his right shoulder, darkening sky ahead. Blood dripped from the bandage. The deep-blue gulf merged indistinctly into the dense lavender of the eastern horizon. *Hurry!* The landing would be difficult in twilight, impossible in darkness and he did not know if he could last. The agony!

Wham! He jumped at the noise. Cowling tore away from the engine in a final violent spasm. A spray of oil splattered the windscreen. Severe airframe vibration. He could smell fuel. The stick felt heavy. Yawing to the left...he could not reach the rudder trim near his blood-soaked left knee. He jammed the right rudder. The engine coughed, another loud bang, a smoky explosion, ripping itself apart, fragments slammed against the wing. Black smoke swirled over the canopy blinding him. Confusion and pain. Darkness surrounded his anguish.

And then it was quiet.

36

Major Binh was an energetic man given to frequent bouts of eagerness and he had become bored with counting airplanes. His mental acumen, attuned to the exigencies of a warrior, had found little satisfaction in reconnaissance duty. But he would not return to the long war that had burned such awful scars into his memories. Torn bodies of allies and enemies merged into the horrors residing in the catacombs of his mind. The darkness. The terrors. The war that had formed him and made him into the monster he had witnessed in his dreams. Vivid recollections of anger, of unmentionable horrors, of three murderous decades had reduced him to despair. He was summoned to this question: *How could a schoolteacher, a husband and father, have evolved into this man he now despised?*

He'd begun as a lowly guerrilla fighter against the French and had killed eagerly for revenge and statehood. Idealism…perhaps? Murder…definitely? Killing had become his natural occupation and he had loved it! He had become so easily that which he now hated. He had tortured and maimed the French and each event erased a little of the sorrow. His wife, his child; their ghosts must have witnessed his revenge. And he'd killed Americans with equal fervor. He had grown in the occupation and soon his abilities were discovered. A shrewd mind. Complete ruthlessness. A knack for interrogation, an ability to see through the fog and deception of war. Questions…answers…lies…truth…intuition…and then…*Perception!*

A natural talent had made him an intelligence officer and he had given able and loyal service to the cause. Knowing the enemy mind and seeing truth through lies had made of him a hunter and killer of men. Until recently.

Now he was a mere observer of ships and airplanes and he would continue with the boredom because he had vowed to himself and the memory of his wife that he would kill no more. Binh would find peace and he knew how the elusive blessing would come. Such a simple thing, but it had taken his tormented mind years to perceive it. He would find inner peace by *negotiating* peace. And he would have the deliverance he'd been seeking. *Redemption!*

There was time now to enjoy quiet moments; tired eyes gazed to the west. A brilliant red sunset. The verdant hills of his homeland. Over the distant ridge he recalled a beautiful valley and, if one were to travel its length to the north, a dusty road would eventually pass through his village. High thin clouds skirted to southwest, precursors of monsoon rains. Bright sunstreaks filtered through gauzy tendrils, ghostly images at the end of a day, and the end of a life. Binh lit a pipe and thought of his home long ago, a simple place, a shanty on the outskirts of Hanoi but near his school and adequate for his small family. His wife's delicate face intruded into his daydream, and then an image of their child. Hazy, bittersweet recollections after a quarter-century of loneliness. Her photograph still hung in the shabby Hanoi room he rented, aged and yellow, corners tattered from fingers eagerly seeking, but unable, to span eternity. There had been no photographs of the child and Binh could no longer recall his tiny face in detail.

Major Nguyen Binh arranged his data. Soon the airplanes that had streaked overhead toward the southern portion of his homeland would return. A smaller force consisting of two Skyraiders and one helicopter had departed to the northwest; he assumed that would be a rescue mission. They should be returning within the half-hour and he must be ready with notebook and binoculars. A tally would be made. His report must be prepared and radioed promptly at 8:00pm.

Binh stretched and yawned, ancient bones ached, weary of life but fearing death that he had witnessed too frequently. Death would be such an easy release, but not yet. He had a mission. He ordered his assistant to prepare tea. There would a little time for relaxation once the Sharpsburg's recovery process commenced.

*   *   *

"Mayday…mayday! Shadow One, I got an engine failure. I'll have to ditch." The transmission ripped through Roberts' headset. A call he had feared.

"Roger, Shadow Two. I'm ten miles behind. I'll call for a chopper."

The Sharpsburg answered on the first call. The plane guard chopper was dispatched. ETA, ten minutes.

"Bobby…listen…ten minutes for the chopper. You OK?"

"My left hand's shot off. I don't know…all bloody. I can't reach things very well. The airplane's difficult to control. Aileron boost's gone. Rudder's screwed up."

"OK…OK…slow to one-twenty. Can you do that?"

"No. One-forty…best I can do. Lotsa vibration. Dan, I'm…I can't see very well."

Too fast, Roberts thought. Bobby would hit the water hard.
"OK…just hold that. Drop your hook…when it contacts the water…flare. Got it?"

"Sure…what about Herb?"

"Forget him, Bobby. Let's get you home."

Bobby Thomas twisted his right arm over his left knee. *Try to trim rudder...don't hit the water in a yaw!* He released the shoulder harness. Easier now, he trimmed the rudder. *Hook Down. Canopy open. One thousand feet...only moments to ditching.*

Out of the corner of his eye...a movement. Something in the water. Difficult to see through the oil smear. Something solid...floating...a sail.

A boat!

*   *   *

A smoky trail in the evening sky!

Major Binh watched carefully as the Skyraider banked awkwardly and turned in his direction. He dropped the teacup. It shattered on the wooden deck. Smoke poured from the aircraft's engine. He knew it would splash into the Gulf near his junk. His mind spun quickly to the situation. Was this an opportunity gliding to him in a burning Skyraider? He could not believe his good fortune...at last!

Here was the *Moment*!

37

The boat! A desperate glide. Could he ditch alongside? Would the fishermen rescue him? Bobby's mind labored in the blood-splattered cockpit behind the oil-smeared windshield. The pain. Blood loss. Dim vision. Where was Roberts?

"Dan, I'm gonna ditch by...alongside a junk! Can you see it?" he radioed.

"Negative. Don't do that. It's probably North Vietnamese. Wait for the chopper!"

"I can't. Descending through five hundred feet. Not sure I can get outta this thing by myself."

"Roger...I'll vector the chopper. I'll see you on the ship, Bobby. Good luck."

Find the horizon. So difficult to see and his brain seemed so sluggish. Level the wings. Bobby struggled to think clearly through pain and fatigue and blood loss; he recognized symptoms similar to hypoxia. He was bleeding to death and he would be unconscious soon. Fuzziness, fatigue...then listlessness. *Must overcome the apathy.* Concentrate!

Focus to survive! The junk bobbled in the gulf, dead ahead. Slowly, turn to the right, get some lineup. Ditch alongside the junk's bow. Use the sail as a reference, an orange glow in the sunset. A lonely beacon in the darkness drifting in blurry cinema. Ocean blending with sky in lavender twilight. Gentle, rolling waves streaked with blue darkness. So tired…

Concentrate on the sail, a gleaming sentinel beckoning his injured Spad to sanctuary. No horizon through the oil-smeared windscreen. Impossible to see clearly.

A bright-red flash. What? The radar altimeter telling him he was descending below two hundred feet! A spasm of memory…Roberts arguing about the proper radar altimeter setting. *Use sixty feet, Bobby.*

Where was he? Two hundred feet? Sixty feet? Uncertainty! He pulled back on the stick. Flying on instinct. Flare into the water. A nagging thought…something forgotten. What? Fuzziness. Confusion.

He felt the tailhook strike the water…

Binh pushed the tiller to the right on a direct course to the Skyraider. He watched the aircraft strike the water and ricochet like a stone cast upon a lake. The right wing dug into a wave and spun the airplane violently. A watery explosion. Red sunset reflected through effervescence. The tail section broke away from the fuselage and the aircraft cartwheeled over the waves. Crystal drops of blood-red mist showered over the crumpled airplane.

"Hurry!" Binh shouted at the crewman who scurried forward with the lifeline.

He turned at the clamor of a massive engine when another Skyraider roared overhead. Of course, the wingman. Excellent! He would witness the rescue of his friend. Today, Binh would be hailed as a hero and welcomed aboard the Sharpsburg. Today, his plan would be implemented. Binh quivered with overlapping energies. The ruthless guerrilla warrior, the cruel torturer, the intrepid savior, the gallant peacemaker! He could be all those things, if he had the boldness. Seconds spun by in surreal translucence.

Now, was the Moment!

The wingman's Skyraider pitched up and rolled into a turn to circle his friend. Now Binh could imagine precisely how this event would play. The wingman would witness the rescue and he would radio the ship. Binh would fly a white flag of peace and be welcomed aboard the Sharpsburg. There would be gratitude, introductions. Should he request an introduction to the young Skyraider pilot who had nearly crashed weeks earlier? Of course, it was critical that they meet! He would request an immediate introduction. How could they refuse? They could identify the pilot by the date; it was all in his journal. Two men, an American pilot and an NVA intelligence officer, would talk of armistice. Eventually, they would seek an audience with the Sharpsburg's Captain.

Surely, this day's events had been preordained. This was his opportunity to end the madness. This *must* be the Moment. He would prevail.

And there would be peace!

38

The Spad slammed into the water, with the shock of contact Bobby remembered the premonition of something forgotten during the glide. *Lock the shoulder harness.*

His body lurched forward. G-forces from sudden impact smashed his helmet into the glareshield, the shattered visor slashed into his face. His right hand jerked from the stick and crunched painfully into the instrument panel…he felt his wrist snap. Water sprayed into the cockpit. The fuselage jerked awkwardly and he saw water flying over the wing before the spinning aircraft smacked solidly into the waves.

Blood flowed into his mouth from visor cuts. He grasped desperately at the lap harness quick-release but the broken wrist flopped aimlessly. A simple release to the right. *Do it!* He could not move his fingers. Water rolled over the canopy rail rapidly filling the cockpit and washing over his knees, cleansing the oily, bloody floor plates and removing from his vision evidence of their folly.

Hurry!

Desperate efforts in a watery coffin. The Spad sunk into the blue-green while Bobby thrashed at the release with his broken wrist. Now pushing with his blood-soaked, mangled left hand. No fingers! Twisting with the broken hand. A simple snap hinge trapped the struggling pilot.

Do it! he screamed again.

Water rushed over his shoulders into his face. He could no longer see the lap belt. He flailed desperately at the release in the salty darkness…

*   *   *

Binh watched the wingman's Skyraider circle behind his junk. He looked ahead and saw the burning Skyraider sinking into the Gulf. They must hurry! Only moments remained to accomplish the rescue. He turned to order his crewman to prepare, and saw him swinging the junk's 23MM cannon.

"No! You fool….don't!!!"

Bright muzzle blasts drowned his frantic screams.

Roberts flinched as a tracer stream zipped over his left wing. Hostile fire from the enemy boat. The chopper was two miles from Bobby's crash site. No time to warn them. He kicked right rudder. The gunsight pipper danced across the water onto the junk's sail. He squeezed the trigger.

Binh ducked instinctively, 20MM raced across the water frothing the rolling waves into foaming geysers that smashed into his junk. The tiller exploded, it spun from his hands in a splintery vapor. His right shoulder was torn away. Another 20MM round ripped through his chest; his head exploded in bloody splinters. Binh's shattered body slammed into the bulkhead. Blood and bone mass splashed across the deck and over Binh's foolish crewmember, who died in the same volley.

The junk disintegrated under the onslaught of hundreds of rounds of high explosive and incendiary 20MM. It burst into flames and began to sink.

Roberts skimmed over the junk. It was no longer a threat to Bobby Thomas. He rolled into a turn and watched Bobby's broken Spad settle into the deep-blue darkness. Its shattered tail section floated in the calm gulf current surrounded by a shimmering oil slick that waffled and surged over the spot where the Skyraider slowly descended into oblivion. A moment later, the rescue chopper hovered over the slick, a powerful downwash stirring the smear and scattering it into thousands of foamy wavelets. The chopper circled deliberately and dropped a smoke flare to mark the crash-site. It drifted down into the water and floated for a while, then it too was sucked down into the insatiate depths.

A blood-red sunset faded into a shimmering purple covering the oily blue waves in a gentle iridescent glow, and shrouded in the soft Asian twilight the tragedy of human conflict. Roberts circled the site above the helicopter, straining to see in the darkness the inevitable that he knew and feared.

There was a brief flurry of radio traffic and the helicopter was directed to another duty. It fluttered away after radioing a brief report to the Sharpsburg…a red beacon retreated slowly into the distance. He was alone over the silent ocean. Oilslicks from the sunken vessels merged in quiet testimony to the demise of two good men and he could no longer determine which belonged to Bobby's Skyraider. Roberts caught a movement in the corner of his eye. He looked up. A division of A-4 Skyhawks streaked silently overhead on an easterly course to the Sharpsburg, to home and sanctuary.

Soon, Dan Roberts turned his Spad and followed them into the twilight.

39

Herb finished reading May's letter. He would not shed tears; Herb McGinnis was a prudent man not given to excesses. Just as he had been careful in most things, he must be deliberate in the end. He would not weep during the sunset…his mother would expect that.

When things are at their worst, you must always be the most prudent, Herbert. And he had been.

Caution. Prudence. Excellence. Those had been his bywords. And, for the most part he had been successful. A good student, an excellent athlete, a very good man. In fact he had excelled at everything he had ever attempted.

Except one thing.

A lone Spad had flown over his position and strafed the hillside below his nest, then boldly circled his position for a few moments inviting a hail of ground-fire, Dan Roberts attempting to reestablish contact with that curious, halting speech of his. Searching, risking ground-fire, knowing what Herb would do. But Roberts would be unable to spot him in his tight little fortress. Herb knew that as surely as he knew his day was finished. Only those little bastards surrounding him could ferret him out, and they would do it very soon, their movements revealed that they were experienced woodsmen and manhunters. It was only a matter of time.

One singular skill.

It had frustrated him and that was why he was here. Cornered. Tethered by a busted ankle, otherwise, he could maneuver. Escape and Evade, Sergeant Massey had taught them well at Pensacola's survival school. Situational awareness is the key to survival, Massey had said. Herb was quite aware of his situation but that awareness gave him little solace.

Roberts' Spad roared overhead, wiggled its wings and banked gracefully away into the purpling sky. The last pass. Herb watched the Spad disappear beyond the ridge, and then he was alone.

Goodbye, Dan.

One little skill.

It seemed little, when considered in the larger scheme of the war and of piloting in general. Fear had found his secret flaw…and now it had destroyed him.

Trapped because of a lack of mental concentration during carrier landings. That was it in a nutshell and Herb knew it. The irony was that he *could* fly an outstanding mission; he was one of the best, but then he must return to the ship. He would fly back, see the ship, and it would be there, waiting for him…the fear. Now he was trapped by the NVA on a rugged limestone ridge above a beautiful valley; trapped in a third-world country; trapped in a war that he did not want to be part of and that he did not understand. He was trapped because he had been compelled to prove to himself and others that he was worthy.

Although Herb had denied it vehemently, Roberts had known instinctively of his roommate's weakness. A man with his own handicap can always see more clearly the frailties of others. Roberts had known and eventually he had confronted Herb in halting speech but undeniable logic. *Just land the bastard, Herb. Don't think about it so much.*

Herb frequently descended too low and bombed with relentless, but risk-filled, precision because he had wanted boldness to compensate for the uncertain carrier landing that would follow the mission. A good hit was essential to prove that he was competent...to prove that he was worthy in spite of the boltering problem.

Today he had descended too low.

He had barely felt the impact of the solitary fragment of AAA that had disabled his hydraulic system and left him vulnerable to the SAM that had downed him. But he knew the truth.

It was his own foolish pride that had destroyed him.

A tear of frustration rolled down his grimy cheek and splattered onto May's letter. Herb wept quietly as he burned the letter and May's photo. He watched the flames consume her name. *Love, May.*

A bright flash, the photo ignited, flames curled over her face. Once begun, tears rushed forth, he sleeved them away and cursed himself for senseless pride. Then he removed his watch and smashed it with a rock. He pounded the timepiece over and over to expel the demons of anger and despair.

One lousy skill.

Vanity will kill you someday, Herb. Why do you care what people think? Dan Roberts had said, one of his few complete sentences. *I hope I'm not there to see it.*

He searched his pockets for anything else that might be of value. Empty. Pockets as vacant as desperate hope. As empty as his life had now become. As empty as a fool's conceit. Nothing remained worth salvaging. Nothing but himself. His dignity. His honor. Nothing more.

Bobby said something in that discussion so long ago: Our nation's most consummate warriors might have been the Sioux and Cheyenne and they believed that death in battle was infinitely preferable to life in defeat.

Herb replied: You can't seriously believe that humiliation is worse than death...that's barbaric.

Bobby argued: Maybe? Look Herb, like it or not you are a member of the warrior class. The women of the old South sent their men off to the Civil War with great enthusiasm and no honorable man would dare not go, understand? The Kiowas went into battle against the ferocious Sioux and Cheyenne knowing that returning cowards would be ridiculed and tormented by their own women…hell on earth. In that moment, those elegant Southern women and the Kiowa squaws were quite similar. Here's the question for you to consider. How many Confederate soldiers like those of the 13th Alabama Regiment, who spearheaded Pickett's Charge, and Kiowa dog soldiers who fought the more numerous Sioux, distinguished themselves in battle because their fear of a woman's scorn was greater than their fear of the enemy? Believe me, humiliation can be much worse than death!

There is a famous old journal that I read years ago. An 8th Cavalry officer wrote it, I think. Maybe it was Captain Orsemus Boyd. *'Save the last Bullet for Yourself'*, or something like that. The wisdom was time-less, though. You must never willingly allow yourself to be humiliated by the enemy…remember that, Herb.

The sun had disappeared below the horizon and darkness flowed gently over the small group of men on the ridge trapped by a common predicament. Many men, friend and foe, had died here in the last hour and Herbert McGinnis did not know even one of their names. The chopper crew had died horribly in a jet-fuel inferno. Herb cringed at the recollection; he did not want to die by fire. The North Vietnamese had burned captured aviators before; he had been warned and now the Vietnamese soldiers were moving toward him as the sun slipped below the western mountains. He heard rustling movements to his right, men cautiously tightening the cordon around his bastion. They were moving slowly.

They would kill him slowly.

Now Herb regretted shooting the careless NVA soldier. He should not have done that…it had been a meaningless gesture. His mother would have admonished him for such waste.

On the eastern side of the ridge ghostly shadows crept through brushy recesses and he knew they had surrounded his lair, only yards away. He searched for the Polar Star and thought again of his mother. Would she look for it tonight? That had been one of their favored moments. A clear night. The quiet darkness. The porch's creaking floorboards. His mother's gentle voice calling from her rocking chair.

"Herbert, come with me. Let's look for the Star. If it's there, tomorrow will be right behind. Won't it?"

He smiled at the poignant memory. She frequently said extraordinary things and Herb did not always understand her, but he always went. Then his mind raced with the urgency of the condemned. He thought of a beautiful, erotic dancer entwined about his eager form. Her image quickly evolved into the plain, extraordinary girl that he loved. Memories washed over him and he wondered how he could have been so fortunate in life. Women had always gravitated to him and he had found their company immensely gratifying.

Except for this last inconvenience, life had been good for Herbert McGinnis. A kaleidoscope of images flowed. He remembered cool Sunday mornings in the Baptist Church. The pastor's sermon about a tortured man on a barren hill came to mind. Here was *his* small Golgotha. Here and now. Herbert McGinnis, however, would have none of the pain and humiliation suffered on that hilltop. There was no purpose for it here. Bobby was probably correct about not submitting to degradation, but didn't it make them lesser men, he'd argued? Of course, Bobby said, so what? Now all that seemed unimportant on this jungle hilltop. His decision was final. Herb checked his pistol for the last time.

A rustling in the brush to the right rudely jerked him out of melancholy. It was nearly over. He concentrated to visualize May's face. Herb wanted his last thoughts to be of her. Would she know that somehow?

May's long brown hair combed straight down in the current fashion, dark eyes that flashed with laughter at his shy jokes. May wasn't beautiful, but she had vitality and he loved her.

Finally, he cocked the .38 and placed the cold muzzle precisely against his right temple. This had to be done properly and Herb had always been a careful person. He wiped a tear from his eye and concentrated on a vibrant recollection of long, brown hair, of dark, flashing eyes, of authentic beauty.

It was darkening in the rocky redoubt. The sun had set behind the final ridge in Herbert McGinnis' short life. Dense shadows that had covered his lair now blended into a dismal blackness. He heard a quiet footstep. A hushed whisper nearby. A soldier's face peered through the gloom. Searching for Ensign Herbert McGinnis, USN. Searching cautiously because the Vietnamese had grown to respect his resolve and his marksmanship.

Herb took a deep breath and prepared himself. Bobby had been correct and there would be no pain or humiliation for Herbert McGinnis tonight. He would die here in the darkness, whole, a complete man with pride intact. It wasn't much, but he knew it would have to do. Sometimes the best a man could hope for was to die with honor.

Now it was time to go and he was frightened. The muzzle felt so cold against his temple. Poor May, he stifled an anguished cry. Her world had never included violent death in faraway places. What would she do now?

Perhaps she could sell the ring.

40

Mail call had been a dreaded event for the solitary man who sat at the desk in the silent bunkroom. Helen's letter had arrived. The room seemed to close in on his psyche and overwhelm his thin defenses. It had been three days since his friends had died and it was a lonely room without Herb's presence. God, he thought, how he missed the sunlight. He missed the sunrises and sunsets, buried in the room now filled with the darkness of his soul. *We live in a cave,* he had complained recently. *Good place for a Neanderthal like you,* Herb had replied. And now he recalled the exchange with the clarity of the bereaved.

He had known the letter would arrive and he also knew that an immediate response would be required because he had written too frankly to Helen. Candor should be used sparingly when communicating during war. A worried wife was an impediment and he had little remaining capacity for burden. He reread the letter knowing that her hands had touched the paper, applied the ink, and converted those ordinary things into something magic. Helen's letter. And he felt the mixed emotions of joy and loneliness. The pleasure of holding something that had recently been hers, coupled with the pain of long separation.

The warm humidity closed in on him. A wall fan sloshed the thick air around while he wrote to Helen. Or, tried to write because the words would not come easily, they never did for Dan Roberts and tonight was especially difficult. What could he say about Herb? There were few men he would classify as friends; someone he truly liked and respected. Herb McGinnis had been his best friend and now Herb was dead. The desk provided a haven for his reverie and he tried to write about Herb McGinnis and the loss of something priceless. But it wouldn't come easily because Dan Roberts was not articulate and he knew it.

Another letter, open and unfinished, lay on the desk in front of him also demanding completion. It lay there, inert as a sinners hope for salvation. He'd started it with the best of intentions, but found himself unable to convert his thoughts into lucid prose.

Dear May,
My name is Dan Roberts. I was Herb's roommate on the USS Sharpsburg. He was my friend…

And that was as far as his limited abilities took him. He had been unable to write any more than that simple fact. What more was there to be said?

Plenty!

There were volumes to be said about a person like Herb McGinnis, probably the most honest man Roberts had ever known. The letter *must* be completed. He simply must do it! If only he could do it well, but he had serious doubts.

He was my friend.

How could he express that complex, immutable fact to Herb's distraught fiancée, a woman he had never met? Like most young men thrust into bloody warfare, he had little aptitude for condolence. All he really knew was that Herb was dead. And tomorrow he would engage in combat with an enemy that he could not hate, who had killed a friend he could not replace, in a war that he did not understand. Bobby's death compounded the sorrow. Two friends. Gone. How could he possibly assimilate that knowledge and retain his sanity?

He'd attempted to explain Herb's problems in his last letter to Helen. It was impossible to put his worries into the restricted medium of routine correspondence, especially for a man of limited eloquence. He needed his hands and body language and arcane expressive gestures as linguistic crutches to fully describe his anxieties about a friend whose attitude would surely destroy him one day. Now that day had *come* and he must try to explain why Herb had died.

How could he describe to a woman the unforgiving world he lived in? How could any normal person possibly comprehend the tight-knit, minuscule, sub-culture of carrier aviation? Where the ability to routinely land an airplane skillfully aboard a pitching, rolling carrier deck was everything. Absolutely everything! That single ability overshadowed every other phase of a pilot's existence. Flying was an easy skill, but good carrier landings were an art.

A Naval Aviator might be a clumsy oaf, who could not walk through an open door without bumping his head, Roberts had stated awkwardly in his last letter to Helen. But, if he had that special capacity to accomplish good, dependable carrier landings, then he would be forgiven all frailties. Conversely, if an otherwise highly accomplished Naval Aviator, such as Herb McGinnis, was unable to routinely land his airplane skillfully on the ass-end of a pitching boat, then he was known as a *pilot who boltered*. It was unfair, unforgiving, but absolutely true.

She had written in the letter he just received: *Why is it so important? By the way, I think I know who you are describing, the clumsy oaf. Please don't say that anymore.*

Now he must try to describe the anguish of a good pilot, unfairly judged because he was afraid. Fear had killed Herb McGinnis! Fear of carrier landings had compelled Herb to overcompensate. He had descended too low, as usual, in that last fatal bomb run. Herb had wanted, and absolutely had to have, an accurate bomb delivery on an insignificant fuel dump to prove that he was a pilot worthy of respect. Oh, he had hit the target precisely! But then he had paid the price. The prudent man had committed an imprudent act; had been confounded by chance; had been killed by cruel fate. And, now…

Herb was dead.

How could he possibly make any sense out of that?

Roberts wished he had been on tonight's flight schedule. Flying would have filled the emptiness. Should he go to the wardroom for coffee and there in the company of other pilots, finish the letter? He did not want to talk to anyone, but overhearing conversations might help overcome the loneliness. But he decided that letter writing could not be accomplished in the presence of people who did not know his grief. Herb was dead! And so was Bobby Thomas.

He was my friend…

A slight tapping on the door startled him. The door opened and Commander Isaacson stood there in awkward silence.

"May I come in…Dan?" Isaacson said tentatively…eyes blinked a time or two.

Strange, he thought, shyness and uncertainty had never been Isaacson's weakness and Roberts was surprised to be greeted by his Christian name. How extraordinary!

"Writing home?" Isaacson pointed to the unfinished letters.

"Yes, sir…my wife's pregnant. And, Herb…" He let it drop, what could he say? Isaacson had not known Herb personally.

Isaacson looked around his cramped room. Roberts had not packed Herb's personal effects, not yet. Tomorrow he would pack Herb's things neatly and mail them to his mother with a note. Maybe tomorrow, if he felt competent to do something that was hopeless.

"Dan, I'm…" Isaacson cleared his throat. An awkward silence flowed through the humid air. "I…uhh..think I may have had this room on my first cruise." Roberts recognized the lie. "God, almost twenty years ago. You call it the Tranquillity Room, I hear. We had a different name." Isaacson muttered something to justify the awkward intrusion. "I hung a punching bag from that light fixture…used to poke away my excess energy….a lot younger back then."

"It's usually pretty noisy in here." Roberts stood and he sensed a sudden tenseness in Isaacson, a boxer's natural reflex.

"We sent Bobby's stuff off on the afternoon COD," Isaacson said. "Do you need some help with McGinnis' things?"

"No!" Roberts snapped. Isaacson hadn't cared one whit about Herb McGinnis, who had been his friend. Roberts would handle the job alone when he was damned good and ready.

"Sorry, Dan…these things aren't the easiest…"

Herb's B-4 bag lay opened and empty on his bunk. Waiting. An awkward silence fell over the room. They looked at each other in honest appraisal and knew that they had disliked each other from the beginning. A loud bang, the room shook from the catapult. Isaacson's eyes wandered to Helen's photograph and lingered silently on the evocative image. A slender girl's form draped enticingly over an Austin-Healey, a sponge soaked with soapy water splashed across the silver-blue hood. A skimpy halter-top. A smiling face. Long, graceful legs. Shadows played across the background of her mother's yard in Seattle.

"She's very pretty. First child?"

"Yes, sir."

The skipper's eyelids were etched with fatigue; a vibrant, capable man aged by events beyond his control. Isaacson had been consumed by ambition, thwarted by circumstance and now defeated by an unknown enemy. He had been reprimanded.

Orders had arrived. An urgent and unexpected message relieving Isaacson of his command. No reason was given for the early transfer to shore duty. His ambitions for flag rank were now all but eliminated by the short, insulting, devastating message. But everyone knew.

Ambition impeded by vile circumstance. The unexplained deaths of two sailors, a dead pilot, and a shadowy drug scandal poorly concealed by the sham Inquiry had destroyed Isaacson's dreams. The deaths were not Isaacson's fault, but they had occurred on his watch. Subtly, but deftly, he would be forced into retirement and the scandal would be forgotten. Dan Roberts knew that, so did every man in the squadron.

"Do you suppose Pan Am would hire an old war-horse like me?" Isaacson asked. A cracking voice. A weary, resigned face.

"Yes, sir. And they would be…"

"Lucky to have me?" Isaacson scowled.

"Yes, sir." Roberts could think of nothing more to say.

"Honor is a hard master, Dan. I don't know if you're ready for it," Isaacson said, remembering that he had once been an honorable man.

Roberts' eyes strayed to the pale green wall, clean but aged and thick with numerous layers of paint. The room seemed smaller with Isaacson's presence. Hundreds of pilots had occupied the dismal space since the Sharpsburg had been launched in 1943. A battle-scarred veteran, the Essex-class carrier had been nearly destroyed by Kamikaze's in the Philippine Sea, rebuilt and damaged again. It creaked and groaned, but prevailed. A survivor. The ship emitted an odor of oil and sweat and aviation fuel and paint and age. Had Isaacson occupied this room as a young aviator? Or, was he lying to establish sympathy? How was it possible to trust anyone?

"Can't see myself as a limp-dick airline pilot." Isaacson leaned against the bulkhead.

Roberts pointed to the other chair. The skipper sat down and looked again at the photograph of Helen and her sports car.

A frail memory flashed into Isaacson's melancholy. A recollection of blond, flowing hair. Night music spilling onto the verandah of the Mustin Beach Officers Club. Isaacson had been a new Lieutenant Junior-Grade at Pensacola when he had met his wife on that warm, enchanted Southern evening a millennium ago. Gulf breezes had wafted the scent of Magnolia onto the verandah and the whole world awaited his presence. They had walked on the moon-drenched, silvery beach and embraced in the gardens by the fountain. Moonlight reflected from wave crests splashing on white sugar-sand and palm trees sheltered their magic, youthful world. Gerald Isaacson had proposed that night and told her of his ambitions. One day he would surely return to that verandah as an Admiral, and this beautiful woman would be his confederate. She had been a loyal and valued asset. She had supported him, hoping to become the beautiful and vivacious Mrs. Admiral Isaacson. She had joined his quest and had assisted him at every turn of his successful career.

Successful? He choked on the thought of the injustice.

"My wife has blond hair, lighter than hers." Isaacson pointed at Helen's photo. A vivid flash of his wife's radiant beauty. *A Naval Aviator's wife*, Linda Isaacson had proclaimed frequently at her reflections in a mirror…she was well aware of her physical advantages. Another image intruded. She had attended his last boxing match, a bloody affair that he had won on points. The grainy photograph was her favorite; a blood-soaked robe, his sheltering arm draped over her lissome form, a battle-marked ring in dim background.

Captured by his burning ambition, she had wanted Flag Rank, to be the handsome wife of a distinguished Navy Admiral. But now, it was not to be. She would learn of his fate from other ambitious Navy wives, subtly of course. Small comments, gentle, caring questions like daggers to her heart. Isaacson realized that Linda would know it all before he returned to California. And he also knew that she was a tougher animal than he was.

"I'm sorry about our disagreements, Dan." Isaacson finished what he had started to say in the beginning. "Putting you in hack was unfair, I was probably wrong and I wanted to straighten that out. You did the right thing on the Franklin investigation. I asked for a thorough process and you provided it. Manley's an efficient officer…a little pedantic, perhaps.

And I thought a more innovative approach was needed. I chose you for the job…knew from the beginning that it wasn't suicide. It didn't make sense. Didn't realize what the truth would do to me, though. I think you're correct about the Williamson accident, too. I didn't think Pete would go so far." It all came out in a rush and then he was finished.

"What do you mean, Skipper?"

Isaacson lit a cigarette and leaned back in the chair, fatigue etched on the young-old face. Roberts had never seen him smoke before. It was a human frailty, not Commander Gerald Isaacson's style.

"Now, I'm finished. I might as well be dead like Pete and Franklin and Williamson…Bobby and the others." Isaacson blew a long stream of smoke and looked at the ceiling. "Maybe even you, Dan. It's not over yet."

"What do you mean about Pete?" Roberts asked.

"Who would have ever thought. A smoke…" Isaacson waved the cigarette for emphasis. "…a lousy cigarette. Who would have thought that goddamned reefers could have caused so much trouble?"

Isaacson looked at the photo of Helen Roberts. She represented something. Home. Normalcy in a deranged era. Beauty. Humanity. All of those things held dear by a man who had once played by the rules.

"Williamson, Pete, Franklin all dead…and I'm finished because of goddamn greed and marijuana."

Roberts had never heard Isaacson use profanity. He opened the wall-safe and removed a bottle of Scotch, his last. He poured two drinks and splashed water into both glasses.

"Thing is, I can't really understand the difference between drinking alcohol and smoking pot. Both are stupid, if you think about it," Isaacson said.

Roberts nodded, but he did sense the difference. It had to do with social acceptance, with Naval tradition. The Navy accepted, even encouraged the consumption of alcohol while it condemned other drugs. An officer could jeopardize his career if he refused to drink socially with his contemporaries. It had always been that way.

"Not fair," Roberts said. He shook his head while offering the glass to Isaacson. "Goddam those politicians and their…stupid war, Skipper. We'll all be casualties before it's finished. Just wait and see."

Roberts did not pretend to ignore Isaacson's anguish. It was time to make peace with the defeated man. He decided they had a lot in common.

"To Bobby," Roberts said, and raised his glass.

"And all the others…Williamson…McGinnis…" Isaacson looked at Herb's open locker; clothes stacked neatly, a photo of May still taped inside the door, all of the dead pilot's possessions waiting for Roberts to do something.

Something?

"Who would've ever guessed?" Isaacson's voice cracked; he drained the glass to cover the gaffe. "Pete shouldn't have…"

Knowing about verbal gaffes, Roberts looked away quickly, but both were embarrassed.

"Yeah, goddamn Pete. Bobby was a good man," Roberts said. "He promised to cover for me…the investigation…the report…the Inquiry. Pete…all the rest."

"Oh? Well, Bobby's dead."

"And I'm going to take the fall."

"We both are!" Isaacson nodded and then took a deep breath, "Bobby Thomas. The last of a dying breed." He pressed on. "Bobby was a professional warrior and would have been one no matter when or where he lived. I can easily imagine him as one of Caesar's generals or a Cavalry officer in the Army of the West. I..ummhh…I admired him. He was the best."

"I agree, sir."

"So, here's to you, Dan." Isaacson raised his glass. "You've screwed up royally, but your worst sin was to sink that fishing junk. They could've pulled Bobby out of the water. Mine was to punish a foolish man who made a lotta mistakes. I'll have to live with my decisions. Can you?"

"I…no…" he stammered. Isaacson was absolutely correct.

"Bobby always said you were lucky. He admired you for some reason."

"Lucky? Look, Skipper…I just wanted to fly airplanes and they're letting me. That's all the luck I ever hoped to have."

"Personally, I always thought Bobby was wrong," Isaacson said. "Do you think you can live with your mistakes, Dan? You've hurt many people. If you hadn't sunk that boat, maybe Bobby would have survived. And Pete…."

"Pete? What the hell could I have…"

"Done?" Isaacson smiled. "First of all, you should have arrested Pete. We could have court-martialed him, or a captain's mast…almost anything. Hell, I could have covered it up pretty easily. We could've been cleared, you and I, even Pete." Isaacson scowled. "But, we can't now, too many unexplained deaths…too late. I don't know if you plan to make the Navy a career. Well, don't! We're both finished now."

"But, Bobby…"

"Sure, he could have covered for you but he didn't have a chance, except for that junk, and you sunk it."

Roberts avoided Isaacson's glassy eyes that were moist with unabashed sadness. The skipper would be relieved of command before his normal rotation date and shortly before the completion of the cruise, a major insult. He would be denied the distinction of being the final squadron leader of VA-433, the *last of the Spads*.

"My replacement is Clyde Barron, they call him Ironman with good reason. He was assigned early last week…ought to be enroute from Alameda by now. I know him, fought him once at Annapolis. You won't like him…got a reputation…a hard taskmaster…an astute man. He'll kick ass and take names. Kinda guy CincPac would dispatch to straighten out a troubled squadron." Isaacson stood, paced the room. "Oh, you might be interested, Dan…he's demanded copies of several Personnel Records to review while enroute. Guess whose name is at the top of his suspect list?"

"Mine?"

"Ensign Dan Roberts, USNR. I recommend you keep your mouth shut."

"Damn. How the hell did it ever…" Roberts sloshed Scotch into both glasses.

"Get out? Well, you figure it out; you're so smart. Who was there? Who knew it all?"

"I…don't know!"

"You and I knew and we sure as hell didn't spill the beans. Bobby didn't…I'm sure of that. Smithson swears he didn't and I believe him because I asked him directly…scared him shitless. Who does that leave that knew the truth?"

"Manley? No! I don't think so."

"Ralph was transferred early to CincPac two weeks ago. He's an intelligent, ambitious man." Isaacson stated flatly. "A good politician."

"Ralph, the rodent?" Roberts shook his head in disbelief.

"Why not? Some guys can cruise through a war and slip away unscathed, like Ralph. Others will be marked forever, guys like you and me."

"God, I'm sorry, Skipper. I had no idea. Should I have bought the suicide story like Ralph suggested? I think Pete tried to warn me off before…"

"Ralph's smart, he knew more than he let on."

"I should've kept my big mouth shut. Bobby told me so right in the beginning. Would it have been better if I'd ignored the truth? But, goddammit, Skipper, that's what you said you wanted!"

Isaacson lit another cigarette. "Who knows?" he said. "Maybe? That's a value judgment I no longer feel qualified to make."

"Bobby's dead. Herb's missing…but he's dead too. You've been relieved. And everyone thinks I'm a total…blockhead, if not worse. I'm a damned liar and everybody knows it. Now everything's so goddam hopeless."

"It's not entirely your fault. I said I wanted the truth but sometimes the truth's unmanageable. What we really needed was cover. You should've come to me first. Your real problem is that you're not a team player…no business in an organization like the Navy. You buck the system, and now you've lost…we've all lost."

Now Roberts thought he saw Gerald Isaacson clearly for the first time. The skipper probably thought himself to be a warm, compassionate man, seriously misunderstood. He wore his contempt as a suit of armor, a defense a tough man used against a tougher world.

"Yes, but you see, the thing is, I like the Navy. I wanted to be Regular Navy, like you, Skipper. Like Bobby."

"Forget it. My advice to you is to keep your mouth shut and get out of the Navy at the end of your tour. Best for all concerned."

"But…Jesus, Skipper, where's the meaning in all this? I'm screwed. You're fired. All those deaths? What's been gained? Because we're all losers, aren't we? Where's the…?"

"Justice? My goodness, what an astute question. Did you think of that all by yourself?" Isaacson asked.

"Yes, sir. I did…I really did." And they laughed.

Isaacson picked up the photo of the Austin-Healey and the pretty woman. There was a compelling quality to the scene. Roberts had scrawled something in bold script across the bottom of the photograph. *Helen, the Fair. And her sports car.* He remembered the good times with Linda and his promising career. *On a sunny day in America….where life goes on.* Isaacson completed the sentiment for Roberts, the inarticulate man, during his meditation.

A smudged fingerprint marred the frame. Isaacson wiped it carefully with a handkerchief before placing it precisely on the desk; he would not tolerate untidiness. He diddled with the drink for an awkward moment. He admired the photo, the beautiful woman who belonged to the inculpable man who had ruined his career and whose mistakes had killed two men. He looked scornfully at his wingman. He could beat

Roberts to a pulp with so little effort, and who would not understand? Most would probably applaud his efforts and wonder why he had not done it earlier.

"I wonder about you, Dan. Relentless, and yet, choosy about your targets. But, you're always right in there, aren't you? I think I'm beginning to understand. You're like an old-time gunslinger, a natural killer, and a bloody damned fool. Why do *you* always come back when better men don't? You shouldn't have strafed that junk, but you just couldn't resist, could you?" He blew a stream of pungent smoke into Roberts' face.

Roberts waved the smoke away angrily. "I didn't know you smoked, Skipper."

"I didn't, not until this cruise. Old age, I guess. Stress, the flying was getting too much for me. Needed a crutch. Three or four joints a month helped. Pete gave them to me."

"Pete!!? But, Skipper, I don't…?"

"Understand? Sure you do. I've known Pete for ten years. He's helped me a lot."

"Oh, my God!" Roberts choked.

Isaacson gazed at him with tired eyes, confused about something.

"You don't always have to destroy an opponent, Dan."

"Pete was a murderer and a drug pusher."

"Pete was a good friend, and you killed him."

They watched one another warily without speaking. Roberts blinked first.

"Skipper…I'm tired. I've got to finish some letters…get ready for tomorrow."

"Oh, well…to Bobby." Isaacson emptied his glass.

"He was everything I wanted to be," Roberts blurted.

"But, you'll never be! Now you got his death hanging on you, as well. Keep screwing up, Roberts. You'll look like a frigging Christmas Tree before the cruise is over."

Roberts set his glass down angrily. But, he knew it wasn't an insult, it was the truth.

"Bobby was the best," Isaacson said. His face etched with resignation. "And he tried to stop you."

"Yes, sir. He did. Maybe I should've." Roberts poured the last of his Scotch for the man who might have been an Admiral. "Bobby was a one hell of a Spad Driver."

The room tilted slightly as the ship turned into the wind for the night recovery then flight operations would cease for a few hours. An Alpha Strike was scheduled at dawn on another meaningless target in the beautiful hills of an obscure third world country. Isaacson slugged down the drink.

"See you in the morning?"

"Yes, sir. Guess I'm back on your wing. Boxer Two again…sorry. Why don't you get another guy, Skipper?"

"Don't be sorry. I requested you."

"Why? After all that's happened? I know you hate my guts."

Roberts knew Isaacson would say something and then nod his head, Isaacson's way of closing a discussion. He anticipated the nod. Yearned for it.

"You wanna know something, at first I thought you were a little dull…your speech impediment, I guess. That's why I gave you the Franklin investigation. Manley was too smart. I didn't think you'd ever get it quite right. Bobby warned me you were more complex. Now I understand, you're really quite reckless, Dan."

"Maybe so, Skipper. I'm just what you guys made me…I'm your wingman. Why don't you get somebody else for tomorrow?"

"What did Napoleon say? Keep your friends close and your enemies even closer."

"Which am I?"

Isaacson paused at the door. "Another good question." He glanced back at his reluctant wingman. A fleeting smile played across his lips.

The first genuine smile Roberts had ever seen on the disdainful face. "Define irony, Dan."

"What?"

"Irony…the good guys are dead and the bastard who always skates will probably get a medal. And they say Satan doesn't have a sense of humor." Isaacson laughed bitterly.

"Isn't it time for you to leave, Skipper?"

"How will you ever atone for your mistakes, Dan?" Then he nodded and Roberts could not avoid a caustic chuckle.

"Stick it…sir."

"You sanctimonious, insolent bastard." The vulnerability disappeared, replaced by ruthless boxer's eyes that targeted Roberts with cold contempt. "You think you're bullet-proof, don't you?"

"No. I'll tell you what I think…"

"Shut up before I smash you like a bug! You're no different from the rest of us. I expect you'll die alone and bloody someday. I hope so!"

"Shove off, Skipper!"

They stared in stony silence. Two guilt-consumed men. Two corrupted, wounded, condemned warriors.

"You're one of the *unforgiven*, Dan."

*   *   *

Roberts finished the letter to Helen, poorly, he thought. He looked at the other letter, then set it aside. If Bobby were here, he would help. But Bobby was dead and Isaacson had said he was to blame and now he must find a way to write the letter alone. He would finish it tomorrow. He would pack Herb's belongings and not think about Bobby. Somehow he would finish the letter to May and, if he could manage it, a letter to Herb's mother even though he could think of nothing of value to write to either woman other than that single irrefutable declaration.

He was my friend.

Roberts sprawled on the bunk and attempted to fill the void with a Steinbeck novel but his mind strayed to happier times. When he closed his eyes he kept seeing her, an image of Helen standing there on the beach. He studied her photograph and strained to precisely recall a certain sunlit Puget Sound day spent with her, their last day together before he had departed for the Sharpsburg. A sandy beach flooded his memory, a shimmering translucence. He had helped a boy with a kite. She had laughed at his fruitless efforts. Echoes of sparkling laughter flowed like sweet wine through layers of isolation and he tried to ignore the darkness in his soul that filled the room with an overwhelming emptiness. He held the photograph closely, avoiding a wretched sleep and what awaited him.

If only you were here, he thought. *Just for a moment, then I would know what to say.* His mind spun to the thoughts. *There would be time and we would be together and you could help me make some sense of it all. Somehow, in your presence, I might find some reassurance of my sanity.*

A brisk wind had suddenly whipped sand-swirls across the beach and they ran to a shelter.

You must be sure to come back, Dan. She'd said quietly and deliberately. *Terry and Fred were killed on the Oriskany. They were bachelors, you're not. And there will be two of us when you come home.*

What? He'd asked, not aware of it then.

I'm pregnant.

Ohhh, he replied, and she smiled up at him knowing his difficulty.

He lay there looking at her in the vision. The shelter was a flimsy thing and wind stirred through dark shadows. Her face vanished in the gloom and he strained to see the truth. It was so simple, really. She loved him in spite of himself…and that was his greatest reward. He had tried to tell her that afternoon how much he would miss her, but he hadn't been able to come up with the words.

The wind whisked sand into the shelter and they'd embraced knowing there was so little time. The MAC flight would leave from McChord at midnight.

You mustn't worry about us...just come home.

And then she was gone. He was alone.

Fatigue washed over him and he drifted in reverie under the fan that stirred warm, liquid air over his solitary repose while the ship lolled peacefully in the Tonkin Gulf's eternal current. Tomorrow, the Sharpsburg and its complement of sailors would return to the war and to flight operations on Yankee Station. Isaacson's visit had left him diminished and he longed for the sweet rectitude of a peaceful sleep. Staring ahead into the gloom he saw her languid smile dissolve into mist. He brushed the photo lightly with his fingertips for a moment, then placed it on the desk over an unfinished letter.

Roberts set the alarm for four-thirty and closed his eyes, hoping to ward off the demons that frequented the night. He thought about something Bobby had said: *Sometimes you can look at someone for a long time and not see them truly...until they make their move...then it's too late.* They'd been talking about Pete, and Bobby had said Roberts shouldn't blame himself. But, now Roberts wondered if Bobby had been talking about him.

Helen sounded discouraged in the letter he'd just received. Was it the pregnancy? What an extraordinary thing! He could not get a grip on the enormity of it. A baby. An actual living child that belonged solely to them, an image that made him happy; he decided to think about it at length. He dissected the thoughts into many disparate and pretty parts, thus he drifted into sleep, happy images abounded, dark and peaceful. It would not last.

Soon the monsters rushed in. A blurry image of Ha Long Bay stirring slowly in familiar agony. He saw Bill Jensen's parachute and faces of the rescue mission. Bobby waved a bloody arm at him from his Spad. He saw himself over the village. Black puffs filled with red furies. A junk exploded and a Spad sank slowly into darkness. Shadowy figures twisted and burned in the night. A small black figure came running to him, hair flowing behind a terror-stricken face.

In a vile, watery darkness an arm thrust out of a phosphorescent path, beckoning. Isaacson shoved him over the guardrail into the burning, foamy wake. A girl in black pajamas glided with graceful splendor into his gunsight ring, an evocative image, beautiful, familiar and dreadful. A pretty little face taunted him. She skipped merrily across a dock, smiling up to him before she was consumed by strafing fire and flames. His hand thrust at an illusory control stick to deflect the horror. He moaned and drifted into deeper slumber.

Shadowy figures surrounded him, closing him into an ever-shrinking circle of accountability, the voices of Bobby and Pete and Herb shrieked into the night condemning him for his sins and inadequacies. He tossed in sweat-drenched anguish and then slowly, slowly fell into a darker oblivion of hopelessness filled with strident noise and unfocused images. Lost in his own condemnation, he saw himself. And knew that he *was* unforgiven.

The ship plowed through the warm waters of Tonkin Gulf to an assigned position on Yankee Station waiting for a rose-tinted tropical sunrise. Aircraft were poised on the flight deck and ordnance was being loaded. In the deep warrens of the ship an Alpha Strike was being planned and the torment inside the Tranquillity Room would not long endure…he was scheduled for the early launch.